Taken

Niamh O'Connor

TRANSWORLD IRELAND

TRANSWORLD IRELAND
an imprint of The Random House Group Limited
20 Vauxhall Bridge Road, London SW1V 2SA
www.rbooks.co.uk

First published in 2011 by Transworld Ireland,
a division of Transworld Publishers

A CIP catalogue record for this book
is available from the British Library.

ISBN 9781848270930

Addresses for Random House Group Ltd companies outside the UK
can be found at: www.randomhouse.co.uk
The Random House Group Ltd Reg. No. 954009

The Random House Group Ltd supports the Forest Stewardship
Council (FSC), the leading international forest-certification organization.
All our titles that are printed on Greenpeace-approved FSC-certified paper
carry the FSC logo. Our paper procurement policy can be found at
www.rbooks.co.uk/environment

Typeset in 11.5/15pt Sabon by
Falcon Oast Graphic Art Ltd.
Printed and bound in Great Britain by
Clays Limited, Bungay, Suffolk

2 4 6 8 10 9 7 5 3 1

MIX
Paper from
responsible sources
FSC® C016897

Foreword

Some stories come to newspaper journalists that are impossible to prove. But sometimes you get a sense that a story that does appear in a newspaper is only scratching the surface of something that is far more sinister.

How many times do papers make a splash with an interview with a call girl who has sold the story of her night of passion with a footballer or celebrity? It's almost the norm now for these women to come from privileged, educated, middle-class backgrounds, rather than those of deprivation or desperation, as a reader might expect. It is stories like these that have always made me wonder what it must be like to have the sort of looks that appeal to the very rich, and the brains to make a calculated decision to subjugate the self for cold, hard currency. What are the temptations for very beautiful women who want some of the excesses of the glitzy world for themselves? To whom do the wealthy turn for discretion? And how has the global recession impacted on the sex industry?

This book is an attempt to tease out some of the answers, and it's based on a story that couldn't get into a newspaper; one that keeps coming up through different sources. In essence it's about the model industry in meltdown, and the very real links in the chain between the celebrity circuit, and the gangland horrors – murder, human trafficking, drug importation – that are required to keep the rich and corrupt in their party bubble of excess and decadence. It's the story of the oldest profession in the world.

Because no matter the amount of money that changes hands, or the individuals involved, it's still a story of what happens when sex is for sale.

Niamh O'Connor
April 2011

Prologue

Tara Parker Trench pulled up at the only free pump in the petrol station on Eden Quay, and after a long, hard look through the windscreen wipers, killed Beyoncé's 'Ring On It' and twisted around.

It was nine o'clock on a Sunday night, and pitch dark, but she wasn't worrying about what might happen if she left her three-year-old son alone in the car near Dublin city centre. Not when she was only going to be gone for sixty seconds maximum, and especially not when it was lashing rain. Her stomach ached as she turned, and she pressed her hand against it.

Presley had nodded off, and was purring like a kitten in the back. The Ray-Bans she'd got him had slid to the tip of his nose, his Tommy Hilfiger jacket collar was turned up and the peak of his New York Yankees trucker cap sloped to the side, skateboarder style.

'Such a cool dude,' she said, giving his Nike runner boot a little squeeze.

Clicking her seatbelt off, she stretched between the seats and tried to tilt his head back into a more comfortable position, wincing as she did so with the exertion. It flopped forward again, and she reached for the Snuggly Puppy on his lap to see if she could use it as a pillow. But even fast asleep, Presley's chubby little fingers tightened their grip.

Tara smiled. She'd only been sixteen when she'd got pregnant, and had had to fight to have, and keep, him. She'd no regrets: she and Presley, they were a team. Despite all the rows with her own mum about the future, she had been able to build a good life for both of them. Tara was never going back to the hardship of a just few years back. Presley deserved the best in life, and so did she.

A sharp beep from the car behind told her to get a move on. Tara glanced in her rear-view mirror, patting the air to say 'calm down'. Little Miss Impatient was a Botoxed brunette in her forties with that puckered look around her lips that collagen always gave. She was driving a brand new Jag. Catching sight of her own face, Tara wiped away the smudged mascara beneath her eyes. The sooner she got home and into a hot shower the better, she thought.

Stepping out of her black Mini Cooper with white stripes down the bonnet, she grimaced. The River Liffey stank the way it always did before heavy fog. Screwing off the cap to the car's petrol tank, she gestured to the rest of the bays in the forecourt for the Jag lady's benefit as she began to fill up. They were bumper to bumper and it wouldn't just be this garage that was full, either. Every motorist in the country with an ounce of sense would be filling up tonight. Tomorrow was Budget Day, and the fallout from the bank bailout and the IMF interest rate meant another round of hard-hitting taxes was on the cards.

A wolf whistle rang out, and Tara stiffened. She knew it was for her. Men had been wolf whistling at her since she was twelve years old. Whoever it was had issues with women – it was too drawn-out to be friendly or jokey.

Pushing her long hair out of her eyes, she kept her head

down – feeling self-conscious suddenly about the short, glitzy dress she was still wearing and the six-inch heels. She located the man she thought was responsible for the whistle out of the side of her eye. He was parked at pump number three, sitting behind the wheel of a battered HiAce. There was a white Mitsubishi with flashy hubcaps and a spoiler on the boot between her and him. The bay to her right – the one nearest the road – had a white sheet fluttering from the pump which said it was out of service. On Tara's left the boy racer in the white Mitsubishi seat rolled down his tinted window.

'Here, I know you,' he called. 'You're that model, right? I've got your poster on my wall. You know, the one of you posing like Britney Spears in a school uniform?'

Tara sighed. She remembered the shot he was talking about – it was for a campaign against illiteracy to try and encourage older people to go back to school. The message it sent out about what men could look forward to if they returned to the education system was a disgrace, but she didn't object. Money was money, even if a photo call – the bread and butter of a model's trade – was only worth a pittance. She needed every penny at the moment.

'Looking hot, darlin'. Want to go for a drink?'

Tara felt a flash of anger. 'What's your poison?' she called back. 'Lemonade with ice?'

Two of the kid's mates, who had the same chunky silver chains around their necks, came out of the garage forecourt with armfuls of crisps and chocolate, and laughed as they heard Tara's put-down. The boy racer turned red and revved the engine.

Tara angled the nozzle back in the pump. Stooping, she cupped her hands over her eyes to check Presley through the glass, then straightened up to scan the queue at the till inside which snaked right the way down the aisle. It was definitely best to leave him where he was, she decided. She pointed the key fob at the Mini, but changed her mind in case Presley activated the alarm. If he banged his arm or foot against the window and it went off, he would wake, find himself alone and get upset. The last thing she needed now was him bawling all the way home.

The woman in the Jag gave another impatient beep, and Tara reached into the car for her Vivienne Westwood jacket, held it over her head so she wouldn't get wet, and ran towards the entrance, much to the boy racers' delight. They struck up a round of catcalls, and set off after her, a row of flashing blue lights pulsating along their bumper.

Inside, she hurried past a long rack of convenience shelves stocked with the kind of foods that just needed boiling water added. The place was a dive, but at least the queue was moving quickly and there were only three people ahead of her. Then they stopped. Tara strained sideways to see what the problem was. A customer with a shaved head and a Staffordshire bull terrier in tow was pretending he didn't understand the accent of the Chinese man behind the till. 'What?' and 'Can you say it in English?' he kept saying. Tara sighed. At this rate, she'd be here another ten minutes.

She turned to try and peer out the shop front glass to check on Presley, but couldn't see a thing. It was so dark out the fluorescent bulbs overhead had turned the window fronting the forecourt into a virtual mirror.

She focused on the CCTV screen up over the Chinese guy's head, willing it to flash up an image of her car. For a second, she recognized the stripes on the Mini's bonnet but it flashed to another car before she'd had a chance to study it properly.

Shaved head was being asked to stand aside, and was refusing. A man in a suit, standing directly behind him in the queue, pushed his cash in through the sliding hatch in the counter. 'I'm in a hurry,' he said.

Shaved head jerked the dog's leash. The mutt started to growl.

Tara pointed her key fob out the window at where she estimated the Mini was, and pressed the button. Presley's safety was suddenly more important than him getting upset at the alarm going off. When a set of orange indicators blinked back, she exhaled in relief.

The dog had started to bark. Behind her in the queue someone pushed up against her in a way that made her skin crawl. She buttoned her jacket all the way up before turning around. A spotty teenager with a white hoodie pulled over his head nudged her with his shoulder.

'Bet ya he's got a blade,' he said, nodding at the shaved head guy.

He looked like a junkie – his eyes were glazed and he had a nasal tone, but his accent was too posh to be from around there. There was something weird about the way he was staring at her; it was freaking her out. She stepped as far forwards as was possible to get away from him without bumping into the old man in front of her. A car alarm went off outside, and Tara turned, squinting to see through the glass. Was Presley crying? Frantic at the queue stretching behind her, she aimed the remote through the window again and jabbed. The alarm stopped.

Shaved head was dragging his dog towards the exit, still grumbling to himself about the Chinese guy's accent. Hate had made his face tight. His dog was skidding on its paws, every sinew in its body straining to move in the opposite direction. The Chinese guy shouted back through the Perspex protective glass for shaved head to stay where he was until he'd paid, then bent over to reach some button under the counter.

Tara wrung her hands together, and was giving serious consideration to going back out to the car and bringing Presley in with her, when a Muslim guy in a skullcap burst out of a door behind the counter and asked what the problem was.

Shaved head was parallel to Tara now. Picking up a can of Red Bull from the open fridge, he threw it hard at the till. It bounced off the Perspex, and landed on the floor, the contents spraying up in a high arch. The youth behind Tara whooped in delight. The other customers looked either worried or pissed off. The old man was oblivious. Either he'd seen it all before, or was half-blind with cataracts. Tara had to get out.

Shaved head reached for another missile, his arm blocking her exit. Tara ducked under it and bolted as the second can was catapulted to the top of the shop.

Out in the forecourt, she could see that the can of Red Bull had connected with the head of the man in the suit at the top of the queue, who stumbled, then hit the floor with a crash. The dog jumped free of the leash and leapt straight towards him. Tara covered her mouth and ran to her car.

Ducking to look at the back seat, she saw Presley still snoozing his head off. Tara felt weak with relief. 'Sorry, sweetheart,' she whispered, turning the key in the engine, pressing the clutch with her foot and putting the car in first gear. But a hard rapping on the window made her jump, her foot slipped off the clutch and the car did a bunny hop before cutting out.

The Muslim guy was pressed up against the window, and was rubbing his thumb against his first two fingers to signal that she needed to pay for her petrol.

Tara swung the door open, forcing him to step back. 'I'm only moving it,' she shouted, pointing to the air-and-water area. But the bloke in the HiAce had just swerved out of the bay he was in so hard his tyres screeched. He stalled and blocked her exit, and by the look of things had broken down. His van belched out black smoke. One or more of the plug points had gone, she reckoned. Her ex – Presley's dad, Mick – was a mechanic, and some of what he knew had rubbed off. Tonight, after what she'd been through, she wished they were still together.

The HiAce man was turning the engine over, trying to restart it. It sounded to Tara like he was flooding it, but she wasn't going to get involved. The engine stopped slipping, and he suddenly took off, leaving a trail of dirty exhaust fumes in his wake.

Starting up again, she pulled up twenty yards away, parking alongside the door of a toilet with an 'Out of Order' sign taped to it. She could hear a siren getting steadily louder as she headed back inside the garage to settle the bill.

Miraculously, in spite of all the commotion, she made it to the till within less than five minutes of entering. The dog had been called off, shaved head escorted out of the shop, and by the time the paramedics arrived to tend to the suit, the Muslim manager had mopped up the Red Bull and erected yellow 'Wet Floor' signs around the offending area. As Tara handed over her credit card, she saw the dog being locked in the toilet and a garda pushing the shaved headed guy towards a waiting squad car.

Turning away from the till, Tara nearly collided with the Jag lady, whose mouth was pursed in disapproval. Dressed in a pink cashmere cardigan with stern shoulder pads and gold buttons, and wearing a pair of shades, she looked Tara up and down like she was dirt. Much as Tara wanted to ask what the hell her problem was, she wanted to get back to Presley a whole lot more.

Double-checking her till receipt to make sure she hadn't been short-changed, she pinched open the pack of white chocolate buttons she'd bought along with a packet of painkillers when she'd paid for the petrol, and hurried back to the car. If Presley woke, these would keep him pacified for the rest of the journey home. They weren't good for him, she knew, but she couldn't face any more drama, and anyway she never could resist a chance to spoil him.

Opening the driver's door, she leaned towards Presley, smiling and whispering his name. But Snuggly Puppy was on the floor. And Presley was gone.

Monday

1

Detective Inspector Jo Birmingham was trying to adjust the telly on the wall bracket of her brand new office so she could see the screen. The glare of the winter sun was making it impossible to watch the DVD which had arrived in the post that morning. Not that the sounds were leaving much to the imagination. It was clearly a sex tape of some description.

She stretched to try and swivel the bracket around. If she'd had the man who'd stuck it up that high in the first place here in front of her now she'd have given him an earful. Even at her height – five foot ten – she could barely reach it. And the bracket was at such an inconvenient angle. She'd enough problems with migraines recently to know that focusing on anything at an awkward position would invite them back.

She was also doing her best not to look through the glass partition that separated her from the rest of the detective unit, where a clock said ten to nine. Jo's darkening mood had more than a little to do with the fact that her ex-husband and present boss, Chief Superintendent Dan Mason, was just back from a weekend in the sun, and was holding court in the open-plan office, recounting some story or other. *He always did have the gift of the gab*, she thought sneaking a quick glance. He looked good, his face and hands were tanned, and his hair had grown a bit, too. There were slashes of grey in the sides. The older he got, the more she thought he looked like Jason Statham in the Guy Ritchie films.

Slipping off her heels, she dragged over a plastic chair which she'd recovered from the storeroom about a quarter of an hour ago, when she'd been trying to find things to furnish her office. Plonking it directly under the TV, she hitched up her skirt and stepped on to it, doing her best to ignore the half-dozen grinning detectives turning to have a good gawk and a laugh. In an ideal world, Jo would have flashed them like in that Maltesers ad, to wipe the smiles off their faces, but there was a newly appointed Human Resources manager in Store Street Station, Daphne, and Jo didn't want the distinction of being the one who finally gave her something to do.

Balancing on the chair, which was beginning to wobble precariously, she lifted the telly from its bracket and on to the corner of the desk she'd snaffled from Dan's secretary Jeanie's office, thanks to the fact that Jeanie was now on maternity leave. She'd taken Jeanie's computer, too.

Jo had sworn to the mules who'd hauled the items down the corridor for her ten minutes ago that, of course, they would go back eventually; but because Jeanie was now living with Dan, and carrying his baby, Jo wasn't planning on keeping her word.

Through the glass, she saw Detective Inspector Gavin Sexton stand up from his desk and start to make his way over. *Bloody men, never around when we need them*, she grumbled to herself, stepping down from the chair, and rubbing a twinge that had struck up in the small of her back.

Dan was watching her – she could feel his eyes on her

through the window, but when she turned towards him, he was focused back on his fan club, and was becoming even more animated. Jo hoped her new office wasn't going to make her feel as if she was in a goldfish bowl all the time.

Taking a few steps sideways, she finally made out what was happening on the TV screen. She crossed her arms, and watched as the scene unfolded. A girl with surgically enhanced boobs, wearing only a thong, was standing in the shallow end of an outdoor swimming pool, performing a sex act on a man who was sitting on the ledge, leaning back on his hands.

Within seconds, a group of men burst out of a door just out of camera shot, and started dive-bombing into the water. They were shouting words of encouragement to the first man, who looked up and grinned. The girl carried on regardless. Jo recognized the sound of an Irish accent among the English roars. She reached for the Jiffy bag the disc had arrived in and inspected the postcode. There was no stamp, meaning it had been hand-delivered. It wasn't internal post either, because it didn't have the standard state harp on it.

Her own name was scrawled in capital letters on the outside of the envelope in dodgy green biro under the words 'Private and Confidential'. She had had to borrow scissors from Sergeant John Foxe to get through the multiple layers of Sellotape and staples the Jiffy bag had been sealed with. Foxy had only handed the scissors over on condition that she promised to hand them straight back. His initials were Tipp-Exed on the handle.

As she moved the envelope, a piece of folded paper dropped out. She hadn't spotted it earlier, and she now opened it carefully to view a series of letters and words cut from newspapers and magazines. It read: 'How the other half lives – the justice minister enjoying a night out.'

Jo looked back at the screen, eyebrows raised. The current justice minister was Blaise Stanley, someone she had been dealing with to try and bolster victims' rights in court, but although the party was in full swing in the pool, she couldn't see him. The four men who'd jumped in the water had made a semicircle around the girl, who had stopped what she was doing and was trying to push one of them, who was groping her, away. Jo couldn't see their faces, their backs were all to the camera. The man whose legs the girl had been standing between grabbed her roughly by the hair and forced her head back down in his lap. Jo leaned in closer to the screen. Although the film had been shot at night, she could see palm trees, meaning it had to have been taken abroad. There was a hotel in the background with an onion-shaped roof, and between it and the pool a couple were drinking and chatting. They didn't seem in the least put off by what was going on right under their noses – although the woman looked directly across from time to time.

Jo glanced at the note and back at the screen. *Could that be Blaise Stanley?* She doubted it. It was impossible to tell as his back was to the bloody camera, too. The woman's face was familiar, though. *Who was she?* Jo wondered.

Taking the remote from her desk, she aimed it at the floor where the DVD player had been placed and looked for the 'rewind' button so she could freeze the best shot of the man in the distance, while making a mental note to organize a set of shelves before someone trod on the DVD player.

With a single rap, Detective Inspector Gavin Sexton stuck his head around the door. 'You'll do yourself an injury if you—' He stopped talking as he registered the groans of pleasure coming from the man in the pool. Then, dragging the plastic chair into position in front of the TV, he sat down.

'You could have told me it was starting,' he complained, putting his feet up on the corner of Jo's desk.

Jo slapped his feet down, and went over to the machine to collect the disc. 'Were you born in a barn?' She gave the door a light push to close it.

'Somebody got out of bed on the wrong side,' Sexton said, reaching for the cup of Starbucks Jo had bought on the way to work but hadn't had a chance to drink yet. 'What's eating you, anyway?'

What's wrong with me? Jo thought. *What's eating you, more like?*

It seemed that every day Sexton left work a little earlier than the day before. Come three o'clock he'd be showing signs of getting itchy feet, making a hushed phone call with his hand cupped over his mouth, before announcing he was heading off to meet some anonymous tout whose identity always had to be protected. The next day there was never any information worth relaying when Jo asked him what had come out of it. She thought it a real waste of talent. Without him, she would never have tracked down the Bible fanatic who'd wiped out five people in her last big case.

Just last Friday, she'd come within a hair's breadth of tackling Sexton over his tardiness, because she was knee-deep in trying to find a shred of evidence to link three unsolved rape and murder cases with a rapist currently on trial. But Foxy had stepped in, and had had a quiet word, reminding her it was the second anniversary of Sexton's wife Maura's suicide.

'Do you know what he's carrying around in the inside

breast pocket of his jacket, Jo?' Foxy had asked her. 'Maura's suicide note, that's what. He can't bring himself to read it.'

'How do you know that?' Jo had quizzed.

Foxy had tapped the side of his nose twice.

Now, she studied Sexton over the rim of her coffee cup. She was glad to see him take an interest in a case, even if it was only because he was a red-blooded male. His chocolate-coloured eyes needed to get their spark back.

'Where'd it come from anyway?' he asked.

Jo shrugged. 'There was no stamp . . .' She realized she'd got the wrong end of the stick from the way he was looking around. Sexton meant the office.

She grinned at him. 'Great isn't it? Or at least it will be, when I've made it my own.'

The room had previously been designated the station's smoking room because it was the only section of the entire floor with a window that could actually open, the rest being sealed off to facilitate the air con system. A former smoker herself, Jo hated fags with a passion now.

'Did the chief give it to you?' Sexton asked, looking in Dan's direction.

'As if . . .' She scooped up the tape, note and Jiffy envelope, and packed them into the top drawer of the desk, turning the key, which had a spare dangling on its ring. She'd never had a desk with a key still in it, let alone a Formica-topped surface unmarked by a single scorch mark, coffee ring, or set of initials.

'Then it's positive discrimination,' Sexton teased. 'You've got it because you're the only female DI in the Dublin Metropolitan Area.'

'Or, how about . . . I worked bloody hard and I got what I was due?'

'Not a chance,' Sexton said, nudging her elbow, as silver-haired John Foxe stuck his head around the door.

'There's a woman in reception wants to talk to you.'

'Who, Sarge?' Jo asked.

Foxy was the only one she ever addressed by his title. It was a mark of respect. The only reason he hadn't been promoted over the years was because he'd refused it. His daughter, Sal, had Down's syndrome, and he wasn't interested in pursuing a career that would have required any extra hours.

Foxy shrugged. 'She gets an office, she suddenly wants a secretary,' he joked to Sexton, picking up his scissors from the desk.

'Can you ask her to leave her details? I'm on my way out.' Jo zipped up the leather biker jacket she still hadn't had a chance to take off and hang up yet. Not that she had a coat-stand. She added 'hook' to her mental list of furnishings.

'There's a murder trial on in Parkgate Street this morning,' she explained hurriedly. 'I want to stick my nose in on it. The accused is an ordinary Joe who abducted a woman in broad daylight, bound her with her bra, and gagged her with her tights. I've got three unsolved rapes in my filing cabinet with exactly the same modus operandi.'

In the UK, the information would have been entered in a database and would have thrown up an instant alert. In Dublin, Jo had to rely on her gut. 'I want to interview him when the trial ends. Watching him give evidence today, and seeing what presses his buttons, will be a big help in what comes later.' She didn't add that she could also do with a day out of the office now Dan was back.

Foxy looked concerned. 'Please, Jo,' he said, 'can you tell her yourself? She doesn't want to talk to anyone else. She's—'

'What?' Sexton prompted.

'Well, heartbroken,' Foxy said. 'Poor girl looks like she's been sobbing all night.'

Jo glanced at her watch. It was now ten past nine. The trial was due to kick off at half ten. It would take about ten minutes to get there on the Luas tram, which ran right outside the station, as against at least half an hour if she took her car. Even so, she could forget about a seat in court if she didn't leave immediately – according to the papers the public were queuing up to get a glimpse at the defendant. He was accused of raping and trying to murder a teenage Spanish student who was only in Ireland to brush up on her English over the summer. People were appalled by the case, and their morbid curiosity had taken over.

'OK, OK, I'll talk to her,' she said grudgingly, knowing that Foxy's big heart meant he'd be taking a personal interest in this one. She turned and took one last glance round her new office.

'A clock,' she said, ticking a finger.

'What?' Sexton looked puzzled.

She smiled at her colleagues. 'Shelves, a blind, a coat-stand, a wastepaper basket, that bloody bracket lowered two foot – and a clock –– and this place might just be perfect.'

2

The cocaine had travelled across three continents and four oceans to get to Dublin. It started its journey in Colombia as coca leaves picked by peasants in the eastern plains of the Llanos. It had been carried in sacks on the backs of donkeys to drying-out sheds. In paste pits – holes in the ground lined with plastic – it had been treated with chemicals, and stomped on by workers toiling in the scorching sun. The chunky, light-brown putty-like substance that drained off had then been driven in a convoy of 4x4s through the treacherous mountain passes of the Andes, and along the winding road from Cali to the port of Buenaventura, a city of shacks built on stilts on the sea. There, Afro-Colombian slum soldiers had purchased it for the equivalent of four euro a gram, haggling with machine guns, and testing that the produce was untouched by snorting it themselves.

By the time it got to the streets of Dublin – via West Africa, Spain, and Amsterdam – it was supposed to make more than ten times what it had cost Barry 'King Krud' Roberts, the prisoner on remand, to import it. He might not have been able to point out the countries it had passed through on an atlas, but having just received a phone call on one of the four mobiles which he used to run his business from his cell in Portlaoise, and learned that the consignment which had travelled halfway around the world had been intercepted by gardaí the previous night, he was taking it very personally. And consequently, he was going berserk.

The King was trashing his prison cell on the E1 landing, looking for the listening device he was convinced must have given the game away.

The steroids in his bloodstream, which gave him his bull-dog neck and spotty skin, meant that when he flew into a rage, a powder keg of hate exploded.

The metal bunks made a deafening clang as he upended them. The contents of the slopping-out bucket sluiced all over the tiled floor as he kicked it in a temper. Even his pet canary was in a flap, trying to fly into the highest corner of its cage. If there was no bug in his cell, he was going to have to work out which rat had betrayed him. That rat would have to die, as had nine others in the last year, as the King secured his stranglehold on the south Dublin drug-distribution ring.

Twenty-four years old, he had got his nickname from his habit of smearing his face with faeces before every street slaying, and a bloodlust that had catapulted him from small-time street-corner deals to running a gang of killers willing to do anything to hold on to their new-found status in the underworld. The King was not about to let any of that change just because he'd been remanded in custody pending a murder trial. Throughout every one of his court hearings he'd sung the Bob Dylan song about Rubin 'Hurricane' Carter, a black middleweight boxer in the sixties wrongly convicted of multiple murders.

Not that the King was innocent. He'd done the murder he was in for all right. He'd grown up with Joey Lambert, the man he'd knifed in the heart, and had once considered him a mate. But that hadn't stopped him stabbing Joey in a McDonald's in Stillorgan shopping centre full of horrified south side diners. Why? He'd heard a rumour that Joey wanted to oust him as boss. The King had made sure to twist the knife as he'd plunged it in.

No, he hadn't been singing Bob Dylan because he was innocent. He'd sung it because the gardaí hadn't had a shred of evidence against him – all the witnesses who'd been stuffing their faces that night had suffered from a collective lapse of memory. So as far as he was concerned, it was tantamount to being framed. He'd been wrongly incarcerated, just like Rubin.

He also knew the real reason he was inside was because of what had happened after the killing – a twelve-month tit-for-tat street war as his original gang had split. He himself had opened fire on a pub with both barrels of a sawn-off shotgun, hitting a bouncer and a customer.

This was why the state had locked him up – to quell the feuding. And why this particular shipment of cocaine was extremely dear to him. It was supposed to send out a message on the street that, even banged up inside, he was still the King. It wasn't the size of the consignment he'd lost – he'd imported ten times as much in one single deal in the past – it was that he didn't like what the loss said about him: that he was losing control. That was why this one mattered more than any of the others.

When there was nothing left to smash, rip or tear asunder, the King realized there was no bug in his cell. Which meant that someone had betrayed him. Someone who would soon discover there were worse things than death. There was a hard death.

The ringtone on one of his phones started to play the 50

Cent track: 'Many Men (Wish Death)'. The King was all set to throw the phone, too, against the wall until he saw who was calling.

'Who?' he asked, in his pronounced Dublin accent, then nodded, knelt down on his hunkers, reached for some of what had spilled from the bucket, and spread it across his forehead and cheeks.

Slowly a smile spread across his face. Because, as it turned out, the rat was not a him, but a her.

3

There was no doubt the girl in the public lobby was distressed, but what Foxy hadn't mentioned was that she was also very pretty. Jo sighed, and checked her watch. No wonder he'd been so interested. The girl had perfectly chiselled features, striking green eyes and an expensive hair-cut held off her face with a pair of Gucci sunglasses. She was no more than twenty and dressed in a black blazer, rock-chick T-shirt, a pair of designer jeans and trendy open-toed ankle boots. The studs in her ears sparkled the way only real diamonds can.

'Can you come with me?' Jo asked her, indicating an interview room to the right of the counter. She swiped her card through the pad to open the door, and held it ajar for the girl to enter. Inside, Jo guided the girl by the shoulders into one of the two chairs situated either side of a small square table, noticing as she did so that the girl's toenails had a French pedicure. If Jo had had the time for a pampering, the chances of her squandering it on something like that would have been slim to none.

'You'll think I'm wasting your time,' the girl said.

As she spoke with a cut-glass accent, Jo realized how familiar she was – she had the same sphinx-like quality to her eyes that Kate Moss had. Of course, she'd seen her only the other night on *The Late Late Show*, raising money for charity. Come to think of it, she was a model, and, Jo would bet, one of the country's most well-known ones at that. 'You're Tara Parker Trench, aren't you?' she said.

The girl gave a quick nod.

Why had Foxy not mentioned this, either? Jo wondered. He read every newspaper going, they all came in to the station every day. This girl was one of the It girls of the moment. There was no way her name would have been lost on Foxy. Despite being a stickler for doing things by the book, he loved a bit of gossip. Jo refocused her attention on Tara, who'd begun to weep. She looked unwell; her lips had a bluish tinge.

'Please, it's my little boy, someone's taken him. You have to find him. If anything's happened to him I . . .'

Jo stood, and reached for the phone on the wall. 'We'll have to file a missing persons report. I'll organize the forms we'll need.'

'I've done all that.'

Jo stopped.

'I was in here last night,' Tara explained, wiping her eyes. 'Your lot were right there when he was taken. In the service station around the corner. I told them I wanted you.'

'I don't understand . . .'

Tara sniffed. 'I stopped for petrol on the quays about nine last night, like I already told them. Presley – my son – was in his child seat in the back of the car. I was only gone for a minute, a couple, max . . . he's only three years old. It was lashing . . . he was asleep . . . it was past his bedtime. I didn't want to . . . The gardaí were there because there was trouble . . . There was a squad car parked right beside my car when Presley was taken. I thought he was safe . . .' She fumbled a card out of her pocket. 'That's him, the cop I told everything to. He brought me here last night.'

Jo read Fred Oakley's name on the card. He was a detective sergeant, a great bear of a man with chestnut hair. He was a bit full of himself, but still interested in the job and thorough. Fred was a man's man, he liked swilling the pints and talking about rugby, but as long as he solved crime Jo wasn't about to hold that against him. The fact that this was Fred's case also explained why Foxy had been so scant with details. He'd have known exactly who this girl was, but like the old hand he was, he'd played dumb rather than be accused of muscling in on anyone else's territory. He'd left that to Jo.

'You're in good hands with Fred,' Jo told her.

'But it's you I need,' Tara's voice had risen to a wail. 'I read about what you did in the paper after that reporter's little girl was abducted.'

Jo sighed. Tara was referring to the recent serial killer case she'd worked on, in which the victims had all been connected to the kidnap of a crime reporter's child. She had tracked the killer down by identifying the links between his five victims.

'You have to help me find him. Please. You have to . . .' Tara sounded as though she was about to hyperventilate.

'Is there anything else I should know? Anything about last night? Anything else untoward happen recently? Anyone been giving you bother?'

Tara put her head in her hands. 'Just the row inside the garage shop.'

'What were you driving?'

'My car, it's a Mini Cooper.'

'Colour and reg?' Jo asked.

Tara supplied the details.

Jo made a mental note. 'Did Detective Sergeant Oakley ring someone for you – a friend or partner for you to be with?'

'There's only my mum, and they told her to stay where she was to answer the phone,' Tara answered. 'Please—'

'Look, I'll do what I can, but unless the chief assigns me to the case, I'll only be able to help you on my own time. I'm sorry.'

Tara began to cry again. Feeling a wrench of sympathy, Jo leaned forward and touched her shoulder. Tara flinched.

'The reason why I have to find him . . .' She sobbed. '. . . is because he's got chronic asthma. He takes medication every night. Without it, he'll have an attack. Do you know what that means?' She looked at Jo, fear written all over her face. 'It means he won't be able to breathe.'

Jo asked Tara to wait in the interview room while she headed back out to the public counter. Stretching across the officer on duty, she took the hardback log-book and slid it sideways, flicking the pages backwards till she reached the previous night's reported incidents. Everything had to be logged. She ran her finger up the entries recorded in chronological order. Seconds later, she was tapping the line giving details about a toddler who had been reported snatched from a car in the petrol station a short distance away. The time the information had been received was set at 9.15 p.m., almost exactly twelve hours earlier.

Ordinarily in these circumstances, Jo wouldn't have felt the need to double-check that someone like Tara Parker Trench was telling her the truth, but it wasn't stacking up. *Why the hell didn't I read about the case in the papers this morning?* she wondered. Putting the child's face in the public eye was policing at its most basic. The station should have been buzzing with it, with every available officer drafted in to a conference and put on the case.

Giving the book back to the officer, she headed upstairs to talk to Dan, glad there was no need to knock on Jeanie's door first. The state of the country's finances meant there wasn't even the budget to get a temp in to cover as Dan's secretary. With no one there, Jeanie's old office looked even more abandoned now that her desk and computer were in Jo's new room.

Jo rapped on the inner door, then stepped inside, not waiting for an answer. Dan was on the phone, talking in that low, sexy tone he had when he was in a good humour. His midnight-blue eyes were dancing with mischief, making Jo think that he had to be talking to Jeanie. Jo felt her insides twist in pain. It wasn't too long ago that he used to talk to her like that.

He continued to ignore her, so she stepped up to his handset and pressed 'hold'. 'Sorry, I know that's offside,' she said, 'but Fred Oakley's missing toddler case – I need to insinuate myself on to it. The little boy's poorly.'

Dan pressed 'hold' again and said, 'I'll ring you back,' into the handset, before banging the receiver down. 'Forget it,' he said, his eyes cold and hard. 'That's Oakley's case. He's well able to handle it.'

'I agree, but the mother's asking for me, and I can't walk away.'

'It's not her call,' Dan said, still angry. 'You used to want to be transferred out of this station, remember? And anyway, I trust Oakley.' He leaned back. His stomach was tight, but his shirt was in need of a hotter iron, Jo noticed.

'You done something to your hair?' he asked.

Jo touched her head self-consciously. She'd had it cut into shorter layers while he was away, wanting something easier to manage. The front strands were longer, kinking out at the ends, and the stylist had talked her into a scatter of dirty blonde highlights to lift the brown. Jo hadn't expected Dan to notice it. She sat down in the uncomfortable cup chair he kept for visitors.

'How's Jeanie?' she asked.

Dan looked uncomfortable. 'Good, thanks.' He coughed. 'Keeping me on my toes. She had me painting the nursery all last week. Nesting, I believe they call it.'

Jo studied her shoes. She'd thought they'd separated because he couldn't cope with the shock of her second pregnancy, which had come sixteen years after her first. But by the sound of it he was enjoying Jeanie's. She talked through the lump in her throat. 'I'm worried about last night's missing boy, Dan.'

He exhaled, stood up and walked to the window, turning his back to her. 'Do you know where Oakley should be right now? Home in bed, that's where. He's on nights. Instead, he's out right now looking for the little kid. Knowing him, he'll probably waltz in here any second with the boy in his arms because Little Mizz Up Herself, Tara what's-her-face, has been preventing her ex from seeing his own son.'

Jo swallowed. Tara hadn't told her about her ex. If Dan thought this was a straightforward tug-of-love battle, it was no wonder he'd given the case such a low priority.

'Just give me twenty-four hours on the case, that's all I ask.'

'You know what happened last time you said that? You wanted twenty-four hours on the Bible case after I decided it should go to Sexton. You undermined me.'

'Undermined? I solved it, didn't I?'

He ran a finger inside his shirt collar. 'Oh, you solved it all right, and you made yourself friends in high places in the process.'

'What does that mean?'

'It means while you've been out there lording it over everyone in your own office, I've had to explain to the rest of the team why they're four to a desk. You didn't even have the decency to tell me what was going on. I had a stand-up row with the workmen emptying the room when I got in this morning.'

'But you were on holiday with Jeanie, remember?'

'And you got the minister to organize it behind my back?'

He was referring to Blaise Stanley, who might or might not be on the DVD in Jo's desk. All of a sudden, Jo was glad she hadn't mentioned the sex tape to Dan. 'No! Stanley contacted me to ask if it would help if I had my own office. What should I have said, eh? "No. Wait till I run it by Dan?"'

Dan sighed. 'You could have rung me,' he said gruffly. He crossed the room to stand beside her chair. 'So what did you have to give Blaise Stanley to get it?' he asked, looking down at her.

Jo drew in a long breath. 'Nothing,' she said. 'He's a married man.'

He walked back behind his desk and sat down heavily, reaching for the phone. 'I've made my decision. It's Oakley's case.'

'Please, Dan, just one day. The child is sick, for Christ's sake. Just today, that's all I want.'

But the conversation was over, and Dan had turned back to his phone. Clenching her fists, Jo stood up, and headed for the door.

'And you needn't bother asking your friends in the press to get Tara what's-her-face on the news today, either,' Dan called after her. 'You haven't a hope with the budget. The president could get shot and it would have to be held over till tomorrow.'

Jo didn't turn around to answer him, because she knew if she did she'd bloody well kill him. She'd got an office because she had earned Blaise Stanley's respect for tracking down a cold-blooded murderer. There was no way she was going to let Dan's pride stop her from finding a child.

4

In a café just around the corner from the station, Jo transferred two full Irish breakfasts from a tray and slid a mug of sugary tea in front of Tara, taking the coffee for herself. Circles rippled out through the drinks as a DART trundled by overhead. The café was tucked right under the bridge running into Connolly Station.

Jo watched Tara turn her face away from the smell as she reached for and squirted the plastic ketchup dispenser across her own plate.

'Look,' she said, leaning across the table. 'I need you to stay strong. We've a long day ahead of us, so the sooner you get some food into you, the sooner we get on with it.' Pulling her black-bound pocket notebook and pen from her jacket, she flicked it open on the table, folding a half-slice of toast around a piece of bacon. She took a couple of bites, then checked the pen was working by scribbling on the corner of the blank page.

'Right,' she said looking up in time to see Tara managing some of her fried egg. 'I know you've been through this but I need to go over it again. Where were you coming from last night and where were you going to?'

Tara closed her eyes. 'I'd a shoot at the airport for a

holiday brochure. It wrapped at about eight fifteen, and I headed home. I've an apartment in Citywest.'

'Where was Presley all this time, when you were working?'

'With my mum. She takes care of him when I need it.'

'Why didn't you take the M50 from the airport to Citywest?' The ring road bypassed the city centre.

'Mum lives in North Great George's Street.'

Not far from where the boy disappeared, Jo realized. She made a quick note of the word 'minder' and circled it.

'Who's Presley's father?'

'Mick Devlin. We split up about a year ago.'

'Why?'

'He didn't like me earning more than him. He's a mechanic. Everything's black and white in Mick's book. I'd put on a bikini for work, he'd get jealous and think I was doing it to provoke him. He wanted me to stop modelling. When I wouldn't, he walked.'

'You still get along?'

Tara shook her head. 'Not since he applied for sole custody of Presley.'

Jo put her pen down and stared. 'Why would he do that?'

'Because if I want to get a client's product into the paper, I need to be seen out and about at night so as to get the papers to take an interest in me. But Mick wants me home all the time with Presley. He thinks me having a life makes me an unfit mother.' She blew her nose. 'Look, shouldn't we be out there now, looking?'

'Could Mick have taken Presley?'

'To teach me a lesson? Yes. That was the first thing I thought, too. But he's on holiday in Fuerteventura. He's not due back until tonight.'

'Is there a new man in your life?'

'No. And what's that got to do with anything, anyway?'

'I need to know if you're rowing with any other exes.'

Tara shook her head, and started cutting her food up into small pieces.

'Any women got a grudge against you?' Jo pressed on. 'You get on the wrong side of any of the other models lately? It's supposed to be a bitchy industry. A crime like this has a woman's stamp all over it. Anyone's nose put out of joint because of the attention you've been giving their other half?'

'No. And no.' Tara sighed. 'I don't know anybody who'd do something like that.'

'Someone like you gets invited to great parties, and let into nightclubs for free. You must get a lot of attention from men. There must have been a girlfriend along the way who's got the hump.'

'I get offers, sure. But I don't have time for a relationship. Every spare minute I've got, I'm with Presley, or doing my classes.'

'Classes in what?'

'Acting.'

Jo looked up. *Tara does seem genuinely upset*, she thought. 'Are you practising on me now?'

'What do you mean?'

'Are you acting out a role?'

'Of course not.' Tara lifted her hands to push her hair back, and as she did so her T-shirt slid up to reveal a bare midriff and a range of livid bruises surrounding it.

Jo stared, and Tara sat back down again pulling the top down quickly. 'My son's missing. He's sick. What more do I have to do?'

Jo leaned in to Tara. 'Someone been manhandling you recently?'

'No! I had a fall coming down some stairs, that's all.'

Jo sighed, and stood up, reaching for her jacket and bag. 'If I find out you've lied to me, I'm walking away. Now – are you going to finish that?'

Tara shook her head.

'OK, let's make a start.'

Jo could have walked back to the station for a car, but the garage Presley had disappeared from was only a block away, and with traffic it would have taken a quarter of an hour to drive there.

Five minutes later they were there. The Ever Oil garage had a Methadone clinic on one side, a homeless shelter on the other, a dingy pub two doors up, and a sprawling block of council flats behind it. In terms of a place in which to lose a three-year-old, it was your basic nightmare.

It shocked Jo to see it was business as usual so soon after such a serious crime, with no sign of any area having been cordoned off, and not even a road block in place quizzing passing motorists.

She noted six pumps in the forecourt, all of them in use bar one, with queues developing.

Tara groaned, then ran to a corner of the perimeter and emptied the contents of her stomach behind a scrawny bush. Jo went over and put her hand on her back. 'You OK?'

'I'm sorry,' Tara said, 'the petrol fumes reminded me – oh my God, my poor little boy.'

Jo gripped her arm. 'Show me where it happened.'

Tara gulped a few deep breaths, then pointed a shaky hand towards where she'd parked, just round the corner from the CCTV cameras, and the entrance to the garage store.

Jo walked over to the public toilet door and pressed the handle down. It was locked. She walked around to the entrance of the store, and led Tara through the double-glazed glass door, reinforced with a ridged slab of metal at kicking level.

As convenience stores went, there was a depressed feel to the place. The tiles on the ceiling were missing in parts, leaving cable wiring exposed. The stock was sparse, and the whole interior badly in need of a paint and a clean.

'He was here last night,' Tara said, nodding at a Perspex counter.

Jo looked at the Muslim man behind the till. He had a long wiry beard, and was wearing a skullcap. There wasn't a queue yet, and the man was going through the contents of the till from what Jo could make out.

He registered Jo, let his gaze skirt across Tara, then went back to work. Jo didn't like his attitude. If a small boy got snatched from your premises, you'd ask how the mother was doing next time you saw her.

She led Tara towards him, past the shelves of lads' mags. The man kept counting.

Jo held her ID up to the glass. 'Liquor licence, please.'

He snorted.

'And the key to the outside toilet, while you're at it.'

'Customers only.' His accent was inner-city Dublin.

'Did I say I wanted to use it?'

He threw his eyes up to heaven and headed into the back. A few customers started to file in behind Jo, who was scrolling through the contacts on her phone. She chose Fred Oakley's number.

'Oakley,' she said, as the call connected.

Jo drew a breath. She knew what a voice that was answering from a prostrate position sounded like – so much for Dan's theory that Oakley was out pounding the streets.

'Fred, it's Jo Birmingham.'

He grunted at a pitch that led her to believe Dan must have already briefed him.

'The case of the missing child from last night. Where are we on that?'

He hesitated. 'I'm chasing a few leads. What's it to you?'

'I'm here where it happened with his mother. It's business as usual round at the garage, Fred. Nothing's been sealed off.'

He huffed out a breath, and Jo heard his voice change as he sat up. 'You know who she is, right?'

Jo turned her back to Tara. 'What does that mean, Fred?'

'To put you in the picture, we've had a word with her boss – I believe the correct term is "agent". She's told us on the q.t. that our Tara's got quite a gift for porkie pies. The word actually used was "Munchausen's". I'm amazed Tara Parker Trench's not plastered all over the papers already, to tell you the truth. I'd bet my mother that's what this is really about. I can see the headline: "How My Boy Was Kidnapped." Papers, publicity, profile. All adds up to money. Look at that Jordan one. She's made a fortune out of a pair of tits.'

Jo sighed.

'You know what Munchausen's is, right?' Oakley said. 'It's where mothers present their children at hospital claiming they're sick, so as to get attention for themselves.'

Jo glanced at Tara. She had both her arms wrapped around her belly, and was carrying the same stuffed toy dog that she'd been holding at the station. Jo lowered her voice.

'Yeah, I know what it is, Fred, but it still leaves me with one question. Where's little Presley?'

Oakley paused. 'With whoever was minding him when her ladyship got back from Marrakesh last night, I presume.'

'You presume? Have you checked?'

'You want to watch it,' Oakley said. 'Are you suggesting I haven't? That's basic policing.'

'OK,' Jo said. She didn't want to provoke him unnecessarily.

'I'm sure she knows where the kid is,' Oakley went on. 'If you need any proof that she's an attention-seeker, you don't have to look any further than the kid's poofter name . . . She did tell you she'd been out of the country?'

Jo moved another few feet away from Tara. 'No, she didn't – but it doesn't change anything, Fred. Especially here in the garage where Presley went missing. First thing I'd have done is make a list of every vehicle recorded on the CCTV driving in, and out, at the crucial times – starting from ten to nine, till ten past and working my way back on either side. I'd have listed the drivers' names in one column, and alongside that I'd have put any previous convictions. But you haven't done any of this, and the question I'm going to be asking back at the station is: why?'

She hung up, and turned back to Tara. 'Why didn't you tell me you'd been on a trip? Why did you give me a cock and bull story about a shoot in the airport?'

Tara had begun to shake. 'I did do the shoot when I got back. I didn't think the trip was relevant.'

'You lied to me about the circumstances leading up to the disappearance of your boy. You think that isn't relevant? I told you if you lied—' She stepped closer to Tara, noticing the tiny bloodspots under her eyes and how thin she was under the expensive designer jacket. She remembered the bruises on her stomach, wondered how they'd got there. 'Even your agent says you're a liar. What's she got against you?'

Tara took a deep breath. 'I'm sleeping with her husband.'

Jo blinked. The teller came back, held the liquor licence paperwork up to the Perspex, and dropped a key through the hatch.

'Open the door,' Jo said, pointing past him to the door into the till area.

He looked as if he intended to say no, then moved slowly in that direction.

'Here, I got a delivery to make,' a pizza guy called from the queue behind Tara and Jo.

'Yeah, get on with it, we've all got dinners to make, and kids to collect and feed,' a woman said.

'Quiet, you lot,' Jo ordered, turning round. 'We're looking for a child who went missing from here last night.'

There was total silence.

'What you got under here?' Jo asked, as she entered the till area. Rows of XXX-rated DVDs were hidden from view under the counter by the teller's leg. 'I don't expect you'll be able to produce a licence for this, now will you?' She took the chits he'd been clipping together from his hand. 'Are they from last night?' The date on the top one gave her the answer. 'I'll be needing these,' she said, putting them in her jacket pocket.

She glanced to his left. 'That the door to the loo?'

He nodded.

'Why don't you let me in this way and save me going the long way around?'

Grumbling to himself, he stepped past her and pressed the door handle down.

Inside, the toilet was pitch dark and the air was dank. Concrete walls gave it a cavernous feel, and the sound of the water glugging in the tank was unnerving. The place also stank to high heaven. Jo reached for a string dangling from the ceiling, pulled it and an exposed bulb threw light around a dirty room measuring about twelve foot by fourteen. On the concrete floor painted over with an industrial red-coloured paint, Jo identified the source of the smell as dog faeces smeared all over the floor.

Tara started to wail: a high-pitched keening sound.

'Is the wee child in there?' a woman called from the queue.

'What can you see?' a man said, sounding tense.

On the red concrete floor, a metre out from one of the walls, lay a tiny pair of Ray-Ban sunglasses.

5

Half an hour later Jo had everyone outside the garage, and the whole area cordoned off, as the crime scene examiners arrived carrying their standard black-shell cases. She'd phoned Dan as soon as she'd spotted Presley's shades, demanding that he start taking the case seriously by notifying the Tech Bureau attached to the forensic science lab at HQ. Instead, however, he'd drafted in the local boys attached to the station, which, as far as she was concerned, was the equivalent of giving her the two fingers. It wasn't that the officers weren't highly trained in crime scene preservation – the lads were terrific at what they did, Jo knew that – but they were only ever involved when it was unclear if a crime had been committed in the first place. The green light would only be given to the forensic team at the Tech Bureau after they'd carried out a preliminary examination, all of which was going to add to the delay in finding little Presley.

Jo took a deep breath. She still couldn't understand why first Fred and now Dan were not moving heaven and earth to bring the child to safety. She studied Tara standing on the side of the road, her arms crossed over the toy dog and her whole body shaking. The Muslim manager was shaking too – with anger. His customers were drifting off before he'd had time to collect their payments for fuel.

Jo wasn't having any of it. 'What's your bloody name, bright spark?'

'Hassan,' he answered.

'And what's your problem?'

'She,' he said, jabbing a finger at Tara, 'tried to do a runner last night. That's what I already told your lot. She's the one you want to put under pressure, not me. I'm just trying to make a living.'

Tara had heard what he'd said, and came over. 'How many times do I have to tell you?' she shouted. 'I wasn't going anywhere. I only moved the car because I was freaking out over the shit going on inside; the way that skinhead was throwing stuff left, right and centre. I wanted to check that my son was all right. When I'd moved the car, I was going to come straight back in and pay you.'

'Yeah, well I came out and banged on your window and I didn't see no kid in the back.' He glared at her.

Shocked, Jo turned to face Tara.

'You didn't look in the back!' Tara shouted.

One of the team emerged from the garage and called Jo over. She had met him before. His name was Owen. He was lanky, with an undershot jaw, and he always smelled of soap.

'OK, we're putting the call in to HQ,' Owen said.

'About time, too,' Jo said. She knew none of this was his fault, but she was spitting nails. 'Nothing personal, but we're only about twelve hours late.'

'Yeah, well there's more to this one than meets the eye,' he said.

Jo rubbed the back of her neck. A headache was making itself felt behind her temples. 'What does that mean?'

'Didn't you hear who they found in here last night? Only

Tom Burke, that paedophile they've been hunting for the past twelve months.'

Jo exhaled. 'You're joking.' Everyone had been warned to keep an eye out for Burke, a serial child-abuser who'd been released from prison about a year earlier after a long stretch inside. As a registered sex offender, he was supposed to inform the gardaí of his address, but when an incident in a park was reported involving a seven-year-old boy and bearing all the hallmarks of Burke's previous crimes, they'd discovered he'd moved on. The papers had been baying for him to be found ever since.

Jo glanced over at Tara, who was studying some message on her phone and sobbing again.

'The sick bastard's in hospital now,' Owen continued. 'A dog chewed up his leg in here last night. Pity he didn't finish him off, eh? Good thing Fred Oakley was here. He recognized Burke the second he saw him. Turns out that pervert had been lodging around here all along, right under our noses.'

Of course, Jo thought. If the papers found out that a child had been snatched from under officers' noses while a serial paedophile, who'd eluded them for a year, was right there at the time, it would be the worst kind of publicity for the force. No wonder Dan was being so circumspect.

She walked over to Tara and took her arm. 'I want you to go home to your place in Citywest and try and get a couple of hours' rest.'

'But what happens if Presley has an asthma attack? I must stay—'

'Love, I'm going to have to grill you at length later, so I want you at your best. Go home, shower, change, and make sure you have Presley's medication at the ready in case we need it sharpish.'

48

She flipped open her mobile and started to scroll through for the cab firm the station used, then remembered something.

'I want the names of anyone you gave the key to that toilet to last night,' she said to Hassan.

'Impossible.'

'Nothing's impossible. Either you can sift through your security footage and match the faces up with the times of your credit card transactions to get names for me, or we'll do it for you. And, just so you know, if any harm comes to the missing boy, I'm going to have you charged as an accessory.'

Hassan stepped forward aggressively. 'No, I mean it's impossible. Because the toilet door was open, anyone who wanted could have used it. There's no way I could keep track of everyone.'

'He's lying,' Tara said, over Jo's shoulder. She was about to climb into the taxi Jo had flagged down, and was holding out a scrap of paper in her hand with 'Mum's phone number' scribbled at the top and a mobile listed underneath. 'There was an "Out of Order" sign on the toilet door last night. I saw it. It's gone now. You need to ask him why.'

6

Jeff Cox climbed out of his sleek, black, 7 Series BMW with the morning newspaper tucked under his arm. He jangled a key free from the set as he banged the car door shut, and headed past the fountain feature, towards his imposing mock-Tudor home.

Inside, he cupped his suede loafers off, arranging them neatly at the bottom of the stairs. He knew once his wife, Imogen, realized he was back, she would continue the row they'd had before he'd stormed out and he was going to try and keep that moment at bay for as long as possible. She'd said such horrible things, threatened divorce, told him he wouldn't get a penny. The longer he could put off more abuse, the better. He padded past the giant photograph of her, which dominated the hallway, giving it the customary captain's salute. It had been taken in her modelling days, twenty-odd years ago, when she'd been young and gorgeous. Her dark, kohled eyes smouldered over a scarlet pout. The lipstick ran a couple of millimetres past the outline of her lips. He hadn't been able to keep his hands off her back then. It felt like a million years ago.

Zipping his Abercrombie & Fitch hoodie up as he walked, Jeff headed towards the cold draft of air travelling up the hall, pulling his hands inside the sleeves as he moved. The house was freezing.

He found out why in the kitchen. The sliding patio back door had been left ajar. The wooden slatted blind rattled against it in steady taps.

It didn't make sense to him. Their dog, Molly, always barked at the first sound of his car returning. He'd never have made it from the front door to the back in time to close it before she'd have trundled up to greet him, hips out of sync with the rest of her body, and slavering everywhere.

And if Imogen had taken her for a walk, she wouldn't have left the back door open. Even with a high perimeter hedge around the property and electronic gates at the front, she was still paranoid about security, and guarded their possessions with the zealousness of someone who'd come from nothing. And since the 'burglary', she'd been worse than ever. He couldn't even leave the bedroom window open an inch at night, or she was on his case.

The glass door made a sucking noise as he slid it shut and he stepped awkwardly over the dog's empty wicker basket propped beside it. Molly's sleeping arrangements were an accident waiting to happen, but arthritis was a genetic pre-disposition of Newfoundlands and he was trying to make her life as easy as possible now she was getting on. The fact that the basket was still where he'd last left it was another indicator that Imogen definitely wasn't around, he realized, though he'd just parked alongside her Land Rover in the driveway, and she hadn't mentioned anything about going anywhere when he'd seen her at breakfast. It occurred to him that she might be in one of her sulks over their row, and be giving him the silent treatment.

Jeff hopped back to clear Molly's basket. But if Imogen

had been here she'd have shoved it under the kitchen table
and blocked Molly's access with the chairs, he realized. Jeff
always kicked it straight back out again, as soon as she'd
turned her back.

His eyes skimmed the black marble work surfaces for any
sign of a note. Where had she gone at this hour? When
would she be back? And was a note letting him know really
too much to expect? It was irrelevant, he reminded himself.
Imogen didn't do considerate. He cast an eye over the breakfast dishes, which she could never be arsed to move from the
kitchen table to the Belfast sink. Their dishwasher wasn't
worth a curse because their location on Killiney Hill meant
the water pressure was poor. Jeff only ended up making
work for himself when he used it.

With a heavy sigh, he began to tidy up, groaning as he
realized how long Imogen had left her Rice Krispies to dry in
the bowl – they were a bugger to scrape off. He was sure she
did it to spite him. He angled the tap over it and turned on the
water. The sight of it dripping out didn't help his mood.

He'd be lucky to fit in a trip to the gym, and a swim, at
this rate. He was definitely not going into the office, he
decided, as he began to put away the breakfast dishes. If
Imogen wanted him to be a skivvy at home, she couldn't
expect him to show up for work as well. She only wanted
him in the office so she could order him around there, too.
Well, the mood he was in after everything said between them
this morning, he didn't care what threats she made about
firing him today. The revenue from the business was down
because the world was in recession; it had nothing to do
with him not pulling his weight. She could stick her precious
modelling business where the sun didn't shine. He'd had
enough.

He was still clearing up and putting away things when he spotted her Louis Vuitton handbag under one of the kitchen chairs. He froze. Imogen would never have gone out without her handbag. He stood completely still and listened hard. And then he heard it – what sounded like frenzied barking at the far end of the garden, near the stable block. As he listened, he realized how panicked Molly was.

Heart pounding, Jeff ran to the sliding door and pulled it open again, sprinting to the back of the garden, an acre between him and the pool house. But when he got there, he couldn't believe what he was looking at. Imogen lay face down in the grass, Molly's bark changing to a whimper as she nuzzled his leg.

Jeff's gaze travelled from the blood congealed on the back of Imogen's misshapen head and moved to a bloodstained rock a couple of feet away. He knelt by Imogen and reached for her wrist. She was still warm. He pressed his fingers into her skin and was sure he could feel a pulse. The dark grass around her told him just how much blood she'd lost. His fingers moved to her neck. The pulse was faint, but she was definitely still alive, he realized.

Jeff stood and stared at the house for a second, running his fingers through his hair. 'Come on, girl,' he said, grabbing Molly's collar. If he phoned an ambulance, they might be able to save Imogen. If he gave Molly a feed first, and tinkered about for a bit, perhaps they would not.

7

An hour later, Jo was back in the station and looking for Sexton. He wasn't answering his mobile or the phone on his desk, but one of the guys in the corridor pointed in the direction of the Gents, so this was where Jo headed next. Not bothering to knock, she marched in, shielding her eyes with a hand as she passed two uniforms standing at the urinals.

She called his name. 'Forget it, that's Fred Oakley's case,' Sexton shouted back from behind the only closed cubicle door.

'Well he's making a balls of it,' Jo answered, 'and if you think I'm going to stand idly by when a tot's disappeared from a garage shop where paedophiles were stopping to pick up blue movies, you've another think coming.'

The uniforms glanced at each other, zipped up and made a hasty exit.

Jo heard the toilet flush.

'Where to?' Sexton asked, heading over to the sink, where he squirted the empty soap dispenser and scrubbed his hands.

'We need to talk to the person who's the reason why nobody's taking what happened seriously,' Jo shouted over the drone of the Dyson dryer. 'Tara Parker Trench's agent. We need to talk to Imogen Cox.'

*

The car park was in its usual state of chaos, and they lost a good five minutes trying to get a marked car out of it. Cops on their way into the station dumped their cars, leaving the handbrakes off and the doors unlocked for the cops on their way out to worry about. Tara's Mini, with its striped bonnet, was there today, too. Presumably Fred had had it towed there when he'd decided the case was closed, instead of having the forensic team fine toothcomb it.

Sexton pushed first at the front of the squad car, and then moved to the back while Jo dragged the steering wheel left, then right, her curses growing more explicit by the second. She was about to insist they take the battered Ford she usually drove, and couldn't bring herself to replace because it was a present from Dan, when she finally got enough of a swing to get the squad car out.

Squeezing himself sideways in the passenger door, Sexton read out the address for Tara Parker Trench's boss from a sheet of paper Foxy had handed over on their way out.

'Interesting,' he remarked.

'What?'

'I thought the arse had fallen out of the advertising industry, but judging by where this Imogen Cox lives, she must be minting it,' Sexton added. 'It's Bono and Neil Jordan's neck of the woods – millionaire row.'

He'd barely swung the door shut before Jo was speeding across the Luas tram tracks. Swinging left, she took an immediate right again at the Pig and Heifer, past the green glass and granite IFSC buildings on her left and the city bus terminus on her right, and crossed the Liffey to the south side, turning left on to City Quay at the Matt Talbot Bridge. Only when she had a straight run, in the bus lane on the Rock Road, did Sexton finally speak again.

'You all right?' he asked, gripping the bottom of the seat with one hand, and the overhead handle with the other.

'Fine.' Jo sighed. She wanted to change the subject. 'You're a man about town. Tell me everything you know about Tara Parker Trench.'

'She's a ride.'

'Says you and every red-blooded male in Ireland. What else?'

'She eats microbiotic food that is inedible, she wears Armani that nobody can afford, and she has a stalker, but we won't hold that against her since that's an accessory in the world she lives in. Oh, and she gave her child a ridiculous name, suggesting she has aspirations of winding up in la-la land.'

'A stalker?' Jo said.

Sexton's knuckles were white from holding on to the overhead handle. 'I'm not saying another word until you watch where you're going.'

Jo clicked her tongue, and slowed down. 'You were saying . . .'

'It's nothing. Stalkers are like accessories in the celeb circuit.'

'Sounds pretty scary to me. What I don't understand is why everyone has got it in for her.'

'Who's everyone?'

'Dan and Fred Oakley for starters, and now you. In other words, all the men she's come into contact with at the station, with the single exception of Foxy.'

Sexton slid his finger under his nose to signal what he was thinking – cocaine. 'They've probably heard the rumours about her fondness for you know what. True or not, mud sticks.'

'And do you believe she has got a drug problem?'

'It goes hand in glove with the social set she prefers to hang out with.'

'She works in the fashion industry,' Jo protested half-heartedly. 'Dan and Fred don't think her boy was taken. Do you? If you don't, now's your chance to tell me. Because if I find out you're not focused on this case, you're no use to me, understand?'

Sexton held his hands up in protest. 'She'd been away in Marrakesh, presumably spoiling herself in a flash hotel without the kid, and she left him alone in the car in a grimy garage at night. It's hardly a glowing reference for motherhood.'

'So you don't believe her?'

'I believe you believe her.'

'I do!'

'Well, I trust your instincts. That'll have to be enough.'

'And what's wrong with your own instincts?'

He turned his face away and stared out the passenger window.

'You went through a lot being cooped up like that in the morgue on our last case,' Jo said, her voice softer. 'Maybe you should get some help. It might be good to talk to someone.'

He didn't answer.

'It doesn't have to be a shrink,' Jo went on. 'Are you dating anyone at the moment?'

'I'm not interested in a relationship,' he snapped.

'I'm not asking you to get married again . . .' Jo stopped abruptly, realizing how insensitive the words sounded. She tried to make light of it. 'What I mean is, when was the last time you had sex?'

Much to her relief, this time Sexton took it in the laddish spirit she'd meant it. He grinned, relaxing visibly. 'If I asked you that, Daphne would have me up for sexual harassment.'

Jo glanced across. 'Don't get me started. Human Resources translates as management giving itself a licence to poke around in the personal life of staff, in my book.'

'Politically correct you just don't do, do you, Jo? Well, I got news for you. Daphne's all right.'

Jo felt like she was tiptoeing through a minefield trying to have a conversation with him. She decided to cut through the dross and give him a few home truths. 'Sexton, you're the best cop I ever worked with by a mile. But if Daphne's the one advising you to carry Maura's suicide note around with you – it's bad advice and I should know. I wallowed in grief for long enough over the crash that killed my father. The only way you're going to get your head straight is to get on with your life and let go of the past.'

Sexton turned to stare. 'Who told you about the note?'

'Look, if I tell you something that I've never told anyone about the night my old man died, will you open that bloody thing and read it?'

'The only person I told about it was Daphne.'

'My father died because I opened the passenger door while he was driving down the motorway. I needed to puke and I was too bloody drunk to ask him to stop. It was my fault he died. He was reaching over to try and pull the door closed when he hit the . . .'

Jo stopped. She could feel Sexton's eyes still on her. 'Don't you want to know why Maura died?' she asked softly.

'I know why Maura died,' Sexton said, his voice harsh.

'She died because I wasn't there for her when she needed me. Isn't that enough?'

When they reached the salubrious Sea View Road, sporting palm trees, wilting purple-flowered rhododendron bushes and panoramic sea views, Jo slowed down. She was checking out the house names on the right against Foxy's address, with Sexton scanning the ones on the left, when an ambulance overtook them and swerved into a driveway up ahead. Jo jabbed the accelerator and took off after it. Sexton reached for his grips again, as they pulled up outside a set of wooden gates leading to a mock-Tudor pad where another ambulance was waiting. The name of the property carved into the gate pillar was the same one Foxy had given them as being Imogen Cox's address. The back doors of the first vehicle were open and a female paramedic in navy trousers and a shiny bomber jacket was rooting around in the back. She turned around, clearly stressed.

Jo and Sexton stepped out of the car at the same time. 'I'm DI Birmingham, Store Street,' Jo said.

'That was quick,' the paramedic answered, glancing over Jo's shoulder and giving a thumbs up to the other paramedic. 'Victim's a 43-year-old woman, with two serious head injuries.' She moved towards the second unit as the driver stuck his arm out the window handing over a wad of grey plastic. The paramedic grabbed it, and ran towards the house with it tucked under her arm, looking back and waving Jo to follow.

'The victim's husband rang it in,' she told Jo as they neared the front door. 'Said she'd been attacked by an intruder. We've got three no shocks on the defib. She should have been moved to the hospital by now, but we've only got a fixed stretcher, and her husband says they've lost the keys to the gates for the side entrance. We can't get her out through the house on the ordinary stretcher because of the angles. I'm Ann, by the way, station officer in Dún Laoghaire. Why've they sent Store Street, if you don't mind me asking?'

'Long story,' Jo answered, following her down through the hall and then kitchen. If the defib was flat-lining, Imogen Cox was clinically dead, though only a doctor could pronounce it.

A good-looking man with a silver ponytail and dark-brown eyes was sitting at the table holding an oxygen mask to his face while being tended by another paramedic. His eyes followed Jo's as she and Sexton continued out through some patio doors that led to the garden.

At the back of the landscaped garden, a group of three more paramedics were working on the victim lying on her back beside a pool house. Clear plastic tubes and sterile packaging were strewn in a radius of a few feet around her head. Jo was interested to see what looked like the murder weapon – a bloody rock – lying within easy reach. A clump of hair the same jet-black colour as the victim's was stuck to it. If the killer had grabbed the nearest thing to hand to bludgeon the woman's head in, it suggested to her that this was a crime of passion.

The victim's face did not show her age, Jo reckoned, judging from the wrinkled skin on her neck. Her body looked much younger. Her T-shirt had been cut in a straight line up her breastbone to expose a waist that was tiny. She had scars a couple of inches long at the base of each breast, indicating a boob job. Jo couldn't see her face properly. It was a mask of muck and blood, her hair sticking to places where the blood had congealed into a crust.

Sexton looked away while Jo took it all in. Sticky clear circular pads with metal buds were dotted over the woman's chest. Little red wires with pincers gripped them and led to a machine with several electronic displays. A paramedic with a moustache, wearing the same navy uniform as the girl, was kneeling before the machine. Two more paramedics crouched either side of the victim's head, administering CPR. One, who'd red hair and a red face, was pressing the heel of his joined hands into her chest. After a series of thirty presses, which he counted aloud, he leaned back on his hunkers to allow his bald-headed partner to blow two spurts of air into the woman's mouth, held open at her nose and chin.

'How long has she been here?' Jo asked Ann, who was rolling out the sheet.

'A lot longer than her other half says,' the redhead answered.

Jo glanced at her watch. It was nearing midday. 'She's not dressed for the outdoors, so she must have bolted out here. That's hubby inside, I presume. What's up with him?'

'Shock,' Ann answered.

'Right,' the red-haired paramedic answered, positioning himself at the woman's feet as the bald paramedic moved to her head.

'In three,' said Ann, beginning to count.

After an awkward shuffle, she and the three paramedics managed to heave the woman on to the plastic sheet. Sexton moved to one of the four corners, and together the four men lifted her up and carried her towards the house.

Jo slid the patio door open to full width to help them pass through.

The man at the kitchen table didn't stand up. The mask was gone from his face, but he still looked grey and sick. A big black dog – old by the looks of it – was stretched out by his side, dozing.

'Will she b-b-be OK?' he asked, in a high-pitched voice.

'We're doing everything we can,' Ann answered.

Jo noticed that, along with the newspaper open at the sports pages on the table, there were fliers about adopting an orphan from Africa, and a stack of bank statements, as if someone had been doing accounting.

The men manoeuvred the body through the doorways of the house with difficulty. Some of the victim's hair was pushed off her face with the movement.

Jo gasped.

'You recognize her?' Ann asked, as they walked back towards the ambulance. 'I did, too, when I heard her name. She's always in the VIP mags. It's Imogen Cox.'

But Jo knew the victim as someone else entirely. Imogen Cox was the woman who had been sipping cocktails with an unknown, white-haired male on that morning's sex tape.

8

According to one of the paramedics, the husband claimed to have seen an intruder, so Jo asked Sexton to phone in a request for the air-support unit to scan the fields and coast-line from overhead and search for signs of anyone on the run. Then she headed back into the dead woman's kitchen, where Jeff Cox was now alone, sitting on the edge of the table. She looked at him with interest. Despite his grey hair, he was a good ten years younger than Imogen Cox, and, unlike his wife, physically very fit.

'Sir, I understand you're upset, but this house will have to be combed for forensic evidence, and I'd ask you to keep your movements to a minimum. When you leave here in a moment, it may be a week before you're allowed back in.'

'Yes of course, I'm sorry. I'm not t-t-thinking properly,' he said.

His stutter was slight, Jo realized, and he pronounced 'th' like 't', which told Jo that there probably hadn't been as much money in circulation when he'd been growing up. He took a sip and put the mug down. Jo also noticed his teeth were crooked, another sign she was on the right track. Kids with wealthier parents tended to get orthodontic treatment in their teens.

'I'd like to ask you what happened,' Jo said. 'I'm not look-ing for a formal statement at this point, but I have to caution you that you have the right to remain silent, and anything you do say will be taken down, and may be used against you in a court of law.'

She looked carefully at his black designer T-shirt and denims. Apart from his hair, which needed a cut, he was extremely well groomed, and he smelled of a citrusy after-shave. Interestingly, there didn't seem to be a speck of blood anywhere on him. He'd found his wife, and his natural inclination should have been to touch her. Unless he'd showered since, as she strongly suspected.

'Anything . . . I'll do anything to help. Do you t-t-think she'll be OK?'

Sexton appeared in the doorway. Jo gave him a nod. 'I'm sure they'll let you know as soon as there's any news,' she said, thinking that if he was that concerned about his wife, he'd have asked to accompany the ambulance. 'Now – Jeff, isn't it?' She pulled out her chewed-on biro and a notebook, snapping the elastic off. It opened on the page marked with the word 'minder' from her interview notes with Tara, and she folded it over. 'How did you find her?'

Cox pulled the tip of his nose. 'I, I, I took the dog for a walk, and when I came back I found her lying there, at the back of the garden. She was still conscious, I think – but there was so much blood.'

'Sorry . . . You were coming from where?'

'I went for the newspaper.'

'Where and when?'

'Foley's newsagents, I was b-b-back here about five past ten.'

Jo looked at her watch. 'Really? It's noon now. Why such a long time delay between the time you got home and when the ambulance was called?'

'I t-t-took a shower when I got in.'

'Where was Imogen at this point?'

'Sorry, yes, sh-sh-she was in bed, lying in. I didn't want to wake her, so I went for a wash. I was d-d-due in the office. Business has been slow, we needed to drum up some new clients.'

'What's your business?'

He looked surprised.

'Oh, sorry, I thought everyone knew. We've got a modelling agency – well, Imogen has. She founded it. But I work there, too.'

'What as?'

'S-s-sorry?'

'What do you work as?'

'A photographer. Is this relevant? Shouldn't you be out looking for him, the man who did this?'

'Please answer the questions, Mr Cox.'

He rubbed his eyes. 'I'm a photographer. I'd been working in the field before I met Imogen, but I was let go from a previous company a couple of years ago. T-t-times are tough for everyone. Imogen hired me. She said my experience was an a-a-asset.' He stood up, and the dog stood, too, whining and wagging his tail. 'I was doing the housework when I heard her scream in the garden. I ran out, but I was too late. Her attacker ran, and Imogen was . . . Imogen was—'

The doorbell rang. 'Will you e-e-excuse me?'

'Never trust a man with a ponytail,' Sexton said, once he was out of earshot.

Jo smiled at him, glad to see him taking an interest, and looked around the kind of state-of-the-art kitchen you only ever saw in a *Hello!* magazine spread. Jeff Cox had landed on his feet, but he was now on the verge of losing it all – as prime suspect for the murder of his wife.

9

Tara Parker Trench was in the back of the cab that Jo Birmingham had put her into, but she wasn't heading for her apartment in Citywest. She was going to the five-star Triton Hotel on the south side of Dublin, because that's what the person who had taken Presley had told her to do. A text telling her how to get her son back had beeped into her phone while she'd still been in the garage. That's why she'd given Jo her mum's number – just in case something bad happened before she got Presley back. Tara rested her forehead against the window. The message had said: 'If you want your boy back, come to the spa at the Triton Hotel and I will be waiting for you. Bring anyone with you, and next time you see Presley he'll be in a white coffin.'

She rubbed her eyes with the balls of her hands. *Who hated her so much they would say that?* The question went round and round her head. It had to be someone she knew, because they had her private number. Her stomach constricted. She didn't know which was worse: the thought of someone she knew wanting to hurt her that much, or the idea of her little boy with a stranger. She wouldn't be able to cope if anything happened to him. He was like her lucky charm. Everything she did in life, she did for him . . .

Tara picked up the phone. She'd texted back the

kidnapper that she was on her way, and to take care of Presley, that she'd do anything they wanted, but there'd been no response yet. God – what had happened to her in the last couple of days had been bad enough, but to lose Presley on top of everything – she took several deep, calming breaths. No, as long as she kept her cool, and did what the kidnapper said, everything would be all right.

She sat up straight, and tried to see herself in the driver's rear-view mirror. She needed to look good. Taking a tube of lipgloss from her jacket pocket, she twisted the dip-stick free and applied it liberally. The Triton was the top hotel in the city for visiting celebrities and dignitaries. Anyone who was anyone stayed there, and the manager made sure the papers got tipped off so they could pap the VIPs going in and out. Tara had all the snappers' mobile numbers in her phone anyway. She usually buzzed them herself to let them know what time she'd be heading out, and with whom. She knew each edition time by heart, and had perfected the 'taken by surprise' look for them. It was the way to keep them onside. Press interest meant work. The ad agencies only ever booked girls whose faces were guaranteed to get their product some free publicity.

Combing the ends of her extensions with her fingers, she caught the driver's eye in the mirror. He had that smug look on his face that told her he thought her preening was for his benefit. It reminded her of the way the men had looked at her yesterday in Marrakesh. Like she was irrelevant. *Don't go there*, she told herself. *You haven't got time to think about this now. Presley needs you.*

She lowered the window and tried to take a big gulp of air, but her mouth was too dry for her to swallow. She bit hard on the inside of her cheek to try and control the feelings overwhelming her, tasting coppery blood. If she could just turn back the clock to those two minutes in the garage, and unstrap Presley and carry him inside to pay for the damn petrol! Or if she could just turn the clock forwards till he was back with her again . . .

She covered her face. If something had happened to him, she'd feel it in that sixth-sense way a mother knows. *Wouldn't I?* she asked herself. There were things in her life that she had done that were going to haunt her to the grave, but she could live through anything, as long as she had Presley. In her own mind, he made what she was willing to do to better their situation honourable. Without him, she was something else entirely.

If it turns out Mick has something to do with this, I won't be responsible, she thought, thinking of her ex. Maybe he was trying to teach her a lesson about him needing to see Presley more often. Deep down though, she knew Mick was too soft to have had any hand, act, or part in something like this. And even if he had, at this point it would have felt like a godsend. At least then she'd know Presley was with someone who loved him. She'd know her boy was safe. But if she didn't get Presley back soon, she was going to have to tell Mick that he'd been taken, and he could use it to get Presley away from her for good. And if the papers made her look like a bad mother, it would destroy her party-girl brand. Her modelling days would be over. She was only going to tell Mick as a last resort, she decided. *First I'll do everything I can to get Presley back by myself.*

She craned her neck to see the traffic. She could see the hotel in the distance, but the flow had come to a complete standstill. *What happens if the man who has Presley doesn't wait for me?* she thought. *If I jump out and run, I'll get there quicker.*

'Do you have a boyfriend?' the driver asked, suddenly. She could feel his eyes on her again, and sense what he'd like to do to her.

Tara felt her skin crawl. She wondered if he had had something to do with Presley's disappearance. He was acting as if he had. He hadn't been flagged down by Jo Birmingham at random, she realized. He had pulled into the service station at exactly the right time. She flicked her hair, about to make conversation just to keep him cool, when her phone beeped with another message.

It was from the same number as the kidnapper's text, but this time it was a multimedia message. She pressed 'open' and saw Presley's beautiful face.

Her head lightened with relief. He was OK. He looked happy. She could kiss him better when she had him back. The main thing was it wasn't too late.

'You think you're something big, but you're a nothing and you're a nobody,' the driver was saying. 'I've seen you parade about in your knickers and bra. You get paid for stripping, and that makes you no better than a slag. I wouldn't pay for a hand job from you.'

Tara looked down at the phone and studied the picture of her little boy, because she knew there was something wrong. Then it dawned on her: Presley wasn't wearing the Tommy Hilfiger jacket he'd had on last night. His shirt was different, too. She pushed the phone closer to her face, and recognized it as one she'd bought him a couple of months ago. It hadn't even lasted a day; she'd had to get rid of it the first time he'd worn it because he'd got sick all over it.

The driver was spewing more bile, but the words didn't register because Tara knew exactly who had taken a picture of Presley that day. And now she was really scared.

10

Jo and Sexton were outside the Coxes' house, their conversation drowned out by the air-support chopper whirring overhead. The fact that it was hovering in one place meant it hadn't found anyone to follow. Jo wasn't surprised: the paramedics had suggested the victim had probably died hours earlier. The ambulance was leaving, and in the front garden a uniformed officer, who'd arrived from the local station minutes earlier, was about to set up a cordon. He'd already informed Jo that his inspector and superintendent were on the way, which she took to mean that he was unimpressed by their presence and, having informed his superiors, they'd taken a dim view, too, and were coming to check it out. The competition between stations to crack cases was immense, and Jo knew that she and Sexton were about to be given their marching orders. Not that Sexton was going to need any encouragement to leave. He was looking depressed again, and his mind seemed to be on something else entirely. Jo felt a pang of concern. He'd had a difficult time coming to terms with what had happened to him during the Bible killer case, and now there was the bloody suicide note. But there was a little boy in serious trouble, and that had to be her priority.

Opening the front door, she stepped back into the warmth

of the house. At the other end of the hall she could see Jeff Cox talking to his lawyer. She turned to face a giant image of Imogen Cox.

'I need you to get up there and check every room for any sign of Presley,' Jo told Sexton, pointing to the stairs.

'Why can't you do it?'

Jo sighed. 'Because one of us is going to have to keep whoever appears talking, which someone will any second now – it's bloody well guaranteed. Oh, never mind . . .'

Slipping off her shoes, she ran up the stairs two at a time, moving fast and on the balls of her feet.

Upstairs, the landing branched left and right, with doors on either side.

Jo turned, and opened the only door on the left. It was a large bedroom, and based on the doilies on the locker and the scatter cushions on the bed, probably for guests. After a quick sweep, involving kneeling to look under the bed and opening the empty wardrobe door, she was satisfied the boy was not there. A fine layer of dust everywhere told her that the room had not been in use for some time.

She heard Sexton talking to someone downstairs and moved quickly to the first of four doors on the right-hand side of the stairs. It led to a master bedroom, with a door to an en suite. A giant sleigh bed dominated; the fabrics were pinks and crushed velvets. A giant plasma TV was fixed to the wall opposite the bed, and an extensive wall of wardrobes contained only women's clothes. Jo stepped out on the balcony with its sea views and cocked an ear to see if she could make out what Cox and his solicitor were talking about underneath.

'Just refuse to answer any questions,' the solicitor was saying.

Shaking her head, she carried on into the en suite and put her hand on the shower head. It was cold. There was no sign of Presley, or any of the accoutrements that went with stashing a little boy. Jo slipped out and back into the hall.

She caught a flash of uniform downstairs, heard Sexton telling the cop he'd forgotten his car keys and was heading back into the kitchen to look for them.

The next door along the landing led to what looked like an office, with a desk and computer. She clicked the mouse and the screen burst to life with a list of names, times and numbers. It was impossible to make out what information was contained in the columns, as most of the text was blocked: by a window demanding a memory stick be reinserted. Jo glanced around for one, but thought she heard something, and left the room, running on down the corridor past a giant chandelier. From the hall came the sound of Sexton explaining to the garda why he hadn't realized the keys were in his pocket all along.

The next room was a bedroom, which was sparse and without any flourishes. An Airfix model aeroplane sat on a dresser, along with a one-eyed teddy that looked ancient. A Gibson guitar was lying on the floor in its case. The wardrobe was full of men's clothes, and Jo surmised from them that Jeff Cox liked to dress a lot younger than his years, in designer clobber. He was also clearly sleeping separately from his wife.

She picked up a single page of a bank statement from the locker, which had, as far as she could see, just one cash with-drawal circled with a biro. Jo made a mental note of the branch address, and ducked into the en suite to test the shower head there, too – it was warm. Jeff had washed all right; not hours ago like he'd told her, but while his wife had been dying outside.

Quickly, she moved to the last room. It was the main bathroom with antique fittings. Pulling open the medicine cabinet, she took a quick look at the labels on the vials – noted the presence of Viagra, Prozac and sleeping pills among the other regulars – before flushing the toilet and heading back downstairs.

'Speak of the devil,' Sexton was saying, his forehead furrowed.

Cox's solicitor stood on one side of him, along with Jeff, who was looking agitated. The first officer on the scene had been joined by his superiors, who seemed even less pleased. She knew them both. The Dalkey super's name was Reg. He was all right, in Jo's book, though she was wary of the fact that he was dressed in full uniform, cap included. If he'd taken the time to change his clothes, he was more interested in being on telly than in solving the case, as far as she was concerned.

'Here, Jo, apparently there's a bathroom down here you could have used all along,' Sexton said.

Jo gave him a grateful nod. 'I'll know next time then, won't I?' Glancing at Cox she said, 'I'll see you later.'

'Over my dead body,' Reg muttered. 'You're bang out of order, being here at all.'

Jo turned and gave him one of her killer smiles. 'You're acting like the case is solved. Isn't everyone innocent until proven guilty?' She caught Jeff Cox's eye again, and he looked thoughtful.

When they were outside, Jo turned to Sexton. 'Can you head straight to their bank? I need you to get their accounts to me before Jeff and his solicitor reorganize them.'

When she had them, Jo would be able to establish how much Jeff Cox was going to benefit from the death of his wife. She could read the state of an entire relationship from how a couple spent their money: by looking at their day-to-day lifestyle and their haunts. She could understand what made them tick. Did the Coxes have a standing order to feed an orphan in Malawi, or were they trying to bring one home? Did they eat out? If so, were the meals for one or two? Was the business solvent?

If money was keeping Jeff with his wife, the accounts could show that, too. If Imogen Cox had been a control freak and her husband having an affair with one of the country's most desirable women, it must have led to a lot of tension in the house.

'Why can't you go?' Sexton asked.

Jo threw her eyes up to heaven. 'Look, I know you're not in a good place right now, and I'm sorry Maura did what she did. But we've got a little boy out there who could end up in an early grave if we don't get on top of this case. I'm going straight back to the station to give Dan an earful and get the resources we need to find him. I need you to look for any recent life insurance policies or unusual cash withdrawals. That way, if Jeff Cox did murder his wife, we'll know where to start looking. Can you do that?'

He nodded. 'You think he did it?'

'Despite how it looks, my gut tells me he didn't,' Jo said. 'But he's lying through his teeth, and I want to know why.'

11

Barry 'King Krud' Roberts was snorting one gram off the back of the cistern in the john of the gym to top up. Three lines. Not enough to put him in the party mood, but enough to top up the three grams he'd had already today, and make him feel more like himself. His nose started to tingle. Good, they'd cut it with lignocaine, an anaesthetic used by dentists, like he'd told them to. The muppets had tried to cut corners last time by using lactose. He'd gone ballistic when he had found out. If you used lignocaine, the customers thought the buzz was cocaine-induced, enabling King to mask just how much he'd bulked the stuff out to make more profit. He'd got two dentists on board to buy lignocaine for him. It wasn't hard to recruit professionals. People who had been to college seemed to believe not going down the pit every day carrying a canary entitled them to a lavish lifestyle. King's money always did the talking. He had an accountant to cook the books and keep the Criminal Assets Bureau off his back, and a solicitor to help him hide assets. That was why he was still the King.

He could feel his heart pump harder, and his blood start to race. *Fuck it*, he thought, pulling out another wrap and sprinkling it on the surface, chopping it up with a razor blade. That was the thing about feeling invincible: you always wanted more.

I've earned it, he told himself. He'd been pumping iron for hours. It was vital he stay fit. The easiest place in the world for his enemies to take out a hit on him and have him whacked was in prison. All you needed was a crooked screw to turn a blind eye for ten minutes.

He had a couple of screws on the payroll himself, enabling him to organize phones and the charlie, but the staff were changed all the time to try and prevent corruption, and his men weren't rostered to work today. The only reason he'd managed to get away on his own was because he'd told them he was going to the john. Even the ones who couldn't be bought didn't have the stomach to follow him in there.

He dialled his lawyer, leaving a message when the answering machine came on that he was expecting a visit at half past three that afternoon. It was lucky he was in a good mood, or he'd have phoned one of his runners to check where the brief was. He hated it when the phone wasn't picked up.

While he'd been pumping iron he'd worked out exactly what he was going to tell his lawyer. He wanted to discuss the murder trial, of course – but also tell the brief he held him responsible for the drugs that had disappeared the previous night. That was the way it worked. If you brought someone to the table, as his lawyer had done, you were responsible for recouping any losses and undoing the damage, should they mess up.

The King bent over to hoover up the last of his lines. He'd got the name and address of the woman who'd been making things worse, and was quite enjoying thinking out a way to teach her a lesson; something that would send out a message that he was still the King. It had to be something spectacular to undo the damage of losing his first prison haul.

He sniffed and closed his eyes as the buzz moved to his brain. It was good gear all right. He felt like champion of the world again.

12

In one of the private rooms in the spa of the Triton Hotel, Charles Fitzmaurice was lying on the massage table. The multimillionaire owner of the hotel, he was the man Imogen Cox had turned to for help when the economy had gone into recession. Now that the big money had dried up, and the away gigs that used to be part and parcel of the game had come to an end, the high-escort end of the business was in jeopardy. 'Fitz', as he was known, had been one of Imogen's regular clients, but now that he was bank-rolling her business, he was taking a hands-on interest in every aspect of making it pay. But the recession had hit the hotel industry harder than most, and Fitz was not about to let everything he'd worked for slip out of his hands. As an amateur aviator with a landing strip in the grounds of the hotel, he'd even started flying new VIP clients directly in himself.

'You said you'd tell me where my son was,' Tara said, praying he wouldn't notice the slight quiver in her voice. Fitz got off on fear. He was sixty-odd, overweight and had a flock of seagulls for a comb-over peeling away from his shining bald head. She'd realized in the taxi that Fitz was behind Presley's disappearance – he was the one who'd taken that photograph of him on a helicopter ride, a trip that had made Presley sick. Now all she had to do was find out where Presley was being kept.

She was going out of her way to keep Fitz happy, her fingertips kneading ever increasing circles across his thick skin. Her hands moved in the same rhythm until they met at his spine. Shifting the pressure to the heel of her hands, she changed direction, rubbing down to the tuft of hair sprouting from the base of his back, where a snow-white terrycloth towel covered his buttocks.

There'd been clients who'd revolted her in the past, lots of them, but with enough coke and booze anything was possible, and she got past the lack of physical attraction by concentrating on how she was going to spend the cash-in-hand fee.

She had been nervous when Imogen had first asked her if she was interested in this line of work, of course. But Imogen had claimed that the kind of money men were prepared to pay was the only thing about it that was obscene. And in truth, Tara hadn't needed much persuading. With one job you could go from being broke to flush in the space of an hour, and as Imogen put such an emphasis on discretion, she'd never had to worry about the truth getting out. Both parties had as much to lose if it did, Imogen had said. The clients were only ever going to be celebrities and the filthy rich, she'd promised. She had even managed to make it sound romantic. Tara would be flown by specially chartered planes – and from time to time private jets – to some of the most exotic locations in the world. She would stay in the best hotels, eat in internationally renowned restaurants, be treated like a superstar. She might even meet the man of her dreams and spend the rest of her days living in luxury.

Imogen had also stressed that if any of the girls were

uncomfortable, they had the right to say no at any point in the proceedings, maintaining that this was the crucial differ-ence between a high-class escort and a common prostitute. Anyway, she'd pointed out, just by being models, they were both in the sex industry already.

And for a couple of years, when the money hose had been on, that's exactly what it had been like. Tara had never needed to exercise her discretion. There had been oddball clients with strange perversions along the way, things she was trying to forget, but the excesses had been even more unbelievable. A Russian mining magnate had taken his Rolex off and handed it to her as a tip after celebrating his thirtieth birthday with models from every European capital in his villa on the French Riviera. An Irish rock star, who had hired a yacht and flown a bunch of the girls to the Greek Islands just because it was the weekend, had handed her a bit part in one of his videos – which had given her the dream of one day becoming an actress. A racing magnate had even organized a diamond-encrusted Tiffany's pendant as a gift after she'd admired it in a magazine on his bedside locker.

Some of the girls had landed on their feet. Olga, a six-foot Ukrainian with the face of Anna Kournikova, had been set up with her own apartment in the Boho Club, a hotel and golf club in Meath owned by a property magnate whose permanent residence was in Jersey, and who divided most of his time between the Czech mistress he kept there, and the Cayman Islands, where his wife and children resided. He only ever came to Ireland to play golf, and according to Olga his back was too bad to manage anything other than lying prone while she worked on top.

Tara had had a couple of offers herself to become

exclusive, too. One had involved a five-star suite she could call home – but her son could not. Presley. She caught her breath as she thought of him. She knew that Imogen and Fitz were behind his disappearance – they had to be – but where were they keeping him? This was what she intended to find out.

Fitz gave a low moan of pleasure as her hands slid further down his body. She decided there and then that as soon as she got her boy home she was going to get herself straight. She'd been thinking about getting out for ages. The moment the recession had hit, the fees had halved overnight. In the good old days it had been two grand for straight sex, fifty per cent of which went to Imogen. These days Tara was lucky to get five hundred euro per session. Since nobody was giving out free lines of charlie any more, there were expenses incurred that left a girl with barely anything to show at the end of the night.

Anyway, with the business now mainly concentrated in Dublin, it was just too close to home for comfort. She couldn't afford to be caught in any kind of compromising situation. Some of the models had gone on to get careers in the media, others had become actresses. If what really went on ever got out she'd stop being the darling of the press, and that would be the end of her career.

And last, but by no means least, was the fact that the punters' demands were changing. When Tara had started, anal sex had been a big deal. But now most of the clients considered it obligatory. There was so much of it in porn anyway that they presumed it was a matter of course.

But Imogen had made it sound like the old days might be returning when she had told Tara about the Morocco gig. An Irish-born premiership footballer had wanted to party overnight in the Atlantis, a lavish new hotel in Marrakesh, to celebrate winning a match against his old rivals in Old Trafford. He had specifically requested Tara. The guy was world-famous, married to a pop singer, and had three young children.

A bead of sweat rolled down her back as she remembered the heat of the Moroccan midday sun, and the footballers' harsh faces. Shaking her head, she willed the image away. *Stay focused*, she told herself. *Just get Presley back.*

'Hey!' Fitz grunted. 'Why have you stopped? You give me what I want first, remember? That's the deal.'

Tara closed her eyes – she had to hold it together for Presley's sake. She moved her fingers further down.

He groaned with pleasure. 'You've been a very naughty girl. What were you doing trying to run out on my footballer friends? Who do you think you are?'

'I didn't walk out, Fitz. I did what I was paid to do, and was nearly killed in the process.'

'I don't want to hear about it. A grand you got for that job. Enough to pay for a therapist, and some. Car going well, is it? Apartment nice? Don't forget where they came from, either.'

Tara swallowed. She was not going to cry, was not going to show him that he was getting to her.

Fitz rolled over, and she was struck, again, by how old and ugly he was. 'Don't try to play the innocent with me. I know exactly how rough you like it. Those footballers' wages are the only thing in the world that is recession-proof at the moment. You nearly blew it for us all last night, you know that? What the hell were you doing in that garage, too? You've cost me a bloody fortune. Well, you'll have to work very hard to clear your debt.'

Tara knew where this was going by the way his tone was changing. He couldn't get an erection until he'd hurt her, usually by landing a few punches to her chest and belly. Once, after knocking her to the ground, he'd put a shoe on so he could kick her properly.

'You're going to have to make it up to them, that's all there is to it. The lads are staying in the hotel the next couple of days.'

Fear flooded through Tara's body. 'Where's my son? Where is he? Where's Presley?'

'I'll tell you later. First, you need reminding who's boss. And that's going to take some time.'

'Please, Fitz, just tell me Presley's OK, and I'll do whatever you want. But I have to see him first.'

Fitz clenched his fist, drew his arm back and landed a blow to her side.

She flinched. 'I've been a bad girl,' she said, robotically. She moved back to his shoulders and started to massage.

'Harder,' Fitz demanded petulantly. 'Nothing's happening yet.'

Holding back her tears, Tara thought about her boy, and how she was going to spoil him rotten once she got him back. She'd get him all the toys that she'd told him he'd have to wait till Christmas for – Buzz Lightyear, Woody, Slinky Dog, and that bucket of toy soldiers, and that was just for starters. It didn't matter how much it all cost, she'd get the money somehow. There were always ways.

'I'm going to have to teach you a lesson, you know that, don't you?'

Tara felt herself start to tremble. 'Yes, Fitz.' The last time he'd used those exact words, he'd inserted a bottle of beer into her. There had been a nick out of the top of it, and she'd needed stitching up after.

His fleshy left hand extended and clamped her thigh. Tara was wearing the standard-issue suspenders under her white coat, a uniform that she'd put on as soon as she'd arrived at the Triton.

'I saw for myself what happened in Marrakesh, and you were out of order,' he said, snapping the elastic with his fingers.

'Were you there?' she asked, confused.

'No, I wasn't there, you stupid slag. I saw the film.'

Tara's legs felt like they were going to go from under her.

All the promises about discretion, about protecting the girls and the clients: it was all lies if they'd filmed it.

'We'll make a famous actress of you yet!' Fitz chuckled.

She tried to go back to the toy shop with Presley in her imagination, visualizing which toys could be found in the different aisles, but all she could think about was people finding out about her, and her career being over.

She reached down. His pot belly hung over his penis, which was short and erect, and almost hidden in dense pubic hair.

'Climb aboard,' he invited.

Taking off her white coat, she climbed on to the massage table and straddled him.

'Where's Presley?' she asked softly, putting her hands around his throat and squeezing. 'Where's my son?'

13

It was early afternoon, and for what seemed like an age, Foxy had been staring over the public counter of Store Street Station at a woman draped head to toe in a black burka.

She'd arrived at the station with her husband, Hassan, the garage manager Jo Birmingham wanted interviewed. But for the past three-quarters of an hour, the station's three interview rooms had been in use. Until now, that is. Two officers and a mugging victim had just vacated the room off the public lobby, parking a fire extinguisher in the doorway because the swipe cards were always getting mislaid.

Foxy needed to get in there and start interviewing Hassan before someone else took his slot, but he could not bring himself to leave the woman with her frightened eyes alone – because he'd noticed the sneers, scoffs and muffled insults that had already come from the queue over the past thirty minutes.

'Right, you in there,' he told Hassan, pointing to his left.

Hassan entered without so much as a word of reassurance to his wife. He had a backpack over his shoulder and he took it with him.

Foxy didn't know what depressed him more – the idea that women were still so repressed in some parts of the world, or the fact that all of the racist taunts he'd witnessed had come from middle-class office workers looking to have their passport pictures or driving-licence-renewal forms stamped. 'Would you like a cup of tea?' he asked the woman.

She shook her head.

A skanger in a Millwall jersey fell through the door, slugging from a can of Amstel, shouting and roaring about the squad cars parked on double yellows, and how it was one set of laws for him and another for the pigs. Foxy buzzed the button under the counter for assistance to help get rid of him.

'Here, you!' the drunk called out to the woman, who visibly shrank a couple of inches.

'Lid on it,' Foxy warned him, coming out from behind the counter.

'Me?' He gestured to the woman. 'What about that thing? She could be a shoe bomber for all we know.'

Foxy was all set to kick him out of the station when he spotted his daughter, Sal, walking through the door. Her face was wet from crying.

He hurried over, relieved to see a couple of uniforms emerge behind him. He pointed out the drunk and they moved in on him, leaving Foxy to concentrate on his daughter.

'I thought you had swimming practice this morning,' he said. 'What happened?'

'Philip asked me if I wanted to go into town instead.'

Philip was one of the special needs kids in Sal's group.

'He said we could go to McDonald's,' Sal went on. 'But someone took my money in the queue, and I couldn't buy anything. Philip didn't have enough for both of us.'

'Where's Philip now?' Foxy asked, worried.

'Gone home,' Sal said. 'I'd no bus fare. I said I'd come and see you instead.'

Foxy gave her a big hug. 'Poor love. That was a long walk. You should have phoned me to come and get you.'

Sal hung her head.

'Got your phone, too, did they?'

She nodded.

'Are you hurt? Any cuts?'

'One question at a time, Dad, I've forgotten the first one already.'

'Bruises. Are you sore anywhere?'

She shook her head.

'OK, I'll tell you what. Let me just get you a nice cup of sugary tea for the shock you've had, and then we'll head off. You can tell me everything, one thing at a time, OK?'

'Can we go to McDonald's on the way home?'

'Course.'

'Can I have two Big Macs?'

Foxy hugged her. Sal was his life. Her mother, Dorothy, had left twelve years ago, the night before Sal had had open-heart surgery. He found it hard to remember what Dorothy even looked like now.

After phoning the group Sal was in to tell them what had happened, and to ask someone to wait for Philip at the other end of the bus ride, Foxy held his daughter's hand and started to lead her to one of the quiet rooms upstairs.

The woman in the burka glanced up, and Foxy sighed and waved at her to follow. He'd been going to take them to the detective unit, where he intended to sit them down at a free desk, but then he heard a couple of cops sniggering. So he carried on into Jo's office, pushing a swivel chair along the way, and closing the door behind him.

'I'll get you both a cup of tea,' he said, introducing Sal to the woman, who said that her name was Neetha.

When Foxy returned two minutes later with mugs in both hands, Sal was nattering away happily, using her feet to spin this way and that on the swivel chair. Neetha was still standing in the exact same spot where he'd left her.

'Please, sit down.' He gestured to Jo's chair behind the desk. 'You can stay here till your husband's finished downstairs. Nobody will bother you.' He handed them their tea.

On his way back across the detective unit, one of the cops asked him, 'What's the story with *Not Without My Daughter*?'

The others cracked up. Foxy ignored them and carried on into the corridor, glancing back and noting with relief that inside Jo's office Neetha had sat down and started sipping from her mug.

He was crossing the public lobby when he spotted Jo clipping up the steps. She'd a bunch of DVDs under her arm. Foxy went to greet her.

'Hassan's here,' he told her. 'But I've got a situation I have to take care of. I can't interview him. You'll have to do it yourself.'

He watched Jo push her hair out of her eyes. It looked different, he noticed. It suited her. Made her look younger, somehow. He sighed. He'd like to have stayed, helped out, but looking after Sal was his priority, and always had been. Jo understood that.

'He's in interview room one,' he said, as he went back upstairs. 'His shadow of a wife's waiting, so you'd best make a start.'

*

Jo stared after Foxy for a couple of seconds, then reached under the public counter for a pad of statement forms, tore some pages free and rooted out a pen to bring with her to the interview. She wheeled a TV on a set of shelves with a DVD player underneath out from a control room on the right, and pushed it across the lobby and into the interview room, dislodging the fire extinguisher as she did so.

Inside, Hassan's hands rested on either side of his crotch. From under a bushy set of eyebrows that met in the middle, he watched Jo organize herself at the table.

Strictly speaking, Jo should have had another officer in there with her to witness everything; even a camera wasn't considered watertight protection against a harassment allegation or an assault, but right now she didn't have the time or the patience to go looking.

After cautioning Hassan that he was being recorded, as per regulations, Jo sat opposite and started to quiz him about the previous night.

'I've already told you what I know,' Hassan complained. 'Look, I got tickets to a match in Croker. How long is this likely to go on?'

Jo leaned forward. 'We're talking about a little boy who's missing. You must have seen something. You got kids yourself?'

Hassan didn't answer.

'I've got kids,' Jo said. 'If anyone hurt them and I got my hands on them, I don't know what I'd do.'

'I had a son,' Hassan said solemnly. 'He died of meningitis six years ago. He was three.'

He looked at the floor, his face hard. 'We lived in Iraq at the time. Antibiotics are like gold dust over there because of the sanctions. That's why we came to Ireland. I couldn't face losing another child.'

There were moments in interviews that presented opportunities to exploit a subject's emotions. Sometimes they never returned. Harsh as it might have seemed to an outside observer, this was one of them.

Jo stood up, walked over to the TV and DVD player, and reached for the porno movies she'd taken from his shop.

She pressed the first disc out of the box, and slid it into the drive.

'What are you doing?' Hassan asked.

The sounds from the movie said it all – a woman was crying and wailing in obvious pain, but in-between her pleas a man was making the grunting noises of high arousal. The images were equally despicable – the woman was being raped in a wood, while a line of men waited, laughing and joking. Jo felt ill.

Hassan turned away.

Jo hit 'stop', and 'eject', reached for the next disc from the pile, slotting it in.

'Ah, bestiality,' she said, surveying the cover.

The screen came to life and a naked woman smiled to the camera as she brushed the coat of a German Shepherd.

'Turn it off,' Hassan said.

Jo reached for the next one. 'What age did you say your son was?' she asked, studying the cover. 'Tell you what, why don't we get your wife in to watch with us?'

Hassan held his palms up. 'I'll tell you what you want to know, as long as I don't have to testify in court. I'd be a dead man walking.'

Jo noticed he was sweating.

'The cow who's caused all the trouble, who said her kid

was taken, the one who tried to leave without paying for her petrol – you can't believe a word that comes out of her mouth. She's a hooker.'

'Tara Parker Trench?'

'Yes!'

'Why do you say that?'

He didn't answer.

'Is she in one of your movies?' Jo reached for another DVD, all set to put it in the player.

He looked panicked. 'No, one of the customers told me.'

'Name?'

'I only ever knew him as Marcus.'

'What does Marcus drive?' Jo asked, reaching for the pen.

'A HiAce.'

'Colour?'

'Wine.'

'Year?'

'1998, something like that. You'll get it on the CCTV.' Hassan zipped open his backpack and put two more DVDs on the table. 'This one recorded what was going on inside the shop, this one outside.'

'So you're expecting me to believe someone driving a battered van is able to afford the services of a top model.'

Silence, and then he spoke. 'No, he works with her in some hotel.'

'Where?'

'I dunno.'

Jo raised her eyebrows.

Hassan sighed. 'He's got a cleaning firm. Specialist. It only does pools, hot tubs, steam rooms – that kind of stuff.'

'You know a lot about him.'

'I read it on the side of his van.'

'Bit of a coincidence that Tara should have been in at the same time as him, isn't it?'

Hassan shrugged. 'He was paying for petrol when she came in. I said, "Phoar!" or something like that. He said anyone could have her at this hotel if they'd enough readies.'

'And which one is that, then?'

'I told you, I haven't a clue.'

Jo leaned across the desk, so she was right up close to him. 'Well, you'd better find out, Hassan, and you'd better find out fast, or you and your wife will be on the next plane back to Baghdad. I can guarantee it.'

14

Sexton's stomach rumbled as he was led into Jeff Cox's bank manager's office. He was starving, that was why. He'd had no lunch, and no breakfast, either. Usually he was able to slip out across the road to a little greasy spoon opposite the station for a Danish or an almond croissant to keep him going, but this morning he'd made the mistake of heading in to Jo to see if she needed a hand shifting a television and had been pressed into service ever since. When Jo got her teeth into a case, you couldn't shake her off until she'd solved it. He sighed. He'd been like that once. Before Maura had died. In those days the job had dominated his life, too. Well, he'd learned the hard way where putting work before your home life got a person.

If he'd had his eye on the ball two years ago, his wife and unborn child might still be alive. These days the more he worked, the more guilt he felt. Now, if he cut hours here and there, it was only time he was owed in lieu of all the extra time he had put in over the years. And yet, when he did take afternoons off, he didn't do anything in particular, just kept moving, like the man a few sandwiches short of a picnic he used to pass on the way to work. That bloke had spent the day walking from home to town and back again, just for the sake of it.

The bank manager's office turned out to be a corner of the bank, boxed off by those dodgy blue felt partition-stands that hide nothing from the chest up. The manager had bottle-glass lenses, and examined Sexton's ID an inch from his face, before agreeing to organize a set of the Coxes' accounts. He left Sexton alone to go in search of paper for his bleeping printer.

Sexton rubbed his stomach miserably. He didn't know where his next meal would come from. He didn't keep any food at home any more, as it only went mouldy before he had a chance to eat it. His apartment wasn't really a home in the true sense of the word, anyway, more like just somewhere to put his head down. A home was a place you wanted to go to, and Sexton didn't like being on his own. He hadn't enjoyed getting drunk since Maura had died, either. If he allowed himself to remember the pointlessness of her death – which was all he did when he was on his own or drinking – he got sucked into that way of thinking. He wished someone would explain, in the information leaflets that told depressives to ring the Samaritans or to talk to someone, that actually suicide was the ultimate act of selfishness. It ended the pain for the victim all right, but it devastated the lives of those left behind. What Maura had done had had a domino effect. These days, Sexton spent more time thinking about dying than living.

Daphne had picked up on his state of mind the moment she'd seen him. He'd never been one for counselling, but on her first day in the station she had taken him aside and told him if he needed to talk, she was there. It happened to be the second anniversary of Maura's death, and his head had been all over the place. He'd gone to her boxy little office, not to talk, but so he wouldn't be on his own. He hadn't meant to tell her about the note. It had just come out. She hadn't made him feel like a freak for carrying it around, the way Jo had. Daphne had told him he'd open it when he was ready. And he would. Not to order, as Jo would have it. But when he was ready.

The manager was back with a stack of paper, which he proceeded to insert in the printer, making small talk as he did so. Sexton put his hand in his pocket, and held Maura's note.

'Shite!' The manager cursed.

Sexton looked up. The paper had jammed in the printer again.

'Sorry,' the manager said.

Sorry had to be the most misused word in the English language, Sexton thought. *People used it all the time when they shouldn't, and never when they should.* He wished he'd said it more often to Maura, though. The last time he'd seen her, he'd brought her breakfast in bed. She'd been texting someone, but had stopped when she'd seen him and slipped the phone under the pillow. He remembered how she'd been wearing new lingerie. She hadn't looked right in it. 'What's the occasion?' he'd asked her. But she'd merely smiled. He never had got an answer.

'We have to sign off for every last pencil now, never mind the paper,' the manager said, opening the printer and throwing the screwed-up pages into the wastepaper basket. 'The powers that be are worried we're all about to start a sideline in stationery supplies.'

Do I look like I give a flying shite? Sexton thought. Maura had taken one look at the scrambled eggs he'd made for her that morning, then bolted for the en suite, and knelt in front of the cistern to chuck. Sexton had watched her through the door, as she had held her long brown hair back with one hand. She'd been pregnant, and it tore him up every day to think that he hadn't known or guessed.

'Has something happened to Imogen or Jeff Cox?' the manager asked. 'Is that what this is about?'

'I'm afraid I'm not allowed to go into the details yet,' Sexton answered.

The manager started clicking his mouse. 'Must be serious, then. You guys never release details of a death until the family's been informed. A robbery would be different. You'd want to get the details out as quickly as possible in that case. I saw the gardaí chopper out there earlier and wondered what was going on. I bet it's something to do with this, right?'

Sexton stood up, impatient. 'I am under time pressure here.'

The manager turned back to the screen. 'Just give me a sec . . . Imogen and Jeff Cox. Here it is.' He coughed self-consciously. 'You know I heard on the news there'd been an incident in Killiney and a woman had been hurt. That's where they live . . .'

Sexton sighed, willing himself to relax. It was nothing personal, just his luck that he'd got the most talkative bank manager in the city. 'Like I said, I can't discuss it.'

'I heard the woman was in her forties, just like Imogen Cox, and that she was taken to hospital with head injuries.'

Maura had been going to get her hair done the day she'd died. She'd never kept the appointment. Why had she bothered to book it at all? She had been a little distant with him, yes, but unhappy? No. She'd got herself a little super-market job, which had involved dressing up as one of Santa's elves for work each day.

'Well, I don't have to tell you that they were a wealthy couple,' the banker said.

Sexton tightened his fingers around the note. Of all the feelings – guilt, sorrow, anger – the waste was the worst. Having someone top themselves was worse than having them murdered. At least if someone you loved was murdered you could feel angry at whoever had done it. But how could Sexton be angry at Maura? She was the most inoffensive person he'd ever met in his life. The hardest bit with suicide was having to listen to stories every day on the news: about people looking for transplants; people fighting for their lives after random street-attacks while their families held vigils; people left paraplegic after tragedies – all of them grateful for any small extension to their lives.

'The mortgage on the house was paid. The modelling business had been running at a loss for years, was insolvent, -in fact, but there were frequent cash deposits, and there's two million euro in their current account.'

'Two million euro? How long had the modelling been losing money?'

The manager typed something into the keyboard, then looked at what the computer threw back. 'For as long as we keep records before moving them on to the archive facility – seven years.'

'So how do you know the cash wasn't connected to the modelling?'

The manager shrugged. 'Their business was always cheque-based.'

'Any unusual activity in the account?'

'It depends on what you call unusual,' the banker said, looking at the spreadsheet the printer had just spewed out.

'Well?' Sexton prompted.

'There's been a cash withdrawal of nine hundred and fifty euro every Monday at the same time – 3.30 p.m. – and from the same ATM machine in Sandymount, for the past six weeks. It's not the only cash withdrawal during that time, but the others are for varying amounts, and taken out at different places. The Sandymount ATM is used consistently every time. Nine hundred and fifty euro is also the maximum amount that can be taken out with their card. If it was a payment it would be more usual for it to go through as a direct debit or a standing order.'

Thanking him, Sexton took the printouts, folded them into his breast pocket with the note, and left the bank as quickly as he could.

In the car park, he reached for his phone to dial Jo and tell her about the new development, but the call went straight to her voicemail. He hung up and glanced at his watch. Today was Monday. It was three p.m. If he went to the ATM now, maybe someone would show up.

He turned his key in the ignition. He wanted to impress Jo, show her he hadn't lost it. He didn't ever want to see her looking like she felt sorry for him again, the way she had at the Coxes' house. The ATM it was. And then he'd call her.

15

He stood in the doorway, all six foot four and two hundred and eighty pounds of him. His body was pure blubber, but every bit as powerful as a stack of hard muscle. He also had a walrus moustache of grey, wiry hair over his top lip, and on the bottom a four-inch metal spike screwed into a piercing. Some of the girls didn't believe it when he said it was to impale the testicles of punters who wouldn't pay up, but Tara had seen exactly what he was capable of when she'd been sent to a casino to escort a gambler who'd bluffed about a big win and then been unable to produce the readies. It wasn't just that Big Johnny hurt people – he liked hurting people.

He advanced another step, his tattooed arms moving as if they weren't connected to his body, his huge shoulders leaving no room for a neck.

'That's far enough,' Tara warned him. She'd let go of Fitz, who was gasping for breath on the massage table, his face purple.

Big Johnny's flip-flops stopped squeaking on the tiles. He held up his arms a little, and she could see how wide the damp circles had spread under the arms of his loose, white T-shirt. He flashed a twisted smile, showing a set of gums that were twice the size of his undersized teeth.

Tara held up the razor blade she'd taken from the ladies' changing room, then moved it to Fitz's throat. He gave a harsh gagging sound as she made her first cut. A tiny trickle of warm blood coiled down the steel on to her fingers.

Big Johnny glared. 'If you think you're going to be able to put this one down to PMT you've got another think coming, my darling.'

'My little boy,' Tara said, her voice loud in the silence. 'I know Imogen's behind this – Imogen and Fitz – and I want you to understand that I will do anything – anything to get him back.'

'Put that fucking thing down before you make me really angry.'

'Just get me my boy.'

'You've got five seconds,' Johnny said.

'I want Presley back.'

'You weren't thinking about your little boy before you started this, were you? I'm counting now. Four.'

Tara looked up sharply. 'What have I started? They didn't tell you what happened in Morocco, did they? '

'Three. Don't play the innocent, sweetheart. You have something that doesn't belong to you, so it seems only right and fitting that something of yours was taken out as a little insurance policy to make sure you didn't have any more bright ideas. Good thing, too. Now, put that blade down. Nice and easy now ... two ...' Johnny held out his hand.

'I never took anything, I swear on my little boy's life ...' Fitz thrashed weakly.

'Your car was full of gear,' Big Johnny told her. 'Marcus was supposed to pick the drugs up from the john at the garage. But with all the heat, it was left in your car instead, for safekeeping. And just in case you got any ideas, your boy was taken as well.'

Tara gasped. 'But the police took my car!'

Big Johnny took a step towards her. 'If you'd kept your trap shut, none of this would have happened. You want your boy, you get Fitz's gear back. That's all you have to do. One.'

Tara straightened up and dropped the blade. 'Look, my car's in the station pound. I'll get it back. But you have to let me at least see Presley first. I want my little boy.' She started to sob.

'Good girl,' Big Johnny said. 'Now, come to Daddy.'

16

Jo was not happy. Having let Hassan go, she was standing in her office trying to get through to Tara on the phone. Why the hell wouldn't Tara answer? Banging the phone down, she plugged in the DVD player she'd 'borrowed' from the interview room. Slipping one of the CCTV discs in, she turned the telly on and pressed 'slow fast-forward'. She sat on the edge of her desk, looking between the time on the bottom right-hand corner and the wad of receipts she'd confiscated from Hassan in the station. They were about four inches deep and it took a couple of minutes to sift out any transactions that had occurred between 8.50 p.m. and 9.10 p.m. – fifteen in all, she counted.

Busy night, she thought.

Sitting on a swivel chair that she realized hadn't been there earlier, she ran her finger down each receipt, and, still keeping an eye on the TV, examined the lists of purchases, this time to see if anyone had bought anything unusual. She picked one out: there was no fuel listed. It seemed odd to Jo that the customer hadn't paid for any petrol, but had bought two other items. The first was listed as 'GL' and had cost 22 cents. 'Government Levy' she realized, recognizing the price of a plastic bag. The second was labelled 'Sanitary', and had cost €11.99 – too dear for a bottle of shampoo or a packet of sanitary towels.

She picked up the phone on her desk and rang the service station number cited on the top of each receipt. When the call connected, she identified herself to a man with a Chinese accent, and asked to check the item, calling out the barcode numbers. He told her to hold.

She aimed the remote at the DVD and hit 'pause'.

'It's night pants,' the assistant told her.

'What?'

'Night pants . . . for children at night, that's what the barcode says the product is.'

'Do you mean nappies?'

'Yes, for toilet-training . . . when the toddler goes to bed.'

Jo thanked him, and hung up. She stared at the receipt, perplexed. It could be just a coincidence that someone had bought that particular product on the night Presley had vanished but, as convenience stores went, the garage was pretty uninviting. Maybe the other shops in the area were closed at that hour. Then again, wouldn't most toddlers be in bed by nine at night? She looked at the receipt again, and cursed under her breath when she saw it had been a cash transaction. A visa card number would have led her straight to the purchaser. She'd have to cross-reference the time with the CCTV footage to see if she could ID the person in the shop with the car they'd climbed into; that was presuming they'd driven . . .

She focused on the screen. The time on the bottom right-hand side of the screen read 20.58 p.m., and she could see Tara's car's distinctive striped bonnet in a bay. Ideally, she would have watched the comings and goings building up in the hour before that to see if she could see any suspicious activity, but she was under pressure time-wise and had to be selective. The good news from her point of view was that the garage used a state-of-the-art system to record, so the image wasn't grainy like some of the CCTV systems still in operation around the city. It was like watching TV, but without the sound.

Turning the bunch of statement forms she'd used to interview Hassan upside down so she had some blank sheets of paper – at a premium in the station – she swivelled them to the landscape position and tried to mark up a rough map of approximate distances based on what she was seeing on the screen. Top of the page, in the middle, was the entrance to the store; to the right of that was the door to the public toilet. She drew five lines across the page underneath to represent the six bays, numbering them from left to right. In the fifth she drew a rectangle with an 'x' in it to represent Tara's car.

Using the remote to inch the images forwards, she worked out that the car at the fourth pump, to Tara's left if facing the store attached to the garage, was a white Mitsubishi. Jo drew a box and jotted the registration inside.

In bay three she made out the wine-coloured HiAce whose significance she was beginning to understand, thanks to the interview with Hassan. Again she represented it with a rectangle, making a note of the registration with an arrow between it and the box.

The petrol pump in bay number six – on Tara's right and the one closest to the road – she judged was out of order, having seen two motorists who'd made the mistake of driving in and then tried to reverse and rejoin the queue, causing whatever the equivalent of road rage was when there was no road involved. Jo could imagine the shouts based on the hand gestures and heads being stuck out of windows.

The vehicle in bay number one also got her attention because a camper van was peculiar in this part of the inner city, and at this time of year. The registration was Polish, she noticed. It could just have been someone visiting family the cheapest way possible, she decided, though many of the Poles in Dublin had gone home since the recession.

After a lot of aiming the remote, pausing and playing, she wrote a rough biographical note about the motorists attached to the vehicles, having watched each fill up.

'Teenage male, dressed in baggy jeans with a trucker cap, two male passengers – similar,' she wrote, describing the Mitsubishi occupants.

Marcus, the HiAce driver, didn't get out, and Jo had to rewind to see him filling up five minutes previously. The sign-writing detailing his business, mentioned by Hassan, must have been on the other side of the van, because the side Jo was looking at was blank. She described Marcus as a 'red haired male in his forties wearing a navy fleece, jeans and runners'.

The camper van couple in the first bay were 'in their sixties, with bum bags around their waists, and cameras around their necks', she wrote, thinking: *tourists*.

Then it was Tara's turn. Jo watched her patting the air outside her window, and wondered who she was trying to appease. She fast-forwarded through Tara filling up, to try and ID the car behind.

Jo spooled on to see Tara running into the shop.

A motorcyclist on a high-spec bike pulled into the sixth bay, which Jo had presumed wasn't working. He didn't flick his visor up to read the digital display, or reach for the pump. He just stood there waiting for a few seconds, staring at the garage window. Jo jotted down the registration of his bike. Now he was walking towards Tara's car. Jo sat up. He looked towards the garage again, then stooped to look in the car. The man pulled Presley's door open, pulled a glove off, and seemed to make contact – it was impossible to tell without seeing the child inside. Instead of taking him out, however, he closed the door and went back to the bike before speeding off. Jo exhaled. *What the hell was that about?*

Seconds later, Tara came running out of the station and got into her car, followed by Hassan, who charged out of the shop and banged on the driver's window. The car did a bunny hop, and cut out. Tara shoved her door open, making Hassan flinch as it connected with his body. The HiAce seemed stalled in front of Tara's car. As Marcus got the vehicle going, he sped off, and Tara drove her car out of view. Seconds later she walked back into shot, and entered the garage, Hassan close behind her. The car behind her pulled up, but didn't stop for petrol – it drove straight through and out of shot.

That's odd, too, Jo said to herself, drawing a box on the page behind Tara's car, describing it as a Jag, and noting the registration.

Tara came out of the shop a few minutes later, disappeared momentarily, and reappeared running and in a panic.

Jo numbered on her page which of the drivers she considered most relevant in order of priority, based on what she'd seen. Number one was the man on the motorbike – why was he so interested in Presley? The biker hadn't taken him, but he'd opened the door as if he'd considered it.

Number two had to be the HiAce driver, Marcus, based on what she had already learned from Hassan.

Three, the Jag owner, because it made no sense to queue for fuel if you didn't want any. Jo hadn't been able to make out who was behind the wheel, but she'd have given a good punt it was a female.

Four, the kids in the Mitsubishi, who were only acting the maggot, in her opinion.

She numbered the camper van five.

She pressed 'eject' and slid the disc out. She needed to run all the registrations listed on the page through the computer to ID who each vehicle was registered to, especially the HiAce, which she hoped would lead her to Marcus. But first, she wanted a quick look at what had happened inside the shop, and who was there.

Jo slid the second disc in and fast-forwarded to the time she'd seen Tara first enter the shop, 21.02 p.m.

The camera was positioned behind the teller this time, so, at 21.02 p.m., she had a clear view of Tara, wearing a short dress, entering and joining the queue. There was a row going on at the top between the teller and a guy with a shaved head. Next in line was a man in a suit and looking agitated. Third, an old man Jo hadn't seen entering while the cars were filling up. Jo wondered how long he'd been there and which of the vehicles was his. Tara joined the back of the queue. A short time later, she was followed by a youth with a face Jo couldn't make out because his hoodie was pulled up.

A couple of seconds later, the camper van man came in.

Jo watched the disturbance kick off just as Tara had described, with the man with the shaved head firing cans of drink up at the counter. She could see Tara pointing her key fob at the window, obviously trying to flick her alarm on. Then the shaved-headed man's dog bolted up and started to maul the guy in the suit – the paedophile Tom Burke, she realized. Jo watched Tara turn and make a break for the exit. A middle-aged woman with long brown hair and sixties-style shades nearly bumped into her at the door.

'Where did you come from?' Jo asked, checking her drawing. 'Were you in the Jag?'

On cue, the brunette reached up to one of the shelves. A set of perfectly French-manicured nails, white at the tips, gripped something.

'Bingo,' Jo said, freezing the frame.

The woman held a square packet with 'DryNite' clearly legible across the side.

It looked to Jo like Tara Parker Trench was telling the truth.

17

Sexton was standing across the road from the ATM he was keeping an eye on in Sandymount – a leafy suburb on the south side – leaning against a bus stop. He was the only one waiting, and he took a step back when a double-decker bus started to pull in, straight for a deep puddle that sprayed up, soaking his trousers and socks. *Bloody chilblains to look forward to on top of everything else*, he thought.

It was three thirty, and he decided to give the stakeout another sixty seconds max. He still hadn't managed to get through to Jo, and his heart just wasn't in it today. So far the only people who'd shown any interest in the cash machine were a bunch of school kids messing on the way home. A harried-looking mum was heading towards it now, pushing a buggy. She looked like she was having about as good a day as he was. The rain-cover protecting her toddler blew off suddenly in the wind, and as she stretched over for it, the buggy nearly upended with the weight of her shopping on the handles.

Sexton pulled his phone out of his pocket to try and ring Jo again, but discovered the damn thing was wet through, too. He gave it a shake, but there was no jizz in it at all. He'd had another one that had slipped out of his pocket and into the bog. It had dried out after a couple of days, so he hoped this one would work again, too, but he could forget about using it today. *Fuck this for a game of soldiers*, he thought. He'd had enough.

He had started to walk towards his own car when a big, flash, brand new Audi jeep pulled up directly beside the cash machine, blocking the pathway and forcing the mother with the pushchair to step into the bus lane to get round it. This really pissed Sexton off. She looked like she was a good mum, and had been giving the kid's nose a wipe when the jeep veered in. She shouldn't have to put herself and her kid at risk because a selfish prat who liked spoiling himself couldn't be arsed to park where he was supposed to.

Sexton decided to give the driver a ticket. If he was under forty, he was also going to do him for dangerous driving, he decided. If he was under thirty-five, he was taking the car off him.

Sexton rapped on the driver's window. To do that, he had to stand on the road himself, meaning the driver couldn't do a runner without knocking him down. When the window slid down and the driver grinned out at him, Sexton threw his eyes to heaven, walked around to the passenger door, and climbed in.

'Hello, Gav, how's tricks?' Murray Lawlor said, moving his wallet off the passenger seat and placing it on the dash.

Sexton pointed for him to move out of the bus stop and Murray held his hands up. 'I was just leaving.'

Sexton made sure the mum had angled her buggy back on to the path before studying his companion properly. Murray looked more like an investment banker than a former cop who'd packed it all in to be a bouncer. He was thirty-three tops, with Frankie Dettori slicked-back hair and the jockey's lurid taste in shirts. He'd bailed out of the force a few years back because a nixer he had going in security was proving more lucrative. He now ran his own business, and the secret of his success seemed to be his hiring policy. His staff were all ex-guards he'd coaxed away from the force because they knew the law and, as far as Sexton was concerned, how best to evade it. He'd tried to headhunt Sexton, too, around the time Maura had died, but Sexton's head hadn't been in a place that could take any more upheaval, and he'd declined. Based on the size of Murray's cufflinks, this was a mistake – he was clearly creaming it.

'What are you doing here, anyway?' Sexton asked.

Murray didn't bat an eyelid. 'I had to pull over to answer a call on my mobile.'

Sexton glanced from the expensive hands-free set to Murray's wallet sitting on the dash. 'That right?' he said. 'You wouldn't know Imogen and Jeff Cox, by any chance?'

Murray shifted uncomfortably in his seat. 'Nah. Why?'

'Imogen Cox got whacked this morning.'

Murray looked surprised. 'Murdered?'

'You knew her, then?'

Murray rubbed his forehead. 'Yeah, I knew of her, through some of her models. They're always in and out of one of the clubs I cover.'

'Where's that?' Sexton asked.

'Jesus, shouldn't you be reading me my rights?' Murray reacted, half-joking. 'The Blizzard – the nightclub in the Triton. Imogen's girls all have VIP passes. They come in, so do the blokes.' He glanced at his chunky watch. 'Christ – is that the time? I've really got to get going.'

'I thought you worked nights,' Sexton said.

Murray grinned, and changed the subject. 'Bet you regret

turning down that job offer on wet days like this. You look like a drowned rat.'

Sexton reached for a tissue for his dripping nose from a box Murray kept between the seats – all nice and plumped and ready to be used. He blew hard in it.

Murray grinned again. 'You know, I'm always looking for good people. Tell you what, meet me tonight for a jar, and we can discuss it then.'

Sexton was still thinking about the wallet and what it meant. 'Why would I want to do that?'

Murray rubbed his hands together. 'Because I'll be bringing some girls. Between us, we'll see whether we can persuade you to make a decision you'll never regret.'

Sexton sighed. 'OK,' he said slowly. 'Where and when?'

'Say eight o'clock, in the bar of the Triton Hotel? I'm on the club door after.'

'The Blizzard?' Sexton asked.

'That's the one.'

Sexton nodded, and pulled open the passenger handle. 'What's she like to motor, anyway?' he asked as he climbed out.

'Mate, I'm going to spare you,' Murray said, pulling out into the road. 'See you tonight.'

18

The brief's name was George Hannah, and, physically, he was everything the King wasn't: five foot five, and nine stone tops. The King was only five foot ten but he weighed twice what Hannah did. Hannah was wearing a navy suit, white shirt, and white satin tie; the King – jeans, trainers, and a black T-shirt that looked to have been painted on.

Prison was clearly making Hannah uncomfortable. He was carrying a cardboard folder against his chest in that defensive way only barristers do in court, and was trying to avoid eye contact. The King was carrying a Tesco plastic bag with the possessions he needed when away from his cell – a toilet roll and a bottle of water. He was staring at his lawyer.

'Mr Roberts, in the future I can't just drop everything like this to see you,' Hannah said, looking nervously along the row of ten prisoners and their visitors, facing each other along a long bench, and separated by small partitions. King was in the first seat, beside the screw supposedly monitoring contact – who was actually reading the *Sun*, as he knew better than to start sticking his nose into the King's business.

On their right, a lag was wearing the face off a blonde, who was dressed the way a woman should dress: in next to nothing. She'd looked over at the King more than once during the clinch. Clearly she knew who he was, too.

The King slapped his hands down on the table. The letters tattooed on the tops of the fingers of his right hand spelt 'KILL'. The left one said 'PIGS'.

'Let's get this straight,' he said to Hannah. 'I'm paying you.'

Hannah visibly shrank as he opened his folder.

'I don't want tomorrow's murder case to come to court,' the King said, nodding at the folder.

Hannah looked up in surprise. 'There's nothing I can do to stop it.'

The King frowned. 'Not strictly true. Your friend owes me money. You got him off the hook the last time he was in trouble with the law. I want you to do the same for me.'

Hannah pulled a hankie from a pocket and wiped his forehead. 'I don't know what you mean.'

'Your friend was charged when he was caught in that chopper of his with something he bought off me. You made the case against him disappear. I want my case to disappear, too. And I'm holding you personally responsible. Understand?'

'That was different. He had something up his sleeve.'

'Better tell him to pull it out again, so that he gets me out of here. Tell him that way we'll all be quits. Do you understand?'

Hannah was sweating with fear. The King smiled. 'I've got another bone to pick with you: the consignment that went AWOL on Sunday night. That five million is down to you. You don't get it back, you're in serious trouble.'

19

Jo drove through a set of tall wrought-iron gates and past a gate lodge as she headed towards an imposing Renaissance-revival house set back from the road, with one Grecian nude too many along the driveway. The Clontarf address was listed in the system as the home of the registered owner of the Jag, one Rosita Fitzmaurice.

Jo's boots crunched on the gravel as she climbed out of the car and walked up to the double set of doors. Based on the number of cars parked in the driveway and the fact that the gates had been open, it looked to Jo like someone was entertaining, though half past three seemed a funny time for guests. Jo surveyed the mix of cars as she rang the bell. There were roughly ten, and judging by the models and their varying ages, the owners mixed in all kinds of circles.

It was Rosita who answered; Jo recognized her from the set of her neck and shoulders. Her hair looked different from that of the woman Jo had watched buy nappies on the CCTV footage filmed inside the garage. The realization that Rosita had been wearing a wig and shades in the garage only deepened Jo's suspicions.

Rosita was in her early fifties, with a severe blonde bob. Her make-up was a shade too dark for her skin, her lipstick a pearly pink. Her eyelids had a heavy, sedated look, and her perfume had to be very expensive to smell that bad, Jo reckoned. Rosita put a hand to the side of her face as if surprised to find Jo there, which seemed strange considering the amount of people inside. She had a perfect set of French-manicured false nails, Jo noticed, reaching for her ID. Before she got the chance to produce it, Rosita stepped back, holding the door open. 'Come in,' she said.

Jo stepped into an open, wood-panelled room where people from all walks of life – if their dress sense was anything to go by – sat with their backs to her on chairs facing a temporary dais.

A Filipina girl, shabbily dressed with downcast eyes, was standing on the dais. Jo put her at no more than eighteen years old.

A young man with bad skin, dressed in a sharp suit, walked behind Rosita and put his hands on her shoulders. 'I thought I told you to stay upstairs, Mother,' he said sharply.

'I wanted to get some air,' Rosita said.

'Who's this?' he demanded. 'You should have called me.'

'What's going on here?' Jo asked, still watching the young girl.

The man clicked his fingers, the spectators turned to look, and two women sitting in the front row reacted to him, waving the group away by jumping to their feet and hurrying the Filipina out of the room.

'Wait right there,' Jo told the girl, but she kept walking.

Jo made to follow but the man blocked her path. 'Who are you?' he demanded.

Jo held out her ID.

'She doesn't speak English,' he said about the girl. 'We're hiring new staff for the estate.'

Jo watched her go. 'Your name is?'

'Hugo Fitzmaurice. What's this about? Have you got a warrant?'

'Why would I need one?' Jo asked. 'What's going on here?'

'Who is she?' Rosita asked her son, squinting at Jo's ID.

'A member of the gardaí, mother,' Hugo answered. 'She's called Detective Inspector Birmingham.'

Rosita started to fan the air in front of her face with her palm.

'Is it Charles?' Rosita asked, heading for a chaise longue and taking a seat.

Jo's back straightened as she put 'Charles' with 'Fitzmaurice', and realized she was in the home of the multi-millionaire who owned the capital's glitziest hotel – the Triton. Jo would bet her life that when Hassan came through with the information about which hotel Marcus worked in, it would be the Triton, too.

'Why don't you go take a little nap, Mother?' Hugo suggested.

'Not before we talk,' Jo said. 'You do, of course, have the right to refuse, in which case I will organize an arrest warrant.'

'On what grounds?' he asked.

'Your mother was in a petrol station last night when a little boy was snatched from a car. I'd like to ask her about it.'

'I didn't see anything,' Rosita said.

Jo shook her head. Rosita's natural reaction, if she had really known nothing, would have been surprise. She would have asked what had happened, and expressed interest in the welfare of the child.

'Fine,' Hugo said. 'You can speak to Mother in Dad's private study. I'll come with you.'

'I want you to go and get that young girl back so I can see her paperwork,' Jo said.

'I'll get Lee to show you she's here legally. But she won't thank you for it. She can kiss goodbye to her job if she has to leave with you. I need cleaning done. If she has no work visa, she most certainly will be here illegally – and facing the prospect of immediate deportation back to a life of impoverishment and hopelessness, I'm afraid.'

'Bring her so I can talk to her, along with whatever translator you must have had to help her get through the interview,' Jo replied.

Hugo led Jo and Rosita into a study, also wood-panelled and covered with framed photographs. He took his mother's hands in his own and stared at her. 'Mummy, don't answer anything that you'd rather not. Just tell the nice detective if anything makes you uncomfortable, won't you?'

Rosita nodded, and lowered herself stiffly on to one end of a wine-coloured leather couch.

Jo walked over to the wall of photographs. Fitz was in most of them, schmoozing with well-known faces: riding in golf buggies with a former president of the USA; shaking hands with a former African dictator currently on trial in the Hague for war crimes. Jo had her back to Rosita. 'Your hair looks different from the way it did on the camera in the garage.' She glanced over her shoulder.

Rosita touched it absently.

'It was longer and darker. Why were you wearing a wig?'

Rosita looked startled. 'That's personal. You're making me uncomfortable. Hugo said if . . .'

'Tell me what happened in the garage last night.'

'Absolutely nothing that I saw.'

'It's a bit far out for you, isn't it?'

'Not at all. I'd been shopping in town. I had to collect Fitz from the hotel, he'd been drinking, so I stopped off for petrol on the way.'

'But you didn't buy any petrol.'

'What?'

'Petrol,' Jo said.

'Didn't I?'

'No.'

'That's right, the queue was too long. I was afraid I'd miss Fitz. I knew I'd enough petrol to get me there, there's a garage near the hotel.'

'In which case, why did you go into the shop?'

'Did I?'

Jo sighed.

'Oh, that's right,' Rosita said. 'I thought I saw someone I knew inside.'

'Did you?' Jo asked.

'No,' Rosita replied.

'Why did you buy nappies?'

'I had to buy something. I didn't want them thinking I was a complete lunatic.'

'And you weren't worried about being late for Fitz at that point?'

Rosita sat back. 'Are you married, Detective Inspector Birmingham?'

'Yes. I mean no,' Jo answered.

'Was there another woman involved?'

Jo shifted her weight to her other leg.

'I've been married for forty years,' Rosita said. 'In that time the male ego has become a subject of fascination to me. It's so terribly predictable. From time to time it's necessary to make a man wait. It keeps his ego in check.'

'Ever consider divorce?'

'It may come as a shock to you to learn that some people mean it when they say "for better or worse", Inspector . . .'

Hugo arrived back with the young Filipina and an older Chinese woman.

'Well?' he asked his mother.

She gave a dismissive wave.

Jo turned back to the pictures, and stared at one of Charles Fitzmaurice shaking hands with Blaise Stanley. It looked relatively recent. There were other faces in the background, and Jo's eyes locked on a woman over Fitz's shoulder – Imogen Cox. Jo crossed her arms and walked over to the Chinese woman. 'Ask the girl her name, please.'

The Chinese woman said something sharp. The girl answered, starting to sob.

'Lee Cruz,' the Chinese woman said.

'Ask her why she's crying.'

'She doesn't want to have to go home,' the Chinese woman said.

'Ask her,' Jo instructed.

Hugo sighed.

The Chinese woman said something to Lee, then flatly repeated to Jo, 'She doesn't want to go home.'

'Ask her what age she is.' Jo said.

After the translation, the girl's eyes shot up guiltily before she answered.

'Eighteen,' the translator said, handing Jo a photocopy of Lee's birth certificate. The DOB tallied, but it was only a photocopy. A second sheet was an application for asylum, and it had the necessary immigration stamp.

'Satisfied?' Hugo asked.

Jo ignored him. 'Ask Lee if she wants to come with me

now. Tell her she can stay in my home, and I'll help her find a job.'

The Chinese woman said something. Lee shook her head panic-stricken.

'I'm afraid I'm going to have to ask you to leave, Inspector,' Hugo said. He handed over a card. 'Here's our lawyer's name and number if you've any further requests.'

Jo threw her eyes up to heaven when she read George Hannah's name on the card, and after hesitating, in order to take one last look at the Filipina, she started to make her way towards the door.

'What did you do with the nappies?' she asked Rosita, turning around.

'I dumped them, of course. I had no use for them.'

'If he's here, if Presley is here, he'll need his medication very soon,' Jo said. 'If he doesn't get it he'll go into a coma and could die.'

'I don't know what you mean. Who's Presley?' Rosita answered.

20

Jo figured it was no coincidence that the same solicitor who'd arrived at Jeff Cox's home that morning should also represent the Fitzmaurice family. She immediately phoned George Hannah's office, and learned he was in court. After she had emphasized to his secretary how urgently she needed an appointment, Hannah sent word by text that he was willing to meet Jo in the coffee dock of the courts complex just after four. The case he was involved in should have finished by then.

Dublin's Criminal Court had recently moved – from a building with limestone Doric columns blackened by traffic fumes – to a modern, round construction of glass and wood at the entrance to the Phoenix Park.

With twenty minutes to spare, Jo decided to have a quick scope at the proceedings of the rape case she'd been planning to sit in on that morning. Joining the queue at the security check, she emptied her pockets of change and her mobile phone, placing them in a plastic tray, and slipped off her jacket, which had numerous metal zips.

Maurice – the security man, who had a goatee – was arguing with a teenager with a goatee that stab vests could not be worn into the courts, and saying that the teenager could remove his trainers for inspection, too, while he was at it.

Jo walked under the metal detector arch, setting off red lights and bleeps, just as her belongings started to emerge from the conveyor-belt flap. 'It will be my bloody belt, or maybe it's my bangles,' she said.

Maurice looked up, and waved her through. 'I was expecting you this morning,' he said.

'Got bogged down with something else,' she answered. 'What did I miss?'

'Only legal applications for reporting restrictions. The defendant took the stand just before lunch. You should still catch some of it. Court 17.'

The teenager was indignant. 'Here, how come she is setting off every alarm in the building and can get in no problem?'

'She's a hottie,' Maurice answered.

Jo crammed her stuff back into her pockets, then headed across the marble floor towards the two glass lifts with their exposed cables and metal girders.

A barrister a few steps ahead of her, dressed in a full wig and gown, covered his hand with the corner of his cloak as he jabbed the button for the lift.

'You worried about swine flu?' Jo asked.

'No, static shocks,' he replied. 'This building's a health hazard. There are panes of glass shooting straight out from their frames. Oh, and the lift keeps getting stuck – that's when you can get one. The Courts Service says it's all part of the building's "settling-in phase". Can you believe that?'

Jo could believe it all right. She was having her own settling-in problems with the Tara Parker Trench case. On the face of it, the model was an unreliable, self-harming anorexic who could well be suicidal, if, as Jo suspected, she had recently been beaten-up or half-drowned. Not to mention the fact that she was a pathological liar and an attention-seeker to boot. Maybe bloody Oakley had been right all along, and she had Munchausen's by proxy too.

After a minute-long wait, with both lifts permanently working the higher floors, she gave up and took the stairs.

Six flights later, Jo emerged from the stairwell panting, even though she was relatively fit. Every floor in the building consisted of a circular balcony around a central shaft of space that allowed natural light to flood in from the glass ceiling to the ground floors. You could see each of the other floors from the balcony ledge. Jo took in the view, her heart racing like she'd just run a marathon. She wondered if this was what a panic attack felt like, and, for peace of mind, tried to think of the reasons for and against putting Tara Parker Trench's case behind her and concentrating on this one instead.

But before she could come to any conclusions she had reached the door of the court. She pushed through and went inside.

21

Court 17 was a modern take on the old Central Criminal Court. The window behind the judge was a wide rectangle that curved with the building. Quirkily shaped pews had replaced the old colonial-style ones in the central area, and it was all set off by a blood-red carpet. The main difference was electronic. A TV screen could be lowered from the ceiling so protected witnesses could give evidence while cosseted from the accused and the press. Cameras recorded proceedings, which could be screened to the public on the ground floor when the court got too full. The judge even had a computer. Jo watched him check the angle of his wig in the reflection on the screen, and wondered if he had any other use for it.

To the right, the twelve members of the jury were listening avidly to the accused, who sat facing them on the left.

Jo's gaze turned to him. He was in his forties, short and wiry, with a pale face, crooked facial features, and an ill-fitting suit. The only thing remarkable about his appearance was how ordinary he looked. In a crowd, you'd have thought him the kind of person who cold-called at estate houses, trying to sell stuff nobody needed.

Ignoring the custom of giving a stiff bow to the judge on entry or exit, and instead winking at the court registrar, who she knew of old, Jo moved to a back bench and slid into a seat. She put her phone on silent and crossed her legs. Instantly the top one started to jig.

Jo glanced around for the victim. There was only one woman in the courtroom not looking up. Her sleek black hair was pulled sternly off her face, and her clothes were too baggy for her body. She had olive skin, and was sitting between an older couple.

Jo pulled three files from her bag that she'd put into Manila folders, and after reckoning she had fifteen minutes left before her meeting with Hannah, reminded herself of the victims' details. The first had been raped and murdered in Portlaoise five years earlier. She'd been a nineteen-year-old student teacher out having some post-exam drinks in a pub with friends. The killer had waited in the middle cubicle of the pub's toilets and then climbed over when the student had locked herself into one alongside. He had slit her throat. Nobody had heard a thing. The second victim had been twenty-one and worked in a bar. She had been raped and murdered three years ago in Dublin city centre, after travelling to an open-air concert with a group of friends. She'd got a bus back into town with them, and then left to wait at a taxi rank. Her body had been found in the automatic toilet on O'Connell Bridge – her throat had been slit. The third victim had been an eighteen-year-old still in school. She had been raped and murdered after travelling to Limerick on a school trip. Her throat had been slit and her body found in a toilet in a Supermac's restaurant less than a year ago.

The similarities were impossible to ignore.

The defendant on trial for this separate rape was a taxi driver who'd been nominated as a suspect for the three killings by a highly regarded forensic psychologist reviewing cold cases. He had picked this perp as his best bet, because he was so accomplished at what he did, despite having no criminal convictions. Someone who could kill a woman in a public place would have a similar level of competence, the shrink had suggested.

But on first impressions, Jo did not think he was her man. All of the other victims had been around the twelve-stone mark in weight. The man in the box did not look more than ten, maximum, and he had a serious disability. His right arm ended at the elbow. The victim was thin, too, though Jo suspected she might have lost weight since the attack. But how could this man have climbed over a toilet cubicle quickly with only one arm? And there was another crucial difference between this case and Jo's other three. This victim was alive . . .

It was possible that all the victims were linked by his profession, since he was a taxi driver. Cabbies travelled to where the work was, and all of the women had been some distance from home at the time of their murders. Maybe they'd flagged him down, or been approached by him offering transport.

And his handicap hadn't prevented him from abducting this victim, a Spanish student, from a car park, which was a public place. He must have had plenty of practice to have become that brazen. Maybe he was her man.

Jo watched as the accused's barrister, who had his thumbs tucked into the armpits of his black-buttoned waistcoat, finally asked a question she was interested in hearing the answer to.

'Did you rape her?'

Jo sat up.

'Yes, the first time,' the accused answered. 'But the other times she asked me to make love to her.'

The victim gave little shakes of her head.

Her parents were obviously the people sitting on either side of her. A middle-aged woman with the same black hair held the girl's hand, an older man, in his best suit, had his arm around her shoulders. Their faces were etched with the frustration of not being able to give their side of the story. A translator sat alongside whispering to them what was being said.

It made Jo's blood boil the way victims were treated like second-class citizens in court. She willed the state barrister – a woman with long black hair and heavy make-up, taking copious notes – to object, but she didn't seem to have registered what the accused had just said.

The judge, meanwhile, looked on the verge of nodding off. If separate legal representation for victims had been implemented – as Justice Minister Blaise Stanley had promised Jo that it would be – a scene like this would not be happening.

'You say there was an element of consent,' the accused's barrister led.

'Yes.'

'And that you felt the victim was originally flirting with you in the bar. Isn't that right?'

'Yes.'

'It's a pack of lies,' a man sitting behind the Spanish family shouted, jumping up. His face was red. He looked very young. He was probably the student's boyfriend, Jo reckoned. 'That animal was stalking her.'

The judge moved his face close to his microphone. 'Get this man out of my courtroom before I hold him in contempt.' He indicated to the registrar sitting in front of him his intention to leave until order was restored.

'All rise,' the registrar declared.

Jo sighed as she stood. It was impossible for victims and their families to leave their emotions at the door of the court, as required by the system. That was the point she'd been trying to make to Blaise Stanley. But if the justice minister was implicated in a crime – as that note Jo had received with the sex tape had suggested – then it wasn't so surprising that her pleas had fallen on deaf ears.

Jo began to move sideways to exit the court. She was glad she'd come, because her intuition told her the man on trial was not responsible for her stack of unsolved cases. Why wouldn't he have killed this victim, if he'd murdered the others? Didn't serial killers usually become more violent, not less? The modus operandi was different, too: a knife hadn't been used. Instead, the accused had attempted to suffocate the student. Jo felt she could now meet George Hannah without being concerned, as Dan, Sexton and Oakley were, that the Tara Parker Trench case was taking her away from a more important investigation.

She was grateful that she'd been reminded what rape did to a woman: how it left her picking up the pieces, sometimes for the rest of her life. If Tara had been brutalized the way the Spanish student had – or even more cruelly – then she was in a very vulnerable place, and desperately in need of professional help.

22

George Hannah was waiting nervously for Jo at the door to the barristers' restaurant. He pushed it and held it open the instant she appeared on the second floor. He checked his watch when Jo stopped momentarily to salute a member of the court staff she hadn't seen in a number of years.

'What couldn't wait, Detective Inspector?' he asked, as Jo ducked under his arm less than a minute later and sat at a table for two. He put down a cardboard folder and lowered himself into the chair.

'Make mine a latte, and I'll explain all,' Jo answered. She didn't want the coffee, but her time was every bit as valuable as his, and she didn't mind letting him know it.

Hannah could barely conceal his irritation as he headed off towards the counter, sifting through the change from his trouser pocket and making great play of the fact that he might not have enough.

As soon as his back was turned, Jo opened his folder. Inside was an application to the High Court for a judicial review. Jo glanced up and saw Hannah trying to work out what buttons to press on a drinks dispenser She turned the page. The client he was representing was Barry Roberts. Jo scratched her head. Roberts was at the other end of the criminal spectrum from the likes of wealthy business people like the Fitzmaurices and Coxes. Roberts was a drug dealer, nicknamed 'King Krud', who peddled death and misery. He'd been knocking off his adversaries recently, in a feud that had seen some of the worst bloodshed in years.

She turned the page to see what the issue Hannah wanted to thrash out in the High Court on Roberts's behalf was, but was alerted by the sound of a ringing till. She looked up to see Hannah lifting the coffees and turning towards her.

Jo closed the folder, and smiled wanly.

'You were saying . . . ?' Hannah said, looking from the table to Jo suspiciously as he set the coffees down. He turned the folder the right way around.

'How well do Jeff Cox and Rosita Fitzmaurice know each other?' Jo asked.

'This is the first I've heard of any acquaintance,' Hannah answered.

'Jeff Cox was sleeping with the mother of a child taken from a garage last night, and Rosita was in the garage when the child was taken,' Jo said. 'They're both your clients.'

Hannah took a mouthful of coffee. 'So . . . ?'

'That little boy is out there somewhere. You know exactly what people in this city are capable of. I'm appealing to your conscience. Do you know anything that could help me? You must have had a good start in life to end up so highly qualified. You must have had parents who guided you, who wanted the best for you. And to pick law as a profession, you must at some point have believed in the concept of justice.'

Hannah didn't react. 'I don't know anything that can help you, I'm afraid.'

'Then it's too bloody late for you, too,' Jo said.

23

Jo looked up as Dan walked in. He didn't take his hands out of his pockets as he sat down.

'I'm glad you're feeling better,' he said.

It wasn't exactly the apology she wanted, but she knew it was as close as she'd get. She nodded, spotting dark circles under his eyes. 'I would never undermine you, Dan,' she said. In the old days, she'd have added, 'Because I love you.'

He twisted around, giving her office the once-over. 'So how's Rory? I'm sorry I haven't been around much lately.'

'I noticed,' Jo said. It sounded harder than she'd intended. She wished they could stop their constant tit-for-tat sniping. She hated it that she still snapped at him, and that standing anywhere near him still turned her legs to jelly. But she was never going to get over him cheating with his secretary, not now his future was going to be tied to Jeanie's for ever by the birth of their child.

She straightened up. 'And Jeanie. How's she getting along?' It sounded so formal she wanted to tear her hair out.

'Good,' Dan said, putting his hands on his knees. 'Great. Yeah, she's really terrific, thanks.'

This was torture. Jo cut to the chase. 'Why are you here, Dan?'

He scratched the stubble appearing along his jawline. 'I

want to know where Foxy and Sexton are. Have you got anywhere with the rape investigation? We should have a case conference if you have. I don't want to be sidelined any more. I want to be kept in the picture.'

Jo glanced at her watch guiltily. It was five o'clock. She'd made several attempts to get through to Sexton's phone, but had gone straight to his voicemail, and hadn't a clue where he was. Foxy had technically gone AWOL, too. 'We are working on something, but it's not the rape investigation.'

'So what is it?' Dan asked flatly.

'You know exactly what, Dan. It's the same case I've been harping on about all day, the missing tot – Presley Parker Trench.'

He stood up. 'Why am I getting a distinct impression of déjà vu . . . ?'

'I think Imogen Cox, the woman who was murdered in Killiney this morning, was pimping out her models – girls like Presley's mother, Tara. I suspect that's why Imogen's dead. It also means Presley could be in even more trouble than I originally thought.'

'And I know exactly how this one ends,' Dan said, his eyes cold. 'You've just told me you're not undermining me, yet you've already put a team together, ignoring my direct instructions.'

'Can you stop being so bullheaded and contact Dalkey Station? I want to head up the Imogen Cox murder inquiry while I'm at it. We're guaranteed to find Presley if we find who killed Imogen. If she took Presley, whoever killed her may have taken the child, or at least know where he is.'

Dan threw his arms up in the air in frustration. 'You're not listening to a word I'm saying—'

Jo cut him off. 'When I interviewed Tara this morning her

lips were blue. At first, I thought she was cold, but the heat in the station's stifling. So, then I thought maybe she was in shock. But even after I got some breakfast into her, her lips were still as blue as the first second I saw her. The thing is, I've only ever seen lips that colour on people lying on a slab in the morgue, who've drowned.'

Dan stared in disbelief, his mouth partly open.

'I also noticed she had all these little pinprick blood spots under her eyes. The last time I saw anything like that, Professor Hawthorne was examining a drowning victim during an autopsy. He said that little burst blood vessels scattered about under the eyes meant the person had fought for their life. Tara's nose was running as well, also consistent with asphyxiation caused by drowning. Plus, there were bruises on her torso, suggesting she'd been manhandled. My hunch is that whoever left those marks on her either saved her from drowning or had tried to drown her. And since anyone who knows me knows the only rule of policing I've ever really adhered to is that there's no such thing as coincidence, I'd say the chance that two such recent catastrophic events in her life – being attacked, and losing her child – are unconnected is virtually nil.'

Dan sighed heavily. 'Blue lips, blood spots, a runny nose, and a bruised belly. Why don't I ring the commissioner right now? Better yet, why don't you do it? Let's face it, you've more chance of getting through to him than I have. Or, how about this – come back to me when you have some real hard evidence and not just supposition?'

Jo felt a surge of anger. 'Tara's kid goes missing, Dan. A short time later her boss is murdered. And now I can't get in touch with Tara. You have got to put me in charge of this investigation before anyone else gets killed or disappears. I have the hard evidence you want right here. I have a DVD showing that Imogen Cox was involved in the sex industry.'

Dan took a breath and sat back down. 'Show it to me.'

Jo pulled open the desk drawer. It was empty and so was the one under it. She slapped her hand off the top, sides and bottom of both to be sure, then did the same with the two on the other side. There was something stuck to the roof of one of the drawers, but no Jiffy bag, and no DVD. The video of Imogen Cox, and the note that had come with it, had been taken.

'Well?' Dan asked.

Jo walked to the door and called to the detectives working in the office outside, 'Anyone been in here this morning when I was out?'

Detective Sergeant Roger Merrigan's arm shot up like a schoolboy's, much to the other detectives' amusement. He was the office clown, and Jo knew that when he'd worked with her on the Bible case he'd reported her every movement back to Dan. She gave him a stiff nod to enter, and waited with her hand on the door until he was inside before closing it.

Dan's eyes followed her.

'Who's been in here while I was out?' she demanded.

'Here?' Merrigan asked, looking at Dan with raised eyebrows.

Jo put her hands on her hips.

'Can't say I noticed anyone. I thought you were calling the register, that's why I put my hand up.'

'You must have seen if someone came in? There's a new bloody chair in here. Wheel itself in, did it?'

'Oh, yeah, Foxy's daughter was in all right,' he answered. 'The one who's got that—'

'Sal?' Jo asked. 'Her name is Sal.'

'Yeah, the mongoloid one—'

Jo put her hands on his shoulders and turned him back towards the door. 'On your way,' she said.

'I have to go,' Dan said, also heading for the door. 'Jeanie's expecting me. Don't you have to pick up the boys?'

Jo glanced at her watch, reached for her jacket, and remembered something. Turning back to her desk, she picked free the slip of cardboard stuck to the roof of the drawer. It was an antenatal appointment card for Holles Street Hospital with Jeanie's name on it, citing the date of an appointment some months back for a rhesus positive injection.

Sighing heavily, Jo tossed it on to her desk and locked her office door on the way out.

24

The kid was yapping away, it wasn't normal. Not that she knew much about little kids, but weren't they supposed to button it around strangers? He was doing her head in, talking about this, that and the other.

Her room was pokey at the best of times, but the kid hadn't nodded off on the couch till near midnight, and he'd been up again at six, his motor mouth going non-stop. She was sick to the teeth of listening to him rabbiting on. Even now, he was plonked in front of the TV talking right through the cartoons, which she had on at practically full volume to try and drown him out. She couldn't hear herself think. She hadn't had a wink of sleep last night worrying about the trouble she could get in if she was found with him.

Marching between him and the box, she put her hands over her ears, shut her eyes and yelled, 'Quiet!'

His chin wobbled. 'I want my dad.'

Taking him by the hand, she pulled him off the couch. Having him here was turning into a real pain. She couldn't even open the curtains in case someone saw him.

The kid started to wail.

'Shut up,' she said, shaking him roughly. 'Shut the fuck up!'

But snot and tears were rolling down his face and he was

hollering louder. She put her hand over his mouth. 'OK, you want me to ring your dad? I'll do it,' she lied. 'That's it, good boy, keep it nice and quiet and I'll have him here in no time.'

She held him, feeling the little shudders travelling through his ribcage, hearing the tight wheezing sound he made as he gasped for breath. Cursing some more, she put him down, and picked up her mobile, pretending to dial.

'Hello, it's me. Little Presley wants his daddy. Can you come and get him?'

It worked. The kid was calming down.

'You're on the way? That's fantastic.'

'I want to talk to him,' the kid said. 'He's getting me a present on his holidays.'

She put the phone down quickly. 'Sorry, too late. But don't you worry, he's coming right over. Here, if you're a good boy we can get you chips and sausages. Would you like that?'

The kid nodded.

'Your dad asked if I would wash your hair for you to make you nice and smart, so you've got to be a good boy and come into the bathroom with me, OK?' She held out her hand. 'Otherwise he won't give you your present.'

Looking startled, the kid took a step back, opened his mouth and started to cough.

25

Tara sat on a high stool at the bar in the Triton, downing a third glass of Cristal. She needed it after what had happened in the massage room. The emergency wrap of cocaine she'd stashed with her change of clothes was helping to numb the pain of the kicking Fitz had given her for threatening and cutting him. Still, right now she was buzzing as she waited for Big Johnny to bring Presley back like he'd promised. Then she was going to take Presley in a cab to the police station, and she wasn't going to leave until someone gave her back the keys to her car.

She twisted around to look at the bunch of yummy mummies in the corner of the bar. They were sitting at a table, wearing the kind of condescending expressions women only ever got after they had landed on their feet in a single-income household in a nice part of the city, with two big cars parked outside. Tara had gone to a private school, too. She'd been accepted at university, could play piano, and hold her own in conversation with anyone. She wanted what they had, too, one day – a big house, an SUV, and a nanny. *I'm just taking the scenic route*, she told herself, taking another mouthful of bubbly.

'Have some more,' the man who had bought her the drink said, pulling the magnum from the ice and refilling her glass.

She didn't know him from Adam. He was fifty-something, with high-waisted trousers and a black polo neck so tight that the loose skin on his neck dangled over it.

Nico, the barman – an Italian chef who had switched to bar work because of the size of the tips ladies like the yummy mummies gave – headed over and put his fingers to his lips. 'Not too much more, bellissima,' he told her. 'Fitz is around tonight.'

'Yeah, don't I know it,' Tara answered, holding the glass up in a toast, then knocking it back, too. She banged the empty glass back down on the counter, and sniffed.

The man put one arm around her, and rubbed a clammy hand up and down her skin from shoulder to wrist. It was six o'clock, and the cocktail of drink and drugs was starting to wear off. Her mood was becoming maudlin. *Where the hell were Big Johnny and Presley?*

'You're so sexy,' the man told her.

Tara held out her feet in their glossy red, strappy Manolo Blahniks and twisted her ankles around admiringly. The sight of her expensive shoes always made her feel good, no matter what else was going on. Men who moaned at the prices didn't understand that it wasn't about value for money. Shoes like this, designer bags and dresses, they were a status symbol. They reminded her how far she'd come, how much she'd achieved. Even when she got Presley back, she was never going to return to the bad old days when she hadn't had enough to pay the rent. It was all very well Jeff telling her she needed to get herself straight, but how was she supposed to pay for it?

Tara reached for the bottle and poured herself another glass, toasting Nico – he really was gorgeous, but too broke to be an option. *Been there, done that, worn Mick's T-shirt,* she thought. She stood up, almost upending the stool in the process. Flicking her hair, she tottered on to an imaginary dance floor, put her hands above her head and started to pump the air. Tomorrow she was going to wake up with the same problems, but tonight she was determined to be a superstar. She was going to get her boy back.

26

They were home. Rory pushed the passenger door of Jo's car open, grabbing his schoolbag from the footwell before Jo had finished parking in the driveway. He'd been giving her the silent treatment ever since she'd picked him up from school. She hadn't noticed at first, because she'd been too busy talking to Foxy on the hands-free set when Rory had climbed in at the school gates. Normally she'd have put the call off till after she'd chatted to her son about how his day had been, but she needed to make sure Sal hadn't taken the sex tape from the office, as the thought of what Sal might see filled her with dread.

In the course of the conversation, Foxy had picked up on Jo's stress levels and offered to work tonight if Jo could provide a babysitter. She'd told him to bring Sal over to hers, that Rory would do it. Foxy could then head to the airport, as Jo had established from an earlier call in the car that Tara's ex was due to fly back from his holiday tonight. If problems cropped up Jo would have to go to the station, too, to be in on any interview between Foxy and Mick Devlin. She also wanted to spend part of the evening running checks on the registrations she'd lifted from the CCTV in the garage. She had another try at getting Sexton, but his phone went to voicemail again.

Jo unstrapped Harry from his car seat, and as she set him down took his chunky little hand in hers. Harry held a velvet blanket he used as a comforter against his cheek as they followed Rory inside. It made Jo's heart lurch to think how independent her baby had become since Dan had left. She, on the other hand, felt as if she was regressing as the months turned to years and passed without him. It was hard to come home after a day's work, and not be able to sit down over dinner and thrash out the day with him. It was harder still to sit on a couch when the boys were asleep and stare at the TV on her own. She couldn't have a nightcap alone without feeling like an alcoholic – and without a nightcap, or an adult conversation, or a pair of arms wrapped around her, there was nothing to take the edge off the day. She didn't even want to think about how she was ever going to fare when she was ready to meet someone new. She was still relatively young at thirty-six, but how was she going to find the time to get out and about again? Where did you go when you were single and looking for a date these days? And who was going to want to go out with her, anyway, when she had a family ready-made?

Rory was pulling a towel out of the hot press by the time Jo had turned the alarm off, brought in Harry's crèche bag and closed the door behind her.

'Let's get you fed, darling,' she told Harry, kissing his little cheeks as she scooped him up.

In the kitchen, she put a set of blocks on the red and green chequered floor for him to play with while she got his tea ready. He'd be nodding off in under an hour. She hated seeing so little of him during the week, but whatever options she might have had if Dan had still been around, in terms of going part-time, were gone now she was a single mum and paying her own way.

Something struck her suddenly. Running down the hall, she banged on the bathroom door. 'Let me in, I need to ask you something.'

'What is it?' Rory answered, sounding bored.

'You only ever have a shower when you come in if you're planning on going out again. Tell me you're not planning on going out tonight.'

He pulled open an inch of the pine door. 'I'm going to the Mezz with Becky.'

'No you're not. It's a school night.'

'It's her birthday.'

'I need you here. I've got to go out again. And Foxy needs someone to mind Sal.'

'So I gathered in the car. You should have asked me. I'd made plans.'

'Yes, I should have, I'm sorry. But please, ask Becky to come up if you like, or take her out at the weekend instead. I'm working on a case that I can't clock out of. There's a little boy who's missing.'

'I've booked the tickets, Mother.'

'Look, this missing boy, he's only a year older than Harry. He's got asthma, and he has to be found before he needs his inhalers.' She glanced at her watch.

'Seriously, Mum, this is not my problem. You've worked your shift. Let someone else worry about it.'

'You're getting more and more like your father every day, do you know that?' Jo snapped.

He opened his mouth to answer, as she quickly held her hands up. She had, she realized, managed to upset almost everyone she cared about today. 'You're right. I'm sorry. I've been putting work first. You take the car, meet Becky. I'll work something out.'

'What about the little boy?' Rory asked.

'Not your problem,' Jo said, walking away. 'Go out, enjoy yourself. Just get home at a reasonable hour, will you? I don't want your principal on my case again.'

Rory tugged her sleeve. 'Becky will understand if I postpone—'

Jo threw her arms around him and started kissing him on the cheek.

He screwed up his face as he pushed her back. 'And in return I want your Visa card to pay for a meal for two, and a full tank of petrol in your banger of a car.'

'Deal,' Jo said, smiling.

After Foxy had dropped off Sal and agreed to head to the airport, and Jo had settled Harry down for the night, she stuck her head around the sitting-room door to check on Rory and Sal, whom she'd treated to a pizza. They were watching a repeat of *Britain's Got Talent* – Rory looking through spread fingers at a skimpily dressed very old lady singing her heart out.

'I don't think she's out of tune, Rory,' Sal said.

'It's not the tune, it's the dress,' Rory explained, winking at Jo, who gave him a thumbs up. He'd such a good heart, she could forgive him anything.

'What's wrong with the dress?' Sal asked. 'I love red.'

Jo went into the kitchen, switched on her laptop, and began scouring holiday destinations in Morocco on the internet until she found a hotel with an onion-shaped roof like the one she'd seen in the background of the sex tape. It was called the Atlantis, in Marrakesh.

Next, she logged into her remote access to Pulse, the garda computer system, in order to check the registrations she'd noted on the diagram she'd drawn up in her office. The first number she ran belonged to the HiAce. It threw up Marcus's surname and his address in Sandymount, making Jo look upwards and whisper, *thank you*, quickly. With his name and address she was able to get his social security number from another database on Pulse. Tomorrow she would contact the Revenue to find out the names of his clients, which would hopefully include the Triton Hotel. She curled her lip in surprise when she realized he lived in such a nice suburb, unaffected by the slump in property prices. Especially considering he was driving a van that looked like it was about to collapse.

'Mum, Sal is falling asleep in there,' Rory said, arriving in.

Jo stood up and walked into the sitting room. 'Would you like to go to bed now, darling?' she said.

Sal looked up sleepily. She was only twelve, and it had been a very hard day on her. Jo felt guilty about taking Foxy up on his offer to work that night.

'Yes, please, Jo.'

Jo walked Sal down to the spare bedroom.

'Dad packed my night clothes just in case,' Sal said, taking a Miley Cyrus rucksack off her shoulder.

'Good thing, too,' Jo said, plumping her pillows.

'Good night, Jo,' Sal said, putting her arms out for a hug.

'Night,' Jo answered, kissing her forehead.

'Jo?' Sal asked, as she was closing the door.

'Yes, love?'

'What age were you when you had to start wearing a bra?'

Jo scratched her neck. 'Let me think, must have been about your age, I'd say.'

'Right,' Sal said. 'Thanks.'

'Tell you what,' Jo said. 'We can go shopping for one, if you like, at the weekend?'

'That's OK, thanks,' Sal said. 'I just wondered. Don't say I said so to my dad, OK, Jo?'

'Course I won't,' Jo promised. 'That's girl stuff.'

Jo's mobile was ringing as she re-entered the kitchen. It was Reg, the superintendent in Dalkey, who'd treated her shabbily earlier in Howth.

'We've arrested Jeff Cox for the murder of his wife,' he said.

'End to a perfect day . . .' Jo answered, adding, '. . . not,' quickly. 'Has he admitted anything?'

'The only thing he's saying is that he wants to speak to you,' Reg replied. 'Can you get over? We've already extended his detention once, so it's urgent.'

27

In the bar of the Triton Hotel, Sexton looked around at the blinged-up women with tangerine skin, and the men in chinos and deck shoes, their car keys lined up along the bar like a dick-measuring contest. He'd been so hungry he'd bought a takeaway curry after meeting Murray Lawlor at the Sandymount cash machine. He'd eaten it in the car, and fallen asleep, only waking up just in time to rush here. He still hadn't had a chance to ring Jo.

He was sorry he'd come. He felt shabby still dressed in his work clothes – a grey suit, white shirt, skinny pink tie, and a pair of Dr Martens soles. There was a familiar-looking woman dancing at the far end of the room in that stupid way only the very drunk do. It was a scene he'd have expected to see in the early noughties, before the country went belly up. In the current climate it reeked of bad taste. He felt a bad bout of indigestion coming on, and was all set to turn around and leave when he spotted Murray to the back right, in a blue shirt with a white collar opened one button too low, waving him over. Murray's chest had been shaved and oiled, and if he'd squeezed his pecs together you could have used them to open your beer. There was a motorbike helmet with a black-tinted visor on the table in front of him.

Sexton spotted a couple of well-known faces at the bar and a rugby international heading for the john as he walked over. He felt himself breaking out in a sweat. He liked to disappear in a pub, yet everyone in this place wanted to be seen, as far as he could make out. They were all facing the door, looking up to see who'd arrived, with identical bored expressions on their faces. He got the impression that if Angelina Jolie walked through the door, their faces would stay the same.

Murray had his arms around two babes, who seemed to be hanging on his every word. Sexton stared at them. On second thoughts, maybe he should start looking after himself more, join a gym perhaps, get himself a pair of pecs that could take your eye out, like Murray.

Murray stood and put out his hand to make a meal of his arrival. *Well, with birds like that, he's entitled*, Sexton thought. But what tickled him more was the way the girls stood, too. Like bloody geishas they were, like they didn't have minds of their own.

One of the women was a ringer for the Charlie's Angel he'd a crush on as a kid, Sexton realized. She'd the same long black hair and killer black eyes as Jaclyn Smith. The blonde beside her was more of a Farrah Fawcett than a Cheryl Ladd, too much make-up, but a Kelly Brook body built for sin. *And doesn't she know it?* Sexton thought. Her short sequinned dress was cut so low you could see the rim of her bra, satin red.

'Ladies, this is Gavin, a very good friend of mine,' Murray said. 'Better watch what you say, he's a policeman.'

'What happened to your face?' Farrah giggled. She'd spoken in broken English. She sounded Eastern European.

Sexton touched the scab on the bridge of his nose; he'd

completely forgotten about it. 'I headbutted a dirtbag a couple of weeks back.'

She reached for her drink. The ice cubes tinkled as she drew it to her mouth. Looked like a G & T with a splash of lime. He used to work with a cop who said you could tell all you needed to know about what made a woman tick by the drink she wanted. Her choice told you the kind of hit she was chasing, and, from that, you could generally work out why. A girl into shots wanted to forget, therefore she would need lots of fun to keep her mind off the past. A girl into lager wanted a laugh and generally a commitment, in which case – steer clear. But a girl on G & T was perfect – gin made a woman emotional and needy; in other words, anxious to please.

Jaclyn's eyes widened. 'What did he do to deserve that?' she cooed. She sounded like an Essex girl, and judging by the strawberry on the rim of her glass, Sexton reckoned she was drinking champagne, meaning she was high maintenance.

'Gav, give me a hand at the bar, will you? I've got to keep the ladies here feeling refreshed,' Murray said. He was wearing jeans with pleats ironed down the centre and those tan, square-toed poofter shoes Sexton hated. 'Same again, girls?'

Farrah Fawcett shook her head, grinning. 'A Bacardi Breezer for me this time,' she piped up.

'And me,' Jaclyn rowed in.

Sexton felt depressed. Drinks like that were for kids. Kids shouldn't drink.

'Still got the silver tongue, I see,' Murray said when they were out of earshot. 'What are you talking about nutting someone for?'

'She asked me a question.'

'Yeah. Well, let's keep it nice and light from here on in,

shall we? Everything's on a need-to-know basis, understood? Now, which of them do you want?'

'Yeah, like I'm in with a chance.'

Murray rubbed his thumb off his first two fingers. 'Everyone's in with a chance when it's a level playing field.'

'You are joking,' Sexton said. 'They're hookers?'

Murray put his hand on Sexton's back and turned him away from the girls. 'Can you keep it down? Discretion is the key here.'

Sexton looked over his shoulder, and lowered his voice. 'I just don't get it. The women on the street I meet in the job all have baggage – they were abused as kids or have drug problems. These girls have everything, their whole lives ahead of them. How did they—?'

'Questions, questions,' Murray answered, zipping his lips. 'Are you up for it or not?'

'Nah, paying is the last gasp, mate,' Sexton said.

Murray put his weight on Sexton's shoulder, and leaned in close. 'Just so you get it straight, you're not paying them for sex. Any man can get sex any time, anywhere, as long as he's prepared to lower his expectations to fit the situation. You're paying them to fuck off afterwards, to disappear, to forget it ever happened, to be discreet – in other words everything your ordinary woman won't do after sex.

'These girls are really special for another reason. They don't lie in bed expecting you to do the work. They come to bed to spoil you, treat you like a man. And don't start worrying that you can't afford it. Tonight's on me. Consider it a gesture. You come to work for me, this is the kind of life you'll be leading. These girls are one of the perks. Course if you want them both together, you can forget about a month's notice. I want you on the job tomorrow.'

Sexton felt his heart rate step up a pace, not because of what he was being offered – the thought of paying for sex made him feel sick – but because now he knew he had a lead, something Jo would be interested in. It was possible Murray was taking payments from Jeff Cox for supplying him with prostitutes. Jo had suspected Tara of being on the game, and, having seen Murray waiting at the ATM in Sandymount, Sexton was pretty sure that he'd been meeting up with Cox there on a weekly basis. This also meant they now had evidence of a motive for Cox to murder his wife, despite Jo's first thoughts on the subject.

He exhaled as he mulled this over. 'I thought you were driving,' he said, nodding at the motorbike helmet.

'I'm allowed one,' Murray said.

'Why the switch to a motorbike? You were in a car earlier.'

'Questions, questions. I always take it on a job, if you must know. Best way to follow someone in case of traffic.' He nudged Sexton's shoulder with his own. 'Get these in, will you? I'm going for a slash.'

The change Sexton got back from a fifty euro note for the round was only worth sticking into the collection box on the side of the counter. He stared at the handful of copper coins. He didn't want to insult the street kids of Calcutta by dropping it in.

He watched as Murray emerged from the Gents, earlier than he should have, rubbing his nose with his finger once too often, the spring in his step too springy, grinding his jaw.

Sexton was handing out the drinks when his arm stopped mid-air.

Another drop-dead gorgeous female had just come over – the same one Sexton had seen dancing when he'd been on the way in. She threw her arms around Murray's neck.

'Look what the cat dragged in,' Murray said, extricating himself.

Sexton stared in disbelief. The woman was Tara Parker Trench. And her pupils were fully dilated. She was completely out of it.

28

Foxy stood in the arrivals hall of Dublin airport feeling guilty as hell that he was still working. He rarely worked overtime, as Sal always came first, and he didn't like disrupting her routine. But he'd never known Jo to be wrong when she got this worked up during a case. He wouldn't forgive himself if anything happened to an innocent little boy because he hadn't backed her up, especially after he'd had to bail out of work for a chunk of the afternoon.

He scanned the display board over his head, which claimed the flight back from Fuerteventura had arrived twenty minutes earlier. He knew from bitter experience that luggage collection and passport clearance were notoriously slow. He and Sal went to Euro Disney every Christmas. Getting out of Dublin airport regularly took longer than the flight.

He held a sheet of paper against his chest with Tara Parker Trench's ex's name written in bold caps on it. If he'd had a bit more notice, he might have been able to organize a picture of Mick Devlin through Facebook, the greatest asset to police forces around the world because it provided lists of associates as well as photographs. Foxy had done a course in how to use it, but he still couldn't grasp why anyone would want to show complete strangers their treasured family albums. *Must be getting old*, he thought.

He watched couples embrace as they caught sight of each other, and grandparents with arms outstretched as they spotted returning grandchildren. Everybody needed someone to pick them up at the airport, as far as he was concerned.

Ordinarily, he'd have gone through customs and waited for Devlin as he disembarked from the plane, but Jo had specified their inquiries be kept low key, as there'd be hell to pay if Dan found out what they were up to.

He noticed that some of the passengers starting to stream into the arrivals hall were wearing shorts and T-shirts, and he started to study the men coming through the automatic frosted-glass doors behind trollies stacked with luggage. His focus shifted from a black-haired man in a denim shirt to a pot-bellied guy with shades who was much the same age, early twenties. They were heading in different directions, and neither had seen his note. Foxy chose to follow the guy in the denim shirt for two reasons. Firstly, he had model good looks, so would probably have had plenty of experience pulling gorgeous women, and not have been intimidated by Tara Parker Trench. Secondly, he was on his own – no sign of any mates – while pot belly had a bird hanging out of his arm. Foxy thought it more likely Mick Devlin would have given up on women. And last, but by no means least, denim shirt had a remote control car in a box under his arm, which seemed the perfect present for a three-year-old boy.

'Mick,' he called. 'Are you Mick Devlin?'

The guy stopped and turned. He looked from Foxy's face to the sign, and the colour drained from his face.

'What's going on?'

'I need to have a word.'

'Not me mam or dad?' Devlin glanced beyond Foxy, like he half-expected to see the surviving half in the background.

'Let me buy you a coffee.'

'Oh Jesus, it's not Presley, is it? Tell me that cow hasn't done something stupid. Tell me my boy's all right.' He reached into his back jeans pocket and pulled out a mobile phone.

Foxy spoke quickly. 'We haven't been able to contact Tara, and Presley's missing.'

Mick bent double as though he'd been punched, and with his hands on his knees took a few deep breaths. 'What happened?'

'We don't know. I need you to tell me anything you think might be relevant to his disappearance.'

'Like what?'

'Anything irregular about what was going on in Tara's life that might lead us to her and your son?'

Mick straightened, and glared at Foxy. 'You wouldn't be asking me a question as specific as that without knowing the answer.'

'Please, don't hold back on me. It's too important. Why did you two split?'

'I thought she might be on the game.' He checked Foxy's reaction. 'I can tell it doesn't come as a surprise to you. Is she?'

'Why don't you tell me why you came to that conclusion?'

'The hours, the money, the way she was getting dolled up. The fact that there were never any pictures she could show me for all the supposed jobs she was going to. And she stopped . . .' his voice trailed off.

'Stopped what?'

'Liking sex.'

'But you never had any proof of what she was doing?'

'I never caught her with anyone in our bed, no.'

Foxy chose his words carefully. 'Do you know anything about the men Tara might be involved with?'

'Only that they're rich.'

'Any names?'

'I told you, she denied it—'

'If you suspected something, it must have been with good reason. Did you notice any admirers?'

'Yeah, I suspected someone. That old fart who sent his Bentley around to bring her to the airport, because a taxi was never good enough.'

'And who was that?'

'She called him Fitz. He owns some swanky hotel in Dublin, fancies himself as Richard Branson with his helicopter out back. He's a dodgy bastard. He used to send her flowers as well, give her jewellery. I mean, what would you think?'

'Do you mean Charles Fitzmaurice?' Foxy asked.

'Yeah, that's the one.' Mick stepped closer, his eyes wide with tension. 'Now, tell me. What's happened to my son?'

'Hello, love, what a nice surprise,' a woman said, tapping Foxy's shoulder. 'You always did have a thing about being there to collect someone after a flight.'

It took a couple of seconds for Foxy to place her. The last time he had seen her had been the night before Sal went in for open-heart surgery. And yet here she was, larger than life, and acting as if nothing had happened. Dorothy. His wife. The woman he hadn't seen for twelve years, or managed to divorce.

29

Dalkey Garda Station operated out of a converted Edwardian house with sea views, at the end of a quiet cul-de-sac populated in the main by writers and artists. The joke was that if you got stationed here, you needed amphetamines to unwind. It was gone ten in the evening by the time Jo arrived, and as she walked into one of the draughty holding rooms she wondered how its faded grandeur was making Jeff Cox feel. It made her edgy and out of sorts, because of what it said about the justice department's attitude to policing.

Jeff's eyes were bloodshot, the slick look of the morning gone. 'I d-d-didn't do it,' he said. 'I didn't kill Imogen.'

'Yeah, yeah,' Jo answered. She made a talking hand to illustrate. 'I'm innocent. I loved my wife. I wasn't there.' She glanced at the uniformed male sitting at the door. 'Any chance of a cuppa?'

The uniform stood up slowly.

'Tiny drop of milk, ta. You want one?' she asked Jeff.

He shook his head.

Jo looked at the camera lens and winked at Reg, the Dalkey superintendent, now watching intently from the other side.

She examined her nails. Not one of them was worth filing

into anything, but if Jeff Cox wanted her attention, she was going to make him work for it. She suspected he was used to paying for sex, and she knew he was vain, both of which suggested an egocentric and self-serving attitude. He'd be full of remorse, for himself . . .

'I-I- thought you – of all people – believed me. You said so at my house, in front of my solicitor. That you d-d-didn't think I d-d-did it.'

'Not exactly. And, besides, that was this morning, when I thought you were a kept man and incapable of bludgeoning your wife's head in with a rock. That was before I found out you'd a girlfriend on the side, who – from what I hear – was putting it about to anyone who'd pay.' Jo looked around. 'Where is your esteemed brief, by the way? Let me guess – he had to go to watch some cricket match being played live in India. Personally, I'd have gone for a brief based in or around the Bridewell, the sort more likely to be cheering Eric Bristow along, if you know what I mean. They're particularly good at finding ways not to let a mere "bludgeoning someone's head in with a rock" charge stick. Plenty of practice, you see. Your lawyer's strengths are alimony and personal injury suits against plastic surgeons.'

'I d-d-didn't kill Imogen.'

Jo frowned. 'Your wife was older. You hated her. And to add insult to injury, she was your boss – and not just at home, but at work, too. Did she put you down in front of all the beautiful women she managed? It must have been degrading being paid by her. But the lifestyle made it all worthwhile. You couldn't just walk away. And you needed it if you were going to keep a certain young model in your life who was willing to have sex with you. The fact that it was for money was a by the by to you. Tara gave you back your mojo, made you feel like a real man. Not like your wife. You needed to find a way of getting Imogen out of your life, and Tara in.'

His eyes widened. 'I d-d-didn't d-d-do it.'

Jo held up the bank statement she'd taken from his room.

'What happened? Did Imogen decide you were spending too much of her money? Did you have a blazing row? Did you decide to teach her a lesson? Show her what a real man you were?'

A bead of sweat ran down Jeff's face. 'I d-d-didn't kill Imogen.'

'So you keep saying. But if you didn't, who did?'

The uniform came back with the tea.

'Perfect,' Jo told him, walking over. 'Just what I needed. Raining out, is it?' She could see Jeff fidgeting out of the corner of her eye, and she kept the conversation going with the uniform. 'The things men want in bed never cease to amaze me. Do you know what "rimming" is?'

The uniform shrugged.

'It's licking out someone else's . . . well . . . you know,' Jo pointed to her behind. 'The girls have to wear dams on their teeth to avoid catching hepatitis. What about "roasting"? Have you heard of that?'

The uniform shook his head.

'It's a girl who services two men at the same time. Think of a pig, skewered both ends and turning on a spit.' Jo took another sip and spoke over her shoulder to Jeff. 'Course, I'm sure Tara only ever imagines your face when she's working.'

The uniform sniggered.

Jeff stood up, his face tight with anger. 'Tara's not like that,' he shouted, his stammer gone.

Jo turned to face him.

'She was t-t-trying to get out, put all that behind her,' he said, more quietly.

'Job satisfaction missing, was it? Not getting the same kick out of it any more?'

He banged the table with both fists. 'She was gang-raped. You happy now?' After a pause, he sat back heavily in his chair.

Jo walked over to her chair and sat opposite him. 'In Morocco?'

Jeff nodded.

Jo thought of the DVD she'd started to watch that morning. The girl she'd seen in the pool could have been Tara, now she came to think about it. Tara had certainly had enough bruises, by the look of her. 'By whom?'

He put his head in his hands. 'By animals. They could have killed her.'

'Were they businessmen? Or film stars? The kind of men kids want to be like, that they look up to, that women dream of dating? Who were they?'

'Footballers.'

Jo raised her eyebrows. 'What were their names?'

'I don't know.'

'Bullshit. Imogen was there, too, wasn't she? Who were they, and why didn't your wife do anything to stop it?'

'The b-b-business was d-d-disappearing. All the Irish girls were dropping out. The b-b-big money was gone. She needed to keep the clients happy until she sourced new girls.'

'Where's Presley?'

'I don't know. I thought Imogen must have taken him, to keep Tara quiet, and Tara thought so, too, but my wife swore she hadn't. Imogen couldn't have children herself: she got chlamydia when she was young, and that was the end of it. It made her even more of a b-b-bitter, twisted b-b-bitch, if that was possible. She sucked the life out of everyone she met. A vampire, that's all she was – no b-b-better.'

Jo sighed and rubbed her eyes. She believed him about not knowing where Presley was. The Dalkey gardaí had searched the house after he'd been arrested, but found absolutely nothing to suggest the little boy had been brought there.

'Well, the bad news, from your point of view,' she told him, '. . . is that failing to summon emergency services immediately to help your wife is a very serious crime. Your only hope now of leniency from the courts is to cooperate fully with our investigation. If your expensive solicitor was here, he'd tell you the same thing. Do you have the film of Tara being raped?'

'No.'

'Why not?'

'We were burgled. It was one of the things taken.'

'I want the names of the footballers involved in the assault.'

Jeff looked panicked.

'I told you, I don't know their names. It was a club outing. They were all Melwood Athletic, that's all I know. I swear to you—'

'So what was the last row with your wife over, anyway?'

'T-t-the same thing it was always about – me spending our money.'

'On Tara?' Jo asked. She didn't wait for his answer. There wasn't time.

Reg was waiting for her on the other side of the door.

'Well done.'

But Jo was really worried. 'How the hell am I going to get

an APB on all the ports and airports at this hour of the night?'

'I don't follow,' Reg said.

'If Imogen Cox was running out of girls, she might have started sourcing them from abroad. If this case leads to a human trafficking ring, Presley could be absolutely anywhere in the world by now.'

30

Fitz was in his dressing gown, having waved away his private nurse, who was fussing over a blood pressure monitor and the bandage on his neck. He didn't want any distractions while he watched Tara on one of the screens in the control room of the hotel, which was rigged up like the *Big Brother* house.

Tara, he was starting to believe, knew a lot more about what had been going on in the garage than she'd maintained. Well, once he had his drugs back, he'd teach her a thing or two. He wasn't going to take any more chances.

She was cocking her ass at him as she leaned in to take another glass of champagne from Nico. Fitz's champagne. Now she owed him for that, on top of the five million euro which the haul in the back of her car was worth.

'Is she on something?' he asked Big Johnny, who was standing behind him.

'Nothing, boss. She asked, but I refused.'

'She's on something,' Fitz grumbled. 'If she fucks this up, I'm holding you personally responsible.'

'Yes, Fitz,' Big Johnny said.

'Where's the kid?'

'Upstairs. Yolanda's watching him. He's safe, I guarantee it.'

Tara had moved over to the tables. Fitz watched the way she let her tits brush against Murray, how her leg touched another man's thigh while she pretended to be completely absorbed in what he had to say.

She was air-kissing the new guy now, working her magic, running her fingertips along the back of his neck. She threw a worried glance in the camera's direction like she knew he was watching. Good. He wanted her scared. It was part of the turn on.

She sashayed over to some of the other girls in the bar, heels clicking along the tiles, the new guy's hard-earned cash ching-chinging as he paid for a round of drinks. Oh, she really fancied herself, all right; really thought she was some-thing very special. Not for long, though. He was going to take her down a peg or two. No better man. Not here, not yet. But when she found out what he had in store for her, she'd end up begging him for more. He felt his groin spring to life in a way that hadn't happened for twenty-odd years. He smiled at the screen. He was going to give Tara Parker Trench the seeing-to of her life. It would be her last.

He sat up suddenly. 'Who's that guy with Murray?' He jabbed a finger at the screen.

Big Johnny looked surprised. 'I don't know, boss.'

'Well you'd better find out. And you'd better find out quick. Because we have plans for tonight, and we don't want him getting in our way.'

31

In the flesh, Sexton thought Tara Parker Trench even more stunning than in photographs – with her silky shoulder-length sandy hair, olive skin, and jade-green eyes. She wore a skimpy silver dress and red shoes that were so high she had to keep one hand permanently on the bar for balance. She was movie-star beautiful, but that wasn't why Sexton was staring. He couldn't believe she could be out partying when her kid was missing. Or was she? Perhaps Presley had been found. Sexton cursed his sodding mobile for the umpteenth time today. Given Jo's lecture about his heart not being in the job, there'd be hell to pay tomorrow, especially if she had been trying to contact him. But still, if Tara's boy had been found, how could she be on the lash the first night her kid was home safe?

'Got anything for me?' she was asking Murray. She had a gravelly voice that was sexy as hell. Sexton did not like where his instincts were going.

'He didn't show up,' Murray answered.

Tara looked put out.

Murray wasn't giving her the time of day, Sexton observed. He wasn't even looking at her, just standing there straight as a beanpole. Sexton didn't know if he'd be able to stay that aloof if she started fawning over him.

'That's not good enough,' she told Murray. 'Jeff owes me. I need the money.' She whispered something directly into Murray's ear.

'Not now,' he said in a clipped tone, nodding in Sexton's direction sternly.

Tara pursed her lips like she was sulking, then began talking to Sexton. 'Have we met? You look familiar.' She air-kissed him, running her fingers along his neck.

'I was just going to ask you the exact same thing,' he replied.

'A comedian,' she said, pulling a bored face.

'Actually, Gavin's a copper,' Murray said, emphasizing the last word.

The smile fell from Tara's face, and after a drawn-out second, she turned back to the bar and reached for her glass.

Murray stepped into the gap. 'A word of advice,' he told Sexton, lowering his voice. 'Steer clear of that one. It'll only lead to trouble.'

'You two were talking about Jeff Cox, weren't you?' Sexton asked. 'That's who you were meeting today, right? What exactly is your new job description, Murray? What did Jeff owe Tara money for?'

Murray looked around nervously. 'Button it, I'm warning you.'

Sexton was getting sick of his attitude 'Or what? What do you know about Imogen Cox's murder?'

Murray held his hands up and gave a big, false smile, his eyes hard. 'Look, all I'm saying is, Tara's trouble.'

Sexton glanced around for the nearest payphone. He needed to speak to Jo urgently. He thought there might be one in the lobby.

But before he could make a move, a group of men

streamed through into the bar, joking and jostling. In track-suits and carrying holdalls, they managed to bring the place to a standstill. Sexton had been wrong about this bunch – virtually everyone in the bar was now holding their drink mid-mast, and had cut off their conversations to stare at the newcomers. Even Sexton took a step back in surprise. No wonder they had a captive audience. The men were internationally famous footballers.

One of them pointed over at Tara. 'Here, look who it is!'

The guy speaking was called Kevin Mooney. He was probably the greatest living player in the world, in Sexton's opinion. He'd watched every match Mooney had played for the last five years.

Sexton took a deep breath, but before he could say anything, Tara had thrown her arms around him and started kissing him passionately.

'Get a room,' one of the footballers called, amid a sea of whistles.

'We have to leave,' Tara whispered in Sexton's ear. 'We have to leave now.'

32

Foxy stuck the kettle on as Dorothy pottered between the kitchen and the spare bedroom, unpacking her things and getting her bearings. He was counting his lucky stars now that Sal was staying overnight with Jo, and the house was empty. He'd arranged for Devlin to call into the station tomorrow morning to finish up the interview.

Dorothy reappeared and waved a hand down her front. 'What do you think?'

He realized she'd changed into a pink summer dress that was too young for her. It showed a lot of flesh. Her henna-red hair hung loose about her shoulders, and she wasn't wearing any shoes. Her toenails were painted a bright red and she'd a silver ring on the second toe of the right one.

'How have the years treated me?'

He coughed and turned back to the kettle. 'I'd better put the heating on . . . How long did you say you were over for?'

'Hmm? Oh, just a couple of days.' She sat at the table with a heavy sigh. 'God, my plates of meat are killing me.'

'Sorry?'

She pointed down. 'Plates of meat, you know? Feet. Sorry, I've been away too long.' She peered out the window. 'You should plant a creeper to hide that back wall.'

'No. Sal likes to bounce a ball against it.'

*

A couple of minutes later, he carried two of his best china cups and saucers through to the living room and placed them on the glass table. There were jam rings on the saucers – Sal's favourites.

'I don't drink tea with milk any more,' Dorothy said. 'I have to watch my figure these days.'

'Oh.' He turned and carried one of the cups back to the kitchen, refilling the kettle at the sink before returning. 'So who were you planning to visit?'

She took a biscuit. 'You, of course.'

'Were you going to ring first?' he asked, alarmed, wondering what he'd have told Sal if she'd opened the door to her mother.

'Yes. I am nervous, no point lying to you. Especially after everything.'

Foxy frowned. It felt like a betrayal of his daughter now to remember how their lives had fallen apart when they had first found out about her condition. It was the shock of going from expecting everything to be OK, to watching the doctors and nurses whispering around the observation table after Sal had been delivered. Foxy remembered how they were told her ears were set a bit low, and this might indicate the chromosomal disorder Trisomy 21: Down's syndrome.

Dorothy had been distraught. 'Everything will be all right,' he'd promised her. 'She's beautiful. She's our lovely daughter.' But he had known, because Dorothy had taken the news so hard, that it wouldn't be all right for her.

'Tell me how you've been.' She put a hand on his knee.

He stared at it. 'Fine. Busy.'

'Any women I should know about?'

Foxy stood up. 'Do you know, you haven't asked me one thing about Sal since you arrived.'

'Well, you'd have told me if anything was wrong with her – anything else, I mean.'

'There's nothing wrong with her. Sal is Sal. She's still beautiful. Still special. Yet you haven't asked me what her favourite thing to do on a Saturday is, or what she likes and hates to eat, or what TV programmes she enjoys . . . anything.'

'I didn't think she . . .'

'What? You didn't think she could feel or think?' Dorothy shook her head fiercely. 'You know I don't mean that. I love Sal, I always have. I regret what I did every single day. I want to see her again, that's all. And I wanted to see you. We were happy together once.'

Foxy felt a rush of anger. 'Let's get one thing very clear: I don't want you back, not like that.'

Dorothy threw her hands up in the air. 'For your information, I wasn't offering. I have a partner, thank you very much.'

'So why didn't Frank come with you? Give you a bit of support when you meet the daughter you left for dead?'

Dorothy's eyes welled up. She sniffed.

'I'm sorry,' Foxy said with a sigh. 'I'm not judging you. Really I'm not. I just know you, Dot, and I don't think you've changed a bit.' He paused, and looked at her. 'He's left you, hasn't he? That's why you've come back. You never could bear being on your own.'

Dorothy pulled a tissue from her sleeve as the tears started to flow. 'Frank didn't leave me – he died, poor bugger.'

Foxy walked over and put his arm around her. 'I'm sorry.' He gave her shoulders a squeeze. 'I only ever spoke to him on the phone but he seemed . . . reliable.'

She blew her nose. 'I want to come home, John. It wouldn't have to be like old times. I messed that up, I know.

But I could be a companion – cook and clean for you and Sal, make all of our lives a bit easier. Don't answer me straight away. Just give me a couple of days to prove to you and Sal that home life is better with me in it.'

'Look, I can't have you swan in to her life as her mother, then take off again if it doesn't work out. You'd break Sal's heart.'

Dorothy clutched his hand. 'She's the only reason you're saying no, though, isn't she? I can see it in your eyes. If it was down to you, you'd have me back. Right?' She tried to touch his face.

He leaned away. 'You can stay tonight, but tomorrow you have to go. I need time to think this through.'

Dorothy sighed. 'Can I see her tomorrow?'

'No. You should go back to Brighton. That's where you live now, isn't it? If we do arrange a reunion, I need to prepare Sal gently for what's coming.'

Dorothy closed her eyes and gave a resigned nod. She reached into a pocket, pulled out a tiny plastic band, and handed it to him. It was Sal's hospital wrist ID, less than an inch in diameter, he reckoned.

'You might as well have this, too. Maybe you can show it to her when you're telling her about me?'

He took it, read Sal's name on it.

'I kept it to remind me how tiny she used to be. That's the way I like to remember her, everyone still treating her like she was normal because they couldn't tell. My doctor said I had post-natal depression, did you know? He said that was why I found it so difficult to cope.'

Foxy felt a pang of guilt. 'Look, you'll have to leave early tomorrow morning. I'm sorry, but I have to think about what's best for Sal.'

33

In the hotel suite they had adjourned to, Sexton was standing in the shower, tilting his face into a jet of steaming water, and soaping under his arms, keeping one eye on the crack in the door, which he'd left ajar. It was just coming up to eleven at night, and he'd only given into Tara's insistence that he wash because she was frantic, completely convinced that they were being watched. She'd said Presley's life would be in danger if they didn't keep up the pretence that they were about to have sex. She'd agreed to tell Sexton everything if he first went through the motions, as a client would have done.

He'd decided to cooperate to calm her down. There was no point arguing with someone on drugs; and she was definitely on something – completely paranoid, and jabbering away. But some of the things she'd told him on the way up in the elevator about the footballers in the bar had convinced him she was about to come clean. If he played his cards right, he believed he could have this case solved for Jo by the morning. Tara had even slipped her dress and shoes off and handed them to him to convince him she wasn't going to do a legger as soon as his back was turned.

He snapped the head off one of those miniature shower-gel bottles and soaped it through his hair, rinsing the suds out quickly, and stepped out of the shower. He smelt of strawberries, and he shook the water off his hair as he dried himself. There was a dressing gown on the back of the door and he pulled it on. It was too small, and he felt like a plonker, but if all this got Tara to talk to him, it'd be worth it.

He swiped the condensation off the mirror so he could see himself, and spiked his hair to seem younger, or at least trendier. He wasn't bad looking, he supposed. He'd never had any problems pulling before he got married. After Maura died, he just couldn't be bothered trying any more. Even so, a woman like Tara would never have given him a second glance.

He went back into the dark bedroom. She was lying on her back diagonally across the four-poster bed, wearing only suspenders and a pair of stockings. Her breasts were a little too big for his taste. But, overall, she was perfection.

'OK, I kept my side of the deal,' he said, using the towel around his neck to scrub the back of his hair.

But Tara didn't answer, or react.

Sexton stepped in closer, trying, in the dim light, to make out what was wrong. Then he saw it. A trickle of vomit was running from the corner of her mouth. He put two fingers to her neck, and held his breath as he waited. The pulse was faint, but it was still there. Tara Parker Trench wasn't just out cold, she was in a really bad way.

34

It was nearing midnight as Jo swung her car across the East Link Toll Bridge, towards the city centre. Stays tinkled against the masts of yachts in the marina to her right. The other side was the city's preferred spot for suicide jumps.

Steering past the rundown harbour warehouses dotted along North Wall Quay, she mulled over what Jeff had just told her. If Tara had been gang-raped, and the whole thing filmed, that sex tape in the wrong hands could bring down a lot of important people. The amount football clubs paid for top players was probably worth more than the GNP of the bloody country these days, after the interest on the IMF debts had been paid. Those players who had hurt Tara would have to face criminal charges. If they were prosecuted, and went to prison, the knock-on effect on their club's fortunes would be incalculable. Worst-case scenario: relegation, terrible press, even bankruptcy. The sex tape would be the lynchpin of any prosecution. No wonder it had been taken from her office. But by whom?

The streets were empty. Even the homeless had bedded down for the night, Jo realized, scanning the quay. The car's heater was broken again, and her breath fogged in the night air. She'd kept the radio on to help her stay alert, though it was one of those chat shows where callers ring in to abuse each other and the DJ takes the high moral ground to stir them all up. *Who had sent her the tape?* she asked herself. Tara could have done so, but why give Jo only half the story when she was so desperate to find Presley? Jo felt sure Tara had been trying to hide that part of her life when they'd met.

Her phone beeped with an incoming text and Jo angled it at the top of the steering wheel, clicking the message open. She glanced between it and the road ahead, greasy under the streetlights after a recent shower.

It was from Rory, typed in that phonetic way kids had of spelling that was indecipherable unless it was read aloud. He was letting her know Harry and Sal were sleeping soundly and he was off to bed. He ended the text with one of those sleeping head emoticons. Jo smiled to herself. He was a good kid, and she'd make it up to him at the weekend. She always felt she was failing to maintain the work and home balance.

Pulling up on the kerb outside the Ever Oil service station where Presley had been taken, she shifted the gearstick into neutral, turned the radio off, killed the engine, dimmed the lights, and stared in. She needed to see the place at night in order to imagine what it had looked like to whoever had stolen him. It was well-lit, the vivid red and orange brand logo even more garish illuminated in the dark. The forecourt was empty; metal shutters had been pulled behind the doors. A pay hatch with a slot for cash was manned – she could see a shadow moving inside.

Something about this garage had vexed her ever since this morning, when she'd first entered it with Tara; it had niggled at the back of her mind all day. The place itself was so dingy, and in desperate need of basic upkeep, let alone major renovation work. The staff this morning had been foreigners, sometimes a sign of people who were being paid under the counter with lower amounts than the minimum wage.

Personally, she would only have stopped here for fuel out of desperation. All over the country, well-maintained garages were shutting down. It was becoming really difficult to get from A to B without running out of petrol. But this one was right in the heart of the city and, with the right investment, should have been a money-spinner. No matter which way she looked at it, the location just didn't gel with the set-up.

Jo watched a drunk wobble from the street in the general direction of the pay hatch. His smashed-up face gave him a down-and-out look, and made it impossible to estimate his age. His runners curled up at the toes, several sizes too big. She watched him shout through the speaker set in the Perspex, could see his frustration as he banged his fist against it to try and get some attention from the shadowy figure inside.

Her gaze shifted to the state-of-the-art CCTV camera over the door. She thought about the footage she'd watched today from inside and out, how clear the images had been.

That's bloody well it, she said to herself, as she worked it out at last. If all the signs were that the owner didn't give a toss about his staff, and was paying them next to nothing, and if he didn't want to invest in the place, why did he have such an expensive security system? A much cheaper one would have done the same job. Something else was going on in this garage, and Jo suspected it was so lucrative it dwarfed the revenue from fuel.

'That's why Tara was here,' Jo said to herself. 'And that's how whoever took Presley knew she'd be here, too.'

*

Jo kicked her shoes off as soon as she got in the door of her house. She stood and listened to the 2.30 a.m. silence, then carried on into the kitchen. There she pulled open the washing-machine door, fetched a laundry basket, and scooped out a wash she'd put on before heading out that morning. Taking a clothes horse from the hot press, she arranged the wet clothes on it near the embers of the sitting-room fire. No point in putting them out tonight, rain was forecast.

Then she went to the dishwasher and removed the ware, putting it away quietly into the presses, and stacking the contents of the sink into the emptied trays. She wiped down the surfaces with a cloth and anti-bacterial spray, and swept the floor. It needed a mop, and the sitting room needed a hoover, but both would have to wait. It was only day one of the case, and already the domestic chores were backing up.

Rubbing the back of her neck, Jo padded down the hall, sticking her head into Sal's room to listen, before carrying down to the next room – Rory's – where she did the same.

Then she went into her own bedroom, where the sound of Harry snoozing in his cot lifted her heart. Unzipping her skirt, she let it slip to the floor, unbuttoned her blouse, and unhooked her bra. Moving to the wardrobe, she pulled out one of Dan's old shirts, and after burying her face in its homey, safe, manly smell, she pulled it on over her head, and climbed into bed and oblivion. It had been a long, hard day.

Tuesday

35

Jo was back behind her desk by 8.45 a.m., stifling a yawn as she pored over a bunch of witness statements taken at the garage the night Presley had been snatched.

She'd had to get up at six to do the housework – make beds, hoover, sort laundry and clean out the fire – before dropping Sal off at her day centre, Harry to his crèche, and Rory to school on time.

Somehow, she'd found an extra ten minutes to spend on her appearance, and was now wearing her best tailored suit – a matching black skirt and jacket with a pair of killer heels. If she was going to have to persuade Dan that she couldn't continue running around like a blue-arsed fly and find Presley on her own without any back-up, she wanted to feel feminine while doing so.

The skinhead in the service station who'd caused the trouble by throwing cans of drink had been charged with criminal damage and resisting arrest, Jo noted. His name was Henly Roberts, and he'd an address in Portmarnock, a plush suburb on the north side. His DOB was 1969. Jo sat back in her chair and chewed the top of her biro. It wasn't every day you got a skinhead in his forties named Henly from a nice part of town. Maybe he'd gone into the service station with the deliberate intention of causing a disturbance, to distract everyone from what was going on outside. Jo glanced at the detective unit outside her office. Once Sexton arrived in, she was going to send him to Portmarnock to find out. She made a note to remind Sexton that the dog Henly had had with him needed a licence. She was going to ask Foxy to doorstep Marcus Rankin, the registered owner of the HiAce in the garage, who Hassan had mentioned in his interview. Hassan would need to be brought back in for further questioning, too, about what was really going on in the garage he ran, she decided.

She pushed the swivel chair a couple of steps sideways to the computer, and pinged it on. Once it booted up, she was planning to run a check on whether Henly had any previous convictions.

She continued thumbing through the witness statements while she waited. The computer stopped whirring and Jo double-clicked on the Pulse icon on the screen. Sliding her finger across the mouse pad, she entered her ID number. Yesterday, she'd traced and interviewed the Jag's owner, Rosita Fitzmaurice. Now she realized that someone else in the queue at the garage had the same surname. She read the relevant statement more carefully. According to his DOB, Hugo Fitzmaurice was twenty. Jo guessed he must be the young guy she'd seen on the tape, his face partially hidden by a hoodie. Hugo had exactly the same address as Rosita Fitzmaurice, and Jo realized, with a start, that she'd met him: the young man with bad skin and a sharp suit who'd been ordering Rosita around and calling her 'Mother' in Clontarf. But there was absolutely no mention in either of their statements that they'd been at the garage together, which was highly suspicious.

The Fitzmaurices owned the Triton Hotel, and Jo

suspected that the owner of the HiAce van, Marcus Rankin, worked there with Tara, too. If Tara, Marcus Rankin, Rosita and Hugo Fitzmaurice were all linked to the Triton, and if they were all in the same garage on the night that Presley disappeared, then that in itself was an incredible new lead.

She picked up the phone, and ran Marcus Rankin's social security number through the Revenue to check on his employers. She was just getting the details she needed when she stopped short at the sound of a rap on the door. Dan was entering, with a grave expression on his face. Jo cut the call short and put the receiver down.

'OK, you've got your murder and missing boy inquiry,' he said, sinking into the chair opposite. 'Who and what do you need?'

Jo clapped her hands together, then studied him more closely. 'Why the sudden change of heart?'

Dan exhaled. 'Because Tara Parker Trench turned up in intensive care with a suspected drugs overdose last night.'

Jo gasped.

He leaned forward and picked something off her desk. 'Why've you got Jeanie's hospital card here?' he asked, standing up.

'It was in the drawer of her desk,' Jo said. 'Give it back.' She tried to take it from him.

He stretched his hand up out of reach.

'It's old,' Jo said. 'I was about to dump it.'

'So why didn't you?'

'Look around. I haven't made it to IKEA yet. I don't have a wastepaper basket. Can you just tell me what's happening with Tara?'

Dan ripped the card in two, and slipped both pieces in his

trouser pocket. 'Tara was found unconscious in a hotel room in the Triton,' he said.

'The Triton,' Jo said, clicking her fingers. She stopped as she realized Dan was glowering. 'What?'

'Sexton was with Tara when she OD'd,' Dan said.

'You're joking. Where is he now?'

'Donnybrook Station. He was arrested at the scene.'

36

Charles Fitzmaurice stepped into his Bentley and put the radio on, hearing the pips go for 9.30 a.m. It was only a short walk from his Clontarf home to his garage, but, given his weight, he was panting like a sprinter after a race. He was also hung over from the ten-odd units of twelve-year-old Jameson Gold Reserve whiskey he'd consumed the previous night. His fondness for fine cigars meant his sinuses were at him, and on top of that he was hacking his lungs up, as he did most mornings. To cap it all, he was groggy as hell, having tossed and turned all night after yesterday's events. The only thing that could improve his mood now would be the news that the socialite and model Tara Parker Trench had died. That was why the radio was on.

Sixty-two-year-old Fitz was hoping against hope that things would work out. It wasn't just rock and roll stars on massive blowouts vacuuming charlie up with a deviated septum who dropped dead from overdoses. Middle-class, well-bred beauties like Tara, using cocaine as a recreational way of prolonging the party, were going overboard all the time. At least if she died, it would be the end of the problem. Otherwise, it might come back to him, and he could lose everything. Someone's head was going to have to roll, and as far as he was concerned that someone was Murray Lawlor, for getting too big for his boots . . .

He adjusted the tuning and tweaked the volume as he drove along the coast road. He was a bag of nerves. It wasn't so long ago that he'd had to bribe a reporter who'd been commissioned by a newspaper to dig the dirt on him. The dogs in the street were barking about his extra-curricular activities, apparently. His wife, Rosita, had even taken to following Tara, after finding out about what she believed was an affair. That's how Rosita had ended up in the garage the night everything had gone belly up. If she asked for a divorce, the banks were going to start making demands he couldn't meet.

By the time he reached the lock-up in North Wall, Fitz was in a lather of perspiration. His doctor had done a stress test on him some years back, using a pulse monitor and sweat detectors on his palm. This morning, the doc could have multiplied those levels by ten.

At the warehouse, Fitz sank into his black presidential chair, and picked up the phone to phone his lawyer, aware he was going to have to take some drastic measures.

When Big Johnny appeared ten minutes later, Fitz's heated discussion with George Hannah was winding up. The brief was demanding the Morocco sex tape be couriered over for safe storage in his office. When Fitz informed him he didn't have it, that it had been burgled from Imogen Cox's, the lawyer told him he was going to have to come up with five million quid to keep the drug-dealing scumbag, Barry 'King Krud' Roberts, from killing them all. To top it all, Fitz had just learned he'd lost money on a dog at Shelbourne Park the previous night. A lot of money. Money he didn't have.

'The little boy needs a doctor,' Big Johnny announced, as Fitz slammed down the phone.

'Better call an ambulance,' Fitz said, before stretching over and slapping the mobile out of Big Johnny's hand. He jabbed his temple. 'Have you lost the small ounce of sense you've got?'

Big Johnny looked at the pieces of his phone scattered around his feet.

'You should have gone to that room before lover boy called the emergency services last night. What am I paying you for? Not to think, that's for sure.'

Big Johnny spread his arms wide. 'But Murray said he was a pig. If I'd gone in there . . .'

Fitz smoothed his hair sideways over his scalp. 'If he went to a hotel room with a hooker, he had a price. I knew she was on something.'

'I swear to God, Fitz, I gave her nothing.'

'Murray must have, then. I watched him last night. He's getting too big for his boots. They are my girls. I say who rewards them with what. He needs reminding exactly where he comes in the food chain.'

Big Johnny didn't answer.

'What's the matter with the kid?' Fitz asked.

'Yolanda says he can't catch his breath. She went to a pharmacy last night but they wouldn't give her anything without a prescription. They said he needed a nebulizer, steroids, and regular doses of an inhaler. They told her to bring him straight to a hospital before he needed oxygen as well.'

Fitz's eyebrows soared. 'Tell me she didn't do something as stupid as that.'

'No. But she's getting jittery. She's afraid he'll pass out on her.'

Fitz sighed hard through his nostrils. 'He's no use to us any more, now his dozy cow of a mother is in a coma. You make sure she doesn't come out of it. And get rid of him. I'm not risking him getting sick all over the chopper again. You got any idea how much it costs to get one valeted?'

37

Jo felt a chill running down her spine. 'What do you mean, they've arrested Sexton?' she asked.

Dan leaned back in his chair. 'A bunch of guests in the Triton witnessed Sexton snogging Tara in the bar. They then booked a room together. Apparently, Tara was fine, the life and soul of the party, before she went off with him. About half an hour later, Sexton dialled 999 from the room, claiming he thought she'd OD'd. They were both virtually naked when the paramedics arrived.'

'That's ridiculous,' Jo said. 'Sexton wouldn't sleep with a call girl. That's the bloody problem with him.'

Dan looked surprised, opened his mouth to say something, then closed it again quickly. 'You said you couldn't get in touch with Tara yesterday,' he said finally. 'Did you know Sexton was with her?'

'No,' Jo said reluctantly, remembering how she'd tried to contact Sexton in vain the previous day, too. 'But I trust him completely.'

Dan folded his arms. 'But he has been acting differently lately, you have to admit that. He's never around, for starters, and when he is, it isn't long before he disappears again. If he's got a drug habit, it would explain a lot.'

'Of course he hasn't got a drug problem. It's Sexton, for Christ's sake. He lives the job.'

'He's been under a lot of stress,' Dan said.

Jo rolled her eyes. 'Who hasn't?'

'You seem to know a lot about his love life. Maybe there's another reason you can't keep an open mind . . .'

Jo threw her hands in the air. 'Here we go again. I'm supposed to be bloody shagging Sexton now, as well as the justice minister, is that it? God, I've been having a rare old time since you left. '

Dan stood up slowly, then walked over to the door and closed it. Their raised voices had ensured a captive audience outside. His eyes were stony when he turned back to her. 'What I mean is, it's possible you've been working too close to him to see what's staring you in the face.'

Jo shook her head. 'Don't try and turn this around. I know what you meant. If you want to know if I'm sleeping with someone, why don't you just come out with it straight, and ask me like a real man?'

Dan stepped close enough to slip his hands around her waist. 'Are you sleeping with anyone?'

'Mind your own bloody business,' she said, turning away and pulling her jacket from the back of the chair. She caught a glimpse of Tara's Mini, still impounded in the yard outside, as she moved.

'Listen to me, Jo. You still answer to me on this inquiry, and I'm telling you to call a case conference asap.'

'I'll do it as soon as I've spoken to Sexton.'

'Forget it, you can't see him. He's in custody.'

'We'll see about that,' Jo said, pushing past him to open the door.

*

In the car park, Jo headed towards Tara's car and unlocked the door she'd watched the motorcyclist in the garage open the night Presley had disappeared. If the investigation had run its proper course, the car would have been impounded for forensic examination. Given the haste to put the case to bed, Jo suspected it hadn't even been searched. She climbed in and saw the floors and seats were clear. She ran her hand between the joins and the backs of the seats – anywhere something could have been wedged. There was only some loose change and a child's toy car there. She got back out and went around to the boot, pulling out two doors which opened in the middle. She lifted a buggy from the back, and ran her palms along the carpet, finding only a car jack.

She was about to put the pushchair back in when it occurred to her that the jack should have had a compartment of its own. She fiddled with a couple of plastic knobs, lifted the carpet up and out, and stared in disbelief. What looked like clear, plastic-wrapped bricks of fresh snow were wedged in tightly there. She reckoned there were enough to keep south Dublin partying up to Christmas and through the New Year.

Walking purposefully back around to the door she'd just climbed out of, she got in again, and this time scoured the ceiling, the lining, and finally the padding covering Presley's car seat, which she freed from the rear. That's when she found something she'd only ever seen in intelligence bulletins. It was the size of a kid's marble, but no mother would ever risk leaving it where a child might put it in its mouth. It was a tracking device.

38

With one phone call made on the steps of the station, Jo arranged to meet Blaise Stanley for lunch, and asked him to cut through the red tape so she could pay Sexton an unorthodox visit in Donnybrook Station. Tara's car was towed to the forensic lab where it belonged. The tracking device was sealed in an evidence bag and given to Dan, who was put in the picture. And less than an hour later, Jo walked into Sexton's interview room.

'Thank God you're here,' Sexton said. His whole body slackened as he pushed his chair out from the table in the windowless room.

'Interview suspended at ten a.m. to allow subject to speak to Detective Inspector Jo Birmingham, Store Street,' the interviewing officer announced. His sing-song voice told Jo he wasn't happy that strings had been pulled. Jo wouldn't have been either, but her faith in Sexton was non-negotiable.

Clicking his tongue in annoyance, the officer tucked his notepad under his arm, and banged the door on his way out.

Jo leaned on the table with her two hands and lowered her voice as she glanced around for the camera. 'What have you done with the sex tape that was in my desk?'

Sexton looked taken aback. 'I don't have it. I didn't even know you'd lost it.'

'You knew where it was. And when you disappeared yesterday afternoon, it did, too.'

'Jo, I swear to God—'

'So where've you been? I tried to call you all afternoon. What the hell have you been doing?'

'I've been working. I know you don't believe me, but I went to the bank like you asked, and then, based on what the manager told me, I went to an ATM machine in Sandymount to see if I could find out why the Coxes were withdrawing a large amount of cash there every Monday afternoon.'

'So why didn't you ring me to keep me in the picture?'

'I tried, honestly I did, Jo, but my phone was . . . well, it got wet. Look, I know it sounds like one of my pathetic excuses, but, Jo, I wouldn't . . . I mean, I didn't . . . I was working. I swear on . . . on Maura's memory.'

Jo sat down on the side of the desk and crossed her arms. He was telling the truth. 'So what did you establish?'

Sexton told her about his encounter with Murray Lawlor at the ATM – reminding her who Murray was – and went on to say that Tara had been terrified by the sight of a group of international footballers at the Triton Hotel. He told Jo how he and Tara had headed upstairs, and how Tara had then explained what the footballers had done to her in Marrakesh a couple of nights earlier.

'Do you know who they were?' Jo asked tentatively.

'Of course,' Sexton said. 'If Tara hadn't jumped me, I'd have been asking for their autographs. They're all Melwood Athletic.'

Jo gave a little victory clench of the fist, then made him detail exactly what had happened when he'd met Murray in the bar the previous evening. 'Hold it,' she interrupted. 'Did you just say Murray was on a motorbike?'

'Yes. I thought it was weird, Jo, because, like I said, he was in the big flash Audi jeep earlier in the day. But he made a point of saying he always took the bike when he was working.'

'There was a motorbike in the garage the night Presley was taken,' she said as she pulled out her phone and started to dial. 'I haven't had a chance to run the registration yet. But I'll bet you any money when I do it'll come back to Murray Lawlor.' She winked at him as she waited for the call to connect. 'Well, it seems I owe you an apology. In spite of all this' – she indicated the room they were in – 'yours was an afternoon and evening very well spent yesterday. As a matter of fact, what you've discovered might just have given us a major new lead.' She tousled his hair. 'Nice one, my son.'

He grinned, and she saw a flash of the boyish old Sexton back. Jo asked the duty sergeant who answered the call to enter the registration of the motorbike, which she read out from her garage diagram.

She waited, and nodded when the duty sergeant confirmed that Murray Lawlor's name was listed on the system as the registered owner of the bike. Jo thanked the officer and hung up.

'We'll need to pay Murray Lawlor a little visit,' she told Sexton. 'He's in this up to his eyes.'

'Fill me in on what's happened,' Sexton said.

'I found drugs and a tracking device in Tara's car. The drugs should be enough to get you off the hook for now, or at least buy you enough time to have some tests carried out,' Jo said. 'I'll bet you when they're profiled they'll crossmatch in content and purity with whatever Tara took last night. It looks as though Murray Lawlor was making sure he knew exactly where Tara was at all times. Not just for Jeff Cox, either. Jeff was only small fry. Murray must have been concerned about what was in the back of her car. We need to find out who he was working for. Now, hurry up and extricate yourself from this situation you've got yourself into, because I'm calling a case conference in the station this afternoon and I want you on my team.' She straightened her suit. 'But first, I've got a few questions for Blaise Stanley.'

39

Blaise Stanley was tucking into a bread roll when Jo arrived at Patrick Guilbaud's restaurant, having followed a maître d' down some stairs and into a dining area where some of the country's most notable artists were on display on the walls. She'd refused to hand over her jacket. She didn't plan on getting comfortable.

Stanley pulled his napkin free of his shirt collar and, after dabbing the corners of his mouth with it, deposited it on the table. He stood and air-kissed Jo on both cheeks. The first one made her uneasy, the second made her feel she had sold out.

'How's your friend holding up?'

Jo sat down and gave her table napkin a quick flick before smoothing it over her lap. 'He'll be fine. He's innocent.'

'To what do I owe this pleasure?'

'I just thought it time we had a little tête-à-tête. There was no mention in the budget yesterday of funds being allocated to fund the separate legal representation proposals you've backed to make life easier for victims of crime in court.'

Jo had negotiated lawyers for victims in court with Stanley during the Bible killer case, but the policy had yet to materialize.

Stanley plucked a leather-bound wine list from the table

and studied it, his gold dice cufflinks flashing against a pair of starched white cuffs. 'Patience, Birmingham, I always look after my friends. The country is banjaxed, in case you hadn't noticed, meaning certain projects have to be long fingered. Bond holders, IMF, you must have heard . . .'

'We had a deal,' Jo argued, really annoyed.

'As I said, I always look after my friends. Do you like your new office?'

'Meaning?'

'Meaning that I'm doing my best for you, that I have your best interests at heart.'

Jo sat back. 'Tell me what's going on.'

'At ease, Birmingham. I know I don't have to remind you that if I lose my office, and my enemies do manage to bring me down, your campaign to advance the rights of victims goes with me.'

'You make it sound like a threat.'

'Do I? You've got other issues, haven't you?'

'Yes.'

'Well, tell me about one. I'll get my advisers to prepare a paper.'

'You need to end the system that allows prisoners on murder or rape charges out on bail,' Jo said. 'The numbers reoffending while waiting to go to trial are startling. Then there's the fact that even after being sentenced, prisoners earn an automatic entitlement to remission for good behaviour. These things add insult to injury for the victims.'

'You have a point,' Stanley said. 'Now, do you have a wine preference? I've developed quite a taste for the New World lately.'

'I'll pass,' Jo said, putting a hand over her glass.

'Spoilsport.' He chuckled and reached for a bottle of

water, then checked the label. 'Still or sparkling?' he asked.

'Either will do fine,' Jo said flatly.

He poured her a glass, and set the bottle back down.

'How well did you know Imogen Cox?' Jo asked.

'Who?'

'The former model-turned-model-agent. She was murdered yesterday. You must have heard of her. I'll bet your office has been fielding calls all day looking for quotes from you on the country's crime levels.'

'The name means nothing to me.' He lifted the menu. 'Can I recommend the monkfish? It's sensational.'

Jo studied him closely. 'How come nobody ever raves about the chicken? It's always the sole, the cod, the plaice. It's always the fish.'

'What's your point?'

'That people are sheep. They pretend somewhere like this makes them comfortable, when really they'd be much happier in their local. They say the fish is divine, when actually they'd much rather be getting stuck into a plate of chips. It's all appearances, and you – more than anyone else – know how important those are.'

'Have you something on your mind?'

Jo leaned forwards. 'Were you in Morocco on Sunday night?'

'No.'

'What about Tara Parker Trench? Do you know her?'

'The model? No, again. Why?'

'I'm going to ask you one more time, and I'm going to ask you to really consider what I'm asking before you answer. Did you know Imogen Cox?'

Stanley waved to a waiter over the heads of the other

198

diners, then spoke very quietly. 'Let me reiterate, I categorically did not.'

The sommelier arrived over and began the ritualistic uncorking process.

'Pity you won't join me in a toast,' Stanley said, rolling the liquid around the bottom of his glass, sniffing, tasting and then clicking his tongue on the roof of his mouth.

He signalled he was happy for the wine to be poured, the sommelier duly obliged, and Stanley raised his glass. 'I'm going to promote you. Hence the office. How does chief superintendent sound?'

Jo's mind raced. The potential pay rise would be a lifeline – she was struggling to manage the cost of running the house now she was on her own. She might even be able to afford some help. But there was only one chief superintendent per division, meaning she'd have to be transferred.

Jo took a mouthful of her water. 'Where do you have in mind?'

'I want you to replace Dan,' Stanley said coolly.

'Why? Are you promoting him, too?'

'No.'

Jo tried to process what he was saying. 'Hang on. I was the one who wanted a transfer. You can't move Dan.'

'I'm not going to. An internal investigation has found he was completely compromised during the serial killer investigation you solved. Here are their findings.' He reached sideways into a briefcase on the floor beside him and pulled out a spiral-bound set of sheets, which he tossed in front of her.

Stamped 'Private and Confidential', the title read 'Inquiry into Policing Conduct and Standards during the Walter Kaiser Investigation, Store Street'.

Much as Jo wanted to read every page, she wasn't about to give Stanley the satisfaction. There was no question in her mind that Dan's decision to tell no one that Anto Crawley – the country's biggest drug dealer and one of the serial killer's victims – had been one of his informants, had held up her investigation. But the punishment was heavy handed in the extreme.

'He'll think I've had something to do with it,' she said quietly.

'Does it matter? I thought you'd separated.' Stanley reached for another bread roll and sliced it in half.

'He knows already, doesn't he?' Jo said, suddenly understanding Dan's pent-up anger that morning. 'He thinks I'm behind it, that I've been manoeuvring behind his back.' She stood up so quickly the napkin fell on the floor and her glass of water overturned. 'No, I'm sorry, I can't accept on these terms.'

Stanley reached for some more bread, spread a corner with butter, and spoke out of the side of his mouth as he chewed. 'Suit yourself. But if this report gets out – and there's a very real chance it will – somebody's head is going to have to roll, and it's not going to be mine. You solved the case, it seems only right and fair that you should be rewarded. My spin doctors tell me that if you're promoted, we will minimize the negative ripple effect.'

'Dan is a good cop. He made an error of judgement. We all do it. No harm came of it. We got the killer.'

Stanley leaned back and smiled up at her. 'If you don't want the job, I'm sure one of your colleagues will be more than happy to step up to the mark. All I'm doing is giving you first right of refusal.'

40

The prison officers were wearing white Tyvek overalls, and plastic masks over their noses and mouths, so they wouldn't catch anything from contact with the King. He was sitting in the back of the van bringing him to court, smears of excrement caked to his face. The screws had tossed a coin to decide who should sit in the back with him; the smell was that bad. There should have been three officers alongside him, but they had reasoned it down to one – a butty kid sitting opposite, whose eyes watered over his mask. The other two officers were up front with the driver, only a re-inforced Perspex window separating them. The King's ankles had been cuffed and chained to his handcuffs as an extra precaution. There was no garda escort because the resources for organized crime had taken a hammering in the budget. The cops were planning to meet them at the courthouse instead.

Every time the King looked at the screw opposite, he doubled up laughing like he'd just heard a really funny joke.

'What's so funny?' the officer asked eventually, his voice muffled through the mask and his face shiny with perspir-ation. He'd a stab vest on underneath, and the van was reinforced with bulletproof metal. It was like sitting in an oven.

The King was holding on to a handle grip so tightly his knuckles had turned white. 'You look like one of those Tellytubbies my kid used to like to watch,' he answered, cracking up again.

Then, with a sudden, deafening jolt, the van jackknifed at such speed it overturned and did a double spin. The King's grip ensured he did not bounce off the roof. Holding himself steady, he aimed his feet at the young screw's head, building up momentum with the motion, and connected. The screw's face spurted blood, and his eyes rolled up and closed as he passed out.

The van stopped moving, and the King threw himself on the floor, face down.

He listened hard as, up front, the sounds of breaking glass, metal crumpling, and cars piling up drowned out the high-pitched yells of terror.

Then came the staccato thud-thud-thud of a machine gun, as the King's men finished off the screws in the driver's compartment.

When the shooting stopped, the King grabbed the young screw's set of keys he needed to open his restraints, grinning as he did so. He'd taken out an insurance policy in case his brief let him down in court today, and it looked like it'd paid off.

The champion of the world was a contender again.

41

Jo was back in the office by two thirty, holding her door open with her back as the three detectives she'd requested for the first conference filed past, wheeling chairs in front of them. First was Detective Sergeant Aishling McConigle, a plump, rosy-cheeked new graduate in her mid-twenties, who'd already been promoted for her bravery after an undercover vice operation on prostitution. She'd suffered a kick to the torso after a pimp got territorial, and lost her spleen, but against all expectation had returned to the job. Jo had picked her for her mettle and her knowledge of the sex industry.

Behind her, Detective Sergeant Neil D'Arcy looked more like a computer nerd than any cop Jo had worked with. That was exactly why she wanted him. He'd done several courses in mobile phone analysis, and given that the escort business relied so heavily on mobile communication, he could bring invaluable expertise to the table. The fact that he had a reputation as being a closet anorak when it came to football could prove equally useful.

Third in the line-up was Detective Inspector Al Lovett, a hardworking detective in his forties who'd just concluded a secondment to the cold case unit reviewing old missing persons cases, and identifying the flaws in previous investigations. It hadn't made him popular, but that was a character reference in its own right in Jo's book.

Last, but not least, was Dan, who closed the door behind them as he settled into his seat, stretching his legs out in the pokey space and crossing them at the ankle. He didn't need to be there – ordinarily Jo would have briefed him afterwards. But he was making a point, and since meeting the minister, Jo understood why.

Foxy, Jo had learned from a phone conversation minutes earlier, was on his way. He'd been mysterious about where he was, but had promised he'd be back shortly, and had made no apology for not being on time.

Jo had another twenty lower-ranking officers at her disposal for the dogsbody duties that would need to be carried out. Dan had promised to double that number again within twenty-four hours if Presley was still missing. Once the three in front of her had had their instructions, they could draw on those resources – to help complete the jobs Jo set them.

She rolled up her sleeves as the group arranged themselves, Dan behind them and nearest to the door. Sitting on the edge of her desk, a marker in hand, Jo glanced outside to where Oakley and Merrigan clearly had the hump on the other side of the office wall. They were locked in conversation, and taking regular over-the-shoulder glances in her direction. Jo had been quite prepared to let bygones be bygones and invite Oakley to join them, but he'd kicked up when she'd asked him for the photograph of Presley which Tara had given him, and had tried to refuse to hand it over. He hadn't had a leg to stand on, and after Jo had reminded him of as much, she'd had the picture blown up, laminated, and fixed with a coloured magnet to a wipe board 'borrowed' from the detective unit outside. But she had also washed her hands of Oakley. Presley was the only one who would suffer from Oakley's attempt to turn this into a contest.

The image of a cherubic-looking little boy with blue eyes and a mop of blond curls stared innocently over Jo's shoulder, giving everyone there solemnity and focus.

Not wanting to waste any more time, Jo gave the briefest synopsis of the case, sticking to the facts. Some links in the chain of events, such as the allegation that Tara Parker Trench had been raped, needed corroboration, she explained. Some – such as Presley's abduction and the murder of Imogen Cox – were fact. She censored nothing, and gave them the full details, including the allegations against the justice minister, though this raised a worried look from Dan. A team was a team, as far as Jo was concerned. The fact that the station's local pub was shared by four newspapers, operating out of a city-centre office block nearby, was not something she was going to let divide them. There were stiff penalties for breaching the Official Secrets Act, but cross-pollination was inevitable, especially on Friday nights. Anyway, if what Dan was dreading panned out, the story was leaked to the press, and they started to dig the dirt, they'd be doing her a service. Ultimately, they might help her save Dan's job. Jo concluded the summation by telling the team that their goal in sorting the wheat from the chaff was to establish how the various crimes were linked. Only then would they find Presley.

Then she slid a DVD into the player. It was the CCTV footage taken from the security camera outside Store Street Station. She'd asked the officer who'd copied it for her to edit it down to less than a minute, in which a figure could be seen dropping a Jiffy bag into the station's letterbox.

Unlike the quality of the footage filmed in the garage, the graininess made it almost impossible to make out the figure at all. Everything was also in a muddy colour somewhere between dark grey and navy.

'This is the person who delivered the sex tape to the station,' Jo explained.

The time on the lower right-hand corner of the screen said it was 5.10 a.m.

It was hard to tell if they were even looking at a male or a female. The individual was wearing a three-quarter-length coat, the colour of which was impossible to identify, though it had white ridges, which made a large square pattern. A trucker cap pulled low on the forehead made it impossible to see the face, or length of hair.

'And that's all we've got,' Jo said, pressing 'eject' and sliding the disc out.

'Right,' she said, winding it up. 'Aishling, I want you to concentrate on the Atlantis Hotel in Marrakesh this afternoon. We need the hotel's client list and the names of any guests who checked in and out on Saturday and Sunday night. I also want the names of all the passengers aboard Tara's flight to Marrakesh. Oh, and the guest list from the Triton Hotel on Sunday night, too, OK?'

Aishling nodded as she made a note.

'D'Arcy, I know this can't happen overnight, but I'm going to need you to illustrate on a map of the city what masts Tara's mobile was bouncing off, to try and approximate her movements. OK?'

He gave a thumbs up.

'And Lovett, can you organize a press briefing for early evening? We'll need more photos of Presley, as up to date as you can manage.'

'Won't that bring undue pressure to bear on us?' he replied. 'We don't want the press to start dictating what leads should be followed up, and skewing the direction of the investigation, do we?'

'It's a risk we have to take,' Jo told him decisively. She hoped he wasn't going to question every instruction she gave, as this would be time-consuming and annoying. 'Presley's nan lives nearby, but I expect she'll be keeping a vigil at her daughter's bedside. Which reminds me, we need to keep Tara Parker Trench under protection in intensive care asap.'

She took a deep breath. 'Right, Aishling, if I'm bringing in foreign girls to work on the game here, where do I source them?'

Lovett cut in. 'All the newspapers run those classifieds for private masseuses where you get to pick all sorts from Chinese exotic beauties to Caucasians,' he said.

'But that's for punters,' Jo pointed out. 'I'm talking about sourcing girls for work in the first place.'

'We could get on to the ad managers in the papers who are indirectly profiteering.'

'We'd have to prove it, and we don't have time. Aishling . . . ?'

'The internet,' she replied.

Jo stood and wrote it on the board, with an arrow pointing sideways from it to the word 'computers'. 'Now we're getting somewhere.' She turned to Dan. 'We'll need to seize the Triton's computers.' He took the cue and headed for the door. They'd need search warrants, signed by a judge.

Lovett looked deflated, but Jo didn't have time for egos. Drawing a line to the right from the top of the board to the bottom, she created a second column. 'So I'm a pimp with a bevy of exotic beauties that I've sourced from the internet, and plan to fly in. How do I get my girls into the country without work visas?'

'You don't,' Aishling said. 'You set up a front – you know, a company that looks legit.'

'Go on,' Jo encouraged.

'Remember that model in the nineties, Samantha Blanford Hutton?' Aishling said.

'She had a brother who was a jockey?'

'Yeah, that's the one. Well, she was a model-turned-high-class-hooker who set up a cleaning company, registered it, the lot. She sourced all these girls from Brazil by placing ads in newspapers over there, and got the employment visas she needed rubber-stamped. She brought them over, and withheld their passports to force them on to the game. One of the girls went missing, and some of the others broke their silence – that was the only reason it all came to light.'

Jo thought about the young Filipina girl she'd seen at the Fitzmaurices', and remembered how Hassan had said that the HiAce driver, who was in the garage the night Presley vanished, had a specialist cleaning firm. She wrote his name at the top of the second column with a question mark. 'According to the Revenue, Marcus Rankin works at the Triton. Let's find out the name of his cleaning firm, and if he's got anyone working for him. If he has, let's determine their gender, age, and nationality.' She turned to Aishling. 'How do you know so much about cleaning agencies, anyway?' she asked. 'I thought your speciality was street workers.'

'Samantha used to babysit for me. I grew up a few doors down. I could write a thesis about what went on in that house.'

Jo grinned. 'Only in Ireland . . . Right, we also need to establish if the Triton has been recruiting foreign staff for menial labour – waitressing for instance – through a registered firm,' Jo said, drawing a fresh line on the board to create another column. At the top of it she wrote 'Charles Fitzmaurice, owner of the Triton'.

'I want every spit and cough on this man,' she said. 'I want to know if he's got any previous, and if not, why not. If he's ever rung us to so much as ask for directions, I want the details. After the press conference, I'll be heading on to the Triton. Anything you can get for me for that interview could make the vital difference.'

She listed the names of the footballers in a fourth column on the board. 'I also want you to contact Interpol, Europol and Scotland Yard, and find out if there's anything that's ever rung alarm bells about any of these men, proven or not.'

Out of the side of her eye she saw Foxy hurrying towards the office.

'And last, but not least, can you get someone to bring Hassan and his missus, and Marcus Rankin back in here? For the moment we're only requesting their cooperation. I don't want detention warrants running out on us before I've had a chance to speak to them.'

Foxy had reached the door, and once inside he put his hands on his knees and leaned over trying to catch his breath.

'You'll give yourself a coronary if you keep that up,' Jo said.

Foxy straightened up, then reached into the pocket of his donkey jacket and pulled out a disc, which he handed over to Jo. Oakley, outside, was straining to look over his shoulder and get a view of what the object was.

'What's this?' Jo asked.

'Your sex tape from this morning,' he said. 'Hassan's wife took it when she was waiting up here for him.'

'Up here?' Jo said, glancing out angrily at Merrigan.

Foxy nodded. 'It's a long story. I just paid her a visit.'

'Right,' Jo said. 'We'd better watch it, then.'

42

Jo moved to the side of the TV as the DVD started to play. She pointed to the woman on the screen standing with her back to the camera, between the man's legs.

'I haven't watched this through yet, but if our information is correct, that is Tara Parker Trench. If anyone recognizes the man she's with, please pipe up. Again, hopefully we'll get a better view of him shortly. If we're on the right track, he's a Melwood Athletic player.'

'Christ,' Dan said, leaning forwards.

With a burst of shouts from the screen, the group of men in shorts – who Jo had first seen the previous day – started jumping into the pool. 'Again, from our inquiries, we believe these men could also be MA players,' she explained. 'Sexton got two possible names off Tara last night, before she passed out. Let's pray we get a view of their faces at some stage.'

Aishling tucked a strand of hair behind her ear. 'Jo, the man being, um, pleasured, looks like Kevin Mooney . . .'

'You can't see his face at that angle,' Lovett objected.

'No, I know, but the tattoo on his ankle . . .' Aishling leaned closer to point.

Jo jabbed 'pause' on the remote, and they all studied what was not much more than a speck on the screen.

'She's right,' D'Arcy said. 'Mooney's got a football boot

tattooed on his right ankle, exactly the same as that one.' He turned to Aishling. 'I didn't know you were a footie fan.'

Aishling grinned.

'Can we save the chat for later?' Jo asked. 'But that was well spotted, Aishling. And Kevin Mooney is one of the names Sexton got, too.'

Jo pressed 'play' again, pointing to the couple sipping cocktails about twenty feet beyond the pool. 'Meet Imogen Cox, now deceased. Presley was taken the same night she flew back to Dublin from this hotel with Tara.' Jo's finger moved across the screen, 'This man may be Blaise Stanley . . .'

The detectives glanced at each other.

Dan put his hands together at his mouth like he was praying.

Jo spoke directly to him. 'We need to establish where Stanley was on the night in question, if we're going to substantiate the claim.'

'Let's fly someone out to Marrakesh as soon as possible,' Dan said. 'See if we can't find that hidden camera and whoever knew about it.'

'Why do you think it's hidden?' Jo asked.

'There's no way a politician as long in the tooth as Stanley would be naïve enough to allow himself to be filmed with that going on,' Foxy answered. 'If it's Stanley, it's a hidden camera all right.'

The conversation stopped as, on the telly, the men in the pool started to shout crude words of encouragement at the man getting the blow job.

'There's a Yorkshire accent in there,' D'Arcy remarked. 'Greg Duncan is from Barnsley, is black, and plays for Melwood Athletic.'

Jo's eyes moved to the only black man in the pool, to the far right of the group of four who had made a semicircle around the woman. She moved to get a better view of the screen. She hadn't seen much more of the rest herself.

The men were closing in on the woman. One of them started mauling her breasts from behind. As she reached back to push him off, Kevin Mooney grabbed her by the hair and forced her head into his lap again.

The woman shot up, and turned around to give the man feeling her up a shove, her face finally coming into view as her hands landed on the man's chest. It was Tara all right. Jo sighed with relief. It was another piece of the puzzle. She checked on Foxy, who was standing at the door, gazing out with a pained expression on his face. When he spotted Jo looking at him, he tipped his head in the direction of the unit outside. Jo nodded to show it was OK for him to go. Relief spread across his face.

On the screen, the man who had been sitting on the edge of the pool slid in and stood in the water, clearly put out. Nobody said a word, but more than one of the detectives frowned. Everyone recognized Kevin Mooney now – his face was practically iconic. He was never off the telly, given all the brands he endorsed. Standing beside Tara, he looked short but broad, with dense brown hair and light-blue eyes.

The atmosphere changed once he was in the pool, Jo noticed. For a start the laddish feel to what had been happening disappeared, and there were no more high-spirited shouts. Instead the other men stopped messing and began closing in like a pack. The black man moved behind Tara and, gripping her neck in the crook of his arm, dipped her head sideways into the water.

'That's definitely Greg Duncan,' D'Arcy said.

212

'Good,' Jo said. 'Which means we've only two left to identify, if the second name Sexton got is correct.' She withheld telling them what that was, as it would make the verification process better.

The tape was getting harder to watch. Tara was obviously in acute distress. Two of the men moved to her legs, which they pulled from under her and gripped.

Dan grimaced, and looked away.

By now Tara was fully prostrate in the water, which was washing over her face. Mooney moved between her legs and Tara's head was once again dunked back as she attempted to thrash her arms. A couple of long seconds later she re-emerged and gulped a mouthful of air, too winded to shout or scream. The man holding Tara's right leg put a hand over Mooney's shoulder and glanced over at his companion, holding Tara's left leg, who looked back at him. Their profiles were in clear view.

'Watchman and Mansell,' Dan said, with a sigh.

'Yep,' D'Arcy said.

'Melwood Athletic?' Jo asked.

Aishling nodded.

What followed next made Aishling cover her mouth with her hand, Lovett watch through spread fingers and D'Arcy blink rapidly. Dan stood up, knitting his hands behind his head.

Each of the men took turns to follow Mooney's lead. The positions varied, but the result was the same. At one point, screaming and flailing, Tara managed to break free, and made a desperate attempt to escape. She hauled herself up on to the edge of the pool and crawled forwards, water streaming from her hair, before being caught, dragged violently back into the water and raped again. Afterwards her face, half-submerged, said it all. It was completely blank. She had clearly given up.

Jo focused on Imogen Cox in the background. She stood to kiss the man she was with on both cheeks before he headed back to the hotel. The tape ended abruptly, with Imogen walking over to the pool as the last of the footballers hoisted themselves up and out. Behind them, in the shallow end, Tara lay still.

'Was that Stanley?' Jo asked, referring to the man Imogen was with.

'I can't be sure,' Dan answered, slowly.

'I feel sick,' Aishling said.

Jo could tell from the men's faces that they weren't far off, either.

'Sexton saw some MA players in the Triton last night,' Jo said. 'I say we bring them all in right now, while we can.'

Dan nodded.

'Evening paper's in,' Foxy said, arriving back and tossing it on to Jo's desk. The headline got everyone's attention. Jo lifted it up, the team gathering on either side to read over her shoulders. It read, 'Top Model's Tragic Last Interview.' The strap stated, 'Kevin Mooney's Steamy Desert Hat-trick. How My Affair With Striker Left Me Gagging For More.' Jo scanned the article quickly:

Tara Parker Trench, socialite and model, made secret phone calls from Marrakesh to our paper's showbiz reporter, and he was waiting for her in Dublin Airport with a photographer, where he managed to secure more details. An arrangement was made with Tara, where she agreed to sell her full story, in return for a substantial payment . . . The contracts had been drawn up, but were unsigned . . . On discovering from

a tip-off about Tara's condition, which we are attributing to
an overdose, the editor has taken the decision to publish . . .

'And be damned,' Dan cut in.

'Surely it isn't all bad to have it out in the open?' Aishling
suggested. 'It could bring more girls out of the woodwork.'

'Bollocks,' Jo said. 'They've already started to spin it. All
they need now is for Tara to die on them, and those players
will get off scot free.' She clicked her fingers. 'Hang on, Foxy
mentioned that Tara's ex was going on about that hotelier,
Charles Fitzmaurice, paying her too much attention, right?
. . . He's got a bloody helicopter pad down there at the hotel.
Aishling, can you get on to air traffic control straight away,
see if he's booked any flights in or out for today?'

Oakley rapped on the door and poked his head around it.
'Have they got the Barry Roberts story yet?' he asked, pointing to the paper.

Jo continued to scan the article for details but her ears
pricked up. Roberts was one of the city's biggest drug
dealers, and although her concern right now was Tara,
Roberts's name had come up when she'd sneaked a peek in
the file belonging to the dodgy solicitor, George Hannah.

'Why, what's happened?' Dan asked. 'The King's up in
court today, isn't he? Tell me he didn't get off on a
technicality?'

'He never got to court,' Oakley answered. 'He was sprung
from the prison van, and that's not the worst of it. There's
three prison officers dead at the scene, and a fourth in
Beaumont with serious head injuries.'

43

Sexton pressed the intercom and leaned in close to be heard over the city-centre traffic – honking motorists mostly, outraged that they were going nowhere in the pre-rush-hour build-up. He'd been released at three thirty, with the warning that his file was being sent to the DPP to decide whether there was enough evidence to make a charge. He knew that if there'd been any hard proof there wouldn't have been any need to seek legal advice. He wasn't worried about the results of the blood samples he'd given biting him in the ass, either. He had a horror of drugs, and wouldn't have touched them with a bargepole.

But he also knew that in the policing game, mud always stuck. It was as simple as that. His name had been linked to a hooker, and to drugs, and he was never going to live it down. The fallout would be implicit: in all the jobs he would be assigned from now on, ones guaranteed to turn cold because there were no leads; in the promotion lists, where he'd be passed over time and again; and worst of all, from his point of view, in the way other cops would stop talking whenever he entered a room. If that happened, the job wouldn't be worth doing. He'd seen it with better men than him over the years. They'd ended up like zombies, clocking in and out, just passing time to get their pension. All things considered, he'd decided enough was enough. It was time to make sure Jo cracked this one. He wasn't going to go back to the station until he had something to give her, to reward her faith in him. She was right about Maura's note, too: once this case was solved he was going to read it. He needed to start getting on with his life. The crick in his neck he'd woken up with after nodding off in the car earlier had gotten worse after his arrest. He rubbed his neck painfully.

'Pizza,' he said into the buzzing speaker.

'I didn't order a pizza,' came the response. It was followed by, 'Oh, it's you. Come in, then, but it will have to be brief. I've got to wash my hair. Top floor.'

A set of glass doors slid open.

Murray Lawlor's office was located in a converted mill on Camden Street. There was no reception, just a rack of bike stands attached to the exposed stone wall, facing a line of lockers. Sexton took the wrought-iron stairs instead of the lift. He wanted to see what businesses occupied the other six floors. Solicitors, chartered accountants, and an architect, he realized. Murray was a pimp hiding among professionals. He had chosen well.

At the top a set of doors faced him, made of reinforced steel, with a couple of CCTV cameras angled down over them. The place was bright, but the arched window on one wall was disconcertingly low. He'd have had to kneel and stoop to see out. There was another intercom on the wall, which Sexton was stepping towards when Murray pulled open the door of his office. He was wearing another loud shirt, red this time, with a thin white pinstripe running through it, and he had one of those little metal pins joining the two sides of his stiff white collar under a big fat red tie. Gold. His hair was greased back so heavily Sexton thought about asking him how he felt about threatening local marine life.

But Murray got in there first. 'I did warn you to stay away from Tara,' he said.

Sexton drew back his fist, and slammed it into Murray's stomach, shaking his hand as the impact of connecting with sheer muscle reverberated up to his armpit.

Murray barely winced, but as he clenched his right fist in response, Sexton jolted a knee up into his groin, causing him to bend over and yelp.

'Glad we got that out of the way,' Sexton said, flicking his foot to the back of Murray's knee to trigger the reflex, and then hooking his ankle around Murray's to finish the job and bring him down.

Once he had Murray pinned to the ground, his knee pressed into the small of his back, Sexton let out a hard sigh. 'Now, if that job's still on offer, I'm free for an interview, mate.'

Five minutes later, Sexton had Murray handcuffed to the spindles on the back of his captain's chair in his big fancy office, and had started to riffle through the drawers of a stack of filing cabinets.

'Where did it all go wrong?' he asked. 'Eh? Hotshot. It's not an easy life being in the force, I'll give you that. The money's crap, the public hate you, and relationships, well, I'm living proof of what can happen there . . .' He was walking his fingers through the names on the tags as he scanned, and he stopped when he spotted the word 'Cox'. He whipped the file out and had a quick flick through. It contained photos of Tara in the company of various men: at a candlelit dinner; emerging from a car; smooching. Sexton transferred it to the top of the shiny black desk, and went back to the drawers.

'You're going to regret this,' Murray said through a puffed-up face and a bloody nose. His top lip was also swollen. 'You've no idea who you're messing with. You're a dead man walking.'

'Is that a threat?' Sexton asked.

'It's a fact.'

'But at least before you started sneaking around and paying women to tell you what a big man you were, you could hold your head up. Did you know scientists reckon cops have got a community gene? They want to help make things better?'

Murray cleared his throat and spat at him.

Sexton pulled another file. 'What have we here?' he asked. The label read 'Charles Fitzmaurice'. Sexton pulled out a white sheet with grey type on it, and realized he was holding a summons for Charles Fitzmaurice, dated earlier that month and charging him with possession of class A drugs, with intent to sell or supply. According to the document the drugs had been found at an aerodrome in the north of the city.

The last page in the dossier was a court sheet showing the charges had been struck out.

'Jo is going to love this,' Sexton said with a smile, pulling the contents of the two files out, folding them together and tucking them into his inside pocket. He nodded towards Murray. 'Don't go anywhere. We'll be back soon to pick you up.'

44

Big Johnny pulled in on North Great George's Street, and turned to Yolanda, who was sitting in the passenger seat.

'Right, let's get on with it,' he said.

Yolanda took a quick look at the small boy in the back, who was too tiny to even see out of the windows. Pulling the handle, she hurried around to the back passenger door, which she opened so she could pull Presley out. His lungs were whistling between breaths now. His breathlessness had put her heart crossways during the night. Big Johnny had promised her that if anything happened, Fitz would take care of it, but Big Johnny had also assured her he'd tell housekeeping she couldn't work her cleaning shifts while she was minding the boy, and he hadn't. The boss lady had come banging on the door, gunning for her. Then, when Presley took ill, she had started to panic that he might die in the apartment. What if they blamed her for not summoning help? The last thing she wanted was a police investigation. Supposing they asked her about her tax payments?

Yolanda needed her cleaning job. She'd dabbled in the escort work, but it was irregular and unreliable. She was in her early forties, but looked a lot older. She could see the disappointment in men's faces when she showed up. That was why she liked working in the hotel. She liked having her own place, the uniform, and she needed to save every penny she could to send back home to her mother in Buenos Aires, who was taking care of her twin daughters, who would be in their teens soon. Having Presley around had just reminded her of how the months she'd been away from her own children were stretching into years. But she didn't want to go back yet. There was no work at home. The Irish thought they were in a recession, but they didn't know what poverty was. Yolanda could make in a week here what she did in a year at home, had even got herself some nice clothes for the first time in her life.

'That's my nana's house down there,' Presley said, wheezing.

Yolanda squeezed his hand. 'Do you remember what I said would happen if you talked about where you were?'

Presley nodded.

'What did I say?' she pressed.

He looked anxious. 'You'll come back and take me again,' he said, trying to catch his breath.

Big Johnny got out of the car and walked up to the front door. 'Chop, chop,' he said, ringing the doorbell.

Yolanda gave Presley a little push and told him to hurry.

The front door opened an inch, and from behind a safety chain a worried-looking woman's gaze travelled slowly from Big Johnny to Yolanda, and followed her arm down to Presley. Then the woman jolted the door shut, unlocked it, and flung it open, dropping to her knees and putting her arms out. She was younger than Yolanda had expected.

The kid tried to run in. Yolanda gave Presley's arm a rough tug. 'Not yet,' she warned.

Big Johnny pushed the door open. 'Hello, Gabriella,' he said, like he hadn't a care in the world. 'Stick the kettle on, there's a good girl. You and I need to have a little chat about your daughter. How's Tara doing, anyway? Come round yet, has she? Talking, is she? To tell you the truth, she's caused us quite a spot of bother.'

45

The press conference was held in a hotel on Beresford Place, just around the corner from the station. Two mules were standing on either side of the door demanding mobile phones in return for entry. The room was warm and stuffy, with a long table at the top facing eight rows of seats, ten across, with a centre aisle. Two TV cameras on tripods were blocking the access there, cables trailing after them. The front and second rows had been taken by photographers, who were sitting tight, clearly afraid of losing their seats. Jo had regularly seen snappers come to blows while jostling for position outside court, actually knocking each other off their stepladders to get the shot. The journalists were different. It wasn't about one perfect shot for them. They could get more from talking to each other than from hanging around waiting for a single moment.

Jo sat in the centre seat of the big table with the members of her crack team – Lovett and D'Arcy on her left, and Foxy, and Darragh Boyle, a press officer attached to the garda press office, on her right. All bar Jo had changed into their uniforms before heading over, civvies transferred to lockers in the station. Nameplates sat in front of each of them, along with microphones propped on stands – though Jo's was the only one switched on.

Jo had requested Darragh Boyle's presence, because she was convinced the journalist behind Tara's interview was going to show. The byline on the story attributed it to a Frank Maguire. Sure enough, when a short, wiry man in a puff jacket and CAT boots appeared in the corridor while they were waiting outside, Boyle gave her the nod.

Jo watched him walk into the room and place his digital recorder, the size of a cigarette lighter, on the table in front of her, where it joined a cluster of others that had been left there, red lights flashing in anticipation. He headed to the seats to sidle into the third row. The mules outside had been instructed to snaffle his mobile and make copies of his call log and contacts book. Whatever information they gleaned wasn't evidence they were ever going to be able to admit in a court of law, but it would give them a basic steer into whether the Tara Parker Trench story was authentic.

A poster featuring Presley's face had been attached to the front of the desk with the word 'Missing' typed in large print at the top, and giving details of the little boy's height, size and weight. What he was wearing and where he was last seen were detailed in a smaller typeface at the bottom.

Jo and the others had been at their seats for around five minutes when she leaned to her right to tell the press officer she was not prepared to wait any longer, although the room was only a quarter full. Boyle got up to close the door, causing a last trickle of stragglers to appear, cold coffee cups in hand.

'Thanks for coming,' Jo began. 'I'll give you the details first, and then I'll take questions, but for operational reasons I won't be able to answer many. I'm Detective Inspector Jo Birmingham of Store Street Station, and I'm appealing to the public for their help to find this little boy.'

The cameras began to click incessantly, and the flashes made Jo blink more rapidly. Two men, with earphones on and control packs strapped over their shoulders, angled long sound muffs over her head.

'Presley is three years old,' Jo went on, looking intently down the lens of the TV camera. 'He disappeared from the back of his mother's car in the Ever Oil garage on Eden Quay at around 9 p.m. on Sunday night. At this point in time we'd like to withhold the little boy's surname. If you saw anything in the vicinity that night that you thought was unusual, please contact us. Or if anyone knows what happened, and for whatever reason has kept quiet to date about who has taken Presley, please get in touch.'

She leaned forwards. 'But if you are the person holding Presley, please, please talk to us. It's not too late to undo the damage. This little boy needs medication, and we know he must be really missing his mum and dad.'

Jo reached for an enlarged photograph of a pair of miniature running boots from a stack in front of her, and she held it aloft. 'When taken, Presley was wearing a pair of Nike runners just like these . . .' She held up a second photograph. 'A denim jacket with a Tommy Hilfiger label on the inside collar, and a NY Yankees trucker cap, which was white with black lettering.

'We're in the process of contacting everyone in the garage that night. However, we would urge anyone there in the half hour before the snatch, who noticed any unusual behaviour, to get in touch. Did anyone drive by this garage shortly after 9 p.m. and see a car leaving in a hurry or in a haphazard way? Please get in touch.

'We're particularly anxious to connect with employees working at toll bridges, or at ports, stations, or airports.

Again, please, look hard at this boy's little face. We need to get him home. Did you see him on Sunday night or since?

'And that is all the information we can give you at this point. You can contact the confidential garda number on 18000 666 111. Thank you.'

Several voices started to shout at once, but Boyle waved them quiet. 'Hands up, and we'll try to get to all of you.'

Most of the hands shot up. But a couple of reporters began to tiptoe out into the corridor to file, Jo presumed.

'Maria,' Boyle said, pointing to a woman in her late thirties whose hair was cut in a bob and who was wearing a wax jacket.

'Are you following any specific lines of inquiry?' she asked.

It was such a soft question that Jo suspected Maria must have done a deal with Boyle to get leads on the story further down the line in return. She could see the agitation in the other reporters' faces. They wanted to know the child's surname, his condition, why his disappearance was only now being made public – and those were just for starters.

'Several,' Jo answered. 'That's why I would once again appeal to anyone involved in this crime to come to us before we come to you.'

Maguire jumped to his feet. Boyle tried to wave him down, but he wasn't having any of it.

'No, I'm sorry, this is not on,' he shouted. 'If you want us to inform the public, you can start by giving us some real information.'

Boyle tried to point to someone on the other side of the room, but Maguire wouldn't give up. 'I've got a deadline in half an hour. Who was driving the car the child was snatched from, for starters? What was its make, model and registration? And does this case, coupled with the escape of Barry Roberts earlier today, mean that we have now effectively lost the battle for law and order in the city?'

Jo suspected he was trying to confirm that the car belonged to Tara, and that her child was the one missing. But the way he'd connected the Roberts case to what was happening with Tara had sounded an alarm bell in her head, though not in the way the reporter had suggested. Could the drugs she'd found in Tara's car have something to do with Barry Roberts?

'At this point, all I can tell you about the car is that it was a dark-coloured Mini . . .'

A heavy-set female was waving her arm in an agitated manner. 'Where are the parents? We can't write this as human interest without quotes from them.'

Jo opened her mouth to answer, but she was cut off by the sudden opening of the door from the corridor and the appearance of Merrigan, who walked straight up to the podium and hissed something into Boyle's ear.

'What the hell is going on?' Jo whispered to Foxy.

Boyle stood up. 'Good news,' he announced. 'One of the officers attached to the station, Detective Sergeant Fred Oakley, has found the little boy. Thank you all for your patience. It's rare to be able to wind things up this quickly, but extremely welcome, as I know you'll appreciate.'

46

They were in the station ten minutes later. Conscious that the press pack gathering on the steps outside was increasing by the minute, and not knowing why – given that there was no missing child any more – Jo took a couple of officers in the incident room aside, and asked them what had happened. Foxy, Lovett and D'Arcy came with her, all ears.

'Your appeal went out live on one of the afternoon shows. Presley's granny apparently heard it. She rang in immediately to say the boy had been with her all along,' one of the officers – a tall, skinny man – explained.

'Rang in?' Jo said. 'So why was the call put through to Oakley and not to the incident room?'

Lovett shot her a dismissive look that told her exactly why – because of men's blind loyalty to other men when confronted by a female who outranked them.

'It was,' the skinny garda said. 'Oakley was in here, back at his desk the minute you were gone!'

'Oakley doesn't have a bloody desk in this incident room,' Jo retorted. 'He's not part of the team.'

Dan came into the room, looking stressed and uncomfortable.

'The main thing is Presley has been found,' Foxy said, putting a hand on Jo's shoulder.

Jo was furious. 'He can't be. Presley's grandmother must be lying.'

'That's a bit harsh,' Foxy said.

She rummaged through her pockets. 'I've got a number for her somewhere. Tara gave it to me. I'm going to ring her right now.'

'Is this the first time you've made contact?' Dan asked, frowning.

'It's the first bloody chance I've had,' Jo snapped. 'But I'll make it my priority now.'

'I wouldn't bother,' Dan said. 'Oakley's with her now.'

'Well, he'd better make way for me,' Jo answered.

Dan sighed, his eyes dark and troubled. 'What are you planning, Jo? To create a scene in the middle of what may be the only good-news story of the day? Because if that's the case, I guarantee you the press will pick up on it.'

Jo sat down heavily. 'What I can't understand is: why are so many journalists still hanging around now Presley's been found?'

'Maybe it's because they've cottoned on to who he is,' Dan replied.

Jo felt another jolt of fury. 'And who told them that?' she demanded, looking around to see whether Merrigan was still hanging around.

'I have no idea,' Dan said firmly. 'But let's hope they don't look too hard at this case, or we're all going to end up in the doghouse.'

'I don't know what game Oakley's playing,' Jo said. 'He told me he'd checked Presley wasn't with his nan.'

'That's not the way he tells it,' Dan said.

'So what is his story?' Jo said angrily.

'Standard police checks were not done. He was overruled by you.'

'And you believe him?'

Foxy cut in. 'Let it go,' he said. 'Sort it out later.'

Standing up, she walked into her office, closing the door behind her.

Five minutes later, the sound of a cheer from the street outside caused her to step up to the window and peer out. Oakley was out there, beaming from ear to ear, with a little boy on his shoulders, and a handsome middle-aged woman beside him – who looked startled by the photographers bobbing around her.

Jo watched, arms folded.

Merrigan was there too, tousling Presley's hair, slapping Oakley on the back and smiling for the shots.

Presley seemed well enough, Jo observed, feeling the first wave of relief since she'd taken on the case. He was pale, but clean and well dressed, if slightly wary at finding himself in the middle of a bunch of excited strangers. He had one of those rice biscuits in his little hand, which he was half-hiding behind and half-eating. Jo didn't know what she found harder to believe – the idea that Oakley had found him so easily, or that he had gone to the trouble of thinking of Presley's teeth by giving him the least sugary treat he could find.

Her gaze moved back to Presley's grandmother. *What was it about her that didn't quite fit?* she wondered. She had to have been watching telly at home if she'd got to the station this quickly, which meant she hadn't been in hospital, in the intensive care unit, watching over her critically ill daughter. Jo wasn't going to judge her for leaving Tara's bedside, especially as there were no facilities in the hospital for family members. No, it was the sheepskin coat that was bothering her, she realized. It looked expensive, something you'd expect to see on a woman from one of the more affluent suburbs.

'Somebody got to her,' Jo said, thinking aloud.

'The main thing is that Presley's safe,' Foxy said, coming into her office. He waited for her to answer, and when she didn't, said quietly, 'Sometimes the bigger thing to do is admit you're wrong.'

'I'm not bloody well wrong,' Jo said, turning on him. 'You, of all people, should know that. You said it yourself when you saw Tara yesterday morning. She was heartbroken.'

Foxy nodded, then glanced at his watch. 'I'm sorry about this, but I'm going to have to head off.'

'You can't. Not now.'

'I've put in my eight hours, Jo. Now I have to get back to Sal.' He swallowed, and Jo noticed how strained he looked. 'Dorothy's back.'

Shocked, Jo covered her mouth, then went over and put her arm around his shoulders. 'You'd better hurry, then. Let me know how you get on.'

Merrigan appeared in the doorway. 'A couple of reporters want to interview Fred Oakley. Your office is the best place to do it in.'

'I bet it is,' Jo said, bitterly.

'What's the matter, Birmingham?' Merrigan said. 'Aren't you going to give Fred his due?'

There was an uncomfortable silence as Jo absorbed the tone.

'It's the only quiet spot,' Merrigan went on. 'Can they have it?'

Jo was about to answer with an 'over my dead body', when there was a commotion outside, and Oakley, Presley and Presley's grandmother walked into the incident room outside her office. She didn't even know Tara's mother's name, Jo realized. Maybe she was losing her touch . . .

'Getting more like a bloody crèche every day,' a detective called out, triggering a burst of laughter.

Oakley picked the little boy up and swung him up in the air. 'You're a great lad, aren't you, Presley.'

The child wriggled his way back down to the floor.

'Little scamp,' Oakley remarked as Presley took off across the room. 'Here, he'll make an Olympic champion, at this rate.'

Jo made a beeline for Tara's mother, making sure Presley was out of earshot. 'Do you really mean to say that Presley was never in the service station, and that your daughter lied about everything?'

The woman looked scared. But before she had a chance to answer, Oakley put his arm around her and walked her into Jo's office, tipping his head in the direction of a couple of reporters who had just appeared on the floor.

'All's well that ends well, eh?' he warned, keeping up the big man routine, and making Jo's skin crawl. 'Cute little fella, isn't he?'

He signalled for one of the reporters to follow, then closed the door behind him.

Jo walked over to Presley and knelt down beside him. 'You OK, Presley?' she asked, taking his wrist.

The child looked away.

'Where've you been, little man, eh?'

He twisted out of her grip, and started to run around the room.

'You trying to grill a three-year-old now?' Merrigan said, only half-joking.

Jo looked round. The other side of the glass, Dan was zipping up his sailing jacket, looking as though he was getting ready to leave. She stepped outside, and went over to him. 'You can't go. What about Morocco, the footballers, Imogen Cox?'

'Without a missing boy, we've no claim on any one of them,' he answered, looking drained. 'Besides, you said in your briefing Tara was studying to be an actress. For all we know, she was acting for the cameras on that tape. A defence barrister would have a field day. She hasn't even made a complaint. Quite the opposite, in fact. She's sold her story to the media.'

He started to walk towards the door.

'Where are you going?' she asked, keeping up.

'For a drink,' he said, his shoulders hunched and defensive. 'And if you've any sense you'll join me and let it go, too. This case has been a bloody nightmare from start to finish.'

47

Jo sat at a free desk, keeping an eye on how things were panning out in her office. A camera had been set up, and a big floodlight sat on the ground angled upwards. A circle of silver material had been placed on a stand on the other side of the room to bounce the light back. Presley was sitting on Oakley's knee in Jo's chair. His grandmother seemed to have declined to talk, as she was standing behind the camera.

Jo had rung one of the mums with a child in Harry's crèche and called in a favour, asking her to collect Harry and take him home with her, so she could stop watching the clock. She'd also contacted Rory's school to let him know he should stay on for the study hour. Then, she took out the list of the last twenty mobile phone calls Maguire, the reporter who knew so much about Tara Parker Trench, had made and received. As far as she could see, he'd made several to Tara, but she had returned none, at least not from her mobile. Jo would be able to confirm with the phone provider how long the calls to Tara had lasted, which would straight away tell her whether Tara had spoken to him at any length, or cut him off. There were also several contacts to and from an English number that interested her. She dialled it from the phone on the desk, expecting to get through to Melwood Athletic, only to discover it was

234

the office number of a high-profile publicist who handled celebrities when catastrophes struck. The firm had a reputation for damage limitation.

Jo's mobile rang. She answered it and discovered Aishling McConigle was on the other end. 'For the record,' McConigle said, 'Charles Fitzmaurice did book airspace at lunchtime.'

Jo nodded to herself, and thanked her. She turned back to the tape recorder, hoping to become privy to the conversations the reporter had had with the PR man, when something struck her. Standing up, she walked up to her office, and opened the door without knocking, much to the annoyance of the cameraman and the young female reporter in there, who'd been winding up their interviews. Going over to her desk, she picked up the disc she'd watched with the team earlier, showing the CCTV footage taken from the station on Sunday night.

Back outside, she located a CD player, and put the disc in, looking from the image of the shadowy figure on the screen to Presley's grandmother now in her office. Jo checked the screen again, and confirmed what she'd suspected minutes earlier. There was no doubt about it. The squares on the coat worn by the person who'd dropped off the sex tape at the station were the wool ridges you got at the joins on a sheepskin coat.

48

It was five on the dot when Foxy got home, and ten past by the time he'd washed his hands and stuck Sal's dinner on – coddle, her favourite. He hoped the sausage and bacon dish would cheer her up. She hadn't been herself when he'd collected her, though she wouldn't tell him why. When he called to say the food was ready, she wouldn't come to the table, asking to eat it in front of the telly instead. Foxy felt a twinge of concern. It just wasn't like her to mope about like this. He wondered if the incident in McDonald's with Philip might be playing on her mind, and decided to take a few days' leave in the hope that she'd open up when she was ready.

When the doorbell rang, he waited for the sound of her footsteps – Sal loved answering the door – but when they didn't come, he hurried down the hall himself. He could tell as soon as he saw the shade of red through the frosted glass pane that it was Dorothy. He closed the living-room door to his right, and grabbed his set of keys from the hall table to let himself out.

'What the hell are you doing calling here?' he asked, opening the door and stepping outside, glancing over his shoulder.

Dorothy had two shopping bags in either hand. 'I just

236

called around, hoping we could have a cup of tea. You wouldn't have to tell Sal who I am. Just say I'm a friend. I've brought cake and biscuits.' She swallowed, and took a breath. 'I didn't want to leave without meeting her.'

'Well, you'll have to. If you meet, it'll be on Sal's terms and not yours. I'm not going to ask her to—'

He'd caught sight of a movement behind him in the hall. Grabbing hold of Dorothy's arm, he walked her down the short driveway that would be lined with the primroses he and Sal had planted when spring came, and opened the gate.

'All right, all right, I'm going,' Dorothy said, her voice shaking. 'Take the chocolate cake for Sal, though. She wouldn't be her mother's daughter without a sweet tooth.'

The front door opened and they both looked round. Dorothy dropped the bags and froze.

'Hello,' Sal said.

'Hello, my darling,' Dorothy said.

'Sal, this is Dorothy,' Foxy explained. 'A lady I used to know when I was a lot younger.'

Looking puzzled, Sal walked slowly down the path towards her mother. Wordless, Dorothy put out her arms, tears streaming down her face.

Foxy stepped forward to try and intercept his daughter, but it was too late – she and Dorothy were holding on to each other like the world was about to end.

A minute passed, then Sal stepped back. Her glasses were off-centre. The lenses had steamed up.

Foxy put his arm around her. 'Let's go back inside, Sal. It was nice to see you again, Dorothy.'

Sal shrugged him off. 'She's my mum, isn't she?' She turned to Dorothy. 'You sound just like the woman who rang me in the day centre today.'

Foxy's heart skipped a beat. 'How could you?' he asked Dorothy. 'How could you do this to me? And to Sal?'

Dorothy sniffed. 'I have a right.'

Foxy's breath quickened, and he took a step towards her.

'Dad?' Sal said, tugging on his jacket. 'Dad? Is there a cake in that bag? Can we eat it now?'

Foxy looked down at her. She seemed calm and her face was back to normal. 'OK,' he said reluctantly. 'Just the one slice, mind.'

'Would you like some tea?' Sal asked, taking her mother's hand.

Together, they walked towards the front door, leaving Foxy at the gate on his own.

49

Jo opened her office door. 'I'm afraid you'll have to wrap it up now, I need to get back to work in here.'

The cameraman had already started to disassemble his equipment, and didn't seem bothered, but the female reporter who'd been left waiting outside her office was seriously put out. 'I haven't had a chance to interview anyone yet. Can we relocate somewhere?'

'I'm sure Fred would be more than happy to oblige,' Jo said. 'I need Presley and his nan to stay here for the time being, though.'

'We'll have finished up in ten minutes,' Oakley protested.

'I don't have ten minutes,' Jo answered.

The reporter took Oakley's tone as a green light to get bolshie. 'I've told my editor the interview with Gabriella Parker Trench is in the bag. He's marked it in for page one. I'm up against the clock now. I'm only a freelance.'

'If your editor gives you any grief, tell him to ring me,' Jo said. 'And give me your card. I'll have a much better story in a few days, I guarantee it.'

The reporter handed over her card, and they left. Jo closed the door behind the lot of them, and gestured to Tara's mother to take a seat. It was clear where Tara had got her good looks.

'I'm so sorry to hear that Tara is in intensive care. You must be worried sick about her. Have they told you any more?'

Gabriella studied her hands. 'She's . . . she's in a coma,' she said shakily. 'On life support. I don't know what to do—'

Jo leaned forwards. 'I'm so sorry.'

Gabriella still didn't look up. 'My beautiful girl brought sunshine from the moment she came into the world. I can't have her remembered as someone who sold herself for drugs. That's not who she was.'

Jo looked over at Presley, who had curled up on one of her chairs, and appeared to be dozing.

'She never wanted for anything,' Gabriella continued. 'She had brains to burn . . . could play the piano . . . She wanted to be an actress.'

'Yes,' Jo said. 'She told me.'

'You know, I was a single mum, too, but I wanted the best of everything for Tara. I scrimped and saved so I could send her to the best school. She saw what the other girls had, heard about their foreign holidays, got invited to their big houses – and she wanted all that, too. It's natural, isn't it? She was so generous. She'd have given you the clothes off her back if you admired them. That was my Tara. She just wanted everything now. And because she had so much attention from men, she always got what she wanted in the end. Mick was the only man who really loved her.

'I was at the end of my tether when he told me what was going on – the other men, the drugs. So I did the tough-love thing. I thought, *This will bring her back to me. She'll hit rock bottom and come back.* She and I – we had this bond. We were like sisters. I was only a teen myself when I had her.

That's why I was so dead set against her having, well . . .'
She glanced at Presley.

'Like her, isn't he? Got her bad chest, too. The doctors
said her system could have handled the cocaine, or could
have handled the drink, but the combination of both was
too much, and brought on the heart attack.'

A tear ran down her face. 'I'm so frightened that she's not
going to make it.'

Jo took Gabriella's hands in hers. 'I want to bring the
people involved to justice,' she said. 'But I need your help.
Who took Presley? What really happened?'

'Like I said, he was with me,' Gabriella answered, picking
up her bag and searching for a tissue.

'Has someone threatened you?'

Gabriella looked up, startled. 'No.'

'Presley, then?'

'I don't know what you mean.'

Jo sat back, and pushed her hair away from her face. 'It
was you who dropped in that DVD to the station yesterday
morning, wasn't it? You've spent the last few days trying to
protect your daughter, and Tara knew it.' She handed
Gabriella the slip of paper Tara had written on. 'She wanted
me to come to you if anything happened to her or Presley.'

Gabriella was staring at Jo, her face white with shock.

'I'm going to find the people who did this to Tara, with or
without you,' Jo went on. 'I want you to have the satisfaction of seeing them in court.'

But a look of terror had crossed Gabriella's face. 'If you
have children, for the love of God, never say those words
again to anyone,' she whispered. 'Walk away while you still
can.'

50

It was almost six o'clock when Jo met Aishling outside Connolly Barracks, near Heuston Station, a well-known haunt for hookers cashing in on the passing trade along the quays. The army barracks had been decommissioned years earlier, and the building was now a natural history museum known as 'the dead zoo' because of its collection of stuffed animals.

Aishling climbed into Jo's car and rubbed her hands together, blowing into them to warm them up. She'd just spent the last hour or so asking the girls on the street what they knew about any drug dealing going on in the Ever Oil garage further up the Liffey. Jo was really impressed by her initiative. It was lashing rain, and without the windscreen wipers on their fastest setting, impossible to see out.

Jo had bought them both coffee on the way over. Unplugging one of the polystyrene cups from its holder, Jo handed it over. 'Thanks for sticking with the case,' she told the young detective, as Aishling pulled the hood of her waterproof jacket down. Technically, now Presley had been found, Jo had no right to request anyone to do anything.

'That's all right,' Aishling answered, blowing under the cup's lid, and closing the car door. 'I told you, I like keeping an eye on them.'

She nodded in the direction of a woman standing on the steps of the hotel opposite, sheltering under the entrance canopy, and looking up and down the street at the passing traffic. She was wearing a pair of long shiny black boots that came up over her knees, a short tartan skirt that flashed a considerable chunk of white thigh, and a red leather jacket. Her black hair was in a ponytail; it had the static, flyaway look of a wig.

'That's Daisy,' Aishling said, swiping the rain from her face. 'She's got three kids, and a mortgage on a very nice place in Tyrellstown. She was a hairdresser until the recession, got laid off a few years ago. Doesn't look forty-five, does she?'

Jo shook her head. 'How'd she get this spot if she's only new?'

'She's two daughters working round the corner,' Aishling answered. 'There's strength in numbers.'

'You take sugar?' Jo asked, offering a sachet.

Aishling shook her head.

Jo watched as Daisy held her handbag up over her head, and ran towards a Fiat Punto that had pulled up in front of her.

'It's only her pimp, Tom,' Aishling said. 'He's an evil bastard. He'll be asking her what I wanted. Better head off. I don't want to make things any more difficult for her.'

Jo drove around the corner.

'There's Arlene, her eldest,' Aishling said, as Jo parked up. The girl with one hand on her hip, twenty-odd feet in front of them, was dressed in skin-tight red PVC, despite being morbidly obese. She was holding an umbrella that only managed to cover her head and shoulders.

'Crikey,' Jo reacted.

'You'd be amazed by the trade she does,' Aishling said. 'She's busier than the whole lot of them put together.'

'What's her excuse, then?' Jo asked.

'She makes more hooking than she would as a secretary, gets to decide her own hours, and, believe it or not, enjoys it. Now, don't turn around for a look, but behind us is her other sister, Melissa. She's a junkie, and nothing but trouble.'

Jo glanced in her rear-view mirror at the stick insect in denims and a bomber jacket. 'Did any of them have information worth giving?'

'Yeah, but I'm out of pocket fifty euro,' Aishling said, looking worried.

'That's fine,' Jo said, reaching into her own wallet and riffling out a couple of twenties and a ten. 'There you go.'

Aishling nodded gratefully as she folded the notes and tucked them into her jeans pocket. 'Apparently the row in the garage was over protection money which Hassan refused to pay. That's what the trouble was about on the night Presley vanished.'

Jo looked surprised as she sipped at her drink. 'Did you get a name?'

'Daisy mentioned some skinhead named Henry going in there and causing a fuss. Henry is an enforcer for the gang members who broke away from that Barry Roberts's group, after he murdered Joey Lambert in McDonald's earlier this year.'

'Henry,' Jo reiterated, nearly choking on a mouthful of coffee. 'Trust Oakley to get the spelling wrong! He entered his name in as Henly on the system. I thought he must be a toff connected to Charles Fitzmaurice.'

She and Aishling shared a giggle.

'Has Roberts got some connection to the garage?' Jo asked.

'Funny you should mention that,' Aishling said.

'Go on,' Jo encouraged.

'OK, you know the way all the trucks were supposed to bypass the city centre after the Port Tunnel opened?'

Jo crinkled her nose, trying to figure out where this was going. 'Yeah?'

'Well, some trucker who owes Daisy money keeps filling up in there. She went in screaming like a dervish telling Hassan she was going to report him, and Hassan warned her that the place was protected by Barry Roberts, and to stay away.'

'No wonder the security system's state-of-the-art,' Jo said.

'And here's the best bit,' Aishling continued. 'You remember those three junkies who died on the street last year, after someone mixed rat poison with their gear?

Jo nodded.

'It wasn't accidental,' Aishling continued. 'The King poisoned the gear because they owed him money. The girls hate him. It could have been any of them. The junkies only owed him two hundred euro between them, and the youngest was barely fifteen. The girls are all willing to testify in court against Barry Roberts. If we can find him, that is.'

51

Dan was sitting on a stool at the bar in Molloy's, with one foot on the brass rail that ran around it, and the other on a free stool in front of him. After dropping Aishling back at the station, Jo had gone looking for him to brief him about the latest developments. She hoped the Barry Roberts link to the investigation would stop him from shutting it down.

He was watching a football match on TV but, judging by the expression on his face, the running commentary from the resident pub expert behind him was doing his head in.

'Come here often?' Jo asked, taking the free stool alongside.

He glanced at her in surprise, and reached for his glass.

Whiskey, Jo realized. Neat. The way she liked it, too, but she couldn't remember the last time she'd seen Dan go to the pub straight after work.

'What are you having?' he asked.

'Just a water for me,' Jo said. 'I'm driving. What's your excuse?'

'I'm staying in a hotel tonight,' he answered. He paused, and looked deep into her eyes.

Jo turned to study the TV. After a few moments she said, 'I never wanted your job, Dan. I'm not saying I don't want to be promoted. I do. Just not at your expense.'

As he knocked back the contents of his glass in a couple of gulps she noticed he needed a shave.

'I wouldn't hold it against you if you did. You've worked hard, made a lot of sacrifices for the job. You should be rewarded. It's only right. You don't owe me anything any more.'

Jo didn't like the way he said it. 'What sacrifices have I made, Dan?'

'Forget it, I wasn't having a go.'

She drew a breath and twisted back around, leaning towards him. 'Dan, we broke up because I wanted another baby, and you didn't. Whatever chance we had of working things out ended when you started seeing Jeanie. For the record, that's our story.'

'That's not how I remember it,' he said, indicating to the barman, who was twisting open a bottle of still water for Jo, that he wanted a top-up.

Jo pounced like a hawk. 'Go on . . .'

'I don't want to fight,' Dan said, as the barman plucked his empty glass off the counter and moved off.

Jo stood up. If she stayed, a row was inevitable; her blood pressure was rising by the second, not to mention her sense of frustration that this bloody man could still affect her like this after everything. She bit the inside of her cheek to hold back. Each time she gave him an inch and tried to reach out to him, in however small a way, he did this – twisted things around. Well, she was sorry she'd even bothered attempting to mend bridges tonight. She couldn't do it any more.

'I just didn't think you were a natural mother,' he said.

She froze, her back still to him, jaw hanging open. Even by the standards their rows had sunk to in the past, the throwaway comment marked a new low.

'All the energy you put into work, you were always so knackered by the time you got in, you'd nothing left to give me and Rory,' he continued. 'I didn't think it was fair to bring another child into it.'

Jo spun around. 'I hope, for your sake, that tomorrow you can put this conversation down to alcohol, because, personally, I couldn't be prouder of the young man I have reared my son to be. Sorry if I wasn't fit to pole dance by the time we got to the bedroom after a day's work. Here's hoping the new mother in your life manages it.'

Dan pinched between his eyes with one hand, and reached out to grab her arm with the other. 'I'm sorry, I've been under a lot of pressure,' he blurted out.

Jo pulled her arm free. He stood and took a step closer to her. 'Jeanie and I, we've called it a day,' he said, urgently. 'I've just taken it out on you. I didn't mean it to sound like it did, so bitter. You were a great mother – are, I mean. I'm feeling sorry for myself, lashing out. I've lost someone I loved. Have a drink with me? For old times' sake . . . please . . . Jo. Please.'

She sat down slowly, against her better judgement. She didn't want to think about how she'd react if it turned out he was talking about Jeanie when he said he'd lost someone he loved. She was kicking herself for giving him the benefit of the doubt again, presuming he was talking about their relationship. But much as she wanted to go home before he could burst that bubble, she never could be clinical when it came to Dan.

'I've got to leave to pick up the boys in ten minutes,' she said, swallowing. 'I'm sure you and Jeanie will work things out.'

He was lifting the fresh whiskey to his mouth, but he

banged it back down. 'Under no circumstances. She's taken me for a right fool. I'm not going back.'

Jo moved her glass of water around in front of her, unable to take a mouthful; her stomach was churning.

'I don't want to end up one of those saddos in a B & B,' he said. 'Can I come home, just until I find my feet?'

The know-all behind Dan tapped him on the shoulder before Jo could answer, the tips of his fingers stained from nicotine.

'Any sign of Barry Roberts?' he asked. 'He grew up just around the corner from here, you know.'

Dan ignored him. He slid his arm round the back of Jo's stool and lowered his voice. 'I forgot to tell you. I'm going to resign at the end of the week.'

Jo felt like ordering a double herself at that point. 'What?' She held her finger and thumb an inch apart. 'We're this close to proving it's Blaise Stanley in Marrakesh,' she said.

'The case is closed,' Dan said. 'Don't you get it? The rape happened in another jurisdiction.' His eyes slid towards the punter behind him. 'The only investigation anyone will care about from here on in is the one finding Barry Roberts. If it's any consolation, I'm going to put you over that one before I go.'

Jo was all set to fill him in, but the busybody interrupted again. 'Between you and me, it's all over some drugs deal that went sour,' he said. 'Some big businessman on the south side owes the King money. The drugs disappeared in the garage just around the corner from here the other night.' He put a wavering finger to a set of pursed lips and winked.

Jo stared at him. 'Who told you that?' she asked.

'My lips are sealed,' he slurred, adding, 'half his gang live in the flats around the corner.'

Dan reached for Jo's hand, and examined it closely. 'I'll tell you the real story of us,' he said. 'I didn't want to have to share you with another kid. I thought we had the perfect family set-up: just you, me and Rory. I wanted you all to myself.'

The sound of his voice close up like that had the same effect on her it always did. Jo closed her eyes and tried to remind herself that a couple of minutes ago she'd been spitting nails. She finally took a sip of water from her glass.

'How many of those have you had?' she asked him.

'That's my fourth,' he said about the untouched drink on the bar.

'Let's go home, Dan.'

His face softened.

'I only want to make one stop off on the way,' she said, pulling a tape recorder out of her pocket. 'Don't look at me like that. If I don't speak to Kevin Mooney before drawing a line under this case for once and for all, it's going to get between me and my sleep. Afterwards, I'm all yours.'

52

The King ran out of the pub, across the road, and towards a motorbike being gunned by a man in black leathers. He was moving in steady, even paces, his right arm stiff at his side, to keep the Glock semi-automatic he was holding concealed against his dark leather trouser leg.

He was wearing a black motorcycle helmet, and he flicked the visor up so that he could see the small screen his getaway driver held in one hand.

'The signal moved, literally seconds after you left,' the driver said. 'I tried to ring you but you couldn't have heard . . . It's heading south side. It'll take us less than five minutes to catch it.'

'No, one of the customers recognized me,' the King said. 'It'll have to wait. We'll pay Fitz a visit now, instead.'

53

They got to the Triton just after seven. Dan flicked on the central locking, then put his arm casually over Jo's shoulders as they headed for the entrance. She was not going to let herself think about the idea that he might want her back. Jo had had two years of being logical and careful, and in all that time she'd never found another man as attractive as her ex.

In the lobby, she watched Dan hold up his ID for the receptionist and tell her that they wanted a word with Kevin Mooney.

The girl was young, and pretty, but plastered in make-up she didn't need, with her hair pulled back in a severe bun. She jabbed at a keyboard officiously before announcing that there were no guests of that name staying in the hotel.

Dan wasn't having any of it. 'Don't waste my time. It's more likely you've seen him on MTV's Cribs than running about on a pitch on *Sky Sports*, but I know you know who Kevin Mooney is, nonetheless.'

A door set in-between rows of pigeonholes for room keys opened, and a huge man with a walrus moustache filled its doorframe. 'Problem, Fern?' he asked, eyeballing Dan.

'The gardaí are here to talk to Kevin Mooney, Johnny,' she replied.

'Haven't you told them he's checked out?' Johnny answered, flatly.

'He's checked out,' the receptionist said, turning back to face them.

Dan put his two hands on the marble counter and vaulted it. He grabbed the man by the scruff of the neck and banged him against the pigeonholes.

'Who the fuck do you think you're talking to, boy?' Dan demanded. 'Unless you want a raid on this establishment within the next twenty minutes, you can tell me which room he's in.'

'614,' the receptionist blurted out.

Dan moved to the pigeonholes, took the card key he needed and walked out from behind the counter.

In the elevator, Jo stared at him in disbelief.

'What?' he asked.

'Nothing,' she answered, slipping her hands around his waist and leaning in for a smooch. She thought he was sexy as hell.

'I reckon we've got about four minutes before security gets reinforcements up here,' he said, as they exited on to the sixth floor and walked down the corridor looking at the door numbers.

At 614, Jo pressed her ear against the door, and nodded to Dan, who gave it a hard knock. When there was no answer, she stood back and let Dan use the key.

It was a suite, reputed to cost a couple of grand a night, and Jo noted that though it was bigger than your average hotel room it was otherwise pretty bland.

They walked down the hall and found Mooney lying on his bed in flip-flops and tracksuit bottoms, talking on his iPhone and watching TV. His bare chest was hair-free.

'What the hell is this?' he asked aggressively, holding his phone away from his ear. He was handsome in a Liam Gallagher way, with similar levels of just-beneath-the-surface anger.

'Gardaí,' Jo said. 'We'd like to talk to you about what happened in the Atlantis Hotel at the weekend.'

'Are you having a laugh?' Mooney asked.

'Rape is not a laughing matter, Mr Mooney,' Jo said.

Dan took the phone from his hand and powered it off.

Mooney looked annoyed, and got up off the bed.

'It wasn't rape. We paid her,' he said indignantly.

'You paid Tara Parker Trench for what, Mr Mooney?' Jo asked.

'To party,' he answered, in a way that made Jo's skin crawl.

'Arrest him,' Dan said.

'For what?' Mooney reacted. 'I've got a taxi ordered to take me to the airport. I'm training tomorrow.'

'You can forget about that,' Jo said, pulling the tape recorder out of her pocket. 'I've got you recorded saying you paid for sex, and I've also got a video of what you consider consensual.'

Mooney went pale. 'Give me that mobile,' he said to Dan. 'I need to call my lawyer.'

'Look, you've got the Champions League coming up. How about you do us a deal, and in return we forget about this conversation?'

Mooney sat down heavily on the bed. 'What do you want to know?' he asked, earnestly.

54

After checking up and down the corridor, Jo pressed her ear to the door of the suite next door, and then glanced over her shoulder at Mooney, who nodded. Swiping the key pad in the lock, she opened the door to find two girls in two double beds, both pulling sheets up to cover their nakedness.

One of the women – a blonde – stepped out of her bed, which was very ruffled. 'Who are you?' she demanded, her accent Russian.

'Police,' Jo said. 'And we want you to produce your passports and paperwork sharpish, please. And then you can tell us all about who paid your airfare, and brought you here.'

The blonde shot a dagger look at Mooney, who tried to back out of the room but was blocked by Dan's arm.

'Is this a joke?' the blonde demanded. She was wearing only panties, and she covered her breasts with her arms as she moved towards the bathroom door.

'Not so fast,' Jo said, pushing past her and swinging the door open.

Standing in the bath, hiding behind the shower curtain, were two naked men. Jo recognized one of them as being Greg Duncan, the black man on the sex tape. They held their hands over their privates.

'Put some clothes on,' Dan told them, reaching for a phone to dial the station.

The brunette in the second bed started to cry. She had the features of a Romanian national – dark eyes and hair, olive skin. 'I can't believe this is happening,' she sobbed.

'Right,' Jo said. 'We're arranging squad cars to bring you back to the station, and we'll be needing statements. You'll be asked about any other bookings for tonight, who you're working for, and whether you've been here before. Let's try and get this over with as quickly as possible.'

Jo walked over to a dresser and looked at the little heap of charlie sitting on the counter. She clicked her tongue. 'We might be able to do a deal on the drugs charges if you all come clean on the prostitution racket.'

'I would have done it for free just to say I'd been with any of them,' the brunette said, weeping loudly.

The blonde walked over and put her arms around her. 'We could have sold our stories to a newspaper and made a fortune. We'll know next time.'

'We're models,' the brunette told Jo.

'Course you are,' Dan said.

'Which reminds me,' Jo said, sliding her hands over the surfaces of the walls, and stepping up on a bed to reach the higher spots.

'You see a camera anywhere?' she asked Dan.

The brunette pointed to the light over a picture on the wall.

Jo high fived Dan as she walked over and spoke directly into it. 'Who's a pretty boy then, Fitz?' she said. 'We'll be after you, next, so don't get too comfortable.'

55

The King was in the Triton, his revolver pressed so hard against Fitz's forehead that the metal had made a red, round ring imprint in the skin. Grunting, he moved the gun to Fitz's lips and pushed it into his mouth. Fitz's eyes bulged out further as he looked over at Big Johnny, who was lying spreadeagled on his front on the hotel bedroom floor, hot blood oozing from a bullet hole in the back of his head.

'This is the last time I'm going to ask you,' the King said. 'And I want you to think very carefully before you answer. 'What are you going to give me back first – the money you owe me, or my drugs?'

Fitz gagged on the gun as he tried to speak, then pointed a trembling hand at the wall. The King lowered the gun, and pulled an ornately framed painting down, tossing it to one side to reveal a small safe.

Slowly he raised his arm and cocked the weapon, then looked over his shoulder and saw the look of hope in Fitz's eyes.

'You should have told me it was bulletproof,' he said, pointing the gun back at Fitz. 'It might have caused me a nasty accident.'

'Wait,' Fitz rushed. 'There's only ten thousand euro in it. But I know a way you can recoup ten times what you lost.'

He told the King about the footballers in the hotel, and the videos he'd made of them with his girls.

The King tilted his head. He wasn't interested in match-fixing. That could take months. He wanted his money or his drugs. Now.

Grinning, he slid on the silencer and squeezed the trigger. The tracker he'd put with the drugs would tell him exactly where they were. He didn't need Fitz any more. It was more important to send out a message: *if you try to double-cross the King, you pay with your life.*

56

After they left the hotel, Jo drove in silence through the bus lanes, negotiating the city's traffic. She'd attached the flashing Special Branch blue light to the roof of the car, to weave in and out of lanes when buses and taxis blocked her path. She didn't talk for a while, either. There was too much to think about. Kevin Mooney had confirmed that Blaise Stanley had been in Marrakesh the night Tara was raped. It was all starting to come together.

'You should give Sexton the Barry Roberts case,' she said eventually, checking Dan's reaction.

'Absolutely no way,' he answered.

'He needs to get his teeth stuck into something,' Jo said. 'Gangland is his speciality. It's the sort of case he'd be really good at.'

Gangland murders accounted, on average, for a third of the annual death rate, but in the last year Barry Roberts had been responsible for increasing that percentage to half. Also, he had to have intimidated at least one judge, and several gardaí, to get around charges in the past. A prison officer who'd fallen foul of him had been shot dead on his doorstep. There was no question about who was responsible, but there was no evidence, either. He was one of those people who made Jo reconsider her views on the death penalty. He'd hurt so many others that he was like a cancer on society. In her view he needed to be removed.

But Dan's face had hardened. 'You don't have to tell me anything about Sexton's needs.'

Jo recalled Sexton had once had a soft spot for Jeanie, and wondered at Dan's tone now. She decided not to pursue it. Every time they talked about Jeanie, she felt a surge of jealousy, and they ended up fighting.

She pulled out her phone at a traffic light and dialled Rory's school, to discover he'd headed home alone. 'I cannot believe there was no escort for the Roberts prison trip,' she complained, dialling Rory's mobile, and screwing up her face as she listened to the sound that meant it was dead.

'That would have been Blaise Stanley's decision, too,' Dan said.

Jo didn't want to think about how they were going to deal with Stanley, or what they were going to have to do next. Her head was already spinning from all the new developments in the case.

She phoned the mum who'd collected Harry and sighed heavily when voicemail cut in. She left a message saying they were on their way.

She tried Rory's number again, but got the same sound. Rory's phone rarely had any credit. She dialled the home number again, which rang out.

Dan switched on the two-way radio, to pick up any dispatches between stations.

'Listen,' he said, tweaking up the volume as Jo disconnected her call.

In-between the static, Jo heard a discussion about Barry 'King Krud' Roberts, who'd been seen in Molloy's pub that evening – the same pub she and Dan had been drinking in.

'What time did they say?' Jo asked Dan.

'About half an hour ago,' he replied, glancing over. 'Must have been in only minutes after we left.'

She felt a jolt of fear and tried her phone again, one-handed.

She noticed Dan was checking his wing mirror. Dan was normally unflappable. If he was worried, so was she.

'The old man in the pub said Roberts was from that area,' she said, trying to be logical. 'Maybe that's why he was there.'

The sound of an urgent message from Donnybrook Station radioing a squad car made Dan glance over at her in concern. There'd just been a double shooting in the Triton.

Jo's fingers tightened on the steering-wheel. They had to get home and find Rory – fast.

57

Foxy was trying to lip-read what the RTÉ news presenter was saying as Sal giggled and repeated her mother's words.

'Do me a cheesy quaver . . . favour. Dad, cheesy quaver means favour, doesn't it?'

'Yes.' Foxy smiled.

Dorothy was fussing, topping up the tea he didn't want after the three-course meal she'd made, and offering more cake. He couldn't make himself comfortable on the chair, but nothing needed doing. The milk jug was full, there were spoons for the sugar – Dorothy had ordered him to sit down, and then seen to everything.

'Sal, maybe you could go to your Irish dancing class this evening, now you're feeling better,' he said.

'Will you collect me, Mum?'

Foxy shook his head and opened his mouth to object, but Dorothy had already agreed. He looked back at the TV. That bastard Barry Roberts had escaped.

Sal was looking at him expectantly, like she was waiting for his answer.

'Sorry, love, what did you say?'

'I asked: do you want to come, too?' she said.

'We'll see,' he answered.

The image on the screen was of a reporter good-looking enough to have been a Hollywood actress, talking to the camera while intermittently gesturing back to a cordoned-off section of the M50. Foxy leaned forward. He reached for the remote and turned the telly up.

A ticker-tape headline flashed across the bottom of the screen, filling him in as the reporter started to interview some shocked hotel guests. Two people had just been gunned down at the Triton Hotel.

'Jesus,' Foxy muttered.

'Do. You. Like. Mickey. Mouse?' Dorothy was asking Sal.

'Sal has the most fantastic hearing,' Foxy remarked, still staring at the box.

'Mickey Mouse is for babies,' Sal answered. 'My favourite band is Westlife. My favourite TV show is *Hannah Montana*. My favourite film star is Robert Pattinson. He's drop-dead gorgeous.'

'Ahem,' Foxy said.

'Oh, except I'm not allowed to watch any of his scary things.' Sal giggled again and put a finger to her lips. 'But I have, Mum. Don't tell Dad.'

Dorothy's face lit up.

'What do you like, Mum?' Sal asked.

'Well, I suppose I like singing most. I used to want to be a singer years back.'

'What stopped you?' Foxy asked, standing, and looking around for the phone.

'There was no *X Factor* back then.' Dorothy sighed.

'That's my all-time favourite programme,' Sal said, contradicting herself excitedly. 'After *Dancing On Ice*, and *Deal or No Deal*.'

Foxy blocked his daughter's hand with his, mid-air.

'That's enough cake, missy,' he said. 'You won't be able to manage your Irish dancing if you keep that up.'

'Last bit,' she promised.

The TV camera flicked to the sight of the coroner arriving at the scene.

'What's up?' Dorothy asked.

'There's been a development in the case I'm working on,' he answered, lifting up the couch cushions. 'I need to ring Jo. Has anyone seen the phone?'

Dorothy walked over to the mantelpiece and lifted it up. 'This it?'

He reached over and took it off her.

'If you need to head off, I can bring Sal to Irish dancing if you like,' she said.

Sal beamed. 'Please, Dad, please, please, please . . .'

Foxy was holding the phone to his ear, having dialled Jo's number, but it was engaged. 'Actually, that would be a great help. Thanks.'

Dorothy smiled, and picked at something on the neck of his jumper. 'You've put it on inside out, you big ninny,' she said.

Sal laughed.

After kissing his daughter on the forehead, Foxy reached for his coat and held his arms out stiffly in protest as Dorothy hugged him.

58

Even though they found Rory safe at home, and getting through his homework in his room, Jo's stomach still churned with anxiety. They had collected Harry, who was nodding off on Dan's chest as he pushed back a corner of the curtain and peered out at the street. Every now and then Dan would glance at the news on the TV, which he'd on in the background, the volume turned down low. Barry Roberts's prison mugshot was in the top right hand of the screen as images – of the smashed-up prison van, the spent cartridges still on the road from the gunfire, and the courthouse – played on the screen. One of Dan's hands was spread across most of Harry's back. Jo held her breath. She felt as if she was looking at what life could have been like if she hadn't spent the last two years alone. She walked over, bent down, and touched Dan's back gently.

'Give him here,' she said, reaching for Harry. Dan stood up to help the transfer, and stretched his arms over his head when it was complete.

'Have you packed what you need?' he asked quietly. 'We have to get the boys out of here.'

Jo held Harry tightly in her arms. They knew from a phone call Dan had made in the car who the victims in the Triton were – Charles Fitzmaurice and a security man called

Johnny, the same one they'd seen in the reception area of the hotel. She needed time to think, but there wasn't any.

'Can we have dinner first?' she asked. 'It is eight o'clock.'

'No,' Dan answered, firmly.

Jo continued down the hall, and laid Harry out on his back in his bed, flicking the night light on as she pulled off his clothes as gently as she could to change him into his pyjamas. He was wiped out, and didn't stir. She looked around for his overnight bag, spotted it on the floor, and lifted it on to the bed, to check its contents. Hearing Dan's voice in Rory's room, Jo lifted Harry as she headed back out, and stuck her head in to see Rory packing up his books.

'How about you take Becky for that dinner tonight, and we'll collect you later?' Jo asked quietly.

Rory looked over to check Dan's reaction.

Dan nodded. 'That's a good idea, son. We need you out of the house for a few hours, just as a precaution. It's probably nothing.'

As Rory left the room to ring Becky, Jo sat down on the bed, rocking Harry gently. 'I don't know why Barry Roberts was in Molloy's so soon after us,' she said. 'But there are any number of reasons why he targeted Charles Fitzmaurice.'

'Yes,' Dan said, taking the overnight bag from her arm, hooking it over his own shoulder, and transferring a bulky folder from his pocket into the bag, before kneeling down beside her. 'Of course.'

Jo closed her eyes as Dan reached for her hands. She rolled her neck.

'What if we could turn back the clock?' he asked. 'Would you have done anything differently?'

She kept her eyes closed. 'I'd have tried harder to make it work between us. What about you?'

'I'd have insisted you take pole dancing classes,' he said, making her smile.

A loud bang outside made her heart skip a beat.

'What the hell was that?' Dan said, jumping up and letting the bag slip to the floor.

As he headed to the front door, Jo picked up the bag, and reached for the item he'd just put in, which was sticking out of the top. Curious, she pulled it out. It was a Manila folder with 'Barry Roberts Case' written across it. She opened it. Inside were a few printouts – and the evidence bag she'd given him that morning, with the tracking device still sealed inside.

59

Five minutes felt like five hours as Jo called for Rory to get in the car. Harry wasn't impressed at being woken, and though she tried to soothe him on the move, he seemed to pick up on her own anxiety – rubbing his eyes and wailing. Jo ran down the hall, grabbing the car keys and her mobile. She opened the front door a fraction, and called Dan's name over the sound of Harry's irate cries, but got no answer.

'What's the matter, Mum?' Rory demanded.

'Get in the car. Now,' Jo ordered.

'Where's Dad? What about Dad?'

Jo didn't answer. It was pitch dark outside and the floodlight that normally came on didn't. She handed Harry to Rory and put the car into reverse the second his door closed. He barely had time to click a belt on.

Dialling Sexton's number, Jo pressed the phone to her ear as she started to drive. If she could get the tracking device out of here, maybe she could lure whoever was around away from Dan.

'I'm glad you rang, I need to brief you about what Murray Lawlor's been up to,' Sexton said.

'Not now,' Jo answered, panic-stricken, as she shifted the car into first gear.

'We can't leave Dad,' Rory shouted.

'What's the matter?' Sexton asked.

'Dan's in trouble,' Jo said.

'I'm on my way,' Sexton answered.

'No! Get a unit over. I'm driving the boys out of here. Dan may be hurt.'

'Why do you say that?' Sexton asked, sounding alarmed.

'He went outside, and he hasn't come back.' Jo said. 'I think Barry Roberts has got him.'

60

Jo was about five miles from home, waiting for a red light at the junction of Foster's Avenue on the N11 to change, when she heard the first faint hint of a siren in the distance.

Rory was giving her the silent treatment, still furious about leaving Dan behind, but at least he and Harry were safe.

As soon as the flashing lights came into view, she flicked on the indicator, locked hard on the steering, and crossed the lanes to U-turn over to the far side of the road, pulling up outside the Radisson Hotel. She waited for the squad car to pass, keeping her car in gear, her right foot pressed to the clutch. She opened the window and half-turned, catching sight of Harry fast asleep in the back as she dropped the tracker on the street. Then she sped off in hot pursuit.

Twelve minutes later she parked up behind the squad car in her own drive to find Sexton already there, standing in her front door, shining a torch out. Every light in the house was on.

'Have you found Dan?' she called, as Rory jumped out and ran up to Sexton, who shook his head in response.

Rory flapped his arms in frustration, and tried to head into the house.

'Stay where I can see you,' Jo told him.

Rory grunted something inaudible back. Goosebumps spread up her back. If anything bad had happened to Dan, he was never going to forgive her.

Oakley climbed out of the squad car she'd just followed. Jo lowered her window a fraction to let some fresh air in for Harry – still asleep in the back – and locked the car doors.

She held her hair off her face as she walked up to join Oakley and Sexton, noticing that the front door looked like it had been kicked in.

'Don't worry, I did that,' Sexton said.

Oakley pulled out his notebook, checked his watch, and noted the time. 'What happened?' he asked, still studying the pad.

Jo felt herself choke up. She took a deep breath and talked through the wobble in her voice. 'Barry Roberts followed us to Molloy's, the Triton, and then here,' Jo said. 'We heard a noise and Dan went outside and Roberts did something to him, I know he did. We've got to sct up road blocks, get the air-support unit out, try and find him.'

'One thing at a time,' Oakley said, pen cocked. 'Did you see Roberts?'

'She didn't see anyone,' Rory complained.

Jo shook her head. 'We're wasting time here . . .'

'Sorry, was that a "no" you didn't see him?' Oakley asked Jo officiously. 'We have to be completely clear about what you're saying here.'

'Why? So you can lie about it later?' Jo snapped.

'No. Because you rate instinct too highly. Police work's about facts,' Oakley said.

Jo gritted her teeth. 'The fact is, no, I did not see Roberts, but yes, he was there.'

Sexton put his arm around her.

'How do you know?' Oakley asked.

'Because there was a tracking device in my car,' Jo said. 'And he was following it.' She hadn't wanted to mention the tracking device, because doing so might get Dan into trouble. But there was no help for it now. She knew he'd had a lot on his mind, but he should have handed it in to forensics.

'So where is this device now, then?' Oakley said.

'I threw it out of my car outside the Radisson Hotel.'

'So we've just got to take your word for it?' Oakley said.

'Use your noggin,' Sexton told Oakley, frowning. 'Where do you think Dan is? I'll call in the request for road blocks. Jo. You get yourself inside and I'll get you a cup of tea.'

Jo looked towards the car. 'I have to get Harry,' she said.

Jo took the sofa, blocking Harry from rolling off it, while Sexton carried in a mug of tea which he handed to her before sitting on the arm of a chair opposite.

'No thanks,' Jo said.

'Drink it,' he insisted.

Jo took it from him and put it on a side table. The room was shadowy, the only light falling in from the kitchen. She wanted it that way so Harry could sleep.

'The main thing is not to panic,' he said. 'We think Roberts may have been on a motorcycle, and if he was he couldn't have taken Dan anywhere. Describe the noise you heard outside for me.'

'It was like a . . . gunshot,' Jo said. 'We have to get out there and look for him! He could be lying out there now, injured, or worse.'

'You're jumping to conclusions, Jo.'

'Please, Gavin, if that moron Oakley is let handle this he'll make a balls of it. Please.'

'Don't worry, there's two emergency response units on their way.' Sexton was referring to the ERU, an elite squad of trained marksmen.

'But Oakley . . . ?'

Foxy arrived in, breathing hard, before Sexton could answer. 'I just heard. What's going on?'

Jo burst into tears.

'They've hurt Dan, I know they have. He wouldn't have left me and the boys alone in the house.'

Oakley came into the room and cleared his throat. 'Has Dan ever gone missing before?'

'No . . . Yes . . . Dan would never have left his boys like that, no matter what was going on between us,' Jo said.

Oakley flicked on the light, and Harry whimpered.

'Turn it off,' Jo said.

'Where did he go the last time?' Oakley asked, moving to the mantelpiece where he picked up a picture of Rory and Harry, angled it into the light coming through the door, and studied it.

Jo felt a stab of anger. She looked at Foxy but knew from his expression she'd have to answer.

'Some hotel,' she said reluctantly.

'For how long?' Oakley asked, making a note.

'Three nights,' Jo said.

Oakley tucked his pen and pad in his pocket. 'When was this?'

'Look, how is it relevant?' Jo demanded.

'He has been under a lot of pressure lately with the report about to come out,' Oakley said.

'How do you know about that?' she snapped.

'Easy, Jo,' Foxy said. He turned to Oakley. 'Why don't you make a start on the neighbours?' he suggested.

The gravel outside the house crunched as another car approached. Oakley moved to the window and drew back the blind. 'It's the dog unit,' he said.

Jo drew a breath. The dogs were trained to pick up the scent of death. 'We need to get Harry out of here,' Foxy said. 'You can bring him to my house, and let him sleep there. Sal's great with him, and Dorothy's there. You can come back later, if you like.'

'Roberts could still be around,' Jo said.

'How do you know that?' Foxy asked. 'He could be any-where by now. He's probably followed the tracker.'

The sound of the dogs barking excitedly made Oakley raise his eyebrows. He and Sexton hurried outside.

Jo stood, but Foxy stopped her from following. 'It mightn't be anything.'

Dazed, she headed down the hallway towards the kitchen, then stopped as Oakley reappeared.

'Do you know what blood type Dan is?' he asked.

61

Foxy put on a brave face for Jo's sake, but secretly feared the worst. The blood the dogs had found a few hundred yards down the road was AB, which was Dan's, but also shared by most of the rest of the population. A DNA analysis could confirm whether or not it was Dan's, but would take days to process.

Rory reacted to the news like the young man he now was. He took Foxy aside and told him that the main thing was to keep his mother busy. He was his father's son, Foxy thought, promising him he'd keep an eye on her.

Jo looked washed out. Foxy didn't try to patronize her by telling her everything would be all right. Jo had been on too many doorsteps herself to know that the only thing worse than coping with sudden loss was being given false hope.

Because she had the boys with her, Foxy was able to persuade her to leave the scene and come back to his place. He wanted her to stay the night, but he only had two bedrooms, and Jo wasn't willing to accept a bed if it meant putting someone else on the floor. She needed her own space, she assured him, and left to go to a hotel several hours later, with the boys.

Foxy looked at Dot with changed eyes after they were gone. She had been a rock during the commotion, keeping the tea on tap, and even though nobody had been able to eat, the smell of her bacon sandwiches had been comforting. Sal had slept through all of it, allaying his main concern, which was that he'd have to explain the concept of evil to an innocent like her. He'd always tried to tell her the truth.

'Come here,' Dot said as he waved Jo off and closed the front door. She patted the seat on the couch beside him. He noticed a bright throw had appeared on the worn green velvet cushions. There was a new picture on the wall, too, he realized.

'They'll find Dan,' Dot promised, rubbing his back. 'I know they will, I can feel it in my waters.'

Foxy pressed his hands to his face. They'd find Dan all right, but if Barry Roberts was involved, he wouldn't be alive.

'I blame this King chap's parents,' Dot said.

Foxy had had too long a day to explain how ridiculous this remark was, especially coming from her.

'We've got ASBOs in England to nip any delinquency in the bud before it takes hold,' she continued.

He knew she was trying to make him feel better, but he just wanted to sleep, and the couch was his only option now that she was going to stay in his bed.

He sighed. 'We've got them here, too.'

'Where did it go wrong, then? For someone like Roberts, I mean? Bet you'll find he was abused as a kid. It desensitizes them. Makes hurting other people easy. Do you think he's mad or bad?'

'Who knows?' Foxy said. He didn't care. He just wanted to stretch out on his side and sleep. Come first light the search would begin again.

'Anyway, cocaine has had its heyday,' Dot said. 'It's all

head-shops now, that's why the drug dealers are burning them out. Too much competition.'

Foxy stood up. 'Look, I need to get some bedding for in here.' He hoped she'd take the hint, and leave him to sleep.

'No need to do that,' Dot said.

'I told you you could have a bed tonight, and a bed you will have,' he said.

'That's not what I meant,' Dot said, putting her hand on his. 'I know you've still got a double. There's more than enough room for the two of us. And you might not need a cuddle tonight, but I certainly want reminding that the world's not all bad.'

62

Deeply shocked by Dan's disappearance, Sexton went back to collect Murray Lawlor from his office. It was tearing him up that someone he cared about, a good, decent person like Jo, should be targeted by the very criminals she was protecting the public against. His emotions hardened to anger as he entered the building, using the set of keys he'd taken with him earlier.

What he saw there made his knees go from under him.

Murray was still in his chair, but now a black circle on his forehead showed exactly how close the gun had been. His jaw hung slack, and his lifeless eyes stared upwards.

Sexton drove to Charles Fitzmaurice's home like a man possessed. Tara had told him that Fitz was in this up to his eyes, and even though Fitz was dead, his family might still be worth talking to.

Hugo Fitzmaurice opened the door.

Sexton burst in, taking him by surprise, and twisted his arm high behind his back, slamming him up against a wood-panelled wall and squashing his face sideways.

'Let me go. I want to find Barry Roberts as much as you do,' Hugo grunted. 'I know exactly where that toerag will surface.'

Wednesday

63

Jo didn't sleep, although she longed to. Staying awake was like a living nightmare. Her thoughts were so dark that her heart felt permanently lodged in her throat. What had they done to Dan? Was he alive and suffering? Was he dead? They must have hurt him, he'd never have gone without a fight. What if he needed urgent medical attention? What if he was somewhere within reach but unable to call out? What if Roberts came back to get the boys? How would she protect them? She couldn't watch over them twenty-four seven, and even if she did, she would be powerless against the King and his cronies.

She sat up in her hotel bed. She couldn't switch on the light, because the boys were asleep beside her, but she couldn't keep still, either. She went into the en suite, shut the door, and sat on the edge of the bath. Something about the sparkling glass and blue tiles in there made happy memories of her life with Dan suddenly flood into her mind. She remembered a dazzlingly hot day on holiday by the sea, and Dan splashing in the water with Rory; lying in bed on a Sunday, a shaft of sunlight across the sheets, her body wrapped in Dan's arms; the warm, intoxicating scent of Dan's skin. She started weeping, wiped the tears angrily from her cheeks, and ran herself a glass of water from the tap. But she was too tense to swallow.

The questions came so thick and fast that she felt as if she'd run a marathon. The 'what ifs' were eating her up inside, and she paced up and down the little room, her emotions ranging from complete terror, to anger, to paralysis. She wanted to curl up and wait for everything to end so she could cope. What if it was already too late? What was she going to do without Dan?

64

Jo pulled in at the Triton just after eight, having dropped Harry off at his crèche and Rory at school, in spite of his protests. He was taking it as an affront that life should go on when his father was still missing, but Jo needed to be able to concentrate solely on finding Dan, without having to look after her children. Her head was not in a good place. The more time passed without him making contact, the worse her fears.

The hotel was sealed off, but Foxy was standing at a mobile chip van handing a fiver over.

'Jo, how are you?' he asked.

She gave him a nod.

He took a coffee and offered it to her. She shook her head.

'Now that's what I call enterprise,' Foxy said about the chip van, talking through the awkward silence between them, as if he hoped it would lift her spirits. 'The driver heard the news and headed here in anticipation of gathering press.' He pointed to the far side of the road. 'There's quite a few already, should be more as the day progresses, I presume. Look, there's something you should know . . .'

Jo glanced over at the reporters. She could make out Ryan Freeman, the crime reporter whose daughter's kidnap had played a part in Jo's last big case. She hadn't seen Ryan since, but she waved back when he saluted her. He was a short, overweight man, his hair in permanent need of a cut. His donkey jacket pockets were always overflowing with rolled-up newspapers and spiral notebooks. 'Oh shit, he's coming over,' Jo said. 'That's all I need.'

'Come on,' Foxy said, pointing the way along a series of gangplanks that had been set up around the hotel so as not to disturb potential evidence.

'I'll just ask him how his daughter, Katie, is. You go ahead. If he sees you, he'll try and get a line out of you.'

'Jo, how are you?' Ryan asked. He took her hand and kissed her cheek.

Foxy turned his back and carried on into the hotel.

'I'm good,' Jo answered. 'How's Katie?'

'She's a different child now, you wouldn't recognize her.'

'I'm glad. And Angie. How's your wife doing?'

Ryan scratched his chin. 'Angie and I ... we're not together any more. We couldn't get over what happened with Anto Crawley.'

'I'm sorry. Well, tell Katie I was asking for her.' Jo turned to follow Foxy.

'So how come you're involved in this one anyway?' Ryan asked after her.

'I was just passing,' Jo said over her shoulder.

'You'll have heard the rumours about what was going on in the hotel Fitz owned?'

Jo stopped in her tracks and turned around.

'Gangland's not your area,' Ryan continued. He sounded like he was still working it out. 'You and I both know this is connected to another of your investigations. Tara Parker Trench. Is there anything else going on I should know about?'

Jo shrugged. 'You tell me.'

Ryan walked up to her. 'For old times' sake, you'd better watch your back, Jo. It's more than my job's worth to tell you this, but I owe you a hell of a lot more than my job.'

'What do you mean?'

'I mean Charles Fitzmaurice was a big fund raiser for the justice minister during his election campaign. Blaise Stanley wouldn't have weathered any association.'

'Christ!' Jo said, unnerved. She was going to need Stanley to approve any dragnet to find Dan.

'I thought you might have guessed something was going on – you know, what with Fred Oakley succeeding Dan.'

Jo took a deep breath to steady herself, then, nodding goodbye to Ryan, walked quickly towards the hotel.

Foxy was in the lobby, waiting for the lift. 'So when were you going to tell me about Oakley?' she asked.

Foxy checked to see how she was taking it. 'I'm sorry,' he said. 'He's been made acting head.'

'Don't,' Jo said. 'Blaise Stanley is the only one who's going to regret it.'

The crime scene was heavily taped, with pools of dark blood on the carpet where Fitz and his security man had been murdered.

'Johnny Nash,' Foxy said. 'He worked at the Triton.'

'Yeah,' Jo answered. 'I met him.'

'He had a few convictions for GBH,' Foxy said.

Jo walked round Fitz's outline and out into the corridor. Two detectives were there, their backs to her.

'You heard about Oakley?' one asked.

'Yeah – and the chief,' said the other.

'I heard his days were numbered even if Roberts hadn't seen him off,' said the first.

When they realized who was behind them, their embarrassment was palpable.

Jo tapped the nearest on the chest. 'You use Chief Superintendent Dan Mason's name and title if you ever mention him again, or I'll have you up before a disciplinary committee,' she said. 'Neither of you was fit to shine his boots.'

What scared her more than her anger – she could have happily swung for them – was her own use of the past tense.

65

Back in her office, Jo put the sex tape safely into her bag, aware that a man's suit jacket was draped over the back of her chair. She sat down in front of the computer and clicked on Jeanie's email logo. She was guessing that if Oakley was now acting head, she wouldn't have this office for much longer.

The computer clock read 10 a.m. Glancing up regularly to make sure no one was coming, Jo used the arrow key to bring the cursor down through the subject lines in Jeanie's email box until she found something she hoped might help her. It had been sent from Dan's email on Monday and was entitled 'Tom Burke complaint'.

A rap on the door made her look up. *Speak of the devil*, Jo thought. Oakley filled the doorway. He was seriously running to fat.

'Great,' Jo muttered, double-clicking the email open. When the computer didn't react, she double-clicked again, aware that the whirring noise it was making as it tried to catch up with her command was not a good sign.

'How many men are you allocating for the search party to find Dan?' she asked, staring at the frozen screen. The bloody cursor wouldn't move, and the little egg-timer logo had stopped spilling grains of sand. *Do not crash on me now*, she willed it, clicking furiously.

'I'm going to have a meeting shortly, to decide just that,' he said, clapping his hands together and looking around.

'Not another meeting!' Jo objected.

'I wanted a word, actually,' he said, shifting uncomfortably. 'I can't put you on the case. You know how it is.'

'Have you lost your mind?' Jo flared, about to put her left thumb and two fingers on the CTRL, SHIFT and Escape buttons, just as the email opened. She scanned the contents.

'You're too conflicted to work on it,' he said. 'You could always apply for compassionate leave, if you're too upset to work, of course.'

The email was addressed to Fred Oakley from Dan, and Jeanie had been cc'd into it. It read:

> Further to the complaint to the garda ombudsman by a member of the public about your failure to investigate vital information, I am informing you that it is claimed that you were told a week ago that a paedophile who'd failed to adhere to the terms of his release and register as per the Sex Offenders Act was living beside a local national school, and that you did not immediately act on this information. Please be advised that no evidence could be found to support this allegation. The complaint therefore has not been upheld.

Oakley was unplugging the DVD player so he could take it from the office. He seemed more concerned with rearranging the furniture than finding Dan, as far as Jo could see. She was about to object again, but the contents of the screen reeled her in. She read:

> PS For your information, Fred, you're only off the

hook because I called someone in the ombudsman's office to tell them about last night, and they agreed to make it look like you did initiate an investigation and found Burke as a result. But let this be a note of caution for the future. Any sightings of criminals, or information on criminal activity that's supplied to any individual officer, must be acted upon or passed on at once to avoid cock-ups. Dan.

'Problem with the computer?' Oakley asked, moving towards Jo's side of the desk.

'Nope,' she answered, reaching round to the wall for the flex, and pulling it out.

Nothing happened for a couple of seconds, but as Oakley leaned over her to have a look at the screen it finally went blank.

Jo stood up and put her finger on his chest. 'I know all about the complaint against you – about your failure to investigate that paedophile, Tom Burke. You may have got away with pretending it was my fault Gabriella Parker Trench wasn't interviewed on Monday, but this time I've proof of your incompetence. If you even suggest taking me off Dan's case, Fred, I promise you, I'll get in touch with the garda ombudsman myself, with my own complaint. Don't get too attached to your new office, I've a feeling it's about to bring you as much luck as mine did.'

Sexton bumped into her as she was leaving the station.

'Jo, I think I know where Roberts could be hiding,' he said urgently. 'I'm going to go and check it out.'

'I'm coming with you,' she answered.

'No, I'll ring you if anything turns up. You need to talk to Tara. She's recovered consciousness.'

66

Tara had been transferred from intensive care to the special observation unit of the hospital. Jo had tried not to cry since Dan had disappeared, but the smell of disinfectant being sluiced along the corridor by a cleaner made her eyes brim. She brushed the tears away. Buried memories of her father's death were never far from the surface. The thought that Dan might end up recovering somewhere like this, because someone had set out to hurt him, chilled her more than any accident ever could. He was a good, decent man and if she got the chance to have the honour of having him back in her life, she was never going to let him go again.

She looked into each room as she continued down the ward. After a couple of passers-by glanced at her curiously she realized she'd been whispering, 'Please let Dan be all right,' to herself as she walked.

Tara was in a private room, propped up in bed wearing a light green hospital robe, the wires of a heart monitor running underneath it to a machine.

She looked much older and very frail, as if the slightest movement now required every ounce of her concentration. Her hair was dank, and her dull, hollowed eyes watched Jo listlessly as she rubbed her hands together under a hospital superbug disinfectant dispenser. Jo sat down on the chair beside the bed just as a monitor started beeping.

A nurse did a double take from the corridor as she spotted Jo and headed over.

'Didn't you see the signs about the winter vomiting bug?' she demanded. 'No visitors allowed.'

'I'm not a visitor,' Jo replied, standing to show her ID.

'Make it quick,' the nurse said, unimpressed, pressing a button on the monitor to stop the beep. 'She's due a feed.'

'Isn't there supposed to be a guard keeping an eye on her?' Jo said, lowering her voice.

'There was one here, briefly,' the nurse answered. 'He said something about being taken off the case by higher powers.'

Jo leaned over Tara as the nurse left. 'How are you feeling?' she asked.

Tara gave a tiny nod. 'Presley?' she asked, feebly.

'Safe with your mum,' Jo replied.

'I want to see him,' Tara croaked, trying to hoist herself up in the bed.

'You'll have to get yourself clean first,' Jo said. 'You need professional help. You may have survived this time, but what's going to happen when you have to cope with the stress of prison life? They're awash with drugs in there. It'll only be a matter of time before you OD in prison, too, the way you're going.'

Tara's eyes widened. 'Prison! What have I done to deserve that?'

'Take your pick. You went to the garage to pick up a haul of drugs, for starters,' Jo said.

'I didn't know about the drugs,' Tara said. 'I swear it on Presley's life.'

'Can you say the same about Imogen's murder?' Jo probed.

A different machine started to beep angrily. Jo realized it was the one monitoring Tara's blood pressure. The equipment used for lie detectors wasn't dissimilar. Stress testing was all based on monitoring heart rate and perspiration levels. Jo knew she was on the right track.

'Jeff told me everything when we arrested him,' she said. 'You thought Imogen had taken Presley, didn't you? That's why you killed her.'

'I want to see Presley,' Tara said stubbornly. 'When are you going to bring him in to see me? Mick won't. Mum won't. Please.'

'I'll have him here this afternoon, if you tell me the truth about what was going on in the garage, and if you promise to get yourself clean. You're going to have to prove to everyone you're fit to be his mother. Presley doesn't need all the expensive, fancy stuff you get him. He needs you.'

Tears rolled down Tara's face, and then she started to talk.

67

'Fitz was disappointed with the escort business,' Tara said quietly. 'He was giving Imogen a lot of stick about it. He said she'd duped him, lied about how much money there was to be made. He said he was the one taking all the risks, and there wasn't much of a return.'

'Go on,' Jo encouraged, taking her hand and giving it a squeeze. She felt like shaking Tara, though. She wanted to get a move on, so she could hook up with Sexton and join in the search for Dan.

Tara gave Jo a look. 'Fitz said if Imogen didn't supply him with more girls, he would count her out as a partner. But Imogen couldn't find any Irish girls willing to work at the new rates. She tried, believe you me. She put so much pressure on us all; well, she got me to go to Marrakesh, didn't she . . .?'

Jo knew she was holding back. 'There must have been something else going on in Marrakesh, other than the foot-ballers' party. Why did Imogen go, too?'

Tara turned away to look at the wall. 'I told you, she wanted to get more girls.'

'From Morocco? Who was the contact?' Jo asked.

'Fitz has this guy working for him – Murray Lawlor – he looks after the door at the Blizzard, makes sure everything ticks over with no trouble. Used to be a cop.'

'I know him,' Jo said.

'Murray is a middleman for a big gangster supplying drugs to the club. This gangster provides protection for the club, protection from his own cronies, mainly, if you want to look at it like that.'

'Go on,' Jo said, drawing her out.

'Murray offered to hook Imogen up with someone who could get her some girls from north Africa. But in return, she had to bring a haul of drugs back from Morocco for his boss, the gangster. Fitz couldn't do it. He'd been caught in his helicopter before, and customs were watching out for him. It was a problem, because the gangster was in prison, and didn't trust any of his own men to do it. He was afraid they'd try and rip him off. But Fitz said that as long as Murray got the drugs over, he'd buy them from him. Fitz was branching out into a lot of other areas because of the way the hotel trade was going. He'd even invested in a lock-up, so as to have somewhere to store the drugs when they came in.'

'You know the location?' Jo asked.

'Somewhere in North Wall.'

'And who's the gangster?' Jo demanded.

Tara shrugged weakly.

'It's Barry Roberts, isn't it?' Jo pushed.

Tara nodded reluctantly.

'So Murray Lawlor wanted Imogen to bring a haul of cocaine back from north Africa for Barry Roberts?' Jo said slowly. 'And in return he was going to front up a few females to work at the Triton?'

Tara sniffed in reply.

'But how was Imogen going to transport the drugs?' Jo

asked. 'There's no way she could have got them through on a chartered flight.'

'She arranged for someone to take them on a ferry to the south of Spain in a camper van,' Tara whispered. 'With the girls . . . And just in case anything went wrong, she brought one of the Triton's VIP clients over for the party with her. A politician. He didn't know what was going on, but he would have been extremely useful to Imogen if anything had gone wrong.'

Blaise Stanley, Jo realized, letting out a long hard sigh. And there'd been a camper van in the garage the night Presley vanished. It was the only vehicle she'd taken no notice of, precisely because it was designed to avert suspicion. She was furious with herself for being so stupid.

'How many girls were involved?' she asked impatiently.

'Two,' Tara said. 'There should have been three, but there was a problem. Imogen went berserk. She said the deal was three girls or it was all off. So they snatched a kid off the street rather than risk Imogen pulling out – just a kid. They couldn't control her, she kept trying to escape. They drugged her, and I didn't see her again after that.'

'Where's she now?' Jo asked, worried.

Tara shook her head. 'Only two girls made it back to Dublin. Murray wouldn't tell me what happened.'

'And finally there was an incident in the garage on the night the drugs arrived,' Jo prompted. 'Something unexpected. A fight. The cops were called. Marcus had been sent to collect the drugs. But they needed to be stashed somewhere in a hurry. Your car.'

'And just in case I got any bright ideas, Presley was taken,' Tara said.

'What was Jeff paying you for?' Jo asked.

'What do you think?' Tara asked. 'He wanted me to visit him after Morocco. I think in his head he thought we had a future. I suppose I used that. I thought he could help me get out of Imogen's clutches. But he was too weak.'

'And the film of you being raped in the pool – how did your mother get hold of it?'

Tara sighed deeply. She was visibly growing weaker, but Jo needed to keep her talking. 'Jeff owed me money. He couldn't come up with the readies. Imogen controlled everything in his life, even the amount of cash in his pocket. He gave me a memory stick and told me to consider it a gift. I didn't know what was on it when I took it. He told me it was the one thing I could use against Imogen if the time came.' She paused, and took a few shaky breaths.

'My mum must have watched it the night Presley was taken, and downloaded it on to a DVD. She's the one who told me about you and what you had done to save that other kid.'

'Did she kill Imogen?' Jo asked.

But Tara was gazing at the door of her room. Gabriella was standing there with Presley. Tara tried to hold her arms out, but she barely had the strength.

Jo gripped her hand. 'Come on, Tara. Give me this last piece of the puzzle and I'll leave you with Presley.'

Tara gave a sob. 'No, I killed Imogen. Early on Monday morning, I went to see her. I told her I wanted my boy back. She said I could have him if I gave her the DVD. I didn't know what she was talking about. I picked up a rock and hit her. If anyone had the right to kill her, it was me, and maybe that missing girl from Morocco.' She turned to Jo, her eyes wide with fear. 'I killed Imogen. Are you satisfied now?'

68

A steady stream of press flowed between Abrakebabra, the kebab shop on the corner, and the road block sealing off the street where Barry Roberts's mother lived in Crumlin.

Sexton had phoned Jo at the hospital with the news.

'Roberts has got a hostage,' he'd explained. 'The ERU SWAT team are here now.'

Jo processed what that meant. 'Roberts is armed, isn't he?' she asked, gripping the phone so tightly her knuckles went white. 'Why am I only hearing this now?'

'Because it's only just happened,' Sexton answered softly. 'Are you going to come over?'

'Come over?' Jo said. 'I want to do the hostage negotiation.'

Half an hour later, Jo was at the road block in Crumlin. She showed her ID to the officer keeping the cordon.

'Inspector, you do know who we believe Roberts has taken hostage in there?' the officer asked.

'Yes,' Jo said.

'You can't go in without a bulletproof vest.'

Jo carried on, ducking under the tape. 'Try stopping me,' she muttered.

The officer pressed a button on his radio and left an urgent message.

As Jo arrived on the scene seconds later, she heard Oakley say, 'Roger that.' He watched Jo walk up to Roberts's front door. 'Officer, I'm warning you to stop now, before you endanger life,' he boomed through a megaphone.

Jo gave him the finger over her shoulder and stayed put.

A shot rang out.

Jo couldn't tell which direction it had come from, but she could hear a commotion behind the front door.

She bent and shouted through the letterbox. 'Two cops are better than one, Roberts. Here I am – yours for the taking.'

Seconds later the door opened and, ignoring Oakley's voice on the megaphone demanding she turn back, Jo stepped inside the house.

69

Dan sat on a kitchen chair, his head slumped on his chest, a length of blue washing-line rope binding his wrists and ankles, and strung to a noose around his neck so that if he struggled it would tighten. A plastic carrier bag covered his face, and the handles were knotted under his jaw. If the bag hadn't made a tiny movement as air passed in and out through a small hole in front of his mouth, Jo would have believed him already gone, there was so much blood on his shirt. Roberts was standing directly behind him with a lighter in one hand, the handle of a Glock poking up from the waistband of his jeans, and a sawn-off shotgun pointed at Dan's head.

'Sit down,' he told Jo.

'Aren't you in enough trouble?' she asked, pulling the chair out.

She thought Dan's back straightened a fraction at the sound of her voice. Jo drew a breath. The smell of petrol was overpowering. She'd sensed it first in the hall, which had one of those clear plastic runners down the middle to protect the carpet from stains. Jo had slipped more than once on the way in from all the brown fluid sluiced there.

There was a bark of laughter from Roberts. 'She's got

spunk,' he said, nudging Dan's shoulder with the sawn-off. 'Bet she's feisty in bed.'

Jo could hear muffled crying from another room. Roberts's eyes darted to the door then moved back.

'That your old mum?' Jo asked.

Roberts didn't answer.

Jo looked around the room. 'She did her best for you, I can tell. You should see the hovels some of the scrotes we deal with grew up in. This is a nice place, clean and warm. What are you going to say to the judge when the time comes, if you can't blame your crimes on your start in life, like the rest of them?'

Roberts puffed out his chest. 'I ain't going back inside, not for no one.'

'You didn't give school much of a chance, either, did you?'

The sound of padded footsteps made her turn, and she saw a grey-haired woman shuffle into the room in a pair of fluffy pink slippers. 'It's not his fault,' she said.

Roberts sighed. 'I'll handle this, Mam,' he said.

Jo crossed her arms and spoke directly to the woman. 'Let me guess, his father was an alcoholic who used to beat you. He's the one to blame. Is that it?'

Roberts's face tightened. 'Don't you dare speak to her like that.' Spit turned to shiny strings at the corners of his mouth.

'It's all right, Barry,' the old woman answered, in a strong Dublin accent. 'I want to tell this one, who thinks she knows everything, what was done to you. Barry was a good boy. He was taken off me, and put into care. One of the staff in the home used to abuse him, my son, who was taken from me.'

'Shut it, Mam,' Roberts reacted.

Jo turned to him. 'How many civilians have you killed?

Nine, plus Murray Lawlor, Big Johnny and Fitz? Ten? Well, if you count those young addicts you poisoned it's even more, isn't it? You arranged for three prison officers to be killed yesterday, too. They didn't abuse you, did they? Where's this going to end, Barry? Do you think they're going to let you walk out of here, maybe catch a flight to some Costa, after all that? Use your loaf.'

The sheen of sweat that had broken out across Roberts's face told Jo that whatever drugs had been in his system were now wearing off.

'He dies next,' Roberts answered, gesturing towards Dan. 'One for the road.'

'They don't care about him,' Jo said. 'He's been working on a case to bring down the justice minister, the same one who'll decide how long your life sentence lasts.'

'You're lying,' Roberts answered.

'It's all on tape. I'm surprised your lawyer didn't mention it. George Hannah, isn't it? He's got a lot of friends in high places. How do you think Fitz managed to evade a sentence? Why do you think they let me come in here to talk to you? They'd be delighted if you did away with me, too. If you torch this place you'll be doing exactly what they want.'

'He's not going to set light to his own home,' Roberts's mother said. 'He's just trying to buy time to think.'

'Shut it!' Roberts yelled. 'I can't . . .'

There was a screeching noise as Dan suddenly shunted the chair back into Roberts's groin, trapping him against the sink. Dan coughed for air as Roberts hauled on the noose.

Jo dived towards the old lady and twisted her arm up behind her back. The old woman yelped in pain as Jo put her neck into the crook of her arm and held fast.

'Let her go!' Roberts yelled.

'I will if you take the bag off his head, cut off his ropes, and let him go.'

Roberts looked at his mother and ripped the plastic bag off Dan.

The state of Dan's face made Jo gasp. His eyes were black, his lip split, and bruises had puffed out everywhere into shades of brown, red and purple. The rope was too tight around his neck: the skin above it was swollen and glossy.

Roberts pulled a drawer open behind him and took a kitchen knife out of it, which he put to Dan's throat.

Jo squeezed the old woman's neck, making her moan. 'Now the rope,' she said.

Roberts started to saw through the rope with the knife, so close to Dan's neck that Dan closed his eyes. After a couple of minutes and several superficial nicks that drew a lot of blood, the noose snapped. Dan took deep gulps of air.

'Now,' Roberts said, 'like I said, let her go.'

But the room had filled with thick, choking, blinding smoke before Jo had a chance to answer.

70

Foxy was making his way through a council estate, which was a maze of cul-de-sacs not mapped by logic, street names, or numbers, to get to Hassan's house. He'd been there before, when he'd managed to recover the sex tape for Jo from Hassan's excuse of a wife.

Foxy wanted to be in Crumlin, where the hostage negotiation was unfolding, but Jo had told him to track down Hassan at all costs, and get a statement to back up what she'd discovered from Tara.

Foxy had just arrived at Hassan's home when the man himself emerged from his front door and climbed into a waiting HiAce transit van – which Foxy could see belonged to Marcus Rankin, the pool-cleaning specialist, because his name and mobile number were written on the side.

Maintaining a safe distance, Foxy decided to follow, cursing the anti-joyriding ramps, which were going to play havoc with the squad car's sump. He allowed the van to drive past, watching it from his rear-view mirror, so Hassan wouldn't spot him behind the wheel. Based on the number of scorched-earth patches and cider cans strewn on the open ground opposite, though, he didn't think the squad car in itself would be enough to arouse much suspicion.

It had been years since he'd done any active policing, and

he was glad of it. The country had changed. The days when the priests and politicians held any moral authority were over. Now, kids growing up with nothing thought that following in the footsteps of the likes of Barry Roberts was a real career option.

Aware that the HiAce had just turned right with a bleed arrow, he tried to switch lanes without using the siren, but the motorists streaming around the corner stubbornly ignored his attempts to cut in. Foxy stuck his hand out of the window and managed to edge in just as the lights changed, leaving him with another quandary. If he jumped them, his cover would definitely be blown – Rankin and Hassan would spot him and change their plans.

He waited, and by some miracle, when he finally rounded the turn he could still see the HiAce ahead. He followed it to a lock-up in North Wall. There he watched as Rankin jumped out of the driver's seat and walked around to the side of the van, sliding the door open.

Two young girls, squinting against the light, stepped out. One was a Filipina, and the other looked Moroccan. Foxy sprinted across, grabbing Rankin and Hassan, and snapping cuffs on their wrists. 'You have the right to remain silent,' he said. 'Anything you do say will be taken down, and may be used against you in a court of law . . .'

71

Jo pulled her shirt up over her nose and mouth, but she still couldn't stop spluttering and spitting at the noxious fumes given off by the tear gas.

The SWAT team were screaming for everyone to lie down on the floor, but that didn't stop Roberts discharging his weapon, or the team firing back.

Jo crawled towards Dan and desperately tugged at the feet of his chair to pull him down to safety. He fell with a thud.

She couldn't see anything, but she knew the slippery substance covering him wasn't petrol. She kissed his face, and whispered the things she'd needed to say to him for a long time directly in his ear. No matter what happened, they were going to be together from now on.

Thursday

72

Sexton sat in his car, parked outside Jo's home, staring at the dog-eared envelope on his lap – Maura's suicide note. Now that there was something he was dreading even more than opening it – calling on Jo to see how she and her family were doing – reading it didn't seem such a big deal. Sexton banged his head against the headrest and stared straight ahead. He wound down his window and let in some cool air as he broke the seal and pulled the note out. No matter what it said, it couldn't be any worse than the pain he knew was waiting for him inside Jo's house. He'd sat with her since they'd recaptured Roberts, listened to her pour her heart out, struggling to contain his own feelings of grief and regret. He didn't think he'd seen anything more heart-breaking than the sight of little Harry, oblivious to everything, dressed up in a waistcoat, shirt and tie, holding his big brother's hand as Jo broke the news to them. Rory's face was red from crying, but he hadn't shed a tear in front of Sexton; he was his father's son all right.

He did his best to keep Jo's spirits up, but he knew only too well how hollow words could sound when you needed them most. He'd promised Jo that if he could get out of bed every morning, so could she. He'd told her she might never get over what had happened, but for her boys' sakes she would have to keep going, and that, for them, she'd find a way to make her peace with it.

Sexton rubbed his face in his hands. He was exhausted. The irony was, it was probably the biggest case the station had ever cracked – a human trafficking and drugs ring, Barry Roberts locked up for good by ballistics that linked him to the murder of Fitz, Big Johnny and Murray Lawlor. Some of the most famous footballers in the world were due to stand trial, and even Justice Minister Blaise Stanley had been exposed. He, Sexton, was in the clear now, too, his investigative work cancelling out the cock-up he'd made earlier, when he'd been found in the Triton Hotel bedroom with Tara. But, by Christ, the price had been high. He didn't know if they'd ever be able to persuade Jo to come back.

He bowed his head and read the note. It consisted of one line. 'I love you, but I can't go on. Patricia.'

Sexton felt the hackles on the back of his neck rise. Why would Maura have signed off a note using the wrong name?

She didn't write it, he said to himself.

He looked at the note again. It was definitely Maura's handwriting, but there wasn't a single tear-stain on it. Maura couldn't manage to sit through an episode of *EastEnders* without bawling her heart out. She'd never have written a suicide note without sobbing. String herself up with the flex of a vacuum cleaner? Take their baby's life while she was at it? His wife hadn't topped herself at all.

Sexton shoved the note in the dash. It was for another day, when Jo didn't need him as much as she did now.

Epilogue

Jo had been given special leave while Dan recovered in rehabilitation. She lost all sense of time in the months away from work. There weren't weeks any more, only good days and bad days. The good days were the ones when he tried to talk to her, and she saw signs of the fighter she knew he was. On the bad days, he'd try to force her away, saying terrible things to try to make her believe he didn't love her; sometimes briefly succeeding, and making her storm away. She'd only ever get as far as the car park, a blast of cold air always bringing her back to her senses. There were worse days – when he could say nothing at all because he was so consumed by his own overwhelming sense of powerlessness and rage at the prospect that he might never walk again.

Then, Jo would grip his hand and tell him that she was not going anywhere, and that she loved him, and that he was going to do everything again, but that it would take time. She would prattle on with meaningless news, just talking for the sake of it, to try and ignore the faraway look in his eyes as he battled to come to terms with his condition.

But hardest on her was the fact that not once since his kidnap had he told her he loved her. That was what scared her the most. She could reason away most of her doubts by

311

remembering the man he used to be. *He hated pity, and didn't want to make me feel fettered to him*, she told herself. That was why he'd begged Jo, sobbing like a child, not to bring the boys in to see him until he knew what his chances were. Until then, he wanted them to remember their father as a man who was strong, and could protect them if they needed it.

Rory had put his fist through a door when Jo had told him Dan wouldn't see him. Her friends had been a godsend. She'd had to accept help, and they'd thrown her a lifeline. Dorothy was living with Foxy and Sal again, and her regular offers to babysit Harry, and the home-made meals she had brought over, had freed Jo up to spend even more time trying to bring Dan around.

But alone in bed at night, she could sometimes feel so lost that the practicalities of what needed to happen next seemed insurmountable. But Jo couldn't leave Dan, not when she'd had a taste of what it might be like to have to live in a world without him.

She parked the car, and walked round to the passenger side. Dan was sitting there, hunched up and tense. He frowned at her as she opened the door and tried to guide his legs on to the pavement.

'I said I'd do it,' he said angrily.

She stepped back.

The front door opened and Rory came out, holding Harry's hand. He froze when he saw his father. Dan had planted his own legs on the pavement and was clutching at the doorframe, trying to heave himself out of the car. Jo knew he didn't want her to help, but it was agonizing watching him struggle.

Finally he made it. He straightened, let go of the car, and took two shaky steps forward.

'Well, aren't you going to give me a proper welcome?' he asked his sons.

Rory smiled widely, and ran towards him with Harry, and Jo thought her heart would burst as Dan clasped them both tightly in his arms.

Acknowledgements

As ever, thanks to the inspirational crime editor Selina Walker for all the guidance and encouragement, and for not letting even several feet of snow, which managed to cut off the power and the post, close down the roads and schools, and shut down the entire month of December, get between us and the finish. Thanks, too, to the rest of the Transworld team – Eoin McHugh, Brian Langan, Madeline Toy, Stephen Mulcahey, Kate Tolley, Helen Gleed O'Connor and Declan Heeney. And to Alison Barrow for the amazing night in Belfast with the fabulous Tess Gerritsen and David Torrans. I also have to thank fellow author and journalist Lucy Pinney for giving me a great idea for the next book, Jenni Murray for going easy on me, and Lisanne Radice and Claire Rourke for helping me think things through.

I owe a major thank you to my agent, Jane Gregory, for taking me into her fold with some of my all-time favourite crime authors, and also to my *Sunday World* editors and friends. Thanks to all my girlfriends, Vanessa O'Loughlin, Carmel Wallace, Sarah Hamilton, and Maria Duffy.

Lastly, but most importantly, my husband Brian, and Peter and Johnny who make everything worth it, my parents Eamonn and Sheila, and all my family who allow me to talk about unsavoury things over dinner.

About the Author

Niamh O'Connor is one of Ireland's best-known crime authors. She is the true-crime editor with the *Sunday World* newspaper, and has written a series of books which were given away with the paper. Her job, in which she interviews both high-profile criminals and their victims, means she knows the world she is writing about.

People with Dementia Speak Out

by the same author

Telling Tales about Dementia
Experiences of Caring
Edited by Lucy Whitman
Foreword by Joanna Trollope
ISBN 978 1 84310 941 9
eISBN 978 0 85700 017 0

of related interest

Nothing About Us, Without Us!
20 years of dementia advocacy
Christine Bryden
ISBN 978 1 84905 671 7
eISBN 978 1 78450 176 1

Dancing with Dementia
My Story of Living Positively with Dementia
Christine Bryden
ISBN 978 1 84310 332 5
eISBN 978 1 84642 095 5

Can I tell you about Dementia?
A guide for family, friends and carers
Jude Welton
Illustrated by Jane Telford
ISBN 978 1 84905 297 9
eISBN 978 0 85700 634 9

PEOPLE with
Dementia
SPEAK
OUT

EDITED BY LUCY WHITMAN

Afterword by Professor Graham Stokes

Jessica Kingsley *Publishers*
London and Philadelphia

First published in 2016
by Jessica Kingsley Publishers
73 Collier Street
London N1 9BE, UK
and
400 Market Street, Suite 400
Philadelphia, PA 19106, USA

www.jkp.com

Library of Congress Cataloging in Publication Data
A CIP catalog record for this book is available from the Library of Congress

British Library Cataloguing in Publication Data
A CIP catalogue record for this book is available from the British Library

ISBN 978 1 84905 270 2
eISBN 978 0 85700 552 6

Printed and bound in Great Britain

Contents

Acknowledgements

First and foremost I want to thank all the people with dementia who have so generously shared their stories.

Second, I am grateful to the family carers who made it possible for me to meet some of the contributors and hear about their experiences: Angela Contucci, Mandi Empson, Hamida Farsi, Joanne Franklin, Gerard Hall, Valerie Hall, Zalihe Hassan, June Hennell, Jennifer Hylton, Chloe Hylton-Evans, Bob Kahn, Jane Moore, Mahomed Mukadam and Derek Norman.

Third, I would like to thank all the friends and colleagues in a variety of organisations who helped to put me in touch with potential contributors, made suggestions or helped in other practical ways: Alli Anthony, Janet Baylis, Sue Benson, Jo Cahill, Abul Choudhury, Alison Evans, Simona de Florio, Kate Hancock, Ming Ho, Susanna Howard, John Killick, Jules Knight (formerly Jules Jones), Nick Maxwell, Geraldine McCarthy, Laura Newey, Manjit Kaur Nijjar, Shirley Nurock, Kathryn Quinton, Steven Reading, Marianne Rizkallah, Sreeparna Roy, Martin Sewell, Ralph Smith, Barbara Stephens, Gill Tan, David Truswell, Joy Watkins, Toby Williamson. Special thanks are due to Professors David Jolley and Graham Stokes.

Organisations that have offered support include several branches of Alzheimer's Society, the Scottish Dementia Working

Group, Age UK Camden, Opening Doors London and the Healthy Living Club in Stockwell.

Thanks to the team at Jessica Kingsley Publishers and in particular to Rachel Menzies who has been extremely patient!

Finally thanks to my family and friends for their encouragement along the way.

The book is dedicated to everyone who has dementia, to all the people who love and care for them, and to all the professionals who support them with respect, integrity and imagination.

Lucy Whitman

Introduction

LUCY WHITMAN

'Spotting a ticket inspector is easy. They look just like you.'
That's what it says at my local train station. The same is true
of people with dementia: they look just like you, just like me,
whatever we look like.

Who is this book for?

This book is for anyone affected by dementia, either personally
or professionally. I hope that people who have a diagnosis of
dementia, or who suspect that they may be developing dementia,
and the family members and friends who worry about and
care for them, will find the stories in this book encouraging,
reassuring and inspiring.

I also hope that professionals who support people with
dementia, whether as consultants, dementia advisors, nurses,
healthcare assistants, social workers, or in any other role, will
take the opportunity to listen to what people with dementia have
to say for themselves. It's equally important for those who don't
specialise in dementia, but work in other fields such as cancer
care, physiotherapy, audiology etc. – and above all in general
practice – to find out more about the experiences of people who

have dementia. With the rapid rise in the numbers of people affected by dementia, all health and social care professionals are coming into contact with more and more people with dementia in the course of their work.

I think that many readers will find these personal accounts of living with dementia surprisingly upbeat. Taken together, this collection of stories reveals remarkably little self-pity and a great deal of optimism – and, dare I say it, *joie de vivre*.

The book shows that with the right support at the right time, and above all with opportunities to contribute to society in a meaningful way, it is possible to live well with dementia, have a purpose in life and be reasonably contented.

One size does not fit all

In this collection, I have tried to show the enormous diversity encompassed in the term 'people with dementia'. People with dementia may come from any social or ethnic background; they may have left school at 14, or studied for many years and become a doctor or professor. Within the pages of this book you will meet people from all walks of life – a van driver, a chef, a solicitor, a builder, a playwright, IT consultants, factory workers, engineers, nurses, a psychologist, a psychiatrist and two GPs – amongst others. Some developed dementia when they were over 70, others before they were 50.

'The thing is,' says Daphne Wallace, in her contribution to this book ('A psychiatrist with dementia'), 'different people experience dementia differently. We are all different, and even if you have the same pathology as the person sitting next to you, it won't manifest itself in exactly the same way.'

Symptoms vary tremendously, depending on which parts of the brain have been affected. Short-term memory loss is the symptom most often associated with dementia, but this may not be the most troubling aspect of the condition, or the earliest sign that something is amiss.

Jennifer Bute ('A doctor in search of a diagnosis') experienced alarming hallucinations, found she could no longer recognise familiar faces, and could not remember the way to the GP surgery where she had practised for years. Graham Browne ('Grandad – can you go and get a new brain?') lost the ability to manage money, and ran up huge debts on his credit cards. Ross Campbell ('I'll ken it when I see it') started having fits and blackouts – terrifying for someone who earned his living mending people's roofs.

Many of the contributors are aware that their language skills are diminishing, but this can take different forms. Some can still speak and write fluently, but realise that their active vocabulary has shrunk. Some can read but not write. Some cannot read or write, but can talk eloquently. Some who became proficient in English as a second language years ago now revert to their mother tongue. Some can only speak with a huge effort, straining to find the words that are eluding them.

Many skills remain, but again, these vary from one individual to another. Ann Johnson ('Love me for who I am') can deliver lectures and speak on the radio about living with dementia, but can't interpret the symbols that denote male or female toilets. Alex Burton ('Are you sure you've got Alzheimer's?') can research the medication he has been prescribed, and point out to his doctors that the dementia drug he has been given is dangerous for someone like himself because of his heart condition, but he cannot remember a five-digit number. Jennifer Bute can run cognitive stimulation workshops for fellow residents with dementia in the care home where she lives, but is unable to judge whether the smell of burning in her kitchen is real or imaginary.

People with dementia may be healthy in other respects, or they may be subject to fits, strokes, falls or infections, or other physically debilitating episodes. They may have other life-limiting conditions such as cancer or heart disease. People with certain rare types of dementia may experience a very rapid deterioration in their cognitive and physical abilities, leading swiftly to death; most people, however, will live for years,[1] with varying degrees of ability and insight, after their dementia first becomes apparent.

Are these stories representative?

I have tried to show that there is great diversity amongst people who are living with dementia, but I am not suggesting that this collection is statistically representative.

A disproportionate number of contributors to this book are dementia activists and educators: so long as they are physically able to, they travel around locally, nationally and in some cases internationally, speaking at conferences or contributing to discussion forums, raising awareness of what it is like to live with dementia and arguing for improved services and support. Needless to say, the vast majority of people living with dementia are not activists, but are quietly getting on with their life in their own home or in a care home, so in this respect the book is not 'representative'.

A significant number of the contributors developed dementia at a relatively young age: between the ages of 49 and 65. Anyone who develops dementia before they are 65 is categorised as having 'young onset' dementia, also known as 'early onset' dementia. Latest estimates suggest that there are about 42,000 people in the UK with young onset dementia.[2] (We cannot be sure of the figure, as dementia amongst younger people is still not always recognised or diagnosed.) One reason why this group is 'over-represented' in this collection may be because younger people with dementia tend to have more energy and fewer physical disabilities and comorbidities than those who are already old before dementia manifests itself. They may also be more articulate and assertive (perhaps because of the types of dementia that tend to affect people earlier; perhaps because of cultural reasons, as part of the 'baby-boomer' generation.) It is certainly the case that many of the more outspoken dementia activists who I have encountered are people who developed dementia at a younger age.

By definition, the following groups of people have not contributed to this book:

- those who have reached an advanced stage in their dementia, and are no longer able to communicate their experiences

- those who are in denial about having dementia, or are very unhappy about it.

Therefore the picture that emerges is of a group of people who are not only extremely articulate, but also incredibly resilient: people who have come to terms with the fact that they are living with dementia, and are, by and large, enjoying life.

So, if these people are not 'typical' of people with dementia, what is the point of this book? What can we learn from these stories?

There is a widespread assumption that all people with dementia have 'gone over to the other side' and can no longer articulate their thoughts and feelings or play any role either in their own care or in society at large. Of course, we know that dementia of any kind is a progressive condition, and that many people with dementia will eventually lose the ability to communicate in words. Indeed, some people have already progressed far along the path to advanced dementia before they come to the attention of health professionals (or researchers). We cannot get answers, from people who have reached this stage, to questions such as: *What does it feel like to have dementia? How did you first become aware that you were losing some of your mental abilities? What was your experience of diagnosis? What kind of support is helpful for you?* and so forth.

But dementia does not happen overnight. It is almost always a gradual process, and people who have a diagnosis of dementia but have not progressed to an advanced stage have much to teach us.

Why is this book necessary?

It is estimated that there are now 850,000 people in the UK who have dementia (whether formally diagnosed or not); this number could rise to over a million by 2025, and to over 2 million by 2051, if current trends continue.[3] In the not-too-distant future, there will not be one family in the country that is unaffected in one way or another. So the more we know about dementia the better.

There are already thousands of scholarly books and research reports about dementia, and an increasing number of books, articles and media stories aimed at the general public, but we still very rarely hear the actual words of people with dementia themselves. With some notable exceptions,[4] in those instances where people with dementia are directly quoted, it is usually in short snippets, or in disembodied, anonymised case studies. We rarely get to hear the whole story, about the whole person, who has, amongst other things in their life, a diagnosis of dementia. We rarely get to hear what someone with dementia has to say about the care and treatment they have received from the 'experts': the clinicians who diagnose them and the people who plan and deliver dementia services.

Too many scholarly conferences about dementia, and too many planning meetings for local dementia services, still lack any representation from the 'experts by experience' – people who actually have dementia. This is changing, but not fast enough.

Themes that emerge from this collection

People who have dementia are all unique individuals, just like people who don't have dementia. But there are certain common threads running through the stories in this book.

Delay in getting a diagnosis

One of the recurring themes is the difficulty of getting a diagnosis, especially for those who develop dementia early or who retain strong skills in certain areas, which may disguise the deficits that are developing.

Lorna Moore ('Who's afraid of the flying bombs?'), a pioneering computer scientist, scored so highly on the MMSE[5] (5) that the first consultant she saw did not recognise the clear signs of early dementia that had so worried her and her family.

'We had to drag the diagnosis out of them,' says Ross Campbell. 'My wife had actually got to drag it out of them. My wife says, "Give him his diagnosis. He's big enough and strong enough to take it. Just tell him. And give me it in writing." And she got it in writing.'

Lack of information and follow-up

Astonishingly, even in this day and age, people who receive a diagnosis of dementia do not automatically receive any information about the condition, let alone any follow-up.

'Altogether, it took about six months to get the diagnosis,' says Graham Browne. 'The only down point – which I have since found out most people come up against – is the fact that although you are told the diagnosis, you are not given any information about it.'

After Alex Burton was given his diagnosis, the consultant simply handed him a prescription. 'I was devastated. I walked out of there. I was on my own. Nobody came with me. There was no follow-up, no "We'll see you in six months' time". It was just, "Here's a prescription." I just stared at it. I didn't know anything about dementia or Alzheimer's at that stage. Not a thing.'

Problems with comorbidities

Another common problem is the lack of coordinated care and treatment when someone has more than one long-term condition.

Medication prescribed to Brian Hennell ('A double diagnosis') by his cancer specialist greatly exacerbated his dementia symptoms, apparently extending his lifespan while ruining his quality of life.

Family support – or facing dementia alone

Many of the contributors acknowledge the support of partners or relatives, which has helped them to keep going in the face of many challenges.

'I don't know what I would have done without my wife,' says Ross Campbell. 'She's a star. And my daughter – she's a star too! They would never ever say it was a burden on them, but I can see now that it must have been terrible for them. It was three year before they got the medication balanced. I was a human guinea pig. It must have been three year of hell.'

But what of those people with dementia who do not have a partner or relative to rely on? Some people are widowed or divorced; some never got married in the first place; some have no children. More than one contributor found that their partner was unable or unwilling to take on the role of carer, and their marriage came to an end, leaving the individual to face the future on their own.

Fear and dread

Several of the contributors to this book have themselves cared for someone with dementia – usually a parent or parent-in-law. Some have worked in the field of mental health or dementia care. Alex Lindsay ('You keep-a-knockin' but you can't come in') vividly describes the shocking way people with dementia were treated in the old asylums where he worked as a young mental health nurse. He also saw his father, who had Alzheimer's, die 'in a painful and undignified manner'. 'Lazarus' ('Deciding to resist') cared for his parents-in-law, who both had dementia. On the whole, the contributors are under no illusions as to what may lie in store for them.

Although most of the contributors are determined to be as positive as possible, and do not dwell on their hardships, they are also very honest, and from time to time we get glimpses of the anguish and the fear that sometimes besets them.

'What is it like living alone?' says Alex Burton. 'It's an actual bleakness that stares at me. There was a little bit of numbness in the early stages. I get periods, as I'm sure most people with dementia do, of being frightened. It's very scary.'

'Please try and understand the sheer distress and terror I live in every day with my Alzheimer's,' says Ann Johnson. 'I have dark moments.'

None of the contributors expresses any fear of death. But there is fear of the deterioration which may precede death.

Carol Cronk ('Riding the rollercoaster') writes: 'My internal trauma at my diagnosis was highlighted in such fear and dread because of the experience I had lived through with my father during his battles and struggles with Alzheimer's and vascular dementia. My immediate devastating feelings were not of dying but having to live in one of those "dementia homes".'

Rebirth

Many of the contributors have lived with dementia for ten or more years, but are still living an active life. In several cases, there has been a similar trajectory: first inklings that something is not quite right, a period of denial, a protracted period of assessment leading eventually to a diagnosis; almost overwhelming feelings of fear and despair, sometimes leading to suicidal thoughts; a gradual coming to terms with the situation, and then almost a sense of rebirth as the person finally accepts the condition and finds a renewed purpose in life.

More than one of the contributors actually says they enjoy their life *more* now that they have dementia than they did before, as dementia can bring about a sense of liberation from the petty constraints of everyday life, or in some cases a heightened intensity of feeling. Mary Tall ('Something better') celebrates the fact that she is now enjoying sex with her husband more than ever before, while Jennifer Bute regards her dementia as a 'glorious opportunity'.

'I can't believe you've got dementia'

One of the things that contributors to this book find most infuriating is when other people refuse to believe that they have dementia.

'It is very difficult when people say I do not look like I have dementia,' says Ann Johnson, 'and they are very surprised they can communicate with me. My problems are a bit difficult to explain because people cannot *see* them. You could have a conversation with me and not realise anything is wrong.'

'When people say, "I can't believe you've got dementia,"' says Daphne Wallace, 'that is almost denigrating really, because I'm a professional. I spent a lot of my professional life diagnosing dementia. I should know if I can't do things that I used to be able to do.'

Jennifer Bute is similarly indignant. 'When people say to me that they can't believe I have dementia, I find it very hurtful.'

Unfortunately, it is sometimes medically trained professionals who refuse to believe what their patients tell them. It took Jennifer Bute five years to get an accurate diagnosis, because the specialists who assessed her simply did not believe that this highly intelligent, still competent GP could possibly have dementia, despite her detailed descriptions of very severe symptoms.

Other contributors who had already had their dementia diagnosis confirmed were not believed by doctors they came into contact with later.

Edward McLaughlin ('The doors of perception') went to A & E with a suspected stroke and told the doctor on duty that he has Alzheimer's: '"Ah," he says, "Right. Count from 20 backwards." Which I did. "You don't have Alzheimer's!"'

What do these examples tell us? They tell us that the stereotype of a person with dementia as someone who is living in a twilight world, totally helpless, unable to think rationally or to communicate with others, is still pervasive, not just in society at large but also within the medical profession: we all find it hard to believe that someone who is intelligent, articulate and assertive could possibly have dementia.

So long as we automatically equate 'person with dementia' with 'tragic lost soul', we do a disservice both to the people with dementia who (like the contributors to this book) still have much to say and much to offer, and to those people who have reached a more advanced stage of dementia, who will still benefit from our love and compassion, and our company, if we have not written them off as 'beyond our reach'.

What kind of support do people with dementia value?

The people with dementia who have contributed to this book make it very clear that they appreciate being treated with respect, listened to, believed and included – both socially, and in terms of discussions about their care and treatment. They don't like being patronised, ignored or excluded. This is hardly surprising.

Learning to live with dementia, accept the limitations it imposes, and welcome the new opportunities it may bring, does not happen by accident. Many of the contributors, as we have seen, are lovingly supported by partners or other family members, and many pay tribute to good local services that have helped them. A lot of them say they have benefited from certain drug treatments, which appear to have had a marked effect on their cognitive functioning. Some say they greatly enjoy activities such as dementia cafés and Singing for the Brain,[6] while others would rather not socialise with other people with dementia, especially if dementia is the only thing they have in common, or there is a very wide age gap.

People with dementia benefit from an approach that makes the most of their remaining strengths and abilities, rather than focusing on what has been lost. Significantly, a high proportion of the contributors are involved in mutual support groups where they get together with other people with dementia, mentor those who have recently been diagnosed, go out and about raising awareness in the community, campaign for improved services (and plot the overthrow of the existing order!) The examples in this book strongly indicate that feeling valued and appreciated, staying connected socially and being involved in purposeful activity help to create a sensation of wellbeing and may help to delay further cognitive decline.

Above all, people with dementia want to be treated as individuals and supported in a way that suits their own personality, background, cultural affinities and interests.

Methodology

How did I go about compiling this anthology?

Finding the contributors

First of all I had to get in touch with potential contributors. I was looking for people who were aware that they had dementia and were able and willing to describe their experiences. (Ultimately, one or two slipped through the net who don't seem to be convinced that they have dementia, but the vast majority are fully aware of their condition.)

Almost the first thing I did was to book a trip to Glasgow to attend a meeting of the Scottish Dementia Working Group.[7] I secured three contributions from this source: Alex Lindsay, Ross Campbell and Edward McLaughlin.

I attend many conferences and other events where people with dementia speak about their experiences. I got into the habit of accosting these speakers and inviting them to contribute to the book. This is how I came by the contributions from Jennifer Bute, Carol Cronk, Brian Hennell, Ann Johnson, 'Lazarus' and Daphne Wallace, and, indirectly, Sylvia Kahn, Peter Mittler and Mary Tall.

I also contacted all the dementia professionals I have met over the years, and pestered friends and colleagues in many different organisations. I am greatly indebted to everyone who helped to put me in touch with potential contributors. Through these contacts, I collected contributions from Graham Browne, Alex Burton, Dizi Conti, Romanina Contucci, Halide Eames, Midge Flint, Clarice Hall, Abdul Haque, Pearl Hylton, Lorna Moore and Rukiya Mukadam.

Gathering the stories

How did I gather the stories? I knew that some people with dementia would be able to write their own account, but that many would not be able to write a full-length chapter about their experiences without help. I suggested that some people might like to collaborate with a partner or trusted friend in order to compose their account, and I also offered to interview people if they preferred. As it turned out, two-thirds of the chapters are based on interviews, which I conducted either in person or by phone, and only a few were written by the contributor without help from anyone else.

Editing the contributions for publication

Some of the written contributions arrived fully formed, requiring only a minimum of editorial input; others needed to be shortened and reorganised to some extent, in order to reveal the author's thoughts and feelings more vividly. One contribution was sent as a series of emails, each describing a particular episode – sometimes re-telling the same episode in a slightly different way – and I enjoyed weaving the material into a continuous narrative.

In those cases where I had interviewed the contributor, the first task was to transcribe the whole conversation. After that, I worked through the transcript carefully, creating a first-person account from the exact words spoken by the contributor – as if the person concerned was talking directly to the reader.

In every case, my aim has been to reproduce as faithfully as possible the person's natural way of speaking, so that it sounds like 'their voice'. I go into more detail about some of the technical challenges, particularly where the contributor speaks a non-standard variety of English, in Appendix I on page 283.

How carers have contributed

I have dealt directly with about half of the contributors to this book. In all the other cases, I have received a great deal of help from family carers, many of whom went out of their way to arrange for me to meet and interview the person with dementia.

I made it clear to everyone involved that as I had already produced a whole book of carers' accounts of looking after someone with dementia,[8] this time round I was not inviting carers to tell me about their experiences or to give their version of events. I was so determined not to let carers take over that I almost painted myself into a corner in this respect. Sometimes family members who I met were able to give me relevant information, for example about the process of diagnosis, which the person with dementia could no longer recall. Where possible I have added in this extra information in the short introduction to each chapter.

In two cases, family carers (spouses) sent me a written account on behalf of their partner. Of course I am aware that in this situation there is a risk that the carer may be tempted to 'correct' or 'improve' their partner's account, thus interfering with its authenticity. I emphasised to family members who wanted to help that what I wanted was the person with dementia's own version of events, not the carer's version, and after that I decided to trust them. After all, where someone is unable to write their own account without help, because of cognitive decline, it seems better to give them the chance to tell their story with someone else's help rather than to deny them the opportunity altogether. And in any case, what these family carers were doing was not so very different to what I myself was doing with all the contributions that are based on interviews.

Getting approval from the contributors

In all cases, of course, I have checked back with the contributor to get their approval for the edited text, either by sending them a copy or by going back to see them and reading it aloud to them. Some asked for one or two minor corrections, but all the contributors have confirmed that they are happy with the version I produced. In some cases, it was clear that the contributor was thrilled to hear their words and their experiences reflected back to them. 'I am very, very happy,' said Pearl Hylton ('Anybody been kind to me, it stays with me') when I asked if she was happy with her chapter, while Midge Flint ('I never get tired of dancing') kept exclaiming, 'And it's all absolutely true!' when I read back to her the anecdotes she had told me a few weeks before.

I should point out that it has taken me much longer than I expected to compile this anthology, and some of the chapters were actually completed about three years before I sent the manuscript off to the publisher. Things may have changed in the meantime. Each chapter should be seen as a snapshot of how things were for the contributor at the time their chapter was written.

Seeing the whole person

I did not intend this book to be a collection of reminiscences about the past by people who happen to have dementia. The whole point of the book was to hear what people with dementia have to say about living with dementia.

However, I did not want to present people with dementia simply as a collection of symptoms, or as problems to be solved. I always asked people to tell me something about their past, so that we could see each person as an individual in their own right, someone who had had a life of their own before the onset of dementia.

As work on the book progressed, I found that I had collected contributions from a large number of people with young onset dementia, many of whom were dedicated dementia activists. I realised that I needed to seek out a much wider range of people, including those who don't see themselves as activists, and those who had developed dementia in old age. I discovered that this second wave of contributions tend to be rather different – closer to oral history or reminiscence, and without so much to say about being 'a person with dementia'.

With some exceptions, the older contributors tend to be at a more advanced stage in their dementia, and to have less recall of recent events. Although almost all of them are aware that they have dementia, some of them have forgotten about the process of assessment and diagnosis, so cannot shed any light on that for the reader.

Midge Flint is a good example: 'Nowadays, I know that I've got dementia,' she says, 'but I can't think – I can't remember how that's happened, in all honesty.'

Similarly, Lorna Moore says, 'A few years ago, I noticed that my memory was getting bad. Other people noticed as well. I can remember having a memory test, but I can't remember how it happened.'

However, what Midge Flint and Lorna Moore and many of the others can do is to tell us in vivid language about their childhood and youth. And so, despite my original intentions, there are passages in this book that probably are best described as reminiscence; and in fact I think they make an important contribution to social and cultural history.

Many of today's generation of elders were children during the Second World War and it is not surprising that this features in several of the chapters. We hear from Dizi Conti ('Liberation'), Lorna Moore and Midge Flint, who were all born in London, about the devastation wreaked by the bombs, and about their experiences of evacuation. Romanina Contucci ('I'm gone older. Everything change') has never forgotten the hunger she endured in war-torn Italy, and her mother's inconsolable weeping for the son who was killed in action. Peter Mittler ('Journey into Alzheimerland') describes his escape from Nazi-occupied Vienna, and how he had to adapt to life in England, where Jewish refugees like his father were routinely interned as 'enemy aliens'.

Others tell us about some of the great migrations of the 20th century, fleeing poverty or unemployment, or war and genocide, or simply taking a step into the unknown, in search of a better life.

What relevance does this social history angle have to the central theme of this book? Apart from its intrinsic interest, it reminds us all that every person with dementia, who may or may not remember all the details of their own life, has a wealth of experiences that the professionals who support them may not be aware of. The teenage girls who – like many of the female contributors – strove so hard to acquire a sound scientific education, at a time or in a place when girls were not expected or encouraged to study sciences, may score so highly in later life on some aspects of the MMSE test that the clinician is unable to recognise or acknowledge the severity of the cognitive decline that is taking place. The experience of living through the Blitz as an infant, or coming to England from another country at an impressionable age, will remain at the core of a person's identity. Knowing about dramatic or traumatic events early in a person's life may help to explain behaviour (possibly the sort of behaviour politely referred to as 'challenging') that is otherwise inexplicable.

At the heart of person-centred care is the commitment to finding out as much about the person with dementia as they are willing to share, through conversations, life story work and reminiscence sessions, as well as from family carers. We cannot deliver person-centred care if we do not know who that person is.

The importance of narrative

Throughout my work on this book I have been encouraged and inspired by the work of Trisha Greenhalgh and Brian Hurwitz,[9] and the principles of narrative based medicine, which I explain in a little more detail in Appendix II on page 287.

One of the tenets of narrative based medicine is that the very act of telling the story of your illness to someone who listens attentively is therapeutic in itself. This seems to be borne out by comments made by the people who have contributed to this anthology. 'I have found writing this piece helpful,' says Sylvia Kahn at the end of her chapter for this book ('Down with dementia!'), 'because it makes me feel more of a person.' Another contributor has told me in an email that 'participating in this project has been an empowering experience beyond all expectations.'

For people with dementia in particular, who may fear that their very identity is disappearing along with their cognitive abilities, the importance of being listened to, and having their experiences validated, cannot be overstated. Feeling valued as a person – someone who still has something to say and a contribution to make – is immensely important for maintaining wellbeing and a sense of purpose in life.

One of the benefits of creating an anthology of this kind is that the therapeutic effect can be multiplied by sharing individuals' stories with a wider audience. Other people with dementia (as well as family carers) will recognise elements of their own experience in the accounts contained in this book. Hearing or reading about others who have faced similar difficulties can help people feel less isolated, and a little less 'mad'. There is still so much stigma attached to dementia that simply finding out about others who are 'in the same boat' can have a transformative effect. '*I'm not the only one! It's not my fault. Life has changed, but life goes on.*'

Greenhalgh and Hurwitz's anthology, *Narrative Based Medicine*, published in 1998, does not mention dementia. But the life story work[10] that goes on in many settings for people with dementia could be seen as one application of narrative based medicine.

Dementia and minority communities

Some writers also talk of the 'biographical approach' to health and social care (which is clearly related to the concept of narrative based medicine), and aver its particular importance for the holistic support of people with dementia from minority groups.

A SCIE report on *Black and minority ethnic people with dementia and their access to support and services* states that, 'The benefits of biographical and life-story approaches for people with dementia are increasingly recognised' and goes on to say: 'This involves practitioners taking account of people's sense of individual identity, and the factors that contribute to it, and considering how these may be influenced by their ethnic and cultural identity.'[11]

In recent years there have been a number of reports, the most comprehensive of which is the All Party Parliamentary Group on Dementia's 2013 report, *Dementia does not discriminate*, that consider the experiences of people with dementia from black, Asian and minority ethnic (BAME) communities.[12]

All these reports confirm that in the UK people with dementia and their families from BAME communities are under-represented amongst service users, compared to people in the majority population. In other words, not enough people from these communities are getting access to the clinical and support services that can make all the difference in the quality of life experienced by people with dementia.

The reasons for this are complex, and include:

- A generally low level of awareness and understanding about dementia within many of these minority communities.

- A correspondingly high level of shame and stigma associated with dementia.

- The lack of culturally sensitive and appropriate services.

In many cases a combination of these reasons leads to families not accessing services until the person has reached quite an advanced stage of dementia, at a point when family carers have broken down under the strain of coping without support.

In some communities, the early symptoms of dementia may be seen as a 'normal' part of ageing. However, when the condition progresses to the point where it can no longer be ignored, it may be perceived as a punishment for past sins, or possibly as the result of a curse or spell inflicted by a spiteful neighbour or relative.

Rukiya Mukadam ('Time to break the taboo'), an Indian GP now living in London, comments on the tendency for Asian families to hush up the fact that one of their relatives has dementia. 'Families feel embarrassed for them to come out in public. So they cover it up. They say, "Oh, he's not feeling well today." Even my own uncle, when he had Alzheimer's, every time I went to visit him, his sons, his wife, they would say, 'Oh no, he has forgotten today only. He's not feeling too well … Don't worry. He remembers everybody." Which was not true.'

Rukiya Mukadam herself is afraid of the discrimination she may face within her own community. 'When I got my diagnosis, I felt very upset…because I imagined myself in few years' time, people calling me "loony". That upset me quite a bit. Because I don't want people looking at me and thinking, "She is mental." I don't want that. I'd rather be dead than be like that.' She says she will be 'very happy' if these taboos can be challenged and misconceptions corrected.

The person-centred approach to the care of people with dementia to which we all aspire requires that we listen carefully to what people with dementia from different communities can tell us about their lives. Elders from minority ethnic communities were in most cases born in another country and may have experienced undisguised hostility and prejudice when they arrived here. Pearl Hylton recalls: 'Some places I go to, to get a room, it would say, "No Irish, no Blacks".' This may have left some people with a feeling of mistrust and a determination to be self-sufficient, which affects their willingness to ask for help from health and social care services when it is needed.

In addition to racism, people who have migrated from one country or continent to another are also likely to have experienced the strains of being separated from beloved family members. Halide Eames ('I still remember') had to leave her daughter behind when she left Cyprus for England. Abdul Haque ('One place to another') had lived and worked in England for nearly 30 years, returning to Bangladesh as often as he could, before he was able to bring his wife and children to live here with him. For those who have fled civil war or genocide, the family separation may have been permanent. Peter Mittler, now in his 80s, points out that whereas he was lucky enough to be reunited with his parents, nine out of ten of the children who came to England, as he did, on the Kindertransport[13] never saw their parents again. Those children are now old men and women, and some of them have dementia.

All of these experiences affect people on a very deep level, and 50, 60 or 70 years later, when more recent episodes have been forgotten, long-suppressed painful thoughts and feelings may resurface.

Publicising the stories of people with dementia from minority communities is an essential tool in the process of educating us all, whatever background we come from, about the realities of living with dementia and about the range of interventions which may be required to ensure that everyone gets the services they need.

Several of the contributors attend the Healthy Living Club in Stockwell, South London, a service where the mix of people with dementia, carers, staff and volunteers fully reflects the multi-ethnic, diverse nature of the local community. Clarice Hall, in her contribution for this book ('They deal with everybody as a individual'), praises the inclusive nature of the service, where everyone whatever their level of ability or disability, and regardless of their role in the club, is equally valued. 'We all cope together,' says Clarice, 'and we look after one another, you understand, which is good – good relationship there. And when you get to the centre, you don't look down on anybody. Everybody is in the same category. Everybody is equal, you understand. It's lovely going there. I look forward to it.'[14]

In other situations, a service tailored to meet the needs of one particular minority ethnic group is more appropriate, particularly if most of the service users do not speak fluent English. One long-established service of this kind is the Meri Yaadein project, which works with South Asian communities in Bradford. Meri Yaadein combines outreach work – to increase recognition and understanding of dementia within Asian communities – with practical and emotional support for individuals and families.[15]

In all cases, bilingual or multilingual staff and volunteers, who are familiar with the cultural needs and reference points of service users, are invaluable.

Other projects supporting people with dementia and their families from different BAME groups now exist in different parts of the country, and there are pockets of excellent practice in terms of culturally appropriate services across the UK. Funding for these projects, however, is often precarious. There is still a long way to go before we will be able to say with confidence that people with dementia from all communities have equal access to care and support that fully meets their needs.

I was able to find contributors for this book from a number of different BAME backgrounds including Jamaican, Indian, Bangladeshi, Turkish Cypriot, Italian and central-European Jewish. Of course many BAME communities are not represented within the pages of this book, and much more work needs to be done to find out about the lives and experiences of people with dementia from all the many different communities that make up the population of the UK.

The 'biographical approach' has also been identified as vitally important for the successful support of older people with significant care needs within the LGBT (lesbian, gay, bisexual and transgender) communities. 'We cannot begin to understand and thereby care for and support individual older people in the here-and-now without being able to understand the life that they have lived and their fears for the future. Achieving such an understanding requires the sort of life course or biographical approach advocated [in this volume],' says Stephen Pugh, in his contribution to *Lesbian, Gay, Bisexual and Transgender Ageing: Biographical Approaches for Inclusive Care and Support*.[16] This is a book I recommend to those who genuinely want to provide inclusive services.

I am sorry that I was not able to secure any contributions for this book from LGBT people with dementia. However, just because they are not visible in this book does not mean they don't exist. In my previous book *Telling Tales About Dementia: Experiences of Caring*[17] I included contributions by a number of lesbians and gay men who had cared for a partner or gay friend with dementia. These issues are discussed further in Appendix III on page 289.

The wider context

The National Dementia Strategy for England was published in 2009, followed by strategies or national plans for Scotland, Wales and Northern Ireland. Since then there have been a plethora of initiatives, both local and national, and some notable achievements. The National Dementia Strategy was followed in 2012 by the *Prime Minister's Challenge on Dementia*, updated in February 2015 as the *Prime Minister's Challenge on Dementia 2020*,[18] which reviews progress to date and sets out ambitious goals to be achieved by 2020.

Public and professional awareness of dementia has certainly increased; people presenting at their GP surgery with possible symptoms of dementia are more likely to have their concerns taken seriously and to get a diagnosis. Thousands more practitioners of all kinds who come into contact with people with dementia have received appropriate training. Much good work has been done to make acute hospitals safer places for people with dementia; good work has also taken place to reduce unnecessary hospital admissions; some care homes fully understand the concept of person-centred care and offer a wonderful environment for people with dementia who need residential care. There are many examples in this book of imaginative local services that make a huge difference to the quality of life for those people with dementia who are lucky enough to access them. Sensitive and high quality end of life care is now available to more people with dementia. Some family carers benefit from information, education and support that was not widely available even a few years ago.

Despite all of this, the fact remains that both diagnosis rates and post-diagnostic support for people with dementia and their family carers remain extremely patchy across the UK. It all depends where you live, and, to a large extent, on which professionals you encounter. Some people receive excellent support from highly trained and committed professionals; others receive hardly any support at all, from practitioners who simply don't understand their needs.

Unfortunately, the National Dementia Strategy was published just as the full implications of the global financial crash became apparent. Since then there have been draconian cuts in funding for public services, in particular for social care services provided by local authorities. Because of the false divide between health services (free at the point of use) and social care services (means tested), and the perverse fact that 'care' needs are distinguished from 'health' needs, even though they derive from a medical condition, people with dementia and their family carers have been particularly hard hit by these cuts.

Two-thirds of people with dementia in the UK live in their own homes in the community,[19] supported by family members and/or paid careworkers. The Alzheimer's Society's most recent *Dementia UK* report[20] estimated the value of unpaid care for people with dementia (that is, the care provided for free by friends and family) at 44 per cent of the total cost – a whopping £11 billion in 2013. Social care accounted for 39 per cent (£10 billion) and healthcare only 16 per cent (£4 billion). It is clear that without the unpaid support from family carers, the whole system would collapse.

It is current policy to try to keep frail elderly people in their own homes for as long as possible, to reduce unnecessary hospital admissions, and to delay the need for residential care. Health and social care services are being asked to work more closely together in order to achieve these goals, but without investing more in community health services and social care, this seems like an impossible dream. It is hard to see how two 15-minute visits per day from a careworker is going to keep a frail elderly person with dementia in the best of health and enable them to maintain their independence.[21] (Not to mention the scandal of low pay for the workforce who are looking after some of the most vulnerable people in our society.)

Where do we go from here?

One of the messages that I hope readers will take from this book is that people with dementia are *experts by experience*, whose voices must be heard if we are serious about providing truly person-centred, inclusive and effective services and support.

A very encouraging development in recent years is the increasing number of campaigning and mutual support groups led by people with dementia. The Scottish Dementia Working Group, which was established in 2002, was the first group of this kind in the UK. Other peer support groups for people with dementia are now flourishing in many parts of the country. Many of these groups have received support from the Dementia Engagement and Empowerment Project (DEEP).[22] DEEP aims to help build the capacity of existing groups, support the emergence of new groups and help develop a network linking these groups together. At the time of writing, the DEEP website lists 39 peer support groups and projects in Britain and Ireland.[23]

One of these groups is Lancashire Dementia Voices,[24] which was set up by contributor Alex Burton, who had previous experience of patient and carer involvement in cancer care and was astonished to find, when he was diagnosed with dementia, that it had not occurred to his local Trust to involve people with dementia and their carers in the planning and delivery of dementia services.

Peter Mittler argues, in his chapter for this book (and elsewhere), that the dementia movement needs to link up with the disability movement nationally and internationally, and should make use of the *United Nations Convention on the Rights of Persons with Disabilities*,[25] which the UK government ratified in 2009, in order to demand a better deal for people with dementia. The slogan *Nothing about us without us*, which was popularised by the disability rights campaigns of the 1990s, was taken up by the UK coalition government in their 2010 statement *Equity and excellence: liberating the NHS*[26] where, interestingly, it morphed into *No decision about me without me*. Whether it is 'me' or 'us', it is now government policy, but I think many people with dementia feel there is still a long way to go before their experience lives up to the slogan.

Referring to the UN Convention on the Rights of Persons with Disabilities, Peter Mittler concludes his chapter with the words:

> The Convention marks a watershed in the slow and painful struggle of people with disabilities to be 'allowed' to speak for themselves rather than having to listen to others speaking for them. A powerful consortium of international Disabled Persons' Organisations, committed to the principle of *Nothing about us without us*, took a full and equal part in the detailed negotiations that created the Convention, and remain active in working for its implementation at national and local level. The time is now ripe for people living with dementia and their supporters to become part of this movement, so that '*us*' can finally become '*all of us*'.

Chapter 1

Grandad – can you go and get a new brain?

GRAHAM BROWNE

Graham Browne *was one of the first people to respond to my invitation to people with dementia to write an account of their experiences. He lives in East Sussex and is active in the Brighton Hope group of people with dementia.*[27] *Members of the group regularly speak to health and social care staff and students, raising awareness about the lived experience of*

dementia. He is an ambassador for Alzheimer's Society and was part of the local organising committee for the Alzheimer's Disease International Conference 2012, which was held in London. LW

My journey – no, our journey, because the family live with it as well – into the world of 'living with dementia', began back in 2005, probably around August time, when I walked into a lamp post. I never done any external damage, but I began seeing split level out of my right eye, having to lean my head to the left to get a good focus.

So off it was to the eye hospital, and sure enough I had torn two muscles which needed to be stitched back, but also at the same time, after looking into my eye, the doctor asked if she could get someone else to check. Well, the second doctor asked us to go and see him after we had finished. He turned out to be a neurologist, and when we walked in and sat down, the first question to Debbie, my wife, was, 'And what else do you think is wrong with Graham?' Well, we didn't know what to say, and I saw my wife well up and cry. (I can't handle that side.)

I used to work as a delivery driver. Christmas Eve 2005, just before my 49th birthday, was the last time I ever went to work. After that, my doctor signed me off every two weeks with a sick note saying, 'Neurological investigation'. After several weeks the company I was working for began to ask questions, and after about two months I was sent to our neurological centre for a week and given tests to do – reflex tests, the normal Alzheimer's tests – but I could do them. Even at this time, I did not realise that something was terribly wrong. Then, after seeing eight consultants and plenty of head-scratching, I saw another one who, after spending time talking to us and doing tests, announced that I had a dementia: it was called Pick's disease, or as he called it, 'frontotemporal lobar degeneration disease'.

At long last we had a name. I came out of the hospital, like I had a weight off my back. We could go back and give people a name – I was not lying or cheating anybody. Waiting for the diagnosis had put a strain on us. While you're waiting, you don't know what's going on. You get the company phoning or sending letters, and you have to say, 'Sorry, it's not me, it's the doctor.' You still feel that you can do the job – but obviously, they don't let you go and do it, especially driving. My consultant was absolutely honest. He said, 'If you were on the road, I wouldn't want to be on the road at the same time.'

Altogether, it took about six months to get the diagnosis. The only down point – which I have since found out most people come up against – is the fact that although you are told the diagnosis, you are not given any information about it, so my wife who works at the local hospital went to work the next day and had to look it up on the computer.

You then have to tell the children: the two daughters went into denial, and the son went on the web page and knows more than I do. I have always said I don't want to know, because I will know in myself when changes start.

So my journey began. I sat and moped for about a week, feeling sorry for myself, and Debbie gave up work, but after two months she went back as she realised I could do things OK. I can still cook and go shopping.

Then I was invited to join a day club for two days a week, and after about six months I was asked if I would be prepared to talk at Brighton University. Immediately I said yes, and then I thought, 'I don't do speeches, or even get up and dance,' so I believe that my dementia gave me a new life, because when I went and talked, there was 200 people – social workers, commissioners, doctors, professors, students – but it went really well.

Then someone from the Alzheimer's Society visited the day club and asked if I would be an Ambassador for the Society, and I must say they have changed my life. I'm not sitting around. I have things to do, talks to give, and I meet the most wonderful people in the world – those living with a dementia, and those who care for them.

One of the battles we had on our hands was banks and building societies, because one of the traits with Pick's is spending, which I could do quite easily. I topped all four cards out. When you get in touch they do not recognise dementia as an illness. In the end we got through to them – except one major bank, which phoned and told Debbie, 'When he dies, you will still have to pay.'

That was the first hurdle. The second was with the local social care services. At the time, I collected erotica – figurines, pictures etc.. – and they were on display in the house. Well, we were having a fight to be able to pay my wife to look after me. In the end the top man came out to see us. Now, bearing in mind what is on view, he asked if we could get a sixteen- or seventeen-year-old to come and sit with me – and that is with everything on display! (I don't think so.)

He then said that if Debbie moved out or divorced me, she could be paid to care for me, but not whilst we lived under the same roof. Anyway, two weeks later I done the talk at Brighton University, and I spoke about this battle we were having with social services, and then Debs spoke about it, and when it come to lunchtime, she never got any lunch, because this man took her outside and sat her down and was talking to her, and three days later we got a letter through saying we had been granted what we wanted – and my wife is now paid to care for me.

I have a very close relationship with my oldest grandson, Kyle. I was at home when he was born, and I went down the hospital, and I just held him. I had emotions within me but I didn't want to let them out.

He's my medicine. We are very close. If he gets told off, I hate it! It's funny, because he knows when I have a bad day, and he's a completely different boy – he's as careful as he can be. And then, other days we get into trouble with each other. It's like being a big kid again with him.

Graham Browne with grandsons
(L to R) Logan, Saul, Kyle.

I got a new phone the other week, and I thought, 'I must do it myself, get it sorted out, know what I'm doing.' And he's five, and he knows how to do it all. And he was going, 'Grandad, I'll do it.' And I'm going, 'No, leave me.' And in the end, I threw the box on the floor in a temper, and just said, 'Look, go away and let me get on with it.' And he went upstairs crying. And his Nan went up after him, and said, 'Look, you understand that Grandad's brain's not really well, and there's times when he gets frustrated.' Then I was in the kitchen and he come down, and he stood on a stool and he went, 'Grandad, I'm ever so sorry, but can you go and get a new brain?'

Your friends, or so-called friends – workmates etc. – are unbelievable. I don't know if it is the thought of the word 'disease', but they disappear. Yet I am still the same person who went for drinks and a laugh, just a couple of weeks earlier. But they just disappear, I believe because of ignorance. Out of 40 people who attended a barbeque we put on to tell them what was wrong, only four remain in touch and we still meet for drinks.

That is why I am aiming to get into schools and give talks, so families and friends have a better future. I am a member of the Hope group, which meets in Brighton and is funded by West Sussex County Council. We're all younger people with dementia, and some carers. We go out to universities and training events and talk about our experiences. We got an award from the council last year for the work we do.

So I now not only represent the Alzheimer's Society as an ambassador but various other dementia organisations as well. It's great, because more and more people are beginning to take it on board now. I have had the privilege to travel to parts of Britain I never imagined, and even to Canada. I just absolutely love it. Dementia has given me something to fight for, for other people.

Yes, I have a dementia, but I still feel like the same person I was ten years ago, and every day when I look into the mirror and see the same me, there is no visual sign I have dementia.

Look dementia in the face, grab it by the horns, and take each day as it comes. You will be surprised what can be achieved.

Chapter 2

Are you sure you've got Alzheimer's?

ALEX BURTON

Alex Burton *is a former naval engineer. He cared for his wife, who had cancer, and through this experience became convinced of the value of carer and service user involvement in health and social care. Since his diagnosis of Alzheimer's disease he has campaigned for people with dementia to be involved in the design and delivery of dementia services.*

After much hard work, Lancashire Dementia Voices[28] came into being in 2014. I interviewed Alex by telephone. LW

It started very subtly. It wasn't loss of keys – it was remembering numbers, such as phone numbers. I couldn't remember what sequence they were in. I come from an engineering background, and since I was 15, I have worked in a highly disciplined area of technology. Technology itself is an exact science. It's not hit and miss. So I started to pick up that something wasn't quite right.

Then I began to get really worried when I found that if I got distracted, I couldn't remember what I had been doing before. Everybody gets distracted – if you're doing something and the front door bell rings, you would answer the door, and then come back and carry on with what you were doing before. The problem that I started to experience was, once I got that distraction, and went to the door, I couldn't remember the previous activity. I'd sit there, thinking, 'What was I supposed to be doing, where was I supposed to be going?' and I'd never get recall. Most people, at some stage, get recall. I didn't. Then I noticed that I was going out to meetings on the wrong day. People would say, 'Yes, Alex, what do you want?' 'It's the meeting.' 'No, that's tomorrow.' Or I'd go at the wrong time. And that's when the alarm bells started to ring.

I went to see my GP. The first time I saw him, he said, 'Well, everybody forgets.' I said, 'But this is different.' At that stage, they weren't prepared to do a mini-mental test or anything. Eventually they made a referral to the memory assessment clinic. It's a long process. From going to see the GP, and getting the first appointment at the memory clinic, it was about eight months.

I had a very intensive memory assessment test, over a whole week, and I scored quite highly, but the bits that I didn't score, were exactly the bits that I'd said, in terms of recall. And I was sent for a scan. That's the only really clinical examination I've had.

After that I was brought back in, and the diagnosis was given to me by the consultant. He just said the tests revealed a shrinkage of the brain, which along with the memory assessment test, led to the conclusion that it was early onset Alzheimer's. Then he handed me a prescription.

I was devastated. I walked out of there. I was on my own. Nobody came with me. There was no follow-up, no 'We'll see you in six months' time'. It was just, 'Here's a prescription.' I just stared at it. I didn't know anything about dementia or Alzheimer's at that stage. Not a thing. Dementia, as far as I was concerned, was people in their 80s and 90s, in care homes, suffering from severe memory loss.

The prescription was for Exelon (rivastigmine).[29] Coincidentally, I had also been diagnosed with a heart condition, and I was worried about any possible interaction with the new drug. I told the doctor at the memory assessment clinic that I needed more information, and he said he had some research papers – very kind of him – and when I looked at this research, it's there in black and white: this drug is not as effective as the world seems to think. As it turns out, the drug only has a very limited time of effectiveness, if it is effective at all. So what are the real true benefits of this drug they want me to take?

Then I went to see the cardiologist, on a routine appointment, and told him about the new prescription, and he said, 'Oh yes, we're going to have to monitor this. Because rivastigmine can actually slow your heart down.'

Obviously, it was a bit shocking. The consultant I had seen was a psychiatric consultant, not a clinical consultant, and he didn't have access to any of my medical records. You can't issue a drug without prior knowledge of a patient's medication! I've brought this up several times. I should not be going to see the cardiac consultant, and then going to see the psychiatric consultant, and then going to my GP, and having to liaise between the three of them!

I've always been very self-sufficient. I joined the navy when I was 15 and spent 11 years in the Fleet Air Arms and qualified as an aviation engineer. They take very young recruits, and teach them to be independent, to think for themselves, even though they're working in a team, and to use initiative at all times. I think my experience in the navy set the scene. The skills and the personal aspects stood me in very good stead for the rest of my life.

I met Dorothy, my late wife, and we got married while I was in the navy. It was really for family life that I left the services. My wife had lived in Lancashire all of her life, and she was whisked down to Cornwall, in isolation in some ways. I spent quite large amounts of time away from her – up to eight months – and my three children were born while I was away.

Then we moved back to Lancashire, to my wife's home town. I applied for several jobs in the electronics industry, and eventually joined a security firm in Blackburn. It took me a while, because although the skills I'd developed in the Royal Navy were transferable to civilian life, it was hard to convince employers that I had those skills – engineering skills, management skills, organisational skills.

My wife Dorothy was diagnosed with cancer in 1998. They had missed the diagnosis up to two years before, on several occasions, because they thought she had arthritis. We found out purely by accident – and that was through persevering. We were visiting my brother, who was in the army, stationed in Cyprus, and she had a fall while we were out in the town. We didn't think anything of it at the time, although she was obviously quite badly bruised, and then she was complaining about pains in her neck and shoulder. When we got back to the UK, she was in so much pain, I short-circuited the system. I went straight to the consultant that had seen her a year or so before, and went to his secretary and she was seen the same day. He scanned her and found out that she had actually broken her neck.

We never really got to the bottom of what type of cancer she had. She went into hospital to have a bone graft, and the bone fragments were sent to histology. That's when we got the bad news. The consultant said, 'That's a metastasis.'[30] They were searching for about six months. She had scans, x-rays, biopsies, but we never really got to the primary site. On her death certificate they put breast cancer, which was very misleading. She was 45 when she was diagnosed. And she lasted almost two years.

Obviously it was extremely upsetting for Dorothy and for me. You get the devastation when you get the news first. But then there was an immediate kick-in from my point of view, to basically run with the thing, rather than go into a corner and have a weep about it.

It's only when the treatment started, the chemotherapy and the radiotherapy, that I started to get quite tense. I'd started a business before Dorothy was diagnosed, and that was still growing. It was a small engineering consultancy, and it involved a lot of travelling down to the south of England. I had to pack that up, a year into her disease, because things were starting to get quite serious by then. It had spread to all the bones in her joints. Her bones were breaking in her back. She had two major operations, trying to find the lymph nodes. I remained upbeat, almost until the end.

She was hospitalised for the last three months, following a collapse. She went into hospital, and I was brought into a side room to see the consultant, who said she had a condition called hypercalcaemia, which is where the calcium in the bones leaks into the bloodstream. It causes delirium and fits. They gave her a drug, and believe it or not, within 24 hours, she was sat up in bed, laughing and joking. Even the children thought, 'This is it, she's been cured.' The day after, she declined dramatically, and I was called in on the Friday by the consultant. The word death was never mentioned. It was just, 'This is extremely serious.' 'How serious?' 'She'll be lucky to last the weekend.' So I made the decision on the Friday to stop in hospital. I sat in the chair all over the weekend – and that went on for seven weeks. I never left the side ward. I slept in the chair. I ate in the chair. In some ways you get caught in a devil and the dark blue sea. 'If I go now, she might just die while I'm away.' She died a week short of we'd been married 30 years. I'd lost a very, very good friend. It takes an awful long time to get over that.

About a year or 18 months after, I wanted to go back to the hospital to do some voluntary work. I was asked to coordinate the very first user involvement project. This is long before the word 'user involvement' was even on people's agenda. We went round the wards and reported back on facilities and services and whether there were any issues. I recruited some volunteers and trained them, and we operated for about a year. The one place I couldn't go to in the hospital was the cancer ward where she died. It was off limits.

During that period, I was in and around the hospital, talking to people all the time, and one of the nurses said to me, 'Have you thought about Macmillan?' I didn't know anything about it. Over the whole two-year period, I wasn't aware of Macmillan Cancer Support. So, it was just a simple telephone call to Macmillan, about getting involved, and I was invited down to London, and I've carried on ever since, working on more and more complex projects, including working with the Gold Standards Framework[31] and speaking at conferences.

Some of us were invited to produce a resource pack for Macmillan – nine carers up and down the country, from different backgrounds, with different stories to tell. We produced that resource, sharing our experience right the way through the journey, right through to death and beyond, the whole lot. And it was a truly inspiring experience. The resource pack is in its fourth edition now. It's called 'Hello, and how are *you*?'[32] It's called that because one of the carers who was involved, said, 'Isn't it strange how when someone goes into hospital, they always ask the patient how they are, and never ask the carer.' So that's how that name came into being. Why don't you ask how *we* are?

And I started to look around, where I live, at 'Where is the carer support?' I know about Carers Direct, and I know about Carers UK, and they're a source of information, but I've always said you cannot expect carers to stop caring to go to places – basically, you have to go to them. So I decided to set up a small self-help support group for carers in cancer[33] in 2008, with a little bit of prime funding from Macmillan.

It was originally set up as a local group, and we set up a website and a telephone line, but within a matter of months we started to get calls from all over the UK. It's people, desperate to talk to somebody, about their experience. They very rarely ask for information. I'll just give you an example. An 80-year-old woman contacted me. She's local to me. She said her husband's dying of cancer. She says, 'I'm not very well, I can't get out, I can't do this and I can't do that.' We have tried to set up a buddying and befriending service but we've never really got the funding in place, but I intervened personally, with this lady, and went out to see her – and the relief on her face just said it all.

Carers who are looking after someone with cancer need better support. They keep saying, 'The information's on the internet.' Well, I'm sorry, we're an ageing population, and you're making an assumption, that everybody over 60 has got access to the internet.

After I got my diagnosis of dementia, I was shocked to discover how behind the times the local dementia services are. I think the most honest statement I've had was one of the corporate managers I met from the trust, and he looked at me and he said, 'Alex, on dementia, we are where cancer was 30 years ago!'

Having done all the research, I went on a fact-finding tour locally. I set up meetings with the Alzheimer's Society, with the memory assessment clinic, with the local mental health trust, with my GP, put all the information together, and was horrified at what I was looking at. I've asked some very awkward questions, at very high places, and caused a little bit of a scurry. Too many people say, 'Yes, you're right Alex.' But I don't want to hear that, I want to hear what you're going to do about it.

I wrote a letter to the chief executive of the trust, not as a complaint, but as a concern: why is this happening, why is the doctor writing a prescription out when he's not checked with my medical records, why is there no information, why is there no follow-up? That was, and still is, my absolute major concern. What I asked was, 'Surely, as an absolute minimum, you should be seeing me once a year.' 'Oh, we haven't got the resources to do that!'

Well, why haven't you got the resources? Have you asked the right people?

I said, 'You must have users involved in planning and design. To have a patient-centred service, you've got to have patients sitting on your committees.' During my time at Macmillan, I sat on loads of committees. There was a bit of tokenism, but you can root that out. And it's embedded in law, under the NHS Constitution[34] and the NICE guidelines:[35] you have to have patient and user involvement. So I said, 'Right, what you going to do about it?' And nearly a year's gone by now.

I spoke to the local lead for dementia services and floated the idea of setting up a Dementia Voices group, made up of patients and carers, to develop services, and help to basically change and improve things. He said, 'Believe it or not Alex, I've been trying to do this for the last two years, saying, "Why are we not getting users involved?"' I produced a simple overview of what I think should take place, and where there was a requirement for funding, and he immediately sent that document out to all the eight new commissioning bodies in the county.

Coincidentally, I was called into a meeting with a lady from the mental health trust, and she said, 'We're thinking of setting up a users and carers group.' I said, 'I'm sorry I'm being cynical, but where did this idea come from?' 'Well we've been thinking about it for some time.' I said 'Really!' She said, 'To be fair, you've sparked off something.' 'That's fine,' I said. 'I just want to see something happen. I don't want to be sat here talking.'

I haven't committed myself, because I'm interested to see the fine print of what they're actually offering. It sounds very good, but obviously, it depends on how much autonomy you would actually have. In any case, whether it's the Dementia Voices group, or the trust's group, I'm only going to do it for a year. I'll get it all set up. I've got the skills to do that.

At the moment, in Lancashire, there are no services for younger people with dementia. There's nothing. That's official. People keep inviting me to the dementia cafés that the local Alzheimer's Society run, and I've said, 'With great respect, what in common have I got with an 80-year-old?' I'm not anti-social, and I've got a lot of time for old people, but what are we going to talk about? The Second World War or what?

There's a complete lack of understanding of dementia. The worst people are the health professionals! You'd think they would have been the best, but there needs to be some serious dementia training going on. Everyone expects people with dementia to be in their 90s – not in their early 60s like me.

Recently I had to go into hospital because of my heart condition. As soon as I was admitted, I said, 'Right, I must tell you now, I've got early onset dementia. I'm not going to walk out the hospital, but I do have several problems that cause me great anxiety.' So they made a note of it on the paper. Then I told the doctor when he came to do the initial interview about my heart problem – no reaction. Absolutely nothing! I was moved about 20 or 30 times during the day – it was a busy ward, different beds, different bays, and I thought, oh my word, what's going on here. I mentioned it several times, but there's no real acceptance in an acute hospital of the needs of patients who have dementia. And right at the end, when I was discharged, it was in such a flurry. I was staggered by it. 'We'll email your discharge documents to your GP.' 'So, can I go?' 'Yes.' I walked out. I can't believe somebody didn't say, 'Well, hang on here, where are you going to? Will somebody come and pick you up?'

I have an ongoing problem with headaches. I went to see a very senior neurologist about this, a year or so ago, and when I told him that I had dementia, his words were, 'Where did you pick that up from?' My jaw dropped. I said, 'Pardon!' Obviously, what I wanted to know was, were the headaches attributable to the Alzheimer's or another medical problem. 'Where did you pick that up from?' I told him I had had a SPECT scan, I had had a memory assessment, and I had a confirmed diagnosis of early onset Alzheimer's.

If I walk with a missing limb, that's a clear sign of disability. But because there's no physical manifestation of the disease, because I look 'normal', then I must be 'normal'. 'Are you sure you've got Alzheimer's?' 'Well no actually, I just invented it one Friday night!' I just laugh it off. I'm sorry, but, ask me to remember a five-digit number!

Living on your own puts you in a completely different place in terms of accessing services. I had a wonderful social services assessment, a year ago, over the telephone: 'Can I get access to some help and support?' 'No.' 'Why?' 'We can only give you help and support if it's a crisis or an emergency now, we don't do normal support.' 'Who's going to know when there's a crisis or an emergency, when I live on my own?'

I'm getting tired of asking the same question. I've almost got to the stage of throwing the towel in. It seems like nobody cares whether I'm here today or tomorrow. I do live in sheltered accommodation, but that's not a guarantee. There is a part-time on-site warden. They keep saying, 'We could install a pull-cord system.' And I say, 'You're making an assumption that a person with dementia will know (a) where it is and (b) what it's for!' This is the problem absolutely in a nutshell.

Services out there, even the housing association I'm with, profess to know about dementia, but they don't understand what it really means, and there's nobody prepared to listen to people like me explaining it to them. This is where the frustration is. Stop making assumptions! I've talked to my GP, and I've told the practice nurse there, you need to repeat things. When you say, 'Oh yes, your appointment's at 7.30 next Thursday,' you need to repeat it. I spoke to the pharmacy. I said, 'Please make sure you explain the label to me. Has the medication changed?'

Now if there was a carer there, they would see all this, a carer would be monitoring my medication. Who's monitoring it for me? Have I taken my medication today?

What is it like living alone? It's an actual bleakness that stares at me. There was a little bit of numbness in the early stages. I get periods, as I'm sure most people with dementia do, of being frightened. It's very scary.

I think that my work with Macmillan, and Carers in Cancer and trying to get this Dementia Voices group off the ground, gets me refocused. I was under great pressure from my children to quit all the activities, to give it all up. And I did. And it was like staring at the bottom of a chasm. I was wandering round the flat saying, 'Well, what am I supposed to do now?' I don't do TV. I'm an outdoor person. So gradually I've brought a few things back in, so that at least gives me a focus.

My mobility is pretty dire, because I have chronic osteoarthritis in all the joints. I had my left foot operated on two years ago, trying to save that. And I had some brand new radical treatment on my right foot, several weeks ago, to try and save that. The shoulder and the neck you can cope with, but you can't do without your feet! My ankles just give way. I will end up in a wheelchair, there's no doubt about that. Osteoarthritis just progresses. I don't have any curable diseases! Can I have something that's curable please? I'm in constant pain all the time, but I try not to be too medicated.

But when you've watched somebody die of cancer, this is nothing! It's an inconvenience. And yes, I'm going to die of one of these conditions. I'll die of Alzheimer's at some stage, if my heart doesn't pack up before then! But seriously, it does not compare at all.

I did get asked a couple of times, about the future. By employment advisers! It is futureless. And that takes a lot of getting used to. I know we're all going to die anyway. It's very easy to say that. But it's undetermined. We don't know... So when I'm looking out of the window each day, I do get concerned

– am I going to be in the same place this time next year? I don't think it's anything to be frightened about, if the right type of support is there. But at some stage, am I going to start ranting in the middle of the street? I really can't deal with that very well.

Challenges! I'm doing my best, to try and change people's perceptions. No, I'm not gay, but I came out last year. I thought, I'm not going to hide behind the curtain. I've got dementia. I'm not saying I'm proud of what I've got, but I've got it! Deal with it!

Chapter 3

A doctor in search of a diagnosis

JENNIFER BUTE

Jennifer Bute, *a retired GP, was the executive partner in a busy practice in Southampton when she began to experience disconcerting symptoms for which her medical training had not prepared her. Since her diagnosis of young onset Alzheimer's disease, she has dedicated herself to educating as many people as possible – in particular health professionals – about*

the different ways dementia can affect people. With the help of her son she has created a website www.glorious.opportunity.org and a series of educational films. I interviewed her at her home in a supported 'retirement village' in Somerset. LW

I didn't realise anything was wrong until August 2004, when I had a TIA (transient ischaemic attack, or mini-stroke), and lost the use of my left arm for a short time. That episode prompted me to make notes, which is why I've got a record of everything that happened after that.

It took five years and three different neurologists before I finally received a diagnosis of early onset Alzheimer's, in 2009. The third neurologist I saw was Peter Garrard (who has done work on how Alzheimer's affected the language used by the novelist Iris Murdoch and Prime Minister Harold Wilson).[36] He told me that the dementia had almost certainly started before the TIA, but it was the TIA that drew my attention to it, and also probably made it worse.

My mother died of a coronary when she was 34. I've inherited her condition, which is called familial hypercholesterolemia. I was taken into a cardiac unit in 1991, and started on a statin but put on two stone in two months, so I refused to take them any more. I didn't take any medication for anything until I had my TIA in 2004, which was probably caused by my inherited abnormally high cholesterol.

I had the TIA when I was 59. Looking back, I must have known something was not quite right even before the TIA. I was the executive partner of one of the largest GP practices in Southampton and involved in teaching medical students and appraising doctors. I realised before Easter of 2004 that things weren't quite as sharp as they used to be. So I passed on the responsibility of being executive partner to another doctor a few months before I had my mini-stroke. Peter Garrard suggested it was because I was beginning to show signs of dementia, but did not realise. I'm glad I did hand over then.

After the TIA, I went to the TIA clinic, and they put me on the standard treatment for a stroke, trying to reduce my blood pressure. But because there was nothing wrong with my blood pressure, this just made me worse. Afterwards, my cardiologist said that the stroke had also affected the part of my brain that controlled the blood pressure, so combined with the blood-pressure-lowering treatment, it just went even lower. They had given me a CT scan, which showed changes in my brain. But they weren't looking for dementia. I also used to have a lot of migraine, and they thought the migraine had caused the damage.

Following the TIA I had begun to get seriously lost. I couldn't find my way to places I'd often been to before. I would go to visit patients, and turn up at the wrong house. So I bought myself a Sat Nav. I didn't tell anybody, because I was a bit embarrassed about it, but it was really quite bad. I'd turn up at the wrong house, and say, 'I've come to see So-and-So,' who wouldn't be there, of course. But once I was at the right house, as a doctor, I could still function. It was just in these other things that I was falling apart.

The word dementia had not crossed my mind at this stage, even though I was medically trained. As doctors, we just used to talk about 'senile dementia', and thought dementia was just about memory. I didn't know that dementia can affect people in other ways. I didn't know about getting lost, and that people with dementia sometimes have hallucinations. My training had never covered that. This is why I am now so keen to educate GPs.

It was only in January 2005, when a frightening episode happened at the supermarket checkout, that I went to my GP. I was standing at the checkout, and I didn't know what to do with the shopping. All my shopping had been put through the till, and I was just standing there looking at it. The girl never offered to help or asked what the matter was. The queue gave up and went to other checkouts, and I just stood there wondering what to do. I was terrified, because I thought, 'This is ridiculous, absolutely ridiculous!' I couldn't understand what was happening, and for some reason, I couldn't even talk. I couldn't even ask for help. So I just stood there. Eventually I tried to put the shopping into the bags. And it was so difficult! It was all in slow motion. It was awful. Before I drove home, I did wonder, 'Am I safe to drive?' But I did drive home, and when I got there, my speech was still muddled. Later, my cardiologist wondered if I had had another TIA.

Anyway, I was sufficiently alarmed to go back to my GP, and say, 'Something's not right,' and he sent me to the first of three neurologists. At that time I was a well-respected local doctor and I knew the first neurologist professionally, and I knew his wife too. My husband and I went to see this consultant neurologist and he said, 'Hullo Jennifer, lovely to see you! There's nothing the matter with you!' Before I'd even sat down! He didn't do any investigations at all.

I don't think he even considered dementia, because he thought I was too young. I was humiliated, because in his letter to my GP, he implied I was just making it all up. He wrote and said there was nothing physically wrong with me, and he thought it was functional – in other words implying that it was 'attention-seeking', or that I was stressed. I was completely humiliated. So I decided that I was never going to tell anybody anything any more. If I had these episodes I was just going to keep quiet about them.

My GP was cross. He said, 'We need to send you to a different neurologist,' and I said, 'I'm not going to be humiliated by anyone else.' And he said, 'Well, I know there's something wrong with you.' But I refused to go back to either my GP or the neurologist.

In the meantime, I found that I did not recognise friends and neighbours if I met them unexpectedly. I needed to use the Sat Nav to find my way to my surgery and even to get home afterwards. I was frequently puzzled because no one else seemed to notice the unpleasant smells that I could smell so distinctly. I had a gas leak check done on our house and got the drains checked at work. I did not realise it then, but I was suffering from olfactory hallucinations.[37]

On my way back from Nepal in late 2005, where we had been visiting our son, I passed out on the aeroplane, because of my low blood pressure and the pressurisation in the cabin. They had to get the resuscitation team on touch-down in Doha, because I was unconscious. It felt awful till I got back to London. They wanted to keep me in Doha but my husband pushed me on to the plane in a wheelchair, telling me to try and look a bit healthier! Once we got back to England, I recovered, and they stopped the medication for lowering the blood pressure.

The defining moment came at the end of 2005, when I was chairing an important case conference at work. I did not recognise the chief mental care officer whom I had known for 20 years, and persisted in asking him and other colleagues who they were and why they were there. It was just terrible. I thought, 'This is affecting my work. I can't carry on like this.'

So in 2006, I agreed to see a second neurologist, who was surprised I had had no investigations, and ordered MRI and SPECT scans and a neuropsychology assessment. The neuropsychology consultant said I did have problems, and was not sure if I was, or would remain, safe professionally. The safety of my patients was paramount so I resigned, much to the annoyance of my medical partners, who seemed to think I had imagined it all.

When I went back to the second neurologist, he was also very annoyed that I'd resigned. He said, 'But you're better than most of the other GPs I know.' I said, 'Whether or not that is true, it might not be true next week, or the week after, and I'm not going to wait to find out.' He said the abnormal results of the scans were of no significance, even though by this stage I was often struggling to behave normally. My cooking had become bizarre. I could no longer do simple tasks, and in the evenings I could not talk sense. I even forgot my son's birthday. But the second neurologist discharged me. It was as if they didn't want to diagnose me because they thought they would lose a good

GP. I also think they thought they were doing me a favour, by pretending it wasn't happening.

My husband didn't want to believe it either. I realised that I had dementia long before he did. The case conference was the turning point for me. When I resigned, I thought I had frontotemporal dementia. I didn't recognise public figures on TV. I didn't know who people were in family photos. I would say to my husband, 'Who's this person?' and he would say, 'Of course you know who that is.' He used to get angry with me. If I forgot to cook something, he would ask, 'Where are the potatoes?' Or he would find the iron still on, three days later, because I'd been distracted and forgotten about it, and he'd be cross about it. He couldn't believe that I really didn't know, or had even forgotten. He loved me dearly, but he didn't want to think that I had dementia. I think he dealt with it by denying it.

By January 2008, I had developed significant visual and auditory hallucinations in addition to the existing olfactory hallucinations. I heard babies crying and children calling for attention, and I was seen conducting conversations with people who weren't there. I had to write myself detailed instructions on how to make a cup of tea, and once I cooked supper twice on the same day. One day I did not even recognise my husband. I knew I had dementia.

I asked for another neuropsychological assessment, and was sent to see the Professor of Neuropsychology. She explained that I had been using non-verbal and contextual clues to work things out, and that my intelligence enabled me to cover up. She suggested I should see the third neurologist, Peter Garrard, and when he gave me my diagnosis in 2009 it was a huge relief, that at last someone believed me.

He started me on Aricept, which to begin with, caused terrible nightmares. Later the Memory Clinic added Memantine, and within three months my family were amazed at my improvement. I believe the combination of Aricept and Memantine is more effective than one or the other. I didn't lose my hallucinations until I was put on the Memantine. My family also think the combination of drugs enabled me to talk better. (If you see me in the evenings, I still sometimes can't talk sense, but in the mornings I'm fine!)

I think everybody with dementia should be tried on both Memantine and Aricept. In some European countries, anybody with dementia gets both. But in this country, only if you have Alzheimer's – not if you have vascular dementia – do you get put on Aricept, and after three months you get tested again to see whether your scores have gone up. If it doesn't work, they withdraw the treatment, and that's fair. But people with vascular dementia and other forms of dementia should also be tried on it. I suspect it is because these drugs are expensive.

Perhaps if I had had a diagnosis earlier, and been given these drugs, I could have worked for longer. I resigned in the end, before I had a diagnosis, because I didn't know whether what was going on would affect my clinical care. And because I cared about my patients, I couldn't risk it! But in fact, I'm absolutely positive that it didn't affect my clinical care, at that stage.

Before my husband died, we moved to a care home in Somerset, which is designed and laid out as a 'retirement village'. Most people have their own flats, and you can live reasonably independently, but there are communal spaces as well. There is specialist care for residents who have dementia, and you can arrange for as much or as little care and support as you need.

I try to live as independently as possible, but there have been two worrying incidents recently, connected with my olfactory hallucinations.

I get confused in supermarkets, so I have an internet delivery. The delivery man very kindly put everything in the kitchen for me, including all over the hob – which is fine, because normally one just moves it away. But on this occasion, I didn't. I just moved enough to put one saucepan on, turned on the hob – but turned on the wrong one of course – and then turned on all four hobs full, with all the plastic bags of shopping on top.

I could see the red hobs, and I could see the plastic melting, and the cardboard turning into carbon, I could see everything happening but did not realise its significance. And then I could smell it – the burning and the scorching – so I just thought 'Hallucination!' And it was only when the bananas exploded – it was only when the third sense, hearing, came in – that I realised what was happening. Even though I could see it and smell it, it didn't mean anything to me!

Then last week I was cooking in the kitchen. And I was being very careful, making sure the hob was clear, and I can't remember whether the door-bell went or the phone went, but I left the kitchen, dealt with the interruption, and forgot that I was cooking. So I came into the sitting room, and sat down. I was probably doing some knitting. After a while I noticed a nice smell of someone cooking supper. And I thought, 'Oh, that's nice. I wonder if it's the people downstairs.' It didn't enter my head that it was my supper. I couldn't remember that I hadn't had my supper – because I often can't remember whether I have or haven't. Then I thought, 'Oh well, maybe it's a hallucination.' Anyway, I didn't take any notice. A little bit later, it began to smell a bit over-cooked, and later still, it began to smell a bit burnt. So then I thought, 'Well, it's definitely a hallucination, you can stop worrying about it now.' And it got worse and worse of course. I even went into the dining room at one stage to check my emails, and I still didn't think of looking in the kitchen. Eventually it got really bad, so I thought, 'Well, I'm obviously suffering from bad hallucinations today. I'll go and make myself a cup of tea.' So I went into the kitchen and – oh dear!

This is a terrible fire-risk. So when I start cooking, I need to put a timer round my neck, set for say half an hour. Then if I get distracted from what I'm doing, the timer will go off, to remind me to go into the kitchen to have a look. I've got to do something, so that I can live independently.

There are new challenges all the time. But I've always had challenges. I worked at an isolated rural mission hospital in

South Africa before I was married. Later on, I worked in Ukraine, after the fall of communism, helping them with family planning clinics, and teaching doctors, who were desperate for knowledge. And I worked in the slums in India as well, when HIV/AIDs was beginning to spread. And being a GP was a challenge. So I've always had challenges, and this is just my latest challenge. You just have to find ways round these things.

My passion is to educate the GPs and medical students. The Royal College of General Practitioners had a conference on dementia some time ago, and I looked at the programme and it said something like, 'Diagnosis of dementia', then 'End of life issues ...' And I thought, 'Well, what about everything in between?' So I wrote to the person who was organising the conference, and told her and they did change the programme a bit.

In 2012 I spoke at a conference in Reading, where there were about 300 doctors, neurologists, psychologists and so on in the audience. In the questions at the end, someone stood up and said, 'I'm a very good doctor. I can tell the difference between different types of hernia, I can tell the difference between one heart murmur and another, but having listened to Jennifer's talk, I now realise I know absolutely nothing about dementia.'

I didn't know either, before it happened to me, and I was a good GP. *I didn't realise I didn't know.* This is why I feel so strongly, that my dementia is a gift, and that I've got to use it to educate other doctors.

I have a relative who I am sure has got dementia, so I encouraged her to go to her GP. She phoned her GP, and the doctor said that she didn't need to go and see him, because he could tell – by listening to her on the phone for 30 seconds – that she didn't have dementia! How could he possibly know?

Possibly doctors often think, 'What's the point of diagnosing someone when there's nothing you can do about it?' Which is not true. But I don't think they realise how much it affects the rest of the family. I had a patient in her early 50s who used to come and see me about medical problems and I couldn't tell that she had dementia, just from the short consultations. It was only when her daughter came to see me and said, 'I can't cope with my mother any more because of XYZ,' that I thought, 'Goodness there's a lot more to this.' You can't tell just by talking. So then I started investigating and we found out that she did have dementia. Sadly some doctors won't listen to what the family say. They think the family are either paranoid or have got it in for their parents.

So, when I go and talk to GPs and medical students, I want them to be aware of things that they weren't before; to consider dementia as a possibility, and to be almost excited about it, and to feel that it is worth doing something about. In other words, to demolish the myth that there's nothing that can be done about it, and the myth that it's just about memory, because it isn't.

I remember a patient coming to see me, and I said, 'You were meant to come and see me last week, and you didn't. What happened?' And she said, 'Oh, you'd moved.' I couldn't understand this at the time, but later it made sense, when I realised she had dementia. Then there was another patient whom I visited. She had a medication dispensing box with a week's supply of tablets, all sorted out by the pharmacist, and the whole lot had been undone and the pills spilled all over the floor, and all put back any old how. Well, at the time, I thought, 'How silly!' but now I would think, 'This lady needs to be tested for dementia.'

My son has helped me make a series of ten short films to educate people about dementia.[38] The finished result makes me look very fluent, but I had a script, and we filmed everything twice. He's edited it so beautifully, you just wouldn't know what a mess it was. When people say to me that they can't believe I have dementia, I find it very hurtful. That's one reason my son has also made a short film of me explaining how it affects me.[39]

It's just amazing where that ten-module teaching video has gone – it's gone all over the world, to America, to Australia, to Germany. It's a privilege that I've learned so much. I'm learning all the time, and living here in the care village, I am always trying to find ways to help other people as well as learn from them. I've done training for the staff here, and they have been very receptive. I see things – for example, a lady who's got dementia turned up for lunch without her handbag. And the staff member said, 'Don't worry, you can pay tomorrow, it doesn't matter.' But the staff member didn't understand that this lady's handbag was not needed in order to pay for her lunch – it was her comforter. It was her guy-rope. It was her 'I'm ok if I've got this!' So I said to the carer, 'I'll wait with her while you go back to her room and get it for her.' 'Oh no, that's not necessary,' she said. She didn't understand that for this particular woman, her bag was not just a bag.

And there are a few folk here whom I realise have dementia, and perhaps they haven't realised, or their spouse hasn't. With couples, often one covers for the other and you don't notice. There's one couple who are always together, and the other day, I saw the wife sitting in the atrium, looking at the newspaper. And I thought, 'She never reads the newspaper.' It wasn't the normal pattern. So I said, 'Hullo, how are you?' and she said timidly, 'Well, not quite right.' So I said, 'Are you going back to your flat soon?' and she looked at me and she said, 'I don't know where I live.' So I said, 'Well I do,' because she's just opposite me. 'You come with me.' It doesn't show when she's with her husband, because her husband always takes her. I can't help it. I wear my medical hat here and I see things that distress me. It's not that the staff don't care, because the staff here are brilliant! It's just that they don't know. So now, I tell the person in charge.

We have all kinds of activities here. We have a tea, so people can get together, and carers bring along people with dementia. Not everybody who lives here has dementia but a lot of them do. One lady with dementia came along, and she was a bit of a trial. She was obviously unhappy. And because I believe passionately that feelings remain, even if facts are forgotten, I went up to her, and I knelt on the floor in front of her, took her hand, and I said to her, 'You've got a beautiful smile.' I didn't know if she had or not. But she looked at me, and she smiled, and she was calm for the rest of the hour. And people said to me, 'What on earth did you say to her?' I said, 'It doesn't matter what I said, I made her feel good. That's all you have to do.'

Sometimes people say, 'There's no point taking Mum out, because she won't know where we've been.' So what! She'll know she had a happy time. And that's what she remembers.

People with dementia can get distressed because they've misunderstood something. There was another lady, who was very agitated, and I went along and sat next to her to find out what the matter was. And it turned out that the carer had come along and left her without smiling, because the carer had had a crisis at home – but this lady thought that she had upset the carer. And then she had forgotten why she was upset. It took me ages to try and find out what had set it all off. But there's always a reason.

You can see this in the film *The Iron Lady*, about Margaret Thatcher. I actually cried when I watched the film because I identified so much with it. In the film she gets hallucinations. And she got fed up with this on one occasion. She turned on every appliance in her flat that she could – the coffee grinder and the food processor and everything – so as to make a terrible noise. Her daughter turned up and turned everything off, but she never asked her mother why she had turned them on in the first place. It was in order to get rid of the hallucinations! However, when her daughter arranged a dinner party with lots of VIPs, and her mother sat at the head of the table she functioned perfectly well, because it was a normal pattern for her.

I can stand up and talk to a group, because I used to lecture at the university, so talking in front of hundreds of people is no big deal for me, because it's a normal pattern.

So the three important things: *There's always a reason. Feelings remain. And patterns continue.*

I saw a presentation by the Japanese neuroscientist Ryuta Kawashima at a conference.[40] Since then I have been running a cognitive stimulation group here at the care village twice a week. The group has grown to about 20 people, enough to split into two groups. Most of the members have got dementia (or I think they have). We meet in the lounge, and we start with reading. One group reads from a book, and the group that I run, for people whose needs are greater, read nursery rhymes, or poems like 'The Owl and the Pussycat', something simple and familiar, from way back. And sometimes we even sing them, because we've had a couple of folk who don't believe they can read any more, but if you sing it, they can remember the words.

So, the first part is reading aloud. The second part is all about stimulating the right and left brain. We have cards... for example it says 'yellow' but it's written in blue; or we have shapes – it's a circle but it says it's an oval. We ask them what colour it is, or what shape it is – not what the word says. This stimulates the different sides of the brain. And we also do simple shape Sudoku and different levels of writing activities, which are fun, and finish with mental arithmetic. (It does not matter if the answers are wrong.)

Some people can't remember their alphabet any more. When I give them the sheet of sums to do, and I say, 'Please write your name on it.' (It is to find out whether they can still write.) Those that can't, we re-teach them their letters. We sing the alphabet song. I've got books that I use for my grandchildren about learning to write and we start again!

I believe that you can retrain the brain. They call it plasticity. After a stroke, people accept that you can re-learn. The damage is still there, but you can re-learn to walk or to talk or to write – not always completely, but often you can. I passionately believe you can also do that with dementia. Bangor University call it 'Rementia'!

Professor Kawashima has shown in his work that the reading aloud, the mental arithmetic, and the writing stimulate the brain, and this positively affects everything else, including mood and behaviour, the rest of the time. Just last week, someone said to me, 'Does So-and-So come to your group?' and I said yes, and they said, 'You can tell the difference already!'

So many people with dementia just give up. People think, 'I can't do anything,' but they can still do some things. There was a lady who was convinced that she couldn't read, and I thought that she could – it was probably that she had lost her confidence. And she's now reading again. It's wonderful. Everyone is different so I am always searching for new ways.

My faith has made a lot of difference to how I view my dementia. I see it as a God-given gift, and I have a responsibility to use it, to help other people, and explain and encourage.

I believe that God does amazing things, and that he's involved in the little things in our lives as well as the big things. I believe in a relationship with Jesus who cares. Some people say, 'I don't believe in God. All he does is tell you off, cause tragedies and punish you!' And I say, 'I don't believe in a God like that either.'

I believe that we have a loving heavenly Father. It doesn't matter what disasters happen here, it's not the end of everything, there's still hope now as well as for the future. When I was working, I was dealing with death all the time – and I believe there's life after death.

So for me, it's essential to how I live. People say to me, 'How has having dementia affected your view of God?' and I say, 'It hasn't altered it at all.' As far as I'm concerned, God exists. And God is moral. But he's also a loving God.

Also, if I deteriorate my family understand – I'm still me. When my father had dementia, he could still talk about God and pray to God, even though he didn't know who I was. I believe the spiritual always remains.

Here in the care village, everyone has to write down their wishes for the future. But the plan needs to cover different possibilities. They say, 'Do you want to be resuscitated?' Well that's not the right question. It depends! I don't believe in prolonging the process of dying. So if I was in a vegetative state and developed pneumonia, I wouldn't want to have antibiotics, I would rather die. But I don't believe in finishing oneself off. If I collapse because my blood pressure's low, then of course I want to be resuscitated.

My family know my wishes. When my husband died, we had to decide when to turn off the ventilator. There was absolutely no hope of him ever recovering consciousness, so what was the point of keeping him on a ventilator? But because we all are Christians, we didn't have any problem with that. We all know that one day, we'll be complete again, physically, even if things seem to be unravelling now. One day I was in church, and someone said, 'How are you?' and I said, 'I'm unravelling. It's getting difficult.' And she wrote me a note in church and passed it along the pew. And she said, 'My grandmother only unravelled things to make them into something that was more useful!'

Chapter 4

I'll ken it when I see it

ROSS CAMPBELL

Ross Campbell *is a former roofer and stone-mason from Falkirk near Glasgow. He has lived with epilepsy and vascular dementia for over 20 years, and is an active member of the Scottish Dementia Working Group.*[41] *He has given talks about his personal experience of dementia on many occasions in Scotland and England, and also at Alzheimer's Disease International conferences in Istanbul and Singapore. He is active locally in the Joint Dementia Initiative (JDI)*[42] *in Falkirk, where people with*

dementia organise their own peer support group, and reach out to others who have recently been diagnosed with dementia. I interviewed Ross at the JDI premises in Falkirk. LW

Before I become ill, I was a roofer and a stonemason. Then things began to go wrong. I didn't notice it, but my wife and my daughter – they began to pick up signs, because my daughter was working with people with dementia.

The most frightening experience I had was on a roof about 40 or 50 feet up. It was a doctor's house, and luckily enough I knew the doctor as a friend. All the scaffolding and safety nets and everything were up, and there was three of us on one side, and three of us on the other side – and I could have swore one of them nudged me, and I ended up down in the safety net! Actually, I had slipped, but at that time, I didn't accept that. I believed that one of them had actually nudged me! And I went up there, and I gave them the bloody devil! Then about three or four days later, I was back up there. But at this point, the other two were on the other side, finishing off, and then again, I slipped, and landed in the safety net. The doctor was just getting out of his car, and he looked up and went, 'You – down!'

And they got me down, and he took me into the small surgery he has in his house, and he did a quick examination of me, and said, 'Right, you'll go to hospital tomorrow.' So I was sent to hospital and I had an MRI, and I was diagnosed with grand mal epilepsy.[43] I was 51 at that point.

The next episode came when I was still working on the same house. I had also been working on another house as well, and I had two and a half thousand pounds for the bank, to go and pay the materials for that job. But I went back down to the doctor's and I was finishing off his house, and I'd been up on the roof, with this two and half thousand pounds, which I'd completely forgot about, in my back pocket. When I'd finished, I slid down the roof – you can walk down the roof if it's dry, but if it's wet, you slide down the roof to get down – and I got home, and my wife said to me, 'Have you paid the materials?'

'I think so.'

'Where's the money?'

'I havenae got it on me.'

'Well, I'll go and check if it's lying in the car, or in the pick-up.'

It wasn't in the car or the pick-up, and we went back to the doctor's house, and the money was sitting in the gutter! It had come out of my back pocket and landed in the gutter when I slid down the roof! So somebody could have picked it up! And this was all in the space of three or four weeks.

Another thing I was doing – I was coming home, and instead of taking the dog for a walk, I'd be leaving him in the back garden, and I'd be going out for a walk, with the lead, but no dog!

And I didn't really notice it, but at that time so many wee niggling things happened. I was putting milk in stupid places. And I was putting other things in stupid places. But the wife, when she seen that, she would just change them round about.

One night, I did take the dog with me, and I took him half way up the hill, and the wife was watching me, and I brought him back. And then, instead of going my normal route, I went away – and I disappeared for ten hours! I usually can remember everything, but this is one night I can't remember a thing. It must have been a kind of blackout seizure. If you take a fit, you can recall a fit after it, but with a blackout seizure, you can't recall it. It goes completely. And I ended up ten mile away! And I can't remember one step of the road, going there. And then, you kind of come back, and focus in, and I knew where I was, because I know the area very well, and I thought, 'Bloody hell, what am I doing up here?'

By this time, everybody was looking for me. Neighbours and brothers and sisters, police, everybody! It was winter, and it was hail and wind and rain. So I walked back all the way, and I can remember every step of the road back, I assure you. And I got within about a mile and a half, and this police car drew up beside me. The sergeant was driving, so the PC got out with a photograph: 'Is that you?'

And I went, 'Who the hell's that?' because I didn't even recognise who it was. 'Who's asking?'

He said, 'It's the police. Look at the top of the car.'

'I can't see the top of the car. Just bugger off and leave me alone.'

So the sergeant could see I was getting agitated, so he told the PC to get in the car. And they drove about half a mile down the road and parked up again. So the sergeant got out, and he said, 'Are you Ross Campbell?' but I wouldnae tell them my name. So they drove about half a mile further again.

So the next time they got out, they said, 'Will you get in the car, son, and I'll take you home.'

And I says, 'Have I done anything?'

And he says, 'No, you've not done anything.'

And I says, 'I'm not getting in the car. I'm quite capable of walking.'

'That's fine,' he says. 'Just you walk.'

And I went furtherer and furtherer, and he went furtherer and furtherer. And then I saw I was near my ain street, and they must have radioed the station, to phone my wife to tell her we were on our way down.
    And when I walks into the house, all these folk were in the house. And I said to my wife, 'What the hell's going on in here?'

And she's very clever. She said, 'It's a surprise! A surprise party!'

I said, 'Who's the surprise party for?'

'For you!'

And I said, 'You never telled me, or I'd have been here.'

'Well if I had telled you it wouldnae have been a bloody surprise would it!'

'Well tell them to keep the noise down and clear up the mess at the back of them.' And I just went away to bed.

About three days later, she tells me actually what had happened. And it was then, the wife said, 'That's it!'

So she's took me along to the doctor I've been talking to you about, who's a friend, and who got me diagnosed with the grand mal epilepsy. And she had a word with him about what had happened. And he said, 'Leave it with me.' And he phoned up a colleague, a doctor who was a senior consultant, and got me to see him. And he diagnosed me with vascular dementia. I had to see the psychologist, the neurologist, the psychiatrist, and then they decided to do a brain biopsy. We were back and forth, back and forth, back and forth, for about two years.

We had to drag the diagnosis out of them. My wife had actually got to drag it out of them. My wife says, 'Give him his diagnosis. He's big enough and strong enough to take it. Just tell him. And give me it in writing.' And she got it in writing.

When I got the diagnosis, I wasnae shocked by it, but when I got home, I went away up the stairs, and sort of thought about it, and about a week went by, and I started withdrawing myself. I wouldnae even go out the house – I'm a great walker, and I wouldnae go walk. It was hell for my wife.

And then one day, I just thought, 'You've only got dementia. And it's not a disease. It's an illness. Just grab the bull by the horns!'

◊ ◊ ◊

They sent us a CPN, a young lassie. She come in, and she said to the wife: 'How's Mr Campbell getting on?'

And I'm sitting here. And she said, 'How's Mr Campbell getting on?'

And I said, 'Fine.'

'Has he had his breakfast this morning?'

And I said, 'Aye.'

'Do you think he's going to get a walk today?' And she didnae ask me directly.

So I turned round, and said, 'Listen here, I don't like being spoken over. Just take your airse out of that chair, and take it out the door you come in.'

So she did – and I never seen that CPN again!

◊ ◊ ◊

When I first applied for respite, they put a suggestion that I should go and have a look at a few 'homes'.

I went ,'You mean, old folks' homes?'

'Yes.'

I said, 'Well, you can forget that!'

But they actually did take me to old folks' homes, and I walked in, and I walked right through them, walked back out and I said, 'No.'

Then they took me to a particular one. And there were a few younger people there, maybe just a wee bit older than me. And I went, 'That's ok, I can craic with anybody. This'll do me.'

And I went there for quite a few year. I went in every eight weeks, I think. And all of a sudden, within one month, all the staff disappeared. One left, and another one left, one was sacked, another one was sacked, and another one left. That was the full team. And they put the new staff in, just young people, who had no idea whatever the hell they were doing. They were bringing in teenagers. At that time, it was, 'You either take the job, or you don't get your dole money.' One night the fire alarm went off, and they were running about like headless chickens. I had to show the lassie the fire alarm, and show her how to switch it off! I switched it all off for her!

In the end I said 'I'm out! I'm off!' And they told me I couldn't go. And I said 'Why?'

They said, 'You'll have to see your social worker.'

I said, 'Get a taxi! I'm off!'

◊ ◊ ◊

Then I met Sheena at the Joint Dementia Initiative (JDI) in Falkirk. This was the best thing that happened to me. She introduced me to groups, and I've never looked back. I was put in touch with Neil, a befriender, who I see twice a week. She also told me about a scheme called 'Time to share'. My befriender Neil and his wife Margaret are part of this scheme. I go to their house every two months and stay for a week. I've been going there that long, they classify it as 'my room'. They give me a key to the house – I'm just one of the family.

Falkirk is one of the most supportive areas anywhere, because of the JDI. I've been through Scotland, England, and quite a few places in different parts of the world, and everybody wants to know about Falkirk, about the support.

In Falkirk, we don't have to fight for anything. It's set up automatically, and it's there till you die. It doesn't stop at 65. In

Glasgow, respite stops at 65 and you've got to go to a different organisation and fight for it individually. But here, it goes straight through. We've got specific support for younger persons. You have the younger persons' supporter, and when you hit 65, you have a one-to-one talk. Everything I've got, I've got through the JDI. The project worker here will fight for your rights. If you come in here and ask something, and they don't know it, they will go away and find out. They are a good team.

There's always something going on. Friday's the day with the café, but there's something going on every day of the week. We have two groups. There's the Second Wednesday group, where we meet up and have a natter, and the Mutual Support group, where if you want a speaker then you ask for one.

When someone is diagnosed, if they get word at the JDI, and if they see you're interested, they'll send someone with dementia to talk to them. If it's a man, we've got men, if it's a woman, it'll be a woman. And they'll ask them if they want to come to one of the meetings, and then if they want to come, it puts them in touch with the service. You don't like somebody pouncing on you: 'You've got dementia, I'm going to tell you all about it.' You ken you've got dementia, you don't want somebody to shove it in your face all the time.

When I speak to people who have a new diagnosis of dementia, I tell them they're not alone. They're definitely not alone. I advise them to read the book *Facing Dementia*.[44] The Scottish Dementia Working Group was involved in rewriting that book, so it was re-written properly. We had a lot of criticisms of the first version. And it's out now. It was given to doctors, to give to patients, but they don't always do it. And that's why we go out, speaking to doctors and nurses, speaking to whoever will listen.

I have been a member of the Scottish Dementia Working Group since it was formed. I've spoken to meetings in Edinburgh, York and Glasgow, and at the Alzheimer's Disease International conferences in Istanbul and Singapore.

◊ ◊ ◊

A lot of people don't realise how much dementia takes it out on your family. You having it, and them helping you. They don't realise. Because I didn't.

I've been married 49 years. You just take your wife for the run of the mill. You don't realise just how dependent you are on them.

I don't know what I would have done without my wife. She's a star. And my daughter – she's a star too!

They would never ever say it was a burden on them, but I can now see now that it must have been terrible for them. It was three year before they got the medication balanced. I was a human guinea pig. It must have been three year of hell. But having said all that, there was never a boo said.

And my grand-daughter Kayleigh has written a few poems about dementia. She's only 12. She's seen it all. That lassie's stood by me, with her mother, and never ever said boo. No matter what happened, she was there. She wrote this when she was eight:

My Papa has dementia

Before he had this terrible illness he was brave, strong, healthy and extremely active. Many people have this terrible illness. It's not fair on them and it's also not fair on their family. Some have suffered many years. Many have suffered from epilepsy. Just a little reminder – dementia is an illness that makes you forget things. It can cause blackouts, double vision and bad headaches. I get worried when my papa is lying on the floor because I think he is unconscious. I feel sad that my papa has dementia because he can't get to do the things he really loves. I sometimes wonder if there is a cure for dementia that can help all the people with dementia.

As he carried on with this my papa met people from the Falkirk Mutual Support Group and the Scottish Dementia Working Group (SDWG). At the SDWG he made lots of friends. With the help of the

SDWG he turned out to be a speaker. My papa speaks for those who can't speak for themselves. My papa has represented Scotland when he went to Istanbul. He has met three ministers of health. I'm glad to see my Papa is leading his happy life. He is Living with Dementia NOT dying from dementia.[45]

When I went to the conference in Istanbul, Kayleigh actually rehearsed my speech with me. One night she caught me reading it in the mirror. She said, 'You're talking to the mirror, but the mirror can't talk back to you. The mirror can't correct you if you're wrong. Give me your speech, and rehearse it, and I'll correct you if you're wrong.' She could recite that speech better than I could recite it!

I walk my grandson's dog three times a day, about three mile. I carry one of those cards which says, 'I have dementia', but I don't think I've ever used it. The people in the shops all know. I don't hide it. Since I have accepted my diagnosis, I've never hid it. I said, 'Well if I can accept it, if they don't like it, they can leave it!'

All my mates that know me, before and after, I've never changed. They're not sympathetic, and that's the way I prefer them. I've told them I don't want any sympathetic bullshit. The one thing I hate is being patronised. You either take me the way I am, or forget it.

◊ ◊ ◊

I've had really funny experiences with dementia. One example was when the fridge-freezer had broke down, on the Friday night, and the wife was on duty with St Andrews First Aid on the Saturday, and she said to me:

'Will you go and get a fridge-freezer on Saturday, a new one?'

I says, 'Aye, all right.'

So on the Saturday morning, I felt this wee numbness on my lip. And I thought, 'Oh no! I'd better not say nothing.'

And the wife says, 'Are you going to get that fridge-freezer?'

I went, 'Aye, fine, I'll go.'

So I gets on the bus, goes into Falkirk, gets off the bus, starts walking into the retail park, and I get this one-eyed double vision. 'Oh, here we go!' By the time I get right into the retail park, I've got the double-eyed double vision. So, I was walking along, and there was a boy walking to meet me, and I said, 'Excuse me, can you tell me where Curry's is?'

And he says, 'Are you taking the piss?'

'Honestly, I'm not. Can you tell me where Curry's is?'

'Can you no see it? Is it not big enough writing?' He must have thought I was drunk, because I was staggering.

I says, 'OK, I get the picture.' And the doors are going in and out, in and out, and this woman's trying to get out, with a plant, and a bairn, and I couldn't get in, and eventually, one of the boys that was working in the shop grabbed me, and yanked me in.

He said, 'What are you doing? Are you looking for the Salvation Army?'

I said, 'What the hell? Do I look like I'm looking for the Salvation Army?'

I just started to laugh, and so did he. And there was an elderly woman over there, serving a customer. And she walked over:

'Is there something wrong, Sir?'

'Aye. I've got dementia.'

So she said, 'Hold on, Sir.'

And the boy grabbed my arm, and she said, 'Would you go and get that man a glass of water, and a chair?'

So I sat there, and when she had finished with the customer, she came over to me and she says to me, 'Can I help you?'

I says, 'Aye.'

'Do you know what you're looking for?'

I says, 'No, but I'll ken it when I see it.'

So she takes me by the arm, and she led me through the entire shop, phones, kettles, mobiles, televisions, everything, till we come to the fridge-freezers. And I says, 'That's it!'

So she takes me right through to the desk. 'How are you going to pay it?'

'I've got a Visa card.' So I gave her my card.

'You canna pay it with that Sir.'

'Why not?'

'It's an electric card.'

I said, 'Sorry,' and put it back in my wallet. 'I'll have another go. Is that my Visa card?'

After I'd paid, she says, 'How are you getting home?'

I said, 'That's the next problem my darling. I've got to get from here up to the taxi rank.'

So the lad that yanked me in, she said to him: 'Take Mr Campbell in the car up to the taxi rank. And she ripped off a bit of paper, which had my name and address on it, and she said, 'Give that to the driver, and make sure he takes him to that address.'

Since I had dementia, I've had some wonderful experiences, I really have. Before that, I used to just eat, sleep, work; eat, sleep, work. I'd be up at seven, I'd need to be on site by half past seven, I'd need to do all the work, come home, and prepare for the next day, advance planning, get advance materials, I'd need to look at the next job, plan it out, order it up, and I wouldnae get to my bed till about 3 o'clock in the morning. Now I have time to myself. It's maybe not the most charming life, but I thoroughly enjoy it.

Chapter 5

Liberation!

DIZI CONTI

Dizi Conti with her husband Derek Norman.

Dizi Conti *is no longer able to describe her experiences at any length in her own words but she was very keen to contribute to this anthology. Dizi is a poet, playwright and theatre director, and before she was affected by the brain tumour that preceded dementia, she started to write an autobiography. The chapter which follows includes extracts from Dizi's memoir and other writings, as well as part of the transcript of an interview with Dizi. Unlike the other chapters which are based on interviews, it* *has not been possible to construct a first-person narrative using Dizi's words alone.*

A mere transcript of the words which Dizi spoke during the interview cannot convey the meaning which she managed to put across in the course of the conversation, which was extremely lively and often hilarious. Words frequently desert her, but she acts out a lot of the meaning, or puts eloquent expression into her face and voice when the words don't come.

Dizi granted me permission to prompt her with suggested words, and made it very clear with an emphatic, 'Oh, yes,' or an equally emphatic, 'No,' whether or not I was on the right track. Her voice still has the rich timbre that was noticed when she was a little girl.

Here is an extract from the interview. Dizi's husband Derek was on hand to help out from time to time, but did not try to take over or to tell Dizi's story for her. As Dizi was an actress and playwright, it seems fitting to set it out like a play. LW

◊ ◊ ◊

Lucy: I am hoping to find out about you, and your work. I know that's been very interesting, your writing.

Dizi: And this… *[hands Lucy a book of music for popular songs]*

Lucy: What, music?

Dizi: Yes.

Lucy: Now, is this music anything to do with you?

Dizi: No, it wasn't mine, but um – it's – um – there for me.

Lucy: For singing. And do you sing from that book?

Dizi: Yes.

Lucy: So do you sing by yourself, or with other people?

Dizi: Um – yes, but er – the best one is the one that my – *[sings in an exaggerated operatic style]* 'La, da di, da di, da' and he does it in a very funny way – *[laughs]*. He does it like that.

Lucy: So it's a bit like opera, but jokey. Do you go to a Singing for the Brain group?

Dizi: Oh yes.

Lucy: And you love it, by the look of it?

Dizi: I love it so much. We all love it.

Lucy: And what kind of songs do you sing?

Dizi: Whatever he –

Lucy: Would it be some pop songs?

Dizi: It could be. It could be almost anything. And he's a very good person. He can do it this way, or that way, and he is my – cuz –

Lucy: Your cousin?

Dizi: No, well, yes, really. Yes, probably.

Lucy: He's a relative?

Dizi: Yes. Very.

Derek: It's your grandson David, isn't it?

Dizi: And he's wonderful. Absolutely.

Lucy: Do you dance at your Singing for the Brain group?

Dizi: I'm the one that *[stands up and demonstrates encouraging the others to dance]* – 'Come on, let's do it!'

Lucy: You like to dance?

Dizi: Yes, yes.

Lucy: Do you do it like the Conga – do you all go round in a circle?

Dizi: Yes, yes. And it's so en – a lot of people. And when we – one of me – Italian, sort of thing – and there's a lot of people coming, and all join in, and that's so lovely.

Lucy: So, would you like to tell me about your work?

Dizi: Right. Now, um. Now, where do I get to?

Lucy: You can start wherever you like, because when I write it up, I can put it in order. So, you were a writer. What kind of things did you write?

Dizi: Poems, and all sorts of things. This is probably the one. *[Hands Lucy a typed manuscript, which also contains photos of her parents, herself as a child, and other family members, and is interspersed with Dizi's poems.]*

Derek: This is what you're working on now. This is Dizi's life story.

[Dizi thumbs through the manuscript pointing out who the people in the photos are.]

Lucy: Is this one of your poems?

Dizi: Yes.

Lucy: *[reads aloud]*

> **To Andy**
> Today, I held you in my arms as once I comforted my tiny child
> as you have always comforted me
> as you give comfort to your children
> and to all those in your care.
> For you give comfort
> to everyone you meet

and to everyone comforted by those that you have comforted. Your smile alone can warm the coldest day.

Who is Andy?

Dizi: Andy is, oh, a lovely person.

Derek: She's your daughter, isn't she?

Lucy: So you wrote this poem, to your daughter Andy. Did you write this poem a long time ago?

Dizi: Quite a long time. Because I don't do it any more. I can't do it – because of my head. Do you know about this thing?

Lucy: Yes, you have dementia. What problems does it give you? Is it just your memory?

Dizi: *[Acts out what she is saying]* Can't remember! Getting cross! 'I can't do it!' Grrr!

Lucy: Frustration!

Dizi: Oh yes!

Lucy: So that's very annoying. And did you have to go to the doctor because of this problem?

Dizi: Oh yes. It was – Look! *[Shows her head]*

Lucy: I think you had a brain tumour.

Dizi: Brain tumour, yes.

Lucy: So that was the first thing – a brain tumour – and then after that, that's when the dementia started.

Dizi: Yes.

Lucy: So, the brain tumour – did you have to have an operation?

Dizi: I can't remember how it went.

Lucy: But since then, you've had this problem with your memory.

Dizi: And I can't do things. All these things that I've got. I can't do it.

Lucy: Can you still read?

Dizi: No.

Lucy: You can't read any more. That must be hard.

Dizi: Oh it was. It was really – you know, for what I had before – gone!

Lucy: Yes, because you were a writer –

Dizi: Yes.

Lucy: And you worked in the theatre –

Dizi: Yes.

Lucy: So words were –

Dizi: Wonderful! Yes. So [acts out puzzlement] 'What did you say?' 'No, I can't – I don't understand what you're saying.' You know, that's what my life is like.

Lucy: So sometimes, do you find it difficult to understand what other people are saying?

Dizi: Yes.

Lucy: What about when you watch television?

Dizi: I do a lot of that!

Lucy: What sort of programmes do you like? Do you like things like Strictly Come Dancing?

Dizi: [emphatically] No.

Lucy: Do you like drama?

Dizi: Yes, it would be.

Lucy: Do you watch anything like *EastEnders*?

Dizi: *[emphatically]* No! Ugh!

Lucy: You don't like soap operas! And do you listen to the radio?

Dizi: I do, sometimes. Yes, I can do that. It's okay. But then, [acts out frustration] *'Derek! Come here! Derek! I can't do this!'* That's what, you know – grrr! *'Please!!'*

Lucy: So you feel frustrated. You feel, 'I wish I could do this by myself, but I've got to rely on Derek.'

Dizi: And, um, my d –

Lucy: Doctor?

Dizi: No.

Lucy: Daughter?

Dizi: No. Derek! What am I talking about?

Lucy: You were saying that you get frustrated when you can't do something and you have to ask for help.

Dizi: Oh yes.

Derek: You can't turn the TV on, or change the channel. I think that's what you're trying to get at.

Lucy: Oh, so you're watching television, and *EastEnders* starts and it's 'Derek, quick! Help! I don't want to watch *EastEnders*!'

[laughter]

Dizi: Yes! Exactly.

◊ ◊ ◊

In her heyday, Dizi was a successful playwright and director, working mainly in Fringe theatre and Theatre in Education in London. She also taught theatre skills. Her speciality was improvisation. She and Derek showed me some of the photos and flyers from her productions, and some of her play scripts.

An ardent feminist, she was also involved in the anti-nuclear movement in the 1980s. One of her plays, The Fence, is set at Greenham Common at the time of the women's peace camp,[46] and portrays an encounter between a woman protester who is living at the camp and one of the American soldiers at the airbase.

Dizi is no longer able to continue her writing, but her creativity lives on. She has recently taken up pottery, and the houses of family and friends are adorned with her beautiful pieces.

Dogs have always been immensely important to Dizi, and she called her memoir Dog Days, in honour of all the dogs she has loved over the years.

Dizi wrote this poem when her mother-in-law Gladys and her dog Bonnie were both old and frail:

A Glad Bonnie
Sunday afternoon
and a warm dog barking
at her own echo.
Now in her dreams
she bounds across the valley
to chase invisible sticks
with lesser spotted dogs.
When she wakes
painful joints
will remind her of her loss,
but
for now, her body twitches
in ecstasy as she runs, unchecked
and young.

A second poem, which Dizi wrote about Gladys in 1999, is especially poignant:

Angrier than the squabbling screeching seagulls
Last night she blew a bitter wind
Through the cracks and crevices of our good intentions.
Dawn found her wandering
Lost – like a frightened child,
Her emotions – become erratic tides –
Crash against the now uncertain rocks of her reality.
Her world is made of disconnected moments
Echoing distortions of her yesterday
And in the mirror in her trembling hands
I am confronted by my own tomorrow.

◊ ◊ ◊

Edited extracts from *Dog Days*

My father Celeste Conti was born in a small village high in the Apennine mountains at a time of extreme poverty. At the age of 14 he joined the exodus of the young men from the North Italian mountains to find work. Most of these young men boarded boats and were used as unpaid crew members. My father disembarked in Scotland and started working in a pub, but it didn't last long as he found himself in prison after a fight with a group of Scottish lads. He then made his way to Little Italy in London, where he worked in various cafés in Clerkenwell. My mother Aride Fabrize was born to an Italian family in Hoxton. They married when she was 20 years old.

I was born in a house in Camden Passage, Islington, on 8 January 1934. When I was five years old the Second World War started and my world was turned upside down.

The starkest memory I have of the sudden change was when the authorities arrested my father as an enemy alien. He was taken away and we did not know when we would see him again, but unlike many other Italians who were interned for the duration of the war, my father very quickly came home to us again. Maybe the fact that two of my brothers, Raymond aged 19 and Ivor aged 17, were already conscripted to the army had something to do with his release. He was restricted to a specific area of London throughout the war. Other families were not so lucky. Thousands of men were taken to camps as far away as Australia, and on 2 July 1940 the *Arandora Star* bound for Canada was torpedoed by a German U-Boat killing 446 Italian men. Many of them were friends of my father. In my nightmares I kept seeing their faces bobbing like big beach balls in the water – just the faces, no bodies, and one face belonged to my father.

I was evacuated with my nine-year-old brother, Danny. The first placing that we had was on a farm, where I would have been less miserable if we had been allowed to take any part in the exciting and extraordinarily smelly life of the place, but we were never given a chance to collect the hens' eggs or play with the farm dog. I do remember that as we walked to school every morning, often in snow so thick that it came over the tops of my wellingtons, we would see the farmer's daughter being driven to school in a pony and trap. Later my imagination was to take this image as proof that I was a natural candidate for a lifelong role as a tragic heroine.

We were moved once or twice, but eventually my parents, unhappy at having so little say in our lives, decided to follow the trend of many of the Italian community in London and Danny and I became boarders at St Dominic's Priory in Hertfordshire. For me it was a magical place, an idyllic setting for my dreams. Set in acres of ground with streams, natural swimming pools, and trees that seemed to my eyes to brush heaven's bottom! From the main house a huge conservatory looked out onto a formal walled garden, called the Sisters' Garden, which had small gazebos and summer houses dotted here and there. It was considered a real treat to be allowed to sit in it when recovering from the infectious childhood diseases that were rife. I was always searching for spots, lumps, bumps and rashes; and was surprisingly willing to sit and hold the hands and soothe the fevered brows of any likely looking candidates for the Sisters' Garden.

While the girls lived in the main house with the nuns, the boys, including my brother Danny, were banished up the hill to the Quadrangle; their dormitories were above the old stables, which now served as classrooms. The quadrangle itself was to be the scene of many of my greatest humiliations, for this is where our PE classes were held, winter and summer. Dressed in navy blue knickers and a scratchy woollen vest, I did my very best to skip, hop and jump, and was an outstanding failure in all three disciplines. Although I had not yet become familiar with the word *swingeing* I was already very familiar with the meaning of it. One nun, Mother Mary Magdalene, would swoop down on unsuspecting children like an angry magpie, in her black and white habit. Squatting with her legs apart she would describe a wide and powerful arc with her cane about 18 inches from the ground, and all legs that could not jump above that height would feel its vicious sting. My legs were black and blue, as I could never get them more than nine inches off the ground, and that was one at a time!

Mother Mary Magdalene and I were not the best of friends until the day when the annual Passion Play was being rehearsed. She discovered that I could cry at will, and that my voice had an unusual timbre for a seven-and-a-half-year-old. I was promoted from 'onlooker' to become the child character whose function was to make the audience cry.

I was a child who felt at home in company, but equally happy on my own. I liked to spend time wandering around the woods preparing myself for apparitions of the Blessed Virgin, which I was sure were going to come my way, and I looked for signs of the *stigmata* daily. I was also hoping that the woodland birds and animals would sit on my shoulders or at my feet, though I could never quite decide whether I wanted to be St Francis of Assisi, or Snow White.

I had a voracious appetite for the written word and my religious fancies were fed by the almost total diet of uplifting works that I devoured. I remember most clearly several volumes entitled *Lives of the Saints*, illustrated with extraordinary pictures of saints with eyes fixed in ecstasy on some vision or other, while lurid scenes of horrible things, like having their skin stripped off were happening down below. By the time I was nine I was reading John Buchan, Charles Dickens, and Robert Louis Stevenson. These latter books, and the cinema trips my romantic mother treated me to, fed my more earthly daydreams.

One day during a lesson I was having one such dream in which a handsome American in uniform boarded a train and sat in my compartment. We were deeply immersed in conversation when he got out a pack of *Lucky Strikes* and asked me if I would like one. I replied, 'I don't smoke, thank you.' At this point my dream was shattered by a stern 'I should think not!' accompanied by loud laughter, and I looked up to see Mother Mary Magdalene standing by my desk, and beyond her the grinning faces of my classmates!

In 1945 I finally left St Dominic's. The war was nearly at an end, and there was a buzz of excitement in the air. I remember the strange new sensations of walking to school each morning, past the Arsenal football ground, and along the bustling busyness of Holloway Road. The mixed smells of petrol, fish and chips and leather from the shoe mender's assailed my nostrils, and my eyes were filled with the extraordinary and shocking images of bomb sites and naked bedroom walls complete with fireplaces and peeling flowered wallpaper. Once I saw a picture of the Sacred Heart still hanging on the wall, the impossible face still gently smiling. I thought it was a miracle. It was only later that I started to question whether the former occupants would agree.

My new school was *Our Lady of Sion*. The sudden freedom of a day school, and the feeling of safety from attacks from the skies came like a breath of fresh air to a child who had become accustomed to the choking nightmares of soldiers coming up through the floorboards with bayonets poised. I was 11 years old and loved my school, and I was no longer afraid now that my family were all at home.

In the summer of 1947 my parents had saved up enough money to take a holiday in Italy and visit their families. They took me with them, leaving my brothers in charge of the Hilltop Café. The trip was a revelation for me! On the very first morning of my stay, my cousin Reno, who was a shepherd, took me up onto the plateau above the village. I had recently learnt Christopher Marlowe's poem 'The passionate shepherd to his love' and would quote lines to him, even though he couldn't speak a word of English, but he did teach me the most exciting Italian words I had ever heard. 'Ti voglio bene': 'I love you.'

Just the sound of the Italian language, and the handsome young man saying that he loved me was intoxicating, and the overwhelming beauty of the mountains and warmth of the sun just added to it. Over the next few days there was a lot of what was called 'heavy petting', but fortunately for my virginity, my parents and I were due to go to Torino for a family wedding on the next stage of our holiday.

We returned home to bad news. My brother Ivor was waiting for us at the station to tell us that our dog Leo had died. I can still remember the hot metal of the train as I leaned sobbing against it as my father tried to pull me away.

I was now growing up rapidly and my experiences in Italy had given me an appetite for dangerous romantic liaisons. I flirted outrageously with any young men that I met, always seeing myself as a film star and femme fatale, when in reality I was a foolish and vulnerable girl. I would still veer at times towards an old desire to become a nun and (of course) a saint. I spoke to one of the nuns in my school who thought she had a novice in her keeping. Strangely it was the Mother Superior who, despite her own lack of intelligence or spirituality, came closer to my likely future. Sixth form girls usually joined a missionary organisation called The Children of Mary. There was one meeting when she said how sad it was that black babies, 'piccaninnies' as she called them, grew up to be so ugly. Her response to my anger was that she expected that I would probably visit the school in a few years with several 'piccaninnies' under my arms.

In 1953 I met an extraordinarily handsome Trinidadian/ Indian singer called Yameen, who swore undying love and promised to marry me. At this time I was working as a trainee stage manager at The New Lindsey Theatre Club, Notting Hill Gate.

I had not heard from Yameen for some time, but one morning I was on a bus on my way to work, when I looked out of the window and saw him walking along with a beautiful woman wearing an exquisite sari. I was immediately sick and almost fainted – and now I guessed that I was pregnant.

I continued working at the New Lindsey and one day Yameen suddenly turned up. I realised that someone had told him that I was pregnant. He offered me some money – a five pound note – and as I was always one for big gestures I tore it up!

I was living at home but didn't dare to tell my parents. I was about three months when my mother confronted me with proof of my pregnancy – and chaos reigned! My mother had been reading all my letters and poems, and screamed, 'He's a black man!'

My father told me, 'I won't hit you, because if I hit you I will swing for you!' My three brothers had various views about what I should do. 'Have an abortion.' 'Have the baby adopted.' I refused. I couldn't bear the thought of anything other than keeping my baby.

I was sent to Bournemouth, and stayed with the lovely maiden aunt of my friend Sylvia. Although I was lonely, I had time as I walked along the beach to get to know my baby. As I walked I whispered her name. I knew she was a girl. I knew as I talked to her in my womb that she would be called Dadia, the name I gave her, because of her Trini*dadia*n lineage. As my pregnancy progressed it was decided that I should return to London, and strangely ended up just a few streets from The New Lindsey Theatre Club – but in a different world.

I was now placed in Loretta House, a Catholic 'Home for Unmarried Mothers'. The home was run by two nuns, whose main function seemed to be the constant castigation of the inmates; they seemed to me more like prison wardens. The young mothers were allowed to visit their family for lunch once a fortnight, leaving other girls to look after their children. On my first home visit my father prepared a lovely meal for me, but as the plate was placed in front of me I saw a tiny poussin that reminded me of a baby. I found myself weeping and unable to stop.

When I returned to Loretta House, I was told that I should not breastfeed Dadia but should use dry milk, so that I would be ready to start the process of finding someone to adopt or at least foster my baby. I suddenly realised that this was what was expected. Within a few days I had Dadia baptised in the chapel with my friend Bianca as her godmother. Now that she was baptised I was allowed to take her out, so I took one of the house prams that we had limited permission to use. I took her for a walk in the park, trying to think how I could find a way of keeping my daughter.

Where most of the other girls had not told their parents, or in some cases had been thrown out by their families, I was probably the only one whose intention was to keep my baby. I knew that I was not going to give my baby away no matter what happened.

I did not tell my family of my refusal to sign the vile papers that all the others seemed to be signing. Many nights were filled with the sobs of expectant mothers preparing to give their unborn babies away.

The day came when I had to leave Loretta House and take Dadia to a woman called Mrs Burns, who fostered children for short periods in an unwelcoming house that I visited two or three times a week. Dadia was about six months old at the time and as I pushed her along in her pram, I would find myself crying, and then I would start to dream about how I would get my baby home.

It was an awful time. Mrs Burns and the Catholic priest were trying to place her in a permanent home. I kept refusing to let her go. After about a month, Mrs Burns told me she was due to have an operation, and I would have to put Dadia into an orphanage. When I got home to my family I used all my dramatic talents to persuade everyone that Dadia had to come home. Within two days my brother and I went to collect her. When my parents got home from work that evening they immediately fell in love with her. With help from my brother Ivor, I went to Mrs Burns and paid off money that I owed her. Then we packed my baby's clothes and left never to return. When we got home I found my own bedroom with a lovely cradle and lots of lovely clothes.

When Dadia was three she started at nursery school and I started work as a waitress in my family's restaurant. I soon met a photographer who used the restaurant at lunch times and showed a keen interest in me. My family were delighted with the possibility of me being married to this well-heeled young Italian man. Somehow or other I found myself in a huge whirlwind of wedding preparations. I knew I did not want to marry this smooth stranger, but I had no way to stop this juggernaut.

My father woke me up with a cheery song and a boiled egg for breakfast. I didn't want to eat, I didn't even want to get up, and I didn't want to look at my beautiful wedding dress. I wanted to think that I had had a bad dream. But as the house started filling with calls to breakfast I sighed with a heavy heart, realising that I would not sleep again in my own bedroom, nor would I hear the warm teasing of my brothers. Instead I was going to move into a cold unwelcoming flat with an unwelcoming bridegroom. I had tried to tell my mother that I did not want to get married, but as I had always made a fuss about things, and as my mother always started to cry when I brought this up, I gave up.

But on this day I was really frightened. My mother helped me with my dress, and when I looked in the mirror, I couldn't deny that I looked beautiful – but my fears were all too obvious. I felt like I was drowning.

The church was full with family members, but I could not summon up any joy. Dadia was not at the wedding, a friend was looking after her. At the ceremony, the groom was very much in control. I cannot remember the journey to the reception, but I am sure that there was no kiss, no smile, no love!

There were at least a hundred people sitting down to the wedding breakfast, with about another hundred invited to come to the latter part of the gathering. As the tables were cleared and the music started playing the fast Italian waltz, my mother and father and my groom and I came on to the dance floor, and whirled around, while everyone else clapped hands and sang.

My mother made Dad stop and they both sat down and were talking to my aunt Polly. She said to Dad, 'Are you happy Con?' and he said, 'It's the happiest moment of my life.' And in that moment he died.

All of a sudden I knew that something was terribly wrong. It was one of those moments when time seemed to stand still. It seemed to me that there were loud drums and everybody was screaming and chaos ensued.

After we left the hospital I was still in my wedding dress. It was a terrible night. Did my husband expect me to allow him his conjugal rights? I honestly can't remember. All I can remember is the fact that I kept waking again and again, reliving the horrors of the night.

But more pain was to come. The financial situation was dire. Pop died intestate and the wedding was very costly. When the landlord heard that we could not pay our rent until some money came through we were thrown out within a week. My new husband was seriously planning to kill the landlord for the insult. I should have realised then what I was in for! My mother and brothers were willing to have us back at home but my husband refused. Instead, he immediately took Dadia to a catholic school in the south of England. I had no say in the matter.

On March 15 1961 I wrote in my diary, 'I am now a married woman of three years. On my wedding day my father died and I really don't think I have had a whole day of happiness since then. My husband is a photographer – very good at his work but often a cruel man at home.'

When I finally left my marital home, with my four children, and very little else, my overwhelming emotion was a sense of wonder at my release and liberation. I remember dancing down the street one morning after dropping my children off at school. But it was not long before I found my delicate freedom being threatened by my ex-husband's attempts to take my three younger children from me.

I was not willing to be scuppered just yet. I set out again and came to rest in Muswell Hill. It was because of my ex-husband's determination to continue his domination that I met the students who lived in the downstairs flat, for within days of moving in I got an unpleasant telephone call and I knew it would not be long before he turned up at my door. The students assured me that he would not get past them! They also took a liking to my children, taught them to play card games and football and most importantly – how to have fun. The students all seemed to me unfailingly happy, and this happiness was infectious. My younger children were soon using the garden (which was only reachable by going through the downstairs flat) and I could always find them there, running and jumping, being loud and free.

My heart was almost overflowing with joy to see them so happy, and I soon had an opportunity to show my gratitude in a practical way. It was the time of the 'Rumble in the Jungle' fight between Mohammed Ali and George Foreman. I had a television and they did not, I could cook real Italian pasta and they clearly could not! We watched the fight, ate the food and became a commune! Within a few weeks we were sharing space in the house and gardens as though we had been there forever.

The electricity between me and Derek could have kept the national grid going for months! After the restrictive marriage that I had endured for nearly 13 years, this was a new freedom, similar to that I had experienced at the end of the war. When the first liberation came, people looked at each other in wonder, smiles came unbidden into their eyes; my second liberation was my divorce; when I found Derek, I found my harbour, and my third liberation.

Chapter 6

I'm gone older. Everything change.

ROMANINA CONTUCCI

Romanina Contucci with husband Marcello,
son Gino and daughter Angela, c.1963.

Romanina Contucci *was born in Italy in 1927 and came to England as a young woman. She has lived in South London for more than 50 years. I interviewed her in the presence of her daughter Angela Contucci, who filled in some of the details, and interpreted from time to time when Romanina spoke in Italian. While I was there, Romanina started to read aloud in Italian from an exercise book where she had written a long prayer that she herself had composed. Angela told me that her mother used to* *be fluent in English, but is now more comfortable speaking in Italian. Romanina attends the Healthy Living Club in Stockwell where she can converse in Italian with some of the staff and volunteers. LW*

I been born in Italy, in the country, near Arpino, four hour from Rome. My parents work on a farm. *Contadini.*[47] They grew everything – tomato, vegetables, fruit – lots of fruit.

My mother very very nice. She used to feed other babies. She fed them with the milk, yes. My mother very fat.

I got one sister and two brothers. One brother lost in the war.

When the war came, it was very bad. Because no money for buy food. In the war, very dear, buy all! We use cornflour for make bread. Sometimes, one week after, it was too hard. Make boil it, boil the bread, make oil, and eat it.

It was very danger. Nobody gone out. The children stay indoors. We live near the big road, coming from Arpino. And the *ferrovia*[48] not very far. When the bombs came, we had to hide in *la casa.*[49] There were no shelters, because I'm in the country! *Nella campagna*[50]!

When I born, the war coming. My two brothers gone in army. No stay in home. My father, myself and my mother – my mother wake me up and wrap a blanket around, and bring me in the country. Because my mother must have gone with my daddy. Work in the country. They cannot leave me in home – nobody home.

I lost my first brother, Gino, died in the war. I never forget my mother crying. In the night sometimes, come and take me up. My mother cry all the time, because she lost her son. My mother very, very upset.

When I got married, I had the first boy quick! I had the children quickly. I not supposed to have the children like that. Because they not give me time!

I put the name to my son my brother: Gino. In the day, I keep the child, because I live in the country. I have the children all the time. Put the blanket.

Then my sister coming in England. Because my sister coming in England, I come in England too. When I come I have got my first son. My husband Marcello coming first.

Gino born in Italy, coming here very little. Then he was ill, so he come back in Italy early, because my mother and father lived there. He was there four or five years.

Marcello, my husband, like a god! He do everything!

He work as a baker in Tooting Bec. After he finish the bread, different job. He work in the night for the bread, and in the day in hospital. He made this pastries and everything for all hospital. And I'm lucky, because when he come in in the morning, every time, bring something home. Every time I eating.

I work all the time, because I wanted a house, I wanted to be somebody! I work very hard for make a house. Because we don't have money. We had a little money, we give a deposit.

I did domestic work. I work in a hospital. I work in a factory. I'm working in a place where you make a cake, biscuit. I make me fat! Because my husband say, 'You gone too fat! No eat so sweet!'

I work in a café. I cannot have somebody look after the children, I take with me.

I work with Italian people, I speak Italian. They tell me, 'You must speak English.'

When you cannot speak, they put the job a different one. I want to learn English. I want to be English. That's why I learn quickly. I no go to school, I just speak with the people. I had to learn English, because I been working in hospital.

After my daughter Angela born, I work at home, making scarf. I make a roll the handkerchief, the big one.

I love my children. They would be at home. Up in the morning, put a blanket on the floor. And sit there. I teach the children from a small one.

I'm a long time frustrated, because I have to work all the time, night and day. I make scarf. My daughter must work now! I don't want to work any more.

When we buy this house, I do my garden. We grow beans, potato, turnips, tomatoes, garlic. I have a tree that apples. We grow pears, plums, figs. A beautiful fig tree! I been born in the country! I remember when I was a small baby. Picking the fruit. But all the time I eat everything!

Now I'm gone older. Everything change. How old am I? 88? It's the memory.

I go to different clubs. I see my friends. When I go to the club, everybody see me. I speak the language, in my way. I no speak right. But the people understand me!

Chapter 7

Riding the rollercoaster

CAROL CRONK

Carol Cronk *received support from Alzheimer's Australia after developing young onset dementia. She became active in the Alzheimer's Australia Fight Dementia Campaign, helping to raise awareness about dementia and campaigning for better funding for research. I heard Carol speak at the Alzheimer's Disease International 2012 conference in London, and invited her to contribute to the book. Soon afterwards, she sent me this account. LW*

In 2008 I was diagnosed with early onset Alzheimer's disease at the age of 62. Two years later, another PET scan showed early signs of overlapping frontotemporal dementia.

I have had a few emotional rollercoasters during the past 14 years: three cancer challenges, the worst a breast cancer which required a mastectomy. However, in all these possible terminal diagnoses, I was given the diagnosis, then an 'action plan' towards recovery. Alzheimer's and other types of dementia don't offer any hopeful outcomes.

I went through a three-month period of brain scans – CAT/ MRI/ SPECT/ PET – and intensive neurological testing. When I went to receive my diagnosis, the neurologist explained the results of the tests, and advised my husband and me to change our lifestyle to accommodate my non-curable terminal illness, and basically to make the best of whatever years were ahead of us.

These changes of lifestyle required my husband Oscar to be home with me to accommodate my needs. This meant early retirement, causing our plans for the future to be drastically changed. Our financial commitments were no longer possible, and our mortgage needed to cease.

We sold everything: our lovely canal home and our island getaway cruising boat. We said farewell to the close network of friends that lived on the canals with us, and left Western Australia in a new Fifth Wheel caravan, to live in transit between three states in Australia, to share whatever quality of health time remains with all my family. We settled in a motor home resort in a town called Casino in New South Wales, close to my second eldest son and his family. My youngest son aged 26 years and his family live in Brisbane, three hours from Casino. Our lifestyle now is travelling back and forth between Casino, Brisbane and Perth to visit my 89-year-old mother, senior sister, two sons and my daughter. I also participate in clinical drug trials in Perth.

My internal trauma at my diagnosis was highlighted in such fear and dread because of the experience I had lived through with my father during his battles and struggles with Alzheimer's and vascular dementia. My immediate devastating feelings were not of dying but having to live in one of those 'dementia homes'.

My father had lived all of his early senior years as a free spirit, absolutely independent. When he had to live in a secure dementia environment this was intensely traumatic for him, and for my sister and me. He spent every day seeking to find a way to escape. On the two occasions that he did abscond, he was shortly after apprehended by the police and returned to a more secure area. Dad never gave up his fight for freedom until the last weeks before he died.

The trauma of enduring this nightmare with our father caused us daughters to make a suicidal pledge, that if we ever got *'that* disease', we would do a 'Thelma and Louise'. *Thelma and Louise* is a movie where two female friends decide to commit suicide, and drive over a cliff in a red convertible to escape being imprisoned for their crimes. I had a red convertible at that time!

For my father, having dementia and being forced to live in this type of environment was like being in prison. When I was diagnosed, my father's world of torment unfolded before me. How was I going to live in his footsteps? I felt those prison walls surrounding me.

I accept now that I have to pick up the cross that my father had to bear on his dementia journey. However, I am working hard at obtaining a higher quality of life. Perhaps I am following in his footsteps, but hopefully, with my loving and supportive husband by my side, my road will be smoother and kinder. Also, I have positive gifts from my father's genes: his strong determined will, and his positive mental attitude to overcome adversity.

I joined the Alzheimer's support group, which has been extremely beneficial for both me and my husband. I participated in personal counselling with a wonderful counsellor from Alzheimer's, who would drive for over an hour to visit me in my home. After a period of time she was able to counsel both Oscar and me together, which was very helpful to us both.

After four years of supportive care from the Alzheimer's services we are now participating with them as advocates in the Alzheimer's Australia *Fight Dementia* Campaign. We are campaigning for: continued government funding for research through drug trials to find a cure; public awareness so families and communities can receive the facts about this disease which will help them understand and cope more easily; and hopefully, to remove the stigma that surrounds those who are living with dementia.

We speak out in seminars when the opportunity arises, in the hope to enlighten the communities about Alzheimer's and other types of dementia. People need to know that dementia can affect younger people as early as in their 30s; it is a terminal disease, not an age-related disease, and it is affecting about 1500 more people each week in Australia. Media exposure needs to show younger people affected by this disease, to help change the stigma surrounding this devastating illness – devastating for the sufferers and devastating for their families.

The Australian government has a pharmaceutical benefit scheme which subsidises anti-dementia medication for the first six months. After that period you're expected to sit a Mini Mental State Examination (MMSE) to prove that this medication has improved your mental functioning. If you fail to show the required 2-point improvement on this test they cease their subsidy, and this medication can then cost up to $200 every four weeks.

As people with dementia understand, during the first year after diagnosis, our lives are in upheaval. Many lifestyle changes are forced upon us to accommodate the illness. I believe that using the MMSE in this way is ridiculous, unfair, inaccurate and unjust. I am an example of that test being wrong. Based on my failure to improve my score by 2 points, I might have ceased taking the medication, believing that the test results showed that the medication was not helping me at that time.

But I am living proof – and my doctor agrees – that this medication is beneficial to my continued ability to function mentally.

Others we have known that 'failed' this test stopped taking the medication. We saw them deteriorate so quickly and enter care facilities at an early age, way before they would have, I believe, had they remained on the medication. We wrote to many government officials including our prime minister regarding this unjust and inaccurate evaluation of the medication's benefit, but received no positive responses from any of them.

However, we did get a positive response from the drug company Pfizer. They agreed to give us a free compassionate supply every six months, if I supply a letter from my neurologist stating that the medication is continuing to benefit me.

These drugs offer people with dementia their only hope of prolonging their mental capacity. The restrictive guidelines need to be revised, and this type of medication should be made freely available. This would assist in keeping people with dementia out of care facilities for as long as possible.

In my former life, I worked for ten years with the Salvation Army, supporting homeless youth and their families, and also did voluntary work with the drug and alcohol service in Perth as a 24-hour emergency phone contact for families dealing with drug issues.

While I worked for the Salvation Army, I acquired training in advanced conflict resolution, behaviour management and counselling skills. This training enabled me to teach these teenagers and their parents to recover from their traumatic relationships and rebuild their lives. I humbly say that I was a highly respected employee, and was seen to have a natural gift in this field. This work was extremely rewarding and fulfilling to me: it made my own world a better world, and my joy was making a better world for those suffering emotional brokenness.

Since my diagnosis of dementia, the skills I learned through my work have helped me to overcome my own emotional brokenness. With the support of the Alzheimer's counselling service, I began to activate and draw from deep within myself those skills that I had been using on others for most of my life. In the past, I had the joy of seeing these skills help so many to overcome their hopeless situations: now it was my turn to become active on myself. I found renewed faith to get out of my negative state of mind and begin working these skills on myself.

Skills which I use to overcome my arising symptoms are, first to accept them, then to find ways to combat them, working not only against them but with them, for a better quality of life amidst them. In the words of the 'Serenity Prayer': 'The serenity to accept the things I cannot change, courage to change the things I can, and wisdom to know the difference'.

Four years now into my dementia journey, the disease has taken away my 'known self', the things I used to enjoy about the person I had evolved into. Socially, I was perceived as somewhat extrovert, and known as a 'party animal'. Dementia has taken that personality from me. I now live a lifestyle of almost complete opposite. I perceive myself as an anti-social, introverted personality. I am only happy and comfortable now with like-minded people – people who have dementia in the early stages like me. I cannot force myself into crowded noisy environments such as restaurants, cafés and theatres. The background music and people's background chatting and laughter causes me to become agitated and stressed and need to exit the environment.

At first I struggled against these symptoms, fighting against the dysfunctional person that was evolving within me. In despair at my failure to overcome these changes, I researched on the internet about my disease and learned about the progressive personality and behaviour changes it would cause. I learned to accept what was happening to me, as it was clear that I could not change anything: this new personality that was taking my known self away could *not* be stopped. Having knowledge about my disease empowered me to understand it more clearly, and to make the decision to work with it and around it for my own well-being and that of my husband.

I have a loving, supportive husband that loves his 'two Carols': Carol 1, the one that he married 13 years ago, before the disease; Carol 2, who he has learned to adapt to in these changes. He continues to love me as he always has, and ensures that we can still have a quality of life together amidst our dementia challenges.

We have a new world now where we live together almost completely alone, quietly. Some would view our lifestyle as somewhat isolated from the rest of the world. However we do try to 'seize our every day.'

Skills and strategies that we have learned to help us cope amidst my dementia symptoms.

I can go to cafés and restaurants where we can sit outside in quiet surroundings. We visit cafés prior to their busy mealtimes, or we get a take-away coffee and food and take it to a park, which is now my favourite environment.

When I go to Alzheimer's Australia gatherings, I warn them that I will have earplugs inserted to cope in the busy noisy environment, although this causes limitations in communication. I will be part of their gathering without being socially involved, which I would previously have enjoyed.

When I'm with close friends or family, I can accommodate four people at one time. I explain my needs prior to our get-together. I ask them to please communicate to each other one person at a time, as cross-talking affects me. I have asked some friends of my past life to let our friendship go, as I prefer them to remember me and our friendships as we were. This was a sad and harsh severing for us all, but I am at peace about that decision. And I am certain that it was beneficial for them also. However a few of my friends would not accept that release and have continued to keep in contact.

Family? Well, thankfully, God has taught us to love each other unconditionally, and that is family love. I allow my children to live in their faith and hope – combined with a little 'denial' –

that a cure will arrive in time for me to be spared the rest of my downward spiral.

Early this year, Oscar and I attended an end of life planning seminar. We learned about the ways that we can legally document how I want to die. Firstly, I could state that I should receive no treatments that would prolong my life, so for example I would receive no antibiotics for infections. A chest infection would cause pneumonia, so, as I interpreted that one, I would drown myself. Secondly, I could request to starve myself or dehydrate myself (no fluids) until I ceased living. And thirdly I could be put to sleep 'whilst I am dying'. None of these self-dying methods made any sense to me.

The lady who presented this talk is someone I highly respect as a powerful and lovely person, but when she had finished speaking, I was so frustrated and angry I asked for the microphone. I asked whether I would be treated in this inhumane manner if I was someone's beloved pet. Would anyone be content to have to endure this slow, horrid death with their little pet?

Where would be the human compassion in any of that dying process? I asked why the terminally ill, during our last horrendous stages of this disease (when our brains have ceased functioning and can never be revived), why can we not have the same humane ending of our lives by euthanasia?

I then added, to all the religious minds in the audience, that I was of strong Christian faith, and that the Jesus that I have learned about and lived by for most of my life would not desire for me and my loved ones to have to endure the terrible death process that our ignorant, inhumane laws remain fixed with. I thought after I had finished speaking, that I would have been rebuked for my response or asked to leave. However, the speaker responded compassionately and positively and thanked me for my courage to speak out. She then gave many accounts of doctors and nurses and other terminally ill people facing this same end of life dilemma, who were in total acceptance that this should be a personal and individual choice.

When I was first diagnosed, I read Christine Bryden's books[51] about her Alzheimer's diagnosis and her life, living in this disease. I contacted her for encouragement and knowledge, and we became great friends. I survived many crises due to being able to contact her during those difficult times. I had no one else who could understand or help me, or who I felt comfortable with to share the worries and issues which came up because of my disease. Others experiencing the same difficulties produce a trust and a confidence to share your most intimate problems, as they have lived through some if not all of them. I value her friendship and support as a heavenly gift.

I would be happy for anyone who wants to contact me, after reading my story, to email me. During the four years since my diagnosis, my husband and I have gained a wealth of knowledge about all types of dementia, and experienced a portion of the knowledge we have learned. Doctors and neurologists give you a diagnosis, but no tools to take away to help you manage your downward spiral journey. We taught ourselves through the internet, and learned through experience. I hope my story will encourage another person that is facing this harsh emotional rollercoaster.

My email address is carolsthwestnet@hotmail.com.

Postscript

Carol Cronk adds:

Since I wrote the above account, nearly three years ago, there have been changes in my physical health, in my diagnosis, and my lifestyle.

I was on the Alzheimer's advisory committee in Canberra for about a year, but I had to resign, because I developed a new neurological condition which caused me intense grief. This condition is called cervical dystonia and it causes continual involuntary head and neck movements. I couldn't sit still or travel or take part in long phone calls to committee members. I was overwhelmed with pain and discomfort. I couldn't hold on to information or stay focused. I became confused and extremely frustrated. This was affecting Oscar, who also became extremely frustrated when I tried to persist; he encouraged me finally to let go of things that now I had lost the mental and physical capacity to continue in.

I also underwent a lot more tests and brain scans, as it appeared that my Alzheimer's diagnosis might not be correct. My dementia issues have now been clarified as the vascular type – which my husband and I already begun to suspect, based on my symptoms. We also found that my symptoms actually fitted the same pattern as my father's. His began with tiny strokes, as did mine. During my father's earlier years almost all dementias were under the banner of Alzheimer's.

I now have a wonderful neurologist who supports me/ us wonderfully. He treats me every three months with botulin injections around my neck and back of skull, in an attempt to stop the spasms which twist my neck and head about in uncontrollable pain, discomfort and embarrassment. These three-monthly procedures will continue as long as I do. Now that we know my issues are of the vascular type, Oscar has bought me a heart monitor to check each day, and of course a blood pressure machine to monitor and raise or restrict medication as required. This gives us encouragement towards prevention of heart and stroke issues.

Our lives these days are lived out as quietly as possible. Apart from family and a few dementia friends, we live an extremely quiet life, just together with husband Oscar. We live to our very best amidst our challenges. And be thankful of our every day.

Chapter 8

I still remember

HALIDE EAMES

Halide Eames *was born in Cyprus in 1931 and came to England in
1959. I interviewed her at her home in North London. Her daughter Zalihe,
known as Sally, became concerned about Halide's memory a couple of years
ago, and asked the GP to investigate. 'I got concerned, because Mum started
to forget this and forget that. And I thought – that's not my mum, because
my mum's very independent. A strong woman.' Since Halide was diagnosed
with early stage dementia, the family have received information and support
from the local branch of Alzheimer's Society. LW*

I grew up in Cyprus. I got married but it didn't work out. Got divorced. Then I fall in love with somebody and I have my daughter Sally. And I did love him very much. I did want to marry him. But his parents didn't want him to marry me. They said no. Different religion. And that's it really.

Then I met Mr Eames. I said, 'I've got a daughter,' and he said, 'Your daughter is my daughter.' He was Irish. We got married in Cyprus and then he brought me to England, in 1959. I left Sally with my Mum. We come here first. And after, I sent for her. She came in 1962 when she was seven.

My Mum was sad to say goodbye to Sally. She didn't want me to bring her here. She said, 'Don't go away with Mummy, she's going to smack you if you're a naughty kid, playing about.'

My parents had to move away from their village, because that was the Greek side. They went to live in another village, which was not mix. Turkish this side, and the Greeks that side.

And my Dad pass away, and my Mum left alone. And she stayed there. And after, I went and brought her here. Everybody pushed her to not come, because it's cold – and I said, 'When it's cold, we don't live outside, like in Cyprus.' And I brought her here. And she pass away here.

When she lived here with me, I used to take her to the market, to go shopping. I used to say, 'Come slowly.' And she could sit down, have a cup of tea. I would buy a few things quickly. She sit down there, by the time she finish her tea, I finish my shopping, and we go home. Because she's fed up by herself at home all the time.

Mr Eames was a policeman, and I was a machinist. When I first came to England, we live in Battersea, and I used to work in the hospital – washing the cups, the tea towels, sweeping, cleaning and polishing. It was nice. But I wanted to be machinist. Mr Eames find me a little machine. I learned the machine. He buy me some white cloth so I could practise at home. Then I got a job in a factory, making clothes. I could buy a coat, a jacket. I can't pay cash, but I pay weekly. It was nice people.

I live in this flat a long time, more than 30 years. I have very good neighbours. The one next door, very nice lady. We see each other outside, we start talking, and that's it. Maybe I could go live with Sally, but there's stairs. You have to go up and down. I can't walk.

My knees are getting very weak. No pain. But I have weakness. I don't go out much. I like to go out every two or three weeks. Sally take me shopping, with my walking stick. I can never find my walking stick! I must not lose my walking stick! My grandson got me a walking frame, but I don't want to go out with that, in case I fall down again! Once I went out on my own and I slipped. Bang my head. I went to the phone, to ring Sally up. It took my 50p, but it was faulty or something. So a young man came along. I said, 'Please can you help me?'

When Sally bring me, it's all right – one arm with Sally, one arm with the stick! We go shopping together, or sometime I send her by herself. Sometimes, even she forgets what I want to buy, and I have to go with her! Sometimes when you get older, you forget sometimes, isn't it. But I still remember, I *still* remember.

I have four grandchildren and three great-grandchildren. They ring me all the time! The oldest girl is my special granddaughter, Sevi. I love her very much. I love them all, but she comes first. When she was young I used to go there, and pick her up, and take her around and around. 'I'm going home now.' 'No, Ninny, no!' She's like my own daughter. She's helping me with anything and everything.

My granddaughter wants to take me on holiday, I say no, because of my cat. She says 'Leave your cat.' But I'm cuddling with my cat. She says my neighbour can feed him. He was a stray. He walked in one day, and that was it. He's scared from the kids. If somebody knocks the door, he hides in the bedroom! We had plenty animals in Cyprus, but they were all outside, not in the house.

I'm very lucky. I love my flat. I go in the kitchen, make some dinner. I've got my stick. I go in the garden. I told you, I had my mum, that's why I've got this flat – two bedrooms. When my mum came here, I had a one bedroom flat. It was on the top floor. I put her in the sitting room. It was very uncomfortable. Specially there were lifts going up and down. And then if you were sitting there watching telly, my mummy wants to sleep, so I can't sit in the sitting room. So I said, I know where I want to move – there's an empty flat on the ground floor!

If I need heavy work, like I say, Sally comes. And if you want the kitchen painted, get the kids to do it! I've got a chair, in the bath, to sit down. It's nice to sit in the chair, going up and down!

I've got a garden. I can sit outside. My grandson helps me. He cut my grass, and cut this and cut that. I used to grow vegetables in the garden. I used to plant beans that side, and potatoes this side. It gets sun all day long.

Back home in Cyprus, people make their own bread, and grow their olives, and put them in the big barrels, saving for the winter, and grow figs, and dry them. We're Muslim, so we can't eat pig. We eat goat, and sheep, and this and that.

I still cook, but sometimes Sally cook for me. She cook at home, and bring it here. I used to do a lot of cooking. Bread, olive bread, pastry, *flaouna*[52]...I don't do anything now. Only watching the telly, and go sleep!

For my age, I have very good health. Still alive – and that's it! I'm 81. 82 this year coming. A good age, isn't it. I have blood pressure tablets, diabetes tablets. And my inhalers. Sally she tell me, don't eat too much chocolate. But I'm going to eat, and I don't care! I'm 81. I've been here every year. I'm not going to be here tomorrow. Don't worry about it! It doesn't hurt me!

They check my eyes as well. I had cataracts removed a few years ago. It wasn't bad, but when they look at it, they said to cut it out, and that's what they done. Now I see properly. And my hearing is very good. I forget things a little bit. To forget is natural at my age. I'll be 82 in July.

I like watching telly. *Deal or No Deal*, *EastEnders*, *Coronation Street*. I used to like *The Bill*. I like *NCIS* – I love the grey-haired one. I say I'm going to go and chase him! I like the old films, Elizabeth Taylor, Charlton Heston, the old fashioned films, cowboys films. They don't make films like that now.

Chapter 9

I never get tired of dancing

MIDGE FLINT

Midge Flint with son Gary and daughter Mandi.

Midge (Maureen) Flint *has lived all her life in North London. She has vivid memories of the Blitz and of being evacuated to Cornwall as a young child. I met her at the Enfield Alzheimer's Society dementia café, and interviewed her at home in the presence of her daughter Mandi. LW*

I was born in 1935, so I was only four when the war started. We lived at Finsbury Park, near the Astoria cinema. During the air raids everybody used to run down and shelter in the tube station. Sometimes they knew the raids were going to come that night, so if they knew there was going to be a raid, my mum used to send me and my sister on ahead, with whoever else was going. We all had a blanket each, and we used to all go down there, to get a space on the platform, where the trains come in. I always remember that, because it was freezing. I would never let go of my sister. We had to be very careful. Some of the boys were older and they used to lark about, you know. And don't forget I was small for my age. That's why my name's Midge, because I was called a midget.

When I was about seven, they collected all the kids from my street and we were evacuated to Cornwall. The people I stayed with were very posh people, very wealthy. I can remember so clearly. It was a lovely house, beautiful, with servants and all that. They had servants to cook for them, do the washing, open the street door, do everything for them. But I didn't like their servants, because they didn't like us. We were extra work. And the woman was middle-aged, and she'd never had any children of her own. And I wasn't a very nice little girl! I was a cheeky little bugger and they didn't really like me after a while. I was a handful! I can remember it now.

When I think back, now I'm older, she had no idea how to bring up children. She was proud to go out and say, 'This is the little girl I've taken in,' and hold my hand, but that was it. And I'm not bragging, but I was a blonde, curly-haired little girl, my hair was in ringlets, very blonde. They called me Shirley Temple. And she used to want to take me out and make me immaculate – well, I didn't want to be like that. She wanted to put me on a pedestal, parade me round. It was, 'Don't sit there, it's dirty.' You wasn't allowed to get on bikes or anything. That's how it was.

She chose me out of a crowd. I remember standing there. I can remember thinking, 'I want to be with my sister!' and I was holding on to my sister, but they didn't let my sister come, and I showed off after that. They split us up, and that was wrong. Now I'm older I think that was cruel. And I did show off a lot. But I remember standing in the line, with all the others, and she said, 'I want that one.' It was like picking out an apple! And I can remember thinking, 'I'm not going without my sister.' And they said, 'She's going to be there.' And of course I went along with that – but she wasn't!

When we went to school in Cornwall, the other children didn't like us. They thought we were common. They looked at you as though you was dirty. I was only young, but it sticks in your memory. I remember one saying to me, 'I'm not going near you because my mum says you've got fleas!' I suppose they said that about all the London kids. But of course, my head was full of ringlets, so anything going, I picked it up! I did have fleas by the time I got home, but I never had them when I went. I remember when I came home from there, my mum took me straight down to the cleansing station, because my hair was matted. I remember that so clearly.

By the end of the war, quite a few houses in our street had been damaged. You'd get these incendiary bombs used to fall, so the roof had to be redone, to stop the rain from coming through.

My dad was in the army in the war. He was a Desert Rat, I think they call them. My mum was all on her own for quite a few years. When he went away, I remember clearly, my brother was a baby. And when my dad eventually did come home, my brother must have been about five or six, and he didn't like my dad, because my dad would say, 'Don't do that!' and 'Pick that up from the floor!' and my brother didn't like that, because my brother was a natural boy! I can remember so clearly now, my brother saying, 'Mum, when's Dad going back to the army?' But later on, my brother and my dad was wonderful friends.

My sister and brother and I are all still mates, still good friends. We see a lot of each other.

My dad was a French polisher, and my mum always worked. She used to go out, sometimes did a bit of cleaning, you know, whatever she could. I was very happy as a child. We never had much, but I've got happy memories of larking about. I didn't like school though. I used to play the hop a lot.

I left school as soon as I could. I must have been about 14. And I've worked ever since. I've always enjoyed working. I've done a bit of factory work, a bit of office work. I've done anything that came along that I fancied. The job I liked the most, and I stayed there for quite a long time till I got married, was at this big variety theatre called the Finsbury Park Empire. They had all the big acts on, and I got to know somebody there, and got a job there in the box office. Which I loved! All the different stars came on, Frankie Vaughan, Billy Cotton and his band, and all the rock and roll stars like Marty Wilde, Cliff Richard, Adam Faith. I never minded going to work. I done overtime, because I loved it.

When I was younger, I'm being honest with you now, I liked to go there so much but I couldn't afford to go. I wasn't working there. We found a door that opened, we knew exactly what door. I'm not ashamed to say it, we used to kick the door, and it loosened the bar, so we used to creep in that way! We just used to go and sit down, we never paid. Many times when I was younger, I used to go there with my mates and kick the door, like that, to get it open. Nearly wore my right leg out, getting the doors open for free! If we got caught, you'd see us skirting up the road!

And I ended up working there. And then I met Lenny, and when I was getting married, they all came – all the theatre management came to my wedding. It was wonderful. I got on very well with them all. After I got married, I didn't do much work then, because I got pregnant, and I didn't believe in working and leaving the baby with anybody else.

Lenny grew up a couple of roads away from me, and he used to go to the YMCA on the corner of my road, and they used to play snooker and all that sort of thing. Sometimes there would be a dance at the youth club. I loved jiving. Lenny can't dance, so I would dance with anybody that was going! I mean, he can do a 'creep' as we call it. I get him on the dance floor, and then I'm guiding him.

Lenny's parents were greengrocers, and he became a greengrocer too. At that time, he used to have a horse and cart to go to the market. We wasn't married then. He lived with his parents and I lived with mine. And he used to come round and call for me, and we used to go out together. Years ago we didn't have cars, but he was considered well off because he had his horse and cart. I used to go with him sometimes to market, sitting on a bag full of potatoes! And his mates used to yell, 'Where you going? On your honeymoon?' And I'm sitting there going, 'Shut up!' And he used to look after the horse, and I'm a great animal-lover, and I used to go with him sometimes to feed his horse. They had a stable nearby.

The horse was called Mary. And when we got married and had children, Mary was getting old. We couldn't have her put down or nothing, so we put her into a lovely stables. And we used to take the kids up there and go and see her every week, and take her little treats. She had her own stable, and she used to be able to look out, and up and down, because she could stick her head out. And because the horse knew Lenny so well, when we got to the stables, he used to call out 'Mary!' and her head used to come out – and you could hear her little hooves going like that, excited. We kept her going for years. We wouldn't let anybody ride her, or put her to work. We paid for her to be there, because we loved her, and she died a natural death. She was an old girl, when she died. There was lots of tears shed in this house over that horse.

◊ ◊ ◊

I'm trying to think when I began to notice that my memory wasn't so good. I've got the feeling it was when I first started being ill with arthritis, in hospital. I'm trying to think when it happened.

At first I used to think, 'Oh, I'm doing too much.' I might have been rushing around with the housework, or whatever. And I always used to think it was that, you know. And I still do sometimes. If I forget things, I always say to myself, 'You're overdoing it.'

Anyway, I went to the doctor. I don't like worrying the family, to be honest, so I went on my own. And my doctor, he just said, 'You're just getting old.' And you accept that, don't you. I thought, well, perhaps I am getting old. And you just take no notice.

Nowadays, I know that I've got dementia, but I can't think – I can't remember how that's happened, in all honesty.

I don't let it hold me back. I'm pretty tough like that. To put it crudely – 'Sod it!' I don't really worry that much about it. When I can't remember something, it drives me absolutely mad, but apart from that, I don't mind too much. Touch wood, I haven't done anything terribly wrong! I mean like some people, who forget to get theirselves dressed and run out with no clothes on, or they don't do their housework. I always say, the day you see me not getting dressed, or me clothes aren't clean, and I've not combed my hair, that's when you've got to worry.

I think my brain's pretty active, because I've got my family around. Some women, they live on their own, and they don't see a soul all day long, do they. I've got a good friendly family. They're in and out. They pop round. My daughter, my daughter-in-law, my son. They're all helpful. I've got a close family. But they've got their own lives to lead! We don't choke each other and drive each other mad.

Mandi, my daughter, is a good girl. I'll be honest with you, I'd be lost without her. She takes me out to different activities during the week, and we go to Singing for the Brain on Tuesdays ('cos the brain ain't working very good these days!) I like all that.

I thoroughly enjoy it. It's happy. We sing all the old songs. I love it.

I go out with Gary, my son, on a Sunday to Hampstead, and we have a long walk. We're out there for hours. He's got his dog Freddie. It's Freddie we go for. We go out in all weathers. I'm exhausted when we get back, because we do the whole of Hampstead Heath.

The thing I miss the most is the driving. I used to be so independent! I don't like asking everybody. If it wasn't for my daughter and my son – it's the hardest thing that's happened to me, that I have to ask.

Lenny can't drive any more either. And it's because the pair of us worked too bloody hard! He worked all his life, and I've always been a worker. And we can't drive any more. In a way it's right. Len hasn't got the control of his legs, because he's had arthritis in the spine, and mine's my memory. It's awful, because sometimes I might be in the car with my daughter, and I'm thinking 'Where are we?' I'm never silly. I always do as I'm told. I don't try and drive or anything like that.

Gary's sons are grown up now, and they take Lenny out. Because he can't get around very much now. They take him for a drive and that, and take him to football. They all go off to the Arsenal together. He goes to all the matches.

I still love dancing. I never get tired of that. We go to the British Legion, just down the road, on a Saturday night and have a drink. Sometimes they have a band, and they play a bit of ballroom, a bit of rock and roll, it's a mixture. I love the music! I'll dance with anyone who asks me, with a bit of luck! Lenny doesn't mind. (Otherwise I'd stop him going out to the races with his mates, and the football!) We're all members, so they're all people I know. I still jive, if there's someone who knows how to do it. It's a pleasant evening. I know it might not be everyone's cup of tea, but it suits me and him.

I've got a bit of arthritis as well. That's something I've always suffered from over the years. I think a lot of that was caused through sleeping on the floor in the Underground when I was a child. Now and then I get a twinge, but I just go and get some pills for it. It doesn't stop me walking, and it doesn't stop me dancing.

Chapter 10

They deal with everybody as a individual

CLARICE HALL

Photo © Sophie di Martino.

Clarice Hall *was a nurse in Holloway Prison for more than 30 years. She has always been active in her local community in South London and volunteered in many capacities for her church in Brixton. I interviewed her at her home in the presence of her son Gerard and one of her daughters,*

Joanne. The whole family laughed when they told me of her nickname, 'Twiggy'. LW

I was born in 1933 in the parish of St Ann in Jamaica. I have five brothers. I had two sisters but I didn't know them at all. They died when they were babies, one after another. And I was the third one. So I survived. I was blessed. I was the one girl, the pet one.

We had a lot of freedom. I'm from the country, so you don't have to worry to be protected, because everybody protects one another, everybody look after one another, so you are free to go. You're not afraid of anyone at all. It was loads of us children, and we just play and play.

We always use to run to school. We couldn't be late for school. They were very strict, and I didn't want to be late either. I enjoy school, very much so.

My mother was a business lady. She has her own business, selling groceries. She had a big shop, a market shop, in the town. She had a proper grocery area, and then one area was cooking area, so she also cook there. It was a long building and she had a café one end, and then one end was like grocery area. I was always in the shop with her, specially at the weekend. I love it. I love people. When I left school, I used to help my mum in the shop, while she at the other end with another lady helping her.

My father used to work on the parochial board. He was road headman. He was in charge of giving jobs to people, street sweeping and maintenance. He was in charge of that, for a certain area.

And then my dad took ill, so he couldn't work any more, so it was only my mum was breadwinner, because she had her business. He was getting a bit of money, because he was from the public works department, but it wasn't the salary that he used to get. So my mum manages very well, and then my two eldest brother, they were trademen and they were qualified, so they use to contribute money to my mother as well. So she was very lucky and blessed. She was a very good businesswoman. Everything she touch, turn into gold. She was one of those ladies. So she was very successful.

Then my mum came to England, because they were recruiting people from the islands, from Jamaica and the other islands, to come to England, and America. So she came to England, and she sent for us one by one. One by one we all came. My two eldest brother, they didn't come to England. They went to America. So the money was coming in from America, from the eldest ones. And then from here. And then, my dad was fine. My father was comfortable, because we could pay for somebody to look after him.

When I first came to England, I thought it was awful! Everywhere was dark, the place foggy. It was cold. I wouldn't get out of bed! I gave my mum such a problem. It was paraffin heater they had in the house. So it's not central heating. But eventually, I got use to it. The landlady, Mrs Erskine, she was very, very good to me. So when my mum's gone to work, Mrs Erskine use to come and bring me food in the bed. I'll never forget that lady. She would come, and she would bang the door, and she would say, 'Are you there?' and she would bring the lunch.

At first, I didn't go to work, because we were looking to do some more education. I go to evening classes. My first job was in a factory. I can remember the little man that was the boss. They used to call it Straw House, and they would make little baskets and thing like that.

Then I got a job eventually working in the hospital. That was something that I really enjoyed doing, because I was helping people. I was there for a while. And after when I left from there, I went into the prison service.

'Twiggy': Clarice Hall as a nurse at
Holloway Prison, 1960s.

I work in the prison service for years and years and years.
Holloway Prison. I was a nurse in the prison hospital. I was there
for a long time – 30 years. I retired from there. I enjoy working
in Holloway.

There was this governor, Doctor Bull, the new governor that
came in just after I got there. She was a short lady like that. And
she just fall in love with me. She fall in love with the black girl!
There was not a lot of black folks there. And every time she gets
on the unit, the first person she asked for was me. So I did very
well there!

They use to call me Twiggy! They call me Twiggy, because I
could run! And if there's an emergency anywhere – Doctor Bull,
she was on the top floor. And she asked me to get something, and
when I took it to her, she said, 'How did you get here so quick?'
Because I was fast! And it sticks! Dr Bull is the one, every time
she come visiting she always asks for me. So we became very
good friends.

Some of the staff there, they a bit rough with the inmates, but
I learned that if you can give them even a sweet, they become

135

your friend, and they will keep calm, no problem. I found a way of being their friend. And sometimes they would call, and if another nurse go there to them, they say, 'No, no, I don't want you. I want Twiggy!'

I enjoy working in Holloway! I didn't have any problem at all. I didn't have any problem thank God. And in myself I think it all depends on how you deal with people, because I've never had a prisoner that attempt to hurt me. And they hurt other staff. They do attack the staff sometimes you know, so it doesn't pay for the staff to be too rough with them. You have to be stern, because there are certain things that you can't allow them to do. But it doesn't mean you mustn't treat them as a human being.

If they ask for a drink of water or something, give it to them, and you can talk to them and calm them down and ting like that. And it's better for us. Because if you don't treat them nice, they can be terrible.

I talk to them, and they tell me all the stories that I didn't know exist – what they do and what could happen. Some of them do very bad things, and tell you how they committed a crime, and how they go about it and all that.

Sometimes women steal, and they get caught, and sometimes it is a need, you understand. They're desperate! Sometimes somebody get in trouble, and they didn't mean to get in trouble or something. Even the murderers! They get a knife or whatever and stab somebody to death – they don't know that that would happen.

But some of them, they're devious too! So you don't know. They're all unpredictable. Unpredictable. So as a staff, and as a prisoner, you have to protect yourself. Don't take any chances, because you don't know what is in the back of their mind. I think some had a mental illness, but some were just bad!

Sometimes the prisoners would be put in a single room, and then you would be watching through the little hole to see if they are okay, because you see sometime they are depressed and they try to commit suicide.

Myra Hindley[53] was there. I didn't want to have anything much to do with her, because I know of her character. I was afraid of Myra Hindley! She was a beautiful girl you know. I was very careful with her, because she was devious – very, very devious. So we were warned about her. 'Don't take any chance with her.' It's not good intentions she had. So she was always in a single room.

As staff we were always warned. The governor would say, 'Be careful of that one!' Because when you get to the door, and you give them their medication through that little hole and ting like that, they can grab! They work they brain faster than us you know! Sometimes when you open the door for them, they stuff things in the door, where the lock goes in. And they get back in, and you lock the door behind them – it's not locked! Oh God, I learned so much there! We have a laugh about it sometime in the office.

I used to take all my children with me to Holloway you know, when they were younger. There's a Christmas party for children and everyone gets a present. I took all my kids.

I have half a dozen children, three of each. When I got married, and I was working, my mum was here and she help us right along. I met my husband here. But he was a Casanova! I can't have somebody running around! My mother's been so good to me. The whole family has. My brothers, they help me, they support me, when things went wrong. Thank God.

I use to be very active in church. I'm not as active as I use to be. I used to be Sunday School Superintendent, and I was Ladies' President for the women. That meant you have to organise different things that is going on, and you have to get ideas. So we have a committee, and everybody throw in what they think we should do. And it was early days, it's not even like now, it was different. Young people at that time, they were like to get involved in something and go to somewhere. Now they're independent, they don't have to depend on anybody.

We used to take the youth and the schoolchildren to the seaside every year, Southsea, Great Yarmouth, Littlehampton, Margate... Every year we take them, and we have about three coaches. It was nice to see the children happy.

I also started the Senior Citizens' Club. We use to do things like handwork – knitting and sewing – and we provided lunch, and then we take them out to the seaside sometimes. I'm not able to go now. But they still have it there.

We have a lot of singing and a lot of music in our church. We have organ, drums, guitars, tambourine, and the young people love that. The older people love it as well, but the young people is actually drawn. They are drawn in, because when they passing by the church and they hear that music, even if they are not associated with our church, that draws them in because that entice them. So we always have people coming in, and they all enjoy.

We have a lot of celebrities that come to the church, people like Gordon Brown. Pastor Nelson – the pastor that we had – was fantastic in inviting them. He was very good. He die now, but he would get everyone, all the different politicians and different people to come, and lecture the young people. And when we had trouble like the Brixton riots, he warn the youth – keep out of trouble. Don't get yourself involve in that.

Pastor Nelson was a man who had a really good brain. He think! And said, 'All these young people running up and down the street, and not doing anything, and get theirself involve and get in trouble and thing like that.' He was a wise man. And he would bring all those young people in. You would see him on the street, and he would stop them and ask them, 'Where do you live? Where do you go in your spare time? Do you go to school?' That type of person.

So we have got a centre there for young people from anywhere. We didn't have any problem with them, although they were from outside the area. They weren't a member of the church, they didn't have any dealings with the church, but because of the thing that was happening there, young people from anywhere, it doesn't matter who you are, you were able to come in, and you would have good time, instead of going on the street and get in trouble.

So the place used to be full. And then every year, he have a concert. And that bring in all the relatives.

Our church is the New Testament Church of God in Brixton. It's in a very good spot. And the minister that is there now, Pastor Parkinson, is very nice, lovely. He understands, and he listens. And he will ring up and find out how you're doing. He's a people-person.

I still go to church sometimes. And sometimes they come here and we have prayer meeting. The church is good. They come and visit me all the time.

◊ ◊ ◊

Nowadays, I can't remember things as I used to. I have to think a lot. It's very frustrating. But it's just one of those things I suppose. I'm just careful what I do. I don't go through that door and then I don't know where I'm going. I have specific place that I will go, and then I return. Unless I am with others, or in a company. And the church is very good, because sometimes we go to the seaside, and we go to different places happening. So we are together, so we are protected. Because looking at me, you wouldn't believe my memory's not so good. And there's other folks in my condition as well. So I really can't complain about that.

I don't really go out on my own now. I actually protect myself. Because I know what can happen if I can't remember where I'm going, and I know that I can say to this person, 'I don't know where I'm going, could you help me?' And that person is not a genuine person that would help me – because a lot of the folks are not trustworthy and thing like that. I'm very careful. I work in the prison service for so long, so I have that little bit in the back of my mind, 'Protect yourself.'

I sometimes find it difficult to walk. I use a stick. I'm not really in good health. I'm not a hundred per cent. How can I put it now? I can do bits and pieces but not a lot. My energy's very poor, number one, but also I've got back pain. I've got diabetes and arthritis. I've got a very good doctor, and my son Gerard makes sure I take all my tablets.

When you have dementia, people just think you're mad! But it is a mental state, and it's not so bad. You are forgetful, you're forgetting and forgetting, you can't remember. You get angry sometime when you can't remember. But you can adjust yourself to it. I know that I've got dementia. I don't try to go anywhere that I don't know. And if I'm going anywhere, I go with somebody. I don't take any chance.

I take my tablets, I take my medication. It slow it down, a little bit, a little bit, until they find a cure eventually. Actually they are doing the research.

Doctors don't always recognise dementia. They wave it off. It's very frustrating when you can't remember anything. And then, you see, you get angry. A lot of people get irritable – and you don't know the reason why they getting so irritable. It is what is happening to them inside there.

On Wednesdays, the car come and pick me up, and I go to a day centre, the Healthy Living Club.[54] It's lovely there. They do different things there, so you take part, and it's fun. You can have a good laugh, I tell you. Loads of people go there.

Simona is very good! And the staff is lovely as well. The staff that works around with her, they're really down to earth, and they've got the right attitude. You couldn't do that job otherwise. They're very patient. Because, to be with people with dementia, is not very easy you know. But you would never know, because they deal with everybody as a individual, and know who they are, and what they will do and what they will not do.

We do chair-based exercise, and singing. They give us a meal, and you get a drink with it. And they give you tea and thing like that. They try to get a lot of entertainers there. It refreshes what you are doing all the time.

I don't know if they have anywhere else like the Healthy Living Club. I was thinking the other day. I haven't heard of any centre like this.

Everybody there know one another more or less. And it's really nice, because each one of us that goes there has a problem. If one can't do certain thing, they help them to do it as well. We all cope together, and we look after one another, you understand, which is good – good relationship there. And when you get to the centre, you don't look down on anybody. Everybody is in the same category. Everybody is equal, you understand. It's lovely going there. I look forward to it.[55]

Chapter 11

One place to another

ABDUL HAQUE

Abdul Haque *is a retired chef who lives in central London with his wife and his adult daughter and son. Their flat is at the top of two steep flights of stairs, which he climbs up and down each day without difficulty. He goes for a long walk every day, and attends a day resource centre run by Age UK Camden once a week. I interviewed him in the presence of his daughter Hamida Farsi who helped out from time to time with interpretation between English and Bengali. Hamida told me that her father was diagnosed with diabetes ten years ago, and since then the whole family have cut down on oily food and all eat very healthily with lots of fresh fruit and vegetables each day. LW*

I was born in 1935. I grew up in Bangladesh, in the countryside. My parents were farmers, growing rice and vegetables, and fish. Bangladesh is close to sea-level, and there are deep ponds. We grow fish in there, and we use those water for swimming and eating and everything. This fresh water.

I had two brothers and one sister. When I was about 12, my mother died, and my father got married again. Then I got another four brothers. My stepmother was all right. Some family's stepmother, there's a jealousy. But she's not jealous.

I came to England in my 20s. My uncle was in this country. He knows I got nothing to do out there. There was no work. So he's been Bangladesh, he saw what I am doing, he saw that I get nothing. He thinking about that. Then on that time, this country, they allow to bring people here, and he pay me my fare, for me to come in this country.

In those days, England was bad weather. My first winter in England, 1963, it was very cold. There was that much snow on the ground. Water froze in the taps.

At first I lived in West Midlands, outside Birmingham, in my uncle's house. Then I get a job. Those day, very hard to get a job. My first job was in Leicester, a factory job. They make parts of aeroplanes, body parts. After I worked there for one year, then I get some problem with a colleague or something. I leave that job. I didn't settle at one place. I get another job. Then I work many place, all in the engineering factory. I never been in the cotton mill, wool mill. In engineering factory they make parts of aeroplanes, in some factory they make part of ships, that sort of thing. I didn't do any college or anything, nothing like that. They put me do that job, they just tell you, carry on. I learned on the job.

I stayed in the West Midlands, between Leicester and Birmingham, about 15 or 20 years altogether. But then I can't get any job – all the factory going closed down. I go Bangladesh, I come back, I can't get my job back. There was no more work. So I came in London.

When I came in London, I get a tip from some people. I know a man, he's not live now. He knows me, I know him, but for long time I didn't see him. Somehow I find his address, I came his house. Then when I get there, his house, it is going to demolish. He nearly leave the house. Then he took me another place, to person he knows, in his house. I live over there about two years. Then it didn't work out over there, but there is office, they help people who need the house. Then they give me house near here, just one bedroom, sharing with the bathroom and kitchen. I been there long time.

I went back to Bangladesh every three or four years and I was married there. All my children were born there – two sons and a daughter. My wife and I, we were connect each other on the telephone. I pay my family, spend everything what I earn, what they need, money for their living. Then I decided. They're over there, I am here, and this is not right! So it is better I call them here. So I apply for bring my family. They came to England in 1990. My sons were age seven and nine, and my daughter was two. We living happily here. God give my children all their luck.

Before they come, I get a job, I was working in a restaurant. My London life, I worked in a lot of Indian restaurants. They're not all originally Indian. 'Indian' means India, Pakistan, Bangladesh; we call them all Indian. I am not a top class chef, but I learned how to make many type of curry.

A few years ago, my wife took me to the doctor because I started forgetting things. My memory – I think it is common to everyone. I remember when I was young, but what I have done yesterday is too difficult!

What is frustrating – sometimes what I hear not good; both ears, some kind of noise comes. It's not every day or every week. I told my doctor once. He said they can't do anything about it. I have to take medication for diabetes and blood pressure. I don't take any sugar. I take sweeteners.

I don't like to sit down in one place. I feel boring. I like company. I like people. But I don't like one place many time. I go out, have fresh air, and walk round.

My daily routine when I get up in the morning, I do pray, then I get my breakfast, then I go out. I go for a walk every day. Near my house is Regent's Park, and I go every morning. I go in through Great Portland Street, that corner. I walk through there. I go up to the zoo. From there, there is a straight path. I walk for about an hour, not more than an hour and half. Even if it's raining, no matter what, it not stop me. I go on my own. I never get lost. If anybody wants to come with me, they're welcome.

Round here, there are many people older than me and many people like me. And I don't see anybody walking. Only me. No white, black or Asian – no one! Only me!

On Fridays I go to the mosque. We go to pray God. So everyone comes there. If you go one place once a week or once a month, regularly, then you make friends already.

On Wednesdays, I go to the Resource Centre. Just talk to people. If you go one place, if you know someone, talk to them, 'Hallo,' 'Hi,' like that. Sometimes we play carrom board. It's like snooker, but you flick the ball with your finger. Sometimes we go on outings to the seaside. Once or twice we've been there. I like travelling, one place to another. It's nice to see.

Chapter 12

A double diagnosis

BRIAN HENNELL

Brian and June Hennell.

Brian Hennell *was diagnosed with prostate cancer two years after his diagnosis of frontotemporal dementia. Brian and his wife June collaborated in writing and publishing three booklets for families affected by dementia*[56] *and have been active in training and research at the University of Worcester's Association for Dementia Studies. I met them at a conference on dementia and end of life care organised by the National Council for Palliative Care. Soon afterwards, June sent me Brian's chapter. LW*

Life had been very full, bringing up three sons and feeling the full effect of being parents as chauffeurs, caterers, entertainers, advisors, nurses, financiers, parent/teacher attendees, committee members of judo groups, scout troops and sea cadet units – I'm sure you know the scene. Suffice to say that our love of theatre, dancing, writing, reading, music and travelling had to be fitted in around two full-time jobs and children's needs. With hindsight, we don't know how we did it, but there is much proof that we did – and with a modicum of success too! We managed, often on a shoe-string, to see most of the world with or without our sons, whilst satisfying our wanderlust and curiosity for what makes others tick.

It was in 1992, after a road crash had caused me to take early retirement from my job in the civil service, that our sons started making their own way in life, and, almost by accident, empty bedrooms started to be filled with students, teachers and professionals from other countries whilst they studied English. Our three visitors' books pay tribute to the bonds which were formed, and many still make contact regularly. Between 1992 and 2009, 502 students from 42 different counties sat at our dining table. Didn't we laugh together, about (but never at) misconceptions. One evening, when dinner had been enjoyed with two Arabs, a Latvian, a Frenchman, a Belgian, a Spaniard and four English, June wrote on a large piece of paper, 'Hello, my name is June. I live with my husband and three sons and I am from England.' The paper was passed around the table with each student writing the equivalent information about themselves in their language. Squealing with delight, last in line, the beautiful Latvian TV presenter declared that she could see how to write her name in Arabic script. Looking at what she had written, the Arabs fell off their chairs laughing, for you can't do that! Deconstructing their words in Arabic and creating another word had produced a *very* rude word indeed! Next day the students were still laughing and told their class tutor about the episode. This took our reputation for being 'special hosts' to new heights and was a favourite story for repetition at every available opportunity.

We loved our life and I made a reasonable job of being a house-husband. Everyone seemed happy, June with her challenging job and the students benefiting from our 'one size does not fit all' approach.

It was in the mid-1990s that I started getting bad-tempered about mislaying things and forgetting simple everyday stuff. I had really slowed down, but isn't that normal after retirement, early or not?

I knew that I was becoming hard to live with, but couldn't see a way back. June was still working hard and loved her job with central government but needed to do so much more in the house because I didn't seem able to organise myself like I used to. She would come home from work and find that I hadn't done what she had asked. She didn't know that it wasn't because I couldn't be bothered, but because I had forgotten. I hated it. I had always had a tendency to be lazy, to put things off until I was in the mood. Was this what was happening? I didn't know one way or another.

One day our good friend commented, 'Brian, June didn't deserve that tirade.' I told him to mind his own business because if I wanted his comments I would ask for them. That made me feel lousy afterwards, but I was struggling enough trying to understand what was happening to me, without others noticing it.

Another time, I got so fed up with trying to get some advice from June whilst she stayed non-committal about using super-glue that I told her I might as well move out because we had nothing left in our marriage. I didn't mean that – I just needed to be told what to do. Of course she couldn't win, because if she had been wrong I would have blamed her. She told me that she didn't know and I didn't want to hear that she was as confused as me. My confusion was making me irascible and unreasonable.

Was it old age? If so, heaven help me. I was only in my 60s, too young to be senile.

One example of difficulty came when we were going to visit friends in Colombia in 2004. We wanted to learn to dance the salsa, having mastered all other dances in our years together. I couldn't do it! To my surprise, June could do it and I couldn't. Yet I had always been the best dancer. I felt awful, a failure. It was a huge shock.

Lots of little things went wrong, but it wasn't until 24 November 2005 that June made a first diary entry which read, 'What have I genuinely done wrong today? Instead of the kind, fun-loving and considerate man I once knew, Brian seems to have a split personality. When he is nice he is very nice, when he is not he is horrid.'

In September 2007 we discovered a research programme being carried out by Bristol University into the effectiveness of Omega 3 on memory loss. June got me a place and, although I was given a placebo which disappointed us, the written report was helpful. It showed that there were problems with my verbal recognition memory and visual memory. However, there was no serious advice to seek further help.

However, we did continue to make diary entries which are the only way that I am able to recall what happened next. Together we kept a note of all the issues which worried us. We both signed each page to say that we agreed the notes, so that I couldn't disbelieve them in the future. June suggested it but I didn't mind because I trusted her implicitly and if she said I had done or said something then I knew I had. She was and is the most honest, caring and trustworthy person you could ever find. We've always been a good team.

The time came to get help. We made an appointment with our GP in the summer of 2008 and sent him a copy of the list, hoping that real detail would save us getting embarrassed or getting the facts wrong. After all, we already felt emotional and confused, so how could we expect to get facts right without having them written down? He gave me some simple tests which I just couldn't do. Of course I didn't know what day of the week it was, which month or which year. These things don't matter when you have retired and June always knew, so why did I have to? I felt stupid but June squeezed my hand and it all seemed better. I did feel pleased knowing that he would refer me for tests with consultants. Eventually, having exhausted everything else, especially the possibility of physical or mental repercussions from the crash in 1990, I saw a wonderful consultant psychogeriatrician. After lots of questioning he made a cautious probable diagnosis of frontal temporal dementia. This is all a haze and I can only remember it because it is written in all the presentations which June and I give at training events and conferences. He prescribed Citalopram and I recall walking out of the consultation holding the prescription and thinking, 'I don't care what I've got as long as something can be done to help me. June is happy, and at least I haven't got a brain tumour and our marriage isn't heading for divorce!'

The worst thing was telling our sons. We composed an email to tell them all at once and they were angry with us. Somehow we were supposed to have told them before – but we couldn't, because we didn't know. The telephone lines between them were red hot and the consensus was that we needed to sell up and move closer to the two who lived with their families in Gloucestershire. They even composed an imaginary rota so that someone could be with us all our waking hours if we lived near them. We quickly said that we hoped that wouldn't be necessary for a very long time. The shock for them was awful, worse than for us, because all we felt was relief. I had been fearing the worst and seemed to have been balancing on a knife-edge of frustration and aggression for ages.

Now I had a way forward, because the specialist said that he had had success treating this type of dementia with Memantine and, although NICE had not approved it yet, he would like to trial it for me. I was the recipient of his experience and self-confidence and I shall be forever in his debt. I wish I could meet him again to show him how right he was and to thank him again.

I started to feel more relaxed and, once the medication clicked in, I felt grounded again. Life was worth living. I managed to visualise where I had put my specs so that I could find them again. My confidence in myself returned and I became nicer to live with. Everyone could see the difference. Friends understood and supported us, maintaining the long friendships we had shared. We made lots of adjustments and they worked.

We downsized, and moved to live near our children and grandchildren. This wasn't easy because we had been in our previous home for nearly 30 years. Agonising decisions had to be made about what to get rid of, and I found this heart-wrenching. I wanted to keep everything.

I was not happy about telling DVLA about the dementia in case they stopped me driving. I love it and still think that I am a capable driver. DVLA review my licence annually.

Life went on and we adjusted to living in our home by a beautiful canal in rural Gloucestershire. Our 12-year-old granddaughter did lots of internet research and learned about how to deal with dementia. She gave me lots of hugs and encouragement. She is fantastic.

We connected with NHS Gloucestershire, Gloucestershire County Council, Carers Gloucestershire and lots of charities and social interest companies helping those with dementia. We became volunteers for lots of organisations and cooperated in writing and delivering dementia training material.

We were living well with dementia, concentrating on what we could do and doing it as much as possible, when I started to experience urinary problems. A spell in hospital for minor surgery on the prostate seemed to put things right. Imagine my shock when six weeks later I was told that I had prostate cancer. How could I? I had no pain or discomfort. By now my memory span was seconds, so I never worried specifically about this second diagnosis. Deterioration in my feel-good factor did worry me though.

I was prescribed hormone therapy to block testosterone from feeding the tumour, and had to wait six months before radiotherapy could be started. I felt lousy, exhausted and very tearful, and started imagining all manner of weird and wonderful aspects in my daily life. We got through 35 days of consecutive visits to Cheltenham for radical radiotherapy and I was as surprised to be going on day 35 as I was on day 1. I still didn't know the way on the last day any more than I did on the first. I do remember that the staff were very kind to me and never called just 'Brian Hennell' but called 'Brian and June Hennell', so that June could come with me and act as my memory. We took them cakes and cards at the end of the course and wrote lots of thank-yous to them.

I felt exhausted, my tummy was upset but all this was to be expected. We survived! But next I started to visit some very bad, dark places. It was like I imagine hell to be, frightening. Re-learning that my mother had died many years ago left me devastated and was something I couldn't handle. I kept re-living what a bad son I might have been. Did she die wanting? Did I do my best? However much June told me about the good job I did for my mother after my father died, it didn't matter. I started confusing June with other people. I couldn't sort out why I was here with her, having an affair behind the back of the mother of my sons whom I knew I loved more than life itself. I kept apologising to my sons for the affair I was having with June, and however much they told me she was their mother and all was well, I couldn't believe it. The house we lived in made me think I was on holiday in our caravan in Wales and I kept expecting to go home. Regularly I worried in case June hadn't told my office where I was and that I might lose my job. I didn't believe her when she said that I hadn't worked since a bad road crash in 1990. What road crash? What early retirement? I didn't know that the year was 2012.

My feel-good factor was at an all-time low. I was getting in an awful muddle, and I felt that my head was going to explode. I kept meeting my father on the canal bank when I walked our dog Jack, and I would be convinced that I was walking in Somerset 45 years before.

It was June who made the connection between my serious deterioration and the hormone therapy I was taking, after a urologist addressing our support group mentioned that there is some evidence that hormone therapy (HT) can have a serious impact on those with memory problems. Learning from the oncologist that I needed HT for another two years caused us horror. Very soon after, I had a very bad spell of hallucinations and we decided to stop the HT, contrary to the advice of the oncologist. We explained that I had lost all my quality of life and that living my last years in a care home on antipsychotics but with the cancer controlled was not our chosen route. We were told that it would take two to six months for it to work out of my system and they were right.

After six months, my feel-good factor started to return. I can now truly say that I feel pretty good. I feel grounded, calm most of the time and secure. I've stopped hallucinating that I have met an old friend on the canal path and gone to his place for coffee. I love my daily walks with my dog and haven't got lost for many weeks. That gives me confidence in my own ability.

Two weeks ago I said to June, 'Aren't we lucky?' She smiled and asked what I meant. I said. 'Look out of the window. There is blue sky and sunshine. We have this lovely home, we have each other and no worries.' I really meant that, and if that seems a silly thing for someone with dementia and cancer to say, then so be it. We go to see shows and movies. We love music and socialising with friends, both those with dementia and without. I do sometimes recognise that someone with dementia is worse than me with their condition. I am grateful for that but sorry for them. I am really grateful when people are gentle and kind with me. I don't take kindly to aggression or unfairness. I like to take my time, disliking hurrying at all costs. Life pleases me, all little bits like animals and flowers and beautiful scenes. I cannot imagine tiring of travelling but these days we confine ourselves mainly to the UK. I cannot imagine becoming disinterested in having new experiences, meeting new folks or attending conferences and training events where we can help others to understand more about dementia.

I love animal programmes on TV and re-runs of old comedies, but I now cannot cope with convoluted plots in the detective series which I used to enjoy. Thank goodness for *Countryfile*, *Blue Planet*, David Attenborough, the Eden Channel and *Mamma Mia*, which I have seen and sung through about eight times.

I've been told that my particular dementia, frontal temporal dementia, is only experienced by about 4 per cent of those with dementia. 'Well,' said I on hearing that, 'if I've got to have dementia, I wouldn't want anything too common, would I?'

We often tell those attending our talks that we've never been a particularly fashionable couple but that it was good to be on trend for just one day when our dementia diagnosis was given on 4 February 2009 – the day that the National Dementia Strategy was announced.

Now that we are not treating my cancer, my dementia drugs are working their miracles.

When I was taking the hormone therapy I had no life, no calm, no security, just unhappiness and a doubt whether I would see tomorrow in the hell surrounding me, let alone have a life. We can go forward for as long as we are able contributing to as many publications, dementia training sessions and conferences as we can fit in. As part of the LINK Group at Worcester University's Association for Dementia Studies, we help to deliver dementia events and spread the word that creating dementia-friendly communities is not about throwing funds at the problem but listening to the needs and advice of those who know! Improving the lot for those who need just a little extra understanding and support can improve the lot for everyone.

Thanks to the good help of Carers Gloucestershire, June can get the support she needs, while through the Alzheimer's Society

'Good2Go Group', I can meet with others with dementia in a supportive environment.

Put together, how lucky am I? How many men, married for 44 years and having been with their partner for 46 years, can truly say that they have everything they need? Dementia or not, I'm lucky, and appreciate that fact every day.

Postscript

June Hennell adds:

Brian died peacefully and pain-free in a hospice on 22 July 2013, six months after this chapter was written. We received wonderful assistance from the Gloucestershire palliative care team.

As for me, I found that the chasm of bereavement grief may surpass any preparation. I am going forward step by step but have been taken aback by the degree of difficulty.

Brian's brain was donated to the Dementia Brain Bank[57] I found this process cathartic and it helped me enormously. I am still involved with the University of Worcester Association of Dementia Studies, and take every opportunity to raise awareness about the needs of people with dementia and their families.[58]

For others affected by dementia, I dream that the horrors of comorbidity be better recognised. Instead of consultants working in their own specialist silos, we need patients to be treated holistically, with potential areas for conflict amongst proposed treatments subject to open discussion and resolution.

I also dream that the postcode lottery of palliative care would end. Every area deserves to have an experienced, professional and adequately resourced palliative care team. Every person at the end of life deserves as much care and attention as we give to bringing babies into the world. And dementia must not be used as an excuse for denying anyone the right to make informed choices.

Chapter 13

Anybody been kind to me, it stays with me

PEARL HYLTON

Pearl Hylton *came to England from Jamaica just after the war. I interviewed her at her flat in Stockwell, South London. Her daughter Jennifer told me: 'Mum's an incredibly brave pioneer. She was so young when she decided to travel to England. Her dad was against it as she was travelling alone, but she was very determined and insisted. She also worked*

as an extra on a few movies in the 1950s, including So Long at the Fair, *with Jean Simmons and Dirk Bogarde.' LW*

Pearl Hylton in the 1960s.

I was born in Jamaica in 1927. We were 12 children, seven girls and five boys, and I was in the middle. My parents was very nice people, very lovely people. Decent, respectable and kind.

I came to England in 1948, on the boat that came after the *Empire Windrush*. It was the banana boat, a little one called *Eros*. It has to come fast, before the bananas ripe, you know. I think I paid £28.

I came here on my own. I wanted to travel, and they were inviting people to come to England, so I came. News get around, you know. It was everywhere – people going to England. They used to send for people to come to do building work. They wanted carpenters and all that, to build up London after Hitler.

Some places I go to, to get a room, it would say, 'No Irish, no Blacks'. But sometimes these people used to phone up for me, and if they said they didn't want any black people, they would say, 'Oh, she's very *refined.*'

I never expected to stay. I think I'd make some money and then go back. But that didn't happen. I'm still here! I'm glad I stayed, very glad. There was a lot of opportunities here. The only thing I miss about Jamaica is the food and the weather. Fresh food! And warm all year round. No winter.

All my brothers and sisters end up here, and end up in America. But my father wouldn't come. He didn't like the plane, and he didn't like the ship either. He was determined. He wasn't going up in the air and he wasn't going on the water. He didn't want to come.

My mother died earlier. She bled to death you know. She lost a baby. She was sick for a while. She went in the hospital. But the doctors, they didn't know what to do with this. They probably know now.

My first job when I came here was in a restaurant at Finchley Road. The man had just come back from the army, from the war. He was a very nice man, the boss. I was washing up in the kitchen, kitchen hand. And sometimes we had dinner outside you know, with everybody, all the staff. I did that job for a long time, a good while.

I've done all kind of jobs. At one time I done cleaning as well, in a care home. Let me tell you something before we go further – when we drink tea, in the morning, everybody just take their cup and shake it over the sink, and the tea marks still there. And this Jamaican lady – she was a West Indian anyhow – she wash she cup, and the woman said she wash out all the glazing, she scrub out all the glazing! And she lost she job, you know, she never tell her to come back. She done it too good!

I have four children, three girls and one boy, and a lot of grandchildren. I was married three times. The first one was very nice, gentle. The other one, he was rough, he was terrible. He died, and I wasn't too sorry at all. The third one – I don't even remember, you know!

I like travelling. I've travelled the world. I've been all over Europe, the USA, South America, the Caribbean, Asia. I've been to Ghana. I've travelled all over Africa. We're Jehovah's Witnesses you know, and I asked one of the brothers there where they come from, because they come from different parts of Africa, and I told one of them that I want to come too.

My mother and father weren't Jehovah's Witnesses. I was Church of England. But one day, when the Jehovah's Witnesses came to the door, the things they were telling me, that is not everybody going to heaven – is 144,000, chosen by Jehovah God, going to heaven. A little white woman came. Her name was Janet Owens. That's how I became a Jehovah's Witness.

◊ ◊ ◊

When I first became worried about my memory, I told the lady in charge at the place where I was living, and she said, that what I said it was, it wasn't. Because she said her father have it, you know, and I didn't have that problem. But then my granddaughter, Chloe, she took me to the doctor, and he said, my memory – it was memory loss.

I had a stroke. It happen in the supermarket. My foot going like this, shaking, so I told the woman next to me, and she said her mother get that. So I didn't go for a while, because she said that's all right. Something of the kind. So I didn't go yet. Till later on, the hand drop down. It was just one side. So, this is serious now, so the man in the supermarket, the one in charge, he said, let he call the doctor. And the ambulance came. He asked me a few questions. I could speak, but not too clear. And he asked me which hospital I want to go to, if I want to go to St Thomas's, or I want to go to this one down here, because this one was nearer. So I went to this one. That hospital good. All of them good. They're very good.

I fell down again, in the house, but I don't know what did happen when I went back the second time. I have to take tablets, but I think I'm in good health. I've got a good appetite.

My daughter Jennifer, she's the one looking after me, and my granddaughter Chloe. And the carers come in twice a day.

I can't walk so easily now. I have a walking frame. I used to like to go around marketplace, like East Street market. It's a big market. But I don't go nowadays.

Twice a week I go to a very nice club. They bring a bus here for us, and pick us up, and take us there. We do different things there. Sometimes they do a little exercise. Sometimes they ask questions and tell them about dementia, and things like that.

And once a week I go to the Healthy Living Club.[59] We do the exercise and the singing. I'm not good at singing you know, but I listen. And I enjoy the poetry group you know, where you do literature. That's a new thing to me.

It's funny, I can remember things from a way back, from I was little. And things that happen to me like yesterday, I can't remember. But I can remember things from I was little. And if people do me very bad thing, it stays with me. And if they do good thing, it stays with me too. Anybody been very kind to me, it stays with me.

Chapter 14

Love me for who I am

ANN JOHNSON

Ann Johnson *lives in Cheshire. She was a nurse and a lecturer in nurse education before she was diagnosed with dementia at the age of 52. She campaigns tirelessly for greater awareness and better services for people with dementia. In 2012 she was awarded an honorary doctorate from the University of Bolton in recognition of her contribution to dementia awareness and education; in 2013 she was awarded the MBE for services to healthcare. Since writing this chapter, Ann's mother has died, and she says, 'I miss her dreadfully.' LW*

Ann Johnson in her doctoral robes, 2012.

I was diagnosed with Alzheimer's disease when I was 52 years of age. I am 59 now.

My first indication that something was wrong was that I was forgetting to take medication for a condition I have. My father had Alzheimer's before me. He was diagnosed at 57, but, in hindsight, I think it had started before that. I was doing things that he had been doing. That set alarm bells ringing in my mind.

I didn't go and see my GP for a year because first of all I had to accept my memory was going and I wasn't functioning, and that was hard.

I went on my own. My GP was very good, and he sent me to the memory clinic. That was in December 2004. In January 2005 I was seen by a memory clinic nurse at my home. He gave me the MMSE memory test and other tests, and then sent me to see a consultant psychologist for a memory test that took one and a half hours.

I saw the consultant psychiatrist at the memory clinic. He took my history and sent me for a CT scan, which showed shrinkage of my brain. Another long memory test showed a further big decline in the space of a month, so he told me my diagnosis was early onset Alzheimer's disease.

My mother, aged 80, was with me at the point of diagnosis. We left the clinic, put our arms round each other and said, 'We will get through this together,' which we have ever since. I feel very sorry for my mother, now 86, who has lived through this with her husband and her daughter.

I finally got the diagnosis in October 2005.

In a strange way the diagnosis was a relief. I now knew what the problem was, and often when one knows the problem one can face up to and deal with it.

The memory clinic nurse came to see me at home and started me on medication. I am on galantamine (Reminyl). Before I started taking the medication it was like living in a mist and a fog all the time. When they put me on the top dose of the medication I became alert again and that meant everything to me.

I have wonderful medical support. I see my consultant psychiatrist every three months and I have a wonderful memory clinic nurse who I see often and she is a great friend to me as well.

I am a trained nurse and was a nurse tutor and lecturer in nursing for a number of years before my retirement. I helped to look after my father, who lost all his physical and mental abilities, and I looked after patients in my clinical practice, so I know what to expect. I know what the future holds for me and I am terrified, but I don't worry because it won't change anything.

Most of my friends are trained nurses. Since diagnosis I do not think my relationships have changed. Nobody has ever shunned me. When my father was diagnosed in 1975, life was very different. A lot of people did not engage with him and he felt isolated. I have never felt isolated. My support is from my mother, some very trusted and dear friends and the staff in the care home where I live.

Diagnosis of Alzheimer's is a sledgehammer, but people still have a life which they must live to the best of their ability whatever stage they are at. I have dementia but I still have a life to live, and I will live my life as much as I am able.

◊ ◊ ◊

It is very difficult when people say I do not look like I have dementia, and they are very surprised they can communicate with me. My problems are a bit difficult to explain because people cannot *see* them. You could have a conversation with me and not realise anything is wrong.

I explain that communication problems might involve simple things like not being able to find words, or forgetting what I have just said. I may lose the gist of the conversation. Try and bring me back to it. Speak to me slowly. Do not shout. Ask only one question at a time. Things in my brain don't work as quickly as they used to, so please give me time and be patient with me.

My short-term memory is very bad. I use a simple Dictaphone to record short messages, but I have to remember I have used it. If it is on the chair in the morning, that means I have used it. I have no idea what is on it until I listen to it – quite a revelation!

I get lost when I am out. I wear a dog tag round my neck. Someone can ring the number on it and get me back home. I have difficulty reading. It is not visual. I can see the words but I cannot put them together and concentrate, so I now use audio-books. I cannot use a normal watch so I now have a digital one which also tells me the day and date. A talking clock helps as well. Numeracy is also a problem. I cannot count money any more. I can tell you it is different shapes, sizes and colours but I cannot put it together.

I cannot tell my right from my left, and I have visuospatial problems. When I am out and about, I find interpreting signs difficult. Toilet doors present a big problem. I can see the picture but I cannot understand the meaning. Taps are also a problem – some you lift, some you turn. Toilet flushing systems are all different.

I am now having difficulty with the basics such as washing and dressing myself in the morning.

Frustration with small things causes me a big problem. I become impatient and intolerant, use bad language and find it difficult to cope. Things become difficult and it is not easy to stay focused. I am terrified of what the future may hold for me.

Please try and understand the sheer distress and terror I live in every day with my Alzheimer's.

I have dark moments. In those and all moments I ask people to love me for who I am, and be with me. That means everything to me.

◊ ◊ ◊

I live in a care home. I am the youngest person here. I live with 80 and 90-year-olds. At the moment I am able to get out every day and that is vital. I do have to stick to the same bus or I get disorientated.

I am divorced, and I lived on my own for 27 years. When I couldn't live on my own any longer because of my Alzheimer's, I moved in with my mother, and we got on very well for three years.

One day she said to me, 'Don't speak to me like that.'

I was apparently becoming impatient, intolerant and using bad language – none of which was me. So often in Alzheimer's, behaviour problems occur, and this was happening to me. I am very pleased she told me, because I didn't know it was happening.

They had just built a new care home near us, so I went in for two weeks' respite – and my Mum got her life back. We both decided that I would stay here, and I have been here ever since August 2009. It was the right decision for both of us. She could not look after me any more. Since then she has been very ill. She now lives in a retirement property. We still have a very good mother/daughter/friend relationship.

It was difficult for me to settle into my new home but the staff were very helpful and caring. It gave them a different perspective, caring for somebody at a younger age. I have spoken to them about living with Alzheimer's and they have told me that because they now understand why and how I am having problems with my Alzheimer's, they can help other residents with their problems better. I regard all the staff as my friends and am very happy to share things with them and talk things through if I have a problem.

Residential care for people with dementia must be handled sensitively. Where I live, not all residents have dementia. We have a reminiscence area for residents with advanced dementia. When I go there, I see and feel the love and care from staff to residents.

I am happy living in a care home. My physical and emotional needs are all met. I have my own furniture around me in my room and am able to spend time on my own in my room when I wish. Activities are available in the home which residents enjoy, so people are encouraged to socialise and be active. We have a dog who came with one of the residents. My activity involves going into the local town and meeting friends, and I do a lot of talks about 'Living with Alzheimer's'.

Residential care gives me security, safety, care and love. It would however be of benefit if there were homes for younger people with dementia, but these do not seem to be available.

◊ ◊ ◊

In a strange sort of way I have a new life with my Alzheimer's. I am an Ambassador for Alzheimer's Society. I have been on BBC *Breakfast* twice and on Sky News, and on the radio including the *Today* programme, *Woman's Hour* and Radio Manchester talking about NICE decisions about drugs, early diagnosis and living with Alzheimer's. I have a very dear friend who comes with me when I go to do my talks. She is able to share it with me and be my support.

I am now involved with the Prime Minister's Champions group about dementia-friendly communities. This involves businesses saying how they will help people with dementia with whom they come into contact. I have been very impressed by their efforts on our behalf.

◊ ◊ ◊

I was asked at a talk I did once what three things keep me going. My answer was: my friends, my faith and doing my talks.

Friendship is vital – what you can do for your friends and what they can do for you – please treasure them.

My faith is very important. I am a practising Anglican and have been all my life.

Doing my talks about living with Alzheimer's and associated subjects throughout the country gives me a purpose for living.

When I go and speak all I ask for is my train fare and a friend to come with me as my support.

◊ ◊ ◊

To give a different perspective I now quote from a very dear friend of mine who comes with me as friend, carer and support, so that she can explain the effect on her.

I was speechless when Ann told me she had been diagnosed with Alzheimer's disease six years ago. However, Ann was very vociferous, making it quite clear to everybody that, while living with this disease, she was determined to have a life. Since then she has courageously turned a negative into a positive.

Ann's great quest in life is devoted to educating society through her talks, raising awareness and trying to dispel the stigma of dementia.

Initially Ann was invited to speak at local organisations about living with dementia. Today, despite having mid-stage problems associated with dementia, she draws heavily on her past experience of being a nurse lecturer and trained nurse. Ann climbs on to a podium. Then from behind the microphone she delivers with great clarity and professionalism her informative talks, just as she did years ago. Now her reputation as a speaker has grown far and wide.

Over the past four to five years, Ann has required assistance when travelling on rail, road or plane to various venues up and down the country and to Ireland. On these occasions, approximately four times a month, Ann remains independent but at times gets very anxious and stressed. It is Ann who liaises with event organisers, makes all travel arrangements and takes charge of travelling documents. I am only too pleased to help with checking timetables, travelling information, money exchanges, telling the time, crossing roads and giving orientation in wash rooms. I see my role as a carer to be supportive and try not to take over in most situations. It has given me the chance to have more understanding about dementia, and also, to meet such interesting people from all walks of life, including those with a high profile in government, media and society.

Apart from general support, I feel emotional support is the most important. She needs lots of reassurance that she is doing the right thing to the best of her ability. I see the tears of anger and frustration, the low frame of mind after the adrenaline levels drop following a talk or other excitement. I give a listening ear, ready to hear Ann's worries, anxieties or grievances, to love unconditionally and give the sense of belonging.

Ann always says that it is her talks, faith and friends keep her going. When the former fades, the latter two will always be there for her.

In relation to end of life, I think we should start preparing now. End of life may mean different things to different people. To some it may mean cessation of life. To others it may be that they are not able to function as they once were able. When I am not able to do my talks any more, that will be end of life for me.

How does one prepare? A final end of life will come to us all and we may wish to prepare for that. Practical aspects such as writing a will are vital. It may be appropriate to write a Lasting

Power of Attorney. At the point of death, who do you want to be there? A minister of faith, family? Are your relatives aware of what you want?

People should not be scared of death. I think we are more worried about the process and *how* we will die. In pain, suffering? I am ready to go when called. I am terrified of the future and do not want to face it – but that is not, and never will be, in my control.

I have a pre-paid funeral plan. The reason is, if I have no money when I die, why should my nephews and niece have to pay for it? I have been able to stipulate where I wish my funeral to be, and that I want to go into church overnight and have a requiem mass the next day. I will be cremated and my ashes will go with my father's ashes.

But between now and death, I will live life to the full and I will do that to the best of my ability and to the glory of God.

◊ ◊ ◊

In conclusion, it is a life-changing situation in which I find myself but I give thanks for the things I can still do rather than moan about what I have lost.

To end on a note of hope: my diagnosis was a sledgehammer and very distressing, but things have happened which allow me to help people understand dementia, and explain how to help people with dementia, sometimes even in the simplest way, which will mean so much to us.

So please do not be afraid of us: just love us, be with us and be our friends.

Chapter 15

Down with dementia!

SYLVIA KAHN

Sylvia and Bob Kahn on their Golden Wedding, 2013.

Sylvia Kahn *overcame many obstacles in order to get the education she desired. She had to leave school and get a job at the age of 16, but she continued her studies at evening classes, and went on to gain an honours degree in economics. After her youngest child was born, she trained as a lawyer, and worked as a solicitor until she was 72. Sylvia is an Orthodox Christian, and lives in Cheshire. Her husband Bob sent me Sylvia's account of her life. LW*

Well, I don't like it, but I have to accept it! No one in my family had it; and it never occurred to me that I might get it.

They take away your driving licence, even though it's 40 years old and not a single mark against it. When I was a child, my family did not have a car. I suppose driving a car had become to me a status symbol that I had moved beyond my working class childhood. And so I remain cross that my driving licence was taken away. What's more, my husband connived with the psychiatrist to take it away. They both thought it was no longer safe for me to drive. I know this is legally required and eminently sensible, but I still don't like it, because it restricts my freedom. On the other hand, I wouldn't want to injure or kill anyone, including myself, so I have to accept it. In any event, my husband can readily drive me to church on Sunday and to the many classical concerts that we enjoy together in Liverpool and Manchester.

Throughout my life, I have pushed very hard intellectually; and I have heard there is some evidence that excessive mental effort provides a basis for the development of dementia in later life. (However, a more important risk factor may have been all the smoke I inhaled travelling to and from school on the top deck of the Coventry Corporation buses, as well as from my parents.) Between the ages of five and six I had two eye operations, but I was still extremely keen to read. As a homecoming present from the hospital, I was given a colouring book with a page devoted to each of the 26 letters of the alphabet, which included both a picture to colour and a sentence in large lettering explaining the picture (e.g. 'a' is for apple; 'v' is for violin; etc.). Colouring in the letters, on the floor in the front room, in front of the coal fire, helped me to memorise how they sounded. Without realising the significance of what I was doing, I learned the alphabet and began to read.

Because of a shortage of space, equipment and well-trained teachers due to the Second World War, there was no possibility at my secondary school of studying physics or chemistry. When it came to O-level choices, one either took maths or biology. My father insisted on me taking maths; and I agreed with his point of view. I got O-levels in English language, English literature, history, scripture, French, Spanish, Latin and maths. However, what I really wanted to do was study astronomy. I used to go out in the garden and gaze at the stars.

I left the grammar school at 16, because my father had tuberculosis, and my family needed me to earn some money. My father had a friend in the Inland Revenue, who suggested that income tax would make a good career; and I agreed, under my father's influence. I joined HM Inspector of Taxes, Coventry 3, in September 1953, where I soon passed the government clerical officer examination, coming 28th – to my surprise – among the several thousand people who sat the exam that year. I worked there for the next four years, while also going to evening classes two or three nights a week at Coventry Technical College.

Although I remained interested in astronomy and went to a lecture at Coventry Tech by the Astronomer Royal, I lacked the scientific background to pursue this interest any further. After an unsuccessful attempt to attain an A-level in physics, and still studying part-time while working at the tax office, I eventually gained A-levels in history, economics and economic history, and obtained a place at Liverpool University to read economics.

My mother died of cancer two months after I left home for Liverpool, which was very unexpected. My father was ready to bring me back home to keep house for him (it was 1957!) but my aunt, his sister, offered to care for him in order that I could remain at university. This was my Auntie Elsie, who had also arrived unannounced at my home in Coventry on 16 November 1940, the morning after the city was bombed so extensively, and had taken me back to Northampton to live with her for the next year, in order to avoid the danger of further bombing.

I gained an Upper Second Class Honours degree in economics from Liverpool University in 1960, and was accepted at the London School of Economics to read for a Master's degree in economics of developing countries. There I met my future husband. I did not attain a Master's degree, but gained a husband, who is still with me 50 years later.

As an only child, I was delighted to be in a position to stay at home and raise our five children, each of whom has brought me great joy. They are very different; and I enjoyed having such a lively bunch of children. As a family, we picked raspberries and blackberries and made jam, as well as going sledging in the winter when there was snow, and going on many happy holidays together.

When my youngest child was three, I started to study law at home, passed all the examinations to become a solicitor, and began to practise law when he began secondary school. I practised as a solicitor in England and then we moved to the United States, where my husband and I worked for seven years in the inner city of Kansas City, Missouri, which for me, involved work as a prison visitor, trying to help prostitutes and their children, as well as being part of a Christian mission group that was providing food and clothing to those in need. However, law in Missouri was an oversubscribed profession; and, with an English accent I could not find a job. I was not employable as a lawyer so I decided to become a nanny and spent four years working for two families and changing several young lives.

Then we went to Israel for two years, where I learned Hebrew, before returning to England and resuming my career at the age of 65 as a trusts, wills and probate solicitor. I enjoyed the work very much, especially the relationships with my clients, clarifying their intentions as they made their wills, and then ensuring that their executors carried out their intentions after death. However, my memory weakened; and at the age of 72 I resigned from my job, because I did not think it was fair to either the clients or the firm to continue to work with a defective memory. At that time I had not received a formal diagnosis, but I knew that I could no longer remember all the details necessary to be an efficient solicitor. Unlike some people who try to hold on to their jobs even though they are losing their short-term memories, I rejected such a possibility.

Furthermore, my husband noticed that I did not remember precisely what happened when my grandchildren visited. For example, I told him that I had rolled a ball into the conservatory; and he pointed out that it was my two-year-old grandson that had done it. The next day I realised he was correct, so we made an appointment to see our local GP in August 2008.

The GP asked me a lot of questions: 'Who is the Prime Minister? What day of the week is it today? What year is it?' I knew the answers; and my husband and I both thought he had not referred me to the local memory clinic. However, nine months later, to our surprise, we received a telephone call asking if a nurse could visit. She gave me a memory test. Since I could no longer remember my home telephone number and disliked being asked to remember strange, disassociated objects, I was referred to the memory clinic.

In December 2010 after a brain scan, I was diagnosed with 'probable Alzheimer's'. As I came home from the memory clinic, I hummed the theme tune from *Bridge over the River Kwai*. I guess I felt that my world was about to be blown apart. The next day I proposed there should be a Society to Protect the Elderly. 'Protect them from what?' my husband asked. 'Doctors,' I replied.

Aricept was prescribed, but I found it upset my stomach; and for some time now I have been using the transdermal memory patch Exelon (Rivastigmine). This seems to have stabilised the dementia; and the local psychiatrist said to me. 'This should work for several years.' I hope that she is right. A close friend said to me, 'Sylvia, if you can get Alzheimer's, anybody can.'

My MMSE score is still quite high, 27 out of 30. I'm not stupid, you know, even if I forget what just happened or what day of the week it is. I can still think. I can still cook as well; however, I do have trouble in the kitchen. I found to my chagrin that I couldn't make a simple cheese sauce. Never mind! I got over that one and now accept that I seldom multitask. More significantly, I not only can think, but also relate very well to my husband, my five children, my four daughters-in-law and my 14 grandchildren, seven of whom live around the corner and are being home-schooled. I find that having all seven at the same time is too noisy and difficult, but two or three is enjoyable both for me and for them. When I visit, the two-year-old twins arrive at the door with books in their hands, wanting me to read stories to them.

Furthermore, I can still pray. I had been brought up by my mother as an Anglican, but at Liverpool University, I became friends with a group of three young women, including a very committed Roman Catholic, named Margaret. We spent a lot of evenings discussing our respective faiths, and I decided to become a Roman Catholic, as I thought Roman Catholicism brought one closer to Jesus Christ than did the Anglican Church. I took instruction from the Roman Catholic Chaplain at the University, and became a Roman Catholic in 1958. It was my decision, made in my second year at Liverpool after prayer and reflection; and I was very happy with my new spiritual outlook.

Eighteen years ago, my journey in faith led me to become an Orthodox Christian. I find this the best way to worship as a Christian because the Orthodox Church remains 'the original' Christian Church and is still faithful to its origins in both its worship and its theology. My faith in God enables me to accept the challenge of dementia; and I remain confident that God will not allow me to be challenged to a greater extent than my ability to cope.

I live very much in the present moment and find my life has value despite the limitations of my memory. I read a great deal, including *New Scientist, The Economist* and *The Tablet* each week, plus lots of books from the local library. My favourite novel is Charlotte Bronte's *Jane Eyre*, and I have recently re-read all of Jane Austen's novels, but I also continue to enjoy non-fiction, such as Stephen Graubard's *The Presidents: The Transformation of the American Presidency from Theodore Roosevelt to George W. Bush.*

My current reading is Peter Ackroyd's *Shakespeare: The Biography*, and I recently finished Sian Evans' *Life Below Stairs: In the Victorian and Edwardian Country House*. I read the latter book because I wanted to understand why my great aunt was so difficult and autocratic when she retired in the early 1940s from her job as the head cook of a large country house owned by an earl and came to live with my Auntie Elsie, who was so loving to me throughout my life.

I continue to pray regularly and spend an hour each day reading the Bible, reading a chapter or two from both the Old Testament and the New Testament and always the Psalms, except when I am travelling and turn instead to that slim volume of the four Gospels in French, *Synopse des Quatre Evangiles* which gathers all the gospels into a single chronological narrative (and helps to keep my French in good order).

I believe that the Second World War motto, 'Keep calm and carry on' applies to a life in dementia. Avoiding anxiety is a foundation for living with dementia, instead of getting all het up about things. You can make a difference to yourself and others by being calm, not grumbling and doing the best that you can under the circumstances. I have found writing this piece helpful, because it makes me feel more of a person. Dementia is not a bed of roses, but you can avoid many of the thorns, especially if you have a loving husband!

Chapter 16

Deciding to resist

LAZARUS

The author of this chapter does not wish to give his real name. His chapter is a combination of a written text he sent me and additional information he gave me when I came to interview him at his home. LW

For most of my adult life, I did blue collar work, working with my hands, sweating a lot, getting injured – I've worked on building sites, in factories; I became a truck driver and then a bus driver and a coach driver. It was mostly temporary or insecure work, and I kept getting made redundant. I was in care quite a lot as a child, in different care homes and foster placements, and I ended up in a youth detention centre in Suffolk – a Borstal, essentially. I got up to scrapes, did some crazy things with my mates, stole cars. We stole a double-decker bus once. It's because we wanted to get home. The bus was sitting there, and we nicked it and drove home. I used to bunk off school. But when I was about 37, I went and did a course called 'Second chance to learn', and I learned to read and write properly. That's when I learned that I wasn't dyslexic, and I didn't have a learning difficulty and I wasn't stupid. Before that I just used to bluff. And then I learned to use a computer, and I got good at it.

But I had nothing on my CV that said I was any good – I had no way of proving it. The only job I could get was working for agencies as a temp, so I got to work in hundreds of different places, a week or a month at a time, and I learned a lot about the different ways that computers were used.

And in my spare time, I started writing code – computer programs – to make my life easier. Every job that I had, I found I could think of a better way of doing it, which would be less labour-intensive and less boring. Eventually, I got taken on by British Telecom and I stayed with them for quite a while. And I started writing applications that would speed things up and make things work smarter. Then BT outsourced all of their IT to an American firm, and I started doing contract work for them, three months at a time, and they just kept renewing my contract, because I was really good at what I was doing.

Then there was a whole series of take-overs and mergers, but I kept getting re-hired and I kept on writing applications. I sold some of my applications to my employers and eventually I became a director of a division which did this work all over Europe, including Eastern Europe and Russia, and the Middle East and Africa.

I was about 50 when dementia symptoms first started to trouble me. I just thought I was tired and overworked, so I took more breaks, but I had to work harder to catch up. It is now apparent that I had been experiencing transient ischaemic attacks (a sort of mini-stroke), but I didn't know that at the time. I was also unaware of an underlying condition which was causing them: I had undiagnosed and uncontrolled diabetes and it was causing small vessel damage deep inside my brain.

I was not prepared in any way for what was going to happen to me. My employers noticed that I was struggling to deliver; my work was sometimes late and increasingly there were errors in it. My clients also noticed that I was becoming increasingly forgetful, confused and chaotic. Things were starting to come apart in my life but I was not prepared for the impact of what the doctors eventually diagnosed. I lost my job, I lost my income, I lost my home; my marriage did not survive, and I no longer live with my children.

I will be 60 on my next birthday. I may live for another 20 or even 25 years with this condition progressively affecting my capacity and my functioning.

This has been a very busy life so far: I have been a lover; I have been a husband; I have been a partner; I am a parent; I have been an employee; and I have also employed myself. I have held babies tenderly in my arms; I have nursed them through childhood illness; I have mopped up mess and I have wiped many bottoms; I have listened to many troubles; I have read bedtime stories; I have walked the floorboards many sleepless nights; I have sung songs and nursery rhymes; I have played in the paddling pool: I have pushed on the swings and the roundabouts; I have held hands and rushed through the autumn leaves with my children kicking them high into the air. I have worried endlessly! There has never been a dull moment!

I've not been a philanderer, but I have had three long relationships. I've got a daughter and a granddaughter from my first marriage, a daughter and two stepsons from my second relationship (we didn't marry), and three children from my second marriage, which has recently come to an end.

The eldest of these three is going to be 20 in August. He's at university doing physics and maths. Our daughter is now 17, and she's at college. Then we have another son who's nearly 15, who has special educational needs. He spends all of the school holidays with me, and he's absolutely obsessed with steam trains and railways, so we go to a family project on a steam railway in Wales at half term and pretty much all through the summer holidays. There are about 20 families, and about half of the children have got special needs. He works as a volunteer there now. He's just started working in the engine sheds, getting the locomotives ready to steam every day. He's absolutely fanatical about it.

For about 22 years of married life I helped to care for elderly relatives – my wife's parents in particular. My father-in-law was a veteran of World War Two; his regiment was deployed in almost every campaign and fought in every major theatre of war. Each time they went in he lost most of his comrades, then they were withdrawn and re-equipped to be sent in again. He was one of the few survivors. He had joined up as a regular in 1937 and he was not demobbed until 1946. He earned many medals including a Burma Star. Among the field rations he lived on during these years he was provided with cigarettes. The addiction calmed his nerves and soothed his fears. The legendary British stiff upper lip prevented him from doing anything else with so many years of fear and trauma.

He died with dementia and emphysema, without dignity, defeated and gasping for air. I sat with him all through his last night with us and I held his hand. I reminded him how much he was loved and appreciated. I reminded him of all the things he could be so proud of and especially the achievements of his daughters, one of whom I had married. I grew to love and respect this man. I spent a lot of time with him. We were mates. I miss him still.

Ten years later, my mother-in-law started to need love and affection more and more. It was a gradual thing. She had always been a stalwart ally, helper and resource to us. We lived really close by. She stepped in to help when we were overwhelmed with our own children – and slowly but surely, she became another of our children. We took her with us on all our holidays because we understood that we couldn't really leave her behind. Eventually we realised that she needed to come and live with us. It was no big deal; we just laid an extra place at table and shuffled beds around. In lots of ways she was a pretty sharp cookie. The war had curtailed her schooling but she could reckon her purse and read the local paper.

Then gradually we noticed that the anecdotes and stories she told us were repeated more frequently; then they were repeated endlessly; then we realised reluctantly that she spent an increasing part of her daily existence in the past; then we had to really insist that she shift her attention to the present to attend to her affairs; then we did that for her too. She went slowly. For the most part she went gracefully and with her days filled with as much joy as we could muster for her. At the end she was increasingly confused and incontinent, and had forgotten how to use a knife and fork. I fed her. I fished her dentures out and scrubbed them clean. I put my finger in her mouth to retrieve any un-swallowed food. I wiped her nose. I wiped her bum. I changed her clothes and I changed her bed. She had her last birthday in hospital. Our children made large iced cakes for her and an extra cake for the nurses. We sang her 'Happy Birthday' and the whole ward joined in. She died in her sleep the following night. There was, regrettably, a huge relief when she went. I miss her too.

When the doctors explained that I also had dementia symptoms, my wife was horrified. At first she ignored it. Then she got angry and resentful. Then she realised that the last 20 odd years might be repeated and it felt like a life sentence in the caring role. She is 13 years my junior. She found a new friend of her own age. He is a nice man. My children like him. He obviously likes them.

I had struggled on from the first signs in 2002 until 2006. In 2005 I had coronary stents fitted, because I started getting angina, and that was the first sign that I had the ischaemic disease. Because I was travelling around so much, I never had a regular GP. I used to live in the Netherlands during the week, and commute home at weekends. In 2006 I had an operation on my abdomen, and my job finished, and I moved back to England and lived at home.

At first when I could no longer work I would get the children off to school in the morning. I prepared meals. I became the family taxi driver; an endless round of after school activities, fetching and carrying for everyone. Then I started getting lost and taking the long way home.

When I first became aware of the TIAs, I didn't know what they were. I ignored the first few. And then I had one where I got out of bed in the morning, and crashed around the bedroom and demolished everything, because I couldn't walk. And I had this numb, tingly feeling inside my mouth. My tongue couldn't feel half of what was there – it felt like I'd been to the dentist. And I thought, 'I must have been lying on my cheek awkwardly or something.' I just didn't pay attention to it. And then my wife said to me, 'Are you all right?' and I couldn't talk. So then we went to the hospital. And then I had another one, a sort of left-side collapse – droopy eye, droopy dribbles, dragging leg and wobbly arm, all on the left side. And I couldn't walk or talk at all. That was a stroke, in 2008. And I had quite a good recovery actually, and was pretty much getting up and about, helping at home, wandering around to do the shopping – until I had another stroke, which was really quite disabling, and I wound up in a wheelchair.

I got depressed. Increasingly I became an irrelevance around the home. My wife got desperate. She started to miss the me that I used to be; she missed my identity, probably more than I actually did myself. My dementia got markedly worse. I moved out. Her new partner moved in.

A while back, a consultant and academic called V.S. Ramachandran gave the Reith Lecture and something from this broadcast had stuck in my mind. He was studying brain traumas, illnesses and injuries and he noticed some things that he thought would point to interventions for neurodegenerative processes in the brain. I became addicted to Radio 4 and listened constantly. I next heard a broadcast about brain plasticity from Professor Susan Greenfield which started me on a hunt for things that might mitigate the worst effects of my symptoms, or better still arrest their progression.

Susan Greenfield's theory is that the brain is malleable. She went back to looking at how we learn, and looked at what happens in the recovery process after a sudden brain trauma like accidental injury. And what she found was that we teach ourselves all over again, and we use the same learning processes that we used as a child. They are innate. We're hard-wired to do it, and by examining that process you can actually improve your learning. You can learn to do things that you have forgotten how to do; you can practise and get better. Repetition is what the brain thrives on. When we practise anything, like practising a musical instrument, practising learning a language, what we're really doing is forcing neural connections. And there's an absolutely immense reserve – about 70 per cent of the neurons in our brain are not under our conscious control, and are sitting there chattering away to themselves – and it's possible to redeploy them.

I decided to resist my dementia. Not to be in denial, not to pretend it's not there, but to fight it. I decided to hunt for what might give me the chance of a life worth living instead of a long and slow goodbye. I enrolled as a participant in a study led by Dr Ruth Bartlett into the lives of people living with dementia who have become dementia advocates and activists. I am currently enrolled as a residential full-time student at Ruskin College Oxford. The college allowed me to enrol provided that a package was in place for adequate health and social care support. They also provided a disabled adapted flat with a bedroom for my PA/ carer. My home local authority assessed me for Direct Payments which enable me to pay for care. I have also been assessed by a doctor employed by the Department of Work and Pensions for a DLA award. This pays a contribution toward care provision and enables me to use a Motability disabled adapted vehicle.

When I arrived at college, I was still in a wheelchair. My carer, J, pushed me to and from my lessons across the campus in the wind and the rain and snow all winter for the first term. I spent a month in hospital at that point for surgery to address another chronic problem. I worked my socks off to catch up with missed work but the experience of several hours under anaesthetic seemed to have seriously impaired my ability to learn fast enough. I didn't pass my first year. I didn't give up either.

I speculated on whether trying to learn to walk would also re-programme my brain; I thought it was worth a try. In the vacations I tried to get out of my chair and use a walking frame. At first I only managed one or two steps. I still can't walk very far. My progress is variable. My experiments in trying to learn to walk were also applied to learning other new skills. I decided to start stimulating the brain all the time and in all the ways that I could imagine. I decided to retrain the millions of cells in that huge unused reserve capacity that we were all born with. I decided that they could be brought under my conscious control. I decided that I needed them.

I decided that I could deploy them to take over from those cells and connections which had been destroyed. I decided to do new things every day that would persuade them to make new connections, new networks and new possibilities. I decided to start giving them new jobs to do. I decided not to give in and not to give up. I live my whole life through those decisions now. Sometimes I have to make the same decision time and time again because I often forget them. I have just got into the habit of making decisions repeatedly.

My decisions are what get me through each minute and each day. I decided that decisions were the way for me because my brain plays these funny little tricks on me and because my emotions are a complete rollercoaster. My feelings were no longer a reliable guide to actions I might take. I felt like staying in bed and waiting until my remaining days had all floated by. I had to decide that I was going to get up next morning and then I had to decide to actually get up and get going. I decided to resist.

I am a fully paid-up member of the dementia resistance movement.

If I had acted on one particular feeling you would not be reading this. I sometimes felt so full of bleak despair that I wanted to end my life. I decided to resist the urge to give in to despair. I decided to claim a full and enjoyable life.

Reflecting on my past, I realised that I had kept myself so incredibly busy that I had seldom sat down to deliberately make decisions, even the really big decisions in my life. Sometimes the course of my life was decided by passivity, by timidity or by apathy. Not making a deliberate decision was a decision to put myself at the mercy of events. Even decisions to get married, to have children, to change my job, to move house were mostly abdication of control over events by taking the easiest course and without much thought to the consequences.

I married because of a rush of hormones to the head; because of a romantic notion about relationships, because of physical attraction and because of almost overwhelming physical needs. We called this infatuation with each other love, but love, devotion, commitment, dedication, came later, fortunately. I had children because of a haphazard and essentially lazy approach to family planning. Moving jobs and moving house has all too often been either opportunistic or a reaction to events overtaking me. On reflection, most decisions were made emotionally, and seldom using a logical or rational approach. I rarely evaluated the relative merit of one decision over another. My response to dementia has been to learn new mental health habits and this has involved new thinking habits too.

The contrast between how I got along then and the need now to be very much in charge of every brain cell is quite marked. Dementia onset has required me to respond differently. I am requiring my brain to learn new tricks and to recover all the old tricks it used to know how to do.

You should not run away with the idea that I arrived at all these insights unsupported and unaided. I would not want you to think that I have achieved these modest gains all by myself. I have had practical help, emotional support, counselling, and information generously shared with me by some simply wonderful individuals. The list of allies, fellow travellers, teachers, trainers, clinicians, practitioners, professionals and inspirational examples is endless. What has been different in my case is that I have not had a family or family member carers to fall back on. I have been forced by circumstance to look around me a lot more to identify resources, support and help that a family support network very often provides for a loved one developing dementia.

Independence, autonomy and self-reliance were already important aspects of my personality before I was diagnosed with dementia. Fortunately for me, I could use these already established aspects of how I live my life to navigate a path through the confusion of dementia together with the maze of government agencies, local authority departments and NHS processes. I became quite expert at advocating for my own needs.

I also shared the information I discovered with people that I met, because others were so generous in sharing tips and tricks with me. Soon we discovered that advocating as a group is more effective than battling alone in isolation. I'd learned quite a bit about how resources were rationed and I could appreciate the fact that the public resisted the imposition of extra taxes to fund better services. We tend to blame governments of whatever persuasion for being stingy with the NHS, and they have certainly been ducking the issue of social care. Report after report and commission after commission have had their findings ignored by a political elite focused on their own short-term electoral success. Weasel words and promises of pie tomorrow is all we have had so far. However we are the real culprits: we don't vote, we don't engage, we abdicate from deciding a better course of action. We are marching blindly into a disaster that will touch all of our lives. With one person in every three likely to be affected by dementia and with the impact on the public purse set to increase alarmingly we can no longer afford short-termism. An avalanche of demand is poised to descend upon the settled order and it will devastate many lives unless we act to prevent it.

Early diagnosis is essential, to enable prompt interventions which will prolong capacity and retard the progression of symptoms: this will powerfully contain and reduce downstream costs involving residential and nursing care. Early assessment, monitoring and intervention in all the cluster of comorbidities that affect the population with dementia will dramatically reduce acute admissions that almost inevitably result in a move to residential care. Early, generous and universal availability of support to family member carers, especially regular and frequent respite breaks, will enable them to continue caring and will prevent burn out, despair, depression or a disabling illness.

We have a tradition in this country of burying heads in the sand. We seldom take the necessary action in time to forestall a disaster. Almost everywhere we see the results of under-investment. We have an infrastructure groaning and limping along every day. We are a first world economy which has created third world domestic social conditions. Our GDP is ranked sixth in the world, yet we permit a third of our older population to die in penury, we allow a third of our children to grow up in relative poverty and then we punish the poor by removing their lifeline. We blame the blameless and we persecute the innocent. These are the criminal acts of a culture without conscience.

I have decided that ranting and fuming in a powerless paralysis is not enough. In the remaining functioning and capacity left to me I'm popping my head over the parapet and I can afford to risk having it shot off. There is nothing more dangerous than a person with nothing left to lose. I am now finally unstoppable. I am invincible. I can take untold risks because there is no income to lose; I don't have one. I can't lose my home; I'm essentially homeless now. I can't lose my marriage because that has ended. I have no reputation to risk; any exposure of past mistakes, crimes or indiscretions will just give additional publicity to what I am trying to do. I can't be threatened with dementia because I've already got that. Short of shooting me or locking me up there is very little that anyone can do to shut me up – and I'm having the time of my life! I've got a very big gob and I'm going to use it. The challenge for me is to keep going long enough to get things done.

Everything takes me so much longer. Writing this has taken days. Reading takes even longer. I've got a reading list as long as my arm. I read a sentence or a paragraph, forget what came just before, go back to re-read it; three steps forward and two steps back. It's the same in conversations. I just lose my thread. My personal arrangements are chaotic. I have a wall board in my kitchen but I forget to write hospital visits or doctor's appointments on it. I double book one day in every three. I seem to be better in the mornings. I am close to passing out by seven or eight. I often put myself back to bed by five in the afternoon. I need much more sleep than ever before but my sleep is fractured and seldom particularly restful. As a male approaching later life my elderly prostate signals urgency three or four times and frequently more often; this in itself it is not especially irksome but the consequences are.

My brain then promptly wakes up and reminds me of all the things I forgot to do. Often these are urgent or very important things. Then I get up and write emails or letters in the middle of the night. I know that if I don't, then by the morning I will have forgotten. When morning comes I am often to be found still at it because progress with almost every task is painfully slow. I spend ages trying to find words or trying to remember where I have put my chequebook, my invoices or my bank statement. I walk out of every visit to the optician with two pairs of glasses and have lost or broken them within months. I lose my mobile telephone and my keys with alarming frequency. The major expenses in my life are no longer associated with just keeping body and soul together but rather recovery from regular dementia disasters.

I get help – of course I get help. I am at the point of almost becoming a danger to myself or the people around me. I need help to keep myself safe now.

Young Dementia UK generously provides a support worker once a week. She comes and helps me with my correspondence. I get hundreds and hundreds of letters. They go in a carrier bag in my bedroom. I open some of them. Some of them don't get opened. She makes sure they've all been opened and filed, and all of the bills are paid – so I don't get arrested or have the bailiffs coming in!

I couldn't do without J, my PA/carer. He has a contract of employment that says, 'Get me out of bed, make me hygienic, feed and water me, put me back to bed.' He does ten times more than that, but he can't do everything. At the moment I am being as independent as possible, because physically I'm getting stronger. But I rely on J largely because of the confusion and the chaos.

J is incredibly cheerful. He wakes up in the morning singing. And some really awful things have happened, life-threateningly serious, and he's coped with it. All three times that I was in hospital, it was an emergency admission. One time, I got abdominal sepsis. I was in the intensive care unit and I was unconscious for quite a long while, and when I came to, J was there, which was really reassuring. And the first thing he said was, 'Phew! They told me last night, "He's proper ill! It's really good you got him in here."'

My GP surgery now recognises that it is easier to liaise with J about prescription medicines; I simply forget. I also forget to take my medicines. Time is meaningless. The pharmacy packages everything in a 'dose-it' box and J serves up my tablets at the required intervals. I have access to a modern and efficient dentist surgery who are remarkably understanding about my disability and dementia needs. The bladder and bowel continence promotion service provide me with containment pants. The district nursing services have supported my carer and me in dealing with post-surgical recovery. Regular monitoring and outpatient clinic appointments help me to keep on top of the non-dementia conditions.

The services that I need the most help from are from the memory clinic and from the consultant neurologist; here the position is not so good. Waiting lists for appointments are very long and the appointments are barely long enough to exchange greetings and get some advice. Clinicians here are cautious and tentative; I also suspect that they have little to offer; NICE guidelines restrict their prescribing. My own type of dementia condition is not especially amenable to many pharmaceutical therapies available even if they could be prescribed. I would like it if the practitioners would think a bit more freely. If they prescribed someone to march me up and down the canal towpath, or round the park or along the river; if they prescribed a replacement carer so that J could take his accrued annual leave and bank holiday entitlement; if they could prescribe singing, dancing and music making; then antipsychotics and mood altering therapies would not be so frequently deployed to sedate people.

My moods cycle through feelings of hopefulness and helpless optimism, dark despair, desperation and determination. About half the time I am capable of purposeful and deliberate self-agency. The other half of my life is a battle not to hide my head under the duvet. Plan A is stave off the collapse of capacity and functioning for as long as possible. Plan B, try and deploy my cognitive reserve and teach it to take over from damaged brain cells. Plan C is to make an advance care plan and find someone who will stand guarantor for my wishes being observed (I don't have willing family member carers) and this is the most difficult. Winston Churchill advocated 'keep-on-buggering-on' and he did. Unfortunately I can't afford his appetite for brandy, port and cigars. I live on a student grant and loan that is rapidly reaching maximum. I'd love to have a job I could do somehow. Any ideas?

Postscript

Lazarus adds:

Since writing the above account, I have left Ruskin College and moved into sheltered housing. J has moved on to another job and I now have a new PA.

My clinicians have definitively excluded the two most prevalent dementia disorders, Alzheimer's type and vascular type, but as yet they have no explanation for my symptoms. My consultant says I am a puzzle. Recently my GP referred me for yet more tests. Mild cognitive impairment has been confirmed.

I continue to resist symptom progression by every means possible. I think this attitude is partially responsible for baffling my consultant. I do not fit the pattern. It is clear that I can no longer function as I once did. I function now in ways that are atypical and anomalous. I defy classification. How long I can keep this up I do not know. I am preserving personhood as long as possible by whatever means. I simply refuse to give up.

Chapter 17

You keep-a-knockin' but you can't come in

ALEX LINDSAY

Alex Lindsay *is a former psychiatric nurse who describes himself as 'an old rocker' who is 'a tad off his rocker'. He enjoys 'fighting the establishment' and exposing hypocrisy wherever he finds it. I met him when I visited the Scottish Dementia Working Group in Glasgow, and he was the first person to respond to my invitation to write about his*

experiences of living with dementia. I received his account in the form of a series of emails describing different episodes in his life. I gradually pieced together the narrative which follows. LW

'Angelic Alex': Alex Lindsay as a little boy.

I was born on 30 June 1940, during the Second World War. I was taken home to my abode in the Gorbals area of Glasgow which was notorious for street fighting and razor gangs. My father was a hardworking man, a baker by trade, with a passion for cowboy books. He was a gentle but firm man with high moral standards, and worked long and arduous hours. My first memory is of the air raid sirens wailing, and being rushed to the air raid shelters with a tiny gas mask and a flask of water. When the all clear sounded the family went back to our humble one-room home with an outside privy and gas lighting. My next memory was being in a hospital ward full of wounded soldiers. This was at the age of two years. I remember the soldiers making me a mascot, and being wheeled round on top of the food trolleys. Happy memories.

My father was no academic but wanted me to have an education. He purchased educational toys from a shop similar to the Early Learning Centre. I started to learn the 3Rs. Aged five

I went to primary school and was called a child prodigy. First day in class the teacher asked if anyone could read and write. I replied yes. When she found out my capabilities I was paraded in the masters' room across in the secondary school. They were amazed to discover that when handed a daily newspaper I could read it from front to back with no errors. This brought with it problems. My tutors in a way favoured me and pushed me to academic limits over the other pupils, incurring jealousy and subsequent bullying. Being tall, slim, shy and wearing spectacles with a patch to correct a squint, I was bullied. Later I learned to fight and became one who dished out the punches. My Uncle Joe still remarks to this day that I was prone to hit first and ask questions later. My problems were to come on 17 August 1945 when my sister Kathleen was born. We had the usual sibling rivalry until she grew older and learned how to manipulate my parents, making me a scapegoat for her sins.

From age seven to nine I walked through hell, which shaped my later life and attitudes. My mother, like most of the girls in her family, was highly neurotic. My sister became an expert at causing problems and with an innocent and angelic face made sure I was punished. I have been thrown out naked at eight years of age on a cold communal staircase, and left screaming for help.

Aged ten, we moved to a new housing estate where I got a modicum of freedom, but not for long. I came first in the qualifying exam for secondary school. I used to arrive home late as I dreaded home and whatever would be awaiting me. I was referred to a child guidance clinic and met a psychologist. After a few sessions with my mother present, he spoke to me alone, and I quote his words: 'Alex, it is your mother who requires treatment.' I ran away from home and slept rough in back alleys and empty houses. When I eventually returned home, our GP prescribed Valium in large amounts, so I was one step away from becoming a junkie.

Aged 15, I passed exams to become a marine engineer but it was not for me. As I was not allowed to wear the latest styles, I had to hide clothing in an out-house and change to go dancing.

Then I decided on nursing as a vocation, and started as a student nurse in a 'poorhouse', as it was called. The wards had about 120 patients, mostly with advanced dementia and doubly incontinent. As most were bed-bound, we had to stimulate them to keep them from sinking into total apathy and dying. Some were past the communication stage but quite a few could respond and converse if I took them back to the past. However there were a few cruel nursing staff whom I disliked. One nightshift an old gent badly soiled himself and this thug poured an ice cold bath and dumped the man into it. Result – instant death.

I left to enrol in an old asylum-type hospital outside Glasgow. Many patients only had physical ailments, but people could be 'certified' – nowadays the word is 'sectioned' – with many illnesses including dementia, Huntingdon's chorea (a disease of the nervous system causing uncontrollable spasms), epilepsy with grand mal episodes, and Parkinson's disease. Any symptom deemed to be socially embarrassing was considered 'certifiable'. I spent many hours chatting with patients and could see no signs of mental illness. Early dementia cases would sit and reminisce, which helped relieve the feeling of isolation and being ignored by nurses and psychiatrists.

I saw many acts of cruelty being inflicted on patients whose only fault was to be different from the accepted norm. All were ill-treated and mostly kept sedated. I studied hard to find out what made these people tick by reading Freud, Jung, Kant, Adler and any other books at hand. The patients' clinical notes were an eye opener as the doctors signed them blindly and gave carte blanche to staff to do as they wish. I rebelled and was disciplined several times for smacking staff who ill-treated helpless patients.

All wards were locked and the staff were a mixed bunch. However, my charge nurse and tutor, Dan McGlynn, had the right ideals and approach: 'See the person first then the illness.'

Other staff on opposite shifts were cruel and vicious. If a patient answered back or queried anything they were dragged into a separate room and given what were called 'the bumps'. This was ECT – electro-convulsive therapy, which used to be used for treatment of depression. The theory was that three or four days of confusion and memory loss would take the patient's mind off his problems. In later years, sedation and anti-convulsive drugs were given to lessen the pain and distress caused by this procedure, but not in those days. The patient was dragged bodily into a private room and a cotton wool bandage put in his mouth. His body was held down by four or five nurses to prevent fractures when the fit was induced. More often than not, no duty doctors were consulted, and no note made in the shift log. This 'treatment' was being used as punishment for disagreeing with staff.

By this time I had met a girl and was introduced to sex. Therefore I fell in love and we married. As the nursing wage was £20 per month, I left nursing and became a paramedic with a much better wage. At nights I worked as a bar steward in a local wine shop until closing time (9pm) then crossed the street to don my bouncer's uniform in the famous Barrowland Ballroom, which was pretty rough – but I could fight, which we often had to. This was me working three jobs per day to buy my house and keep a lazy wife who spent her time sitting with pals smoking and drinking tea. Coming home from my ambulance shift to dirty nappies (*not* disposable Pampers) brought me down. I had taken enough so we parted and divorced.

I resumed my nurse training afresh. As I had passed my first part prelims, I could start where I left off. Practices had not changed so I and the new generation of nurses had to try to bring about change. Not easy when the old guard closed ranks. We had to be devious and disobedient to see changes which we could introduce in our theses and hopefully see being adopted.

The practices I have described were treated as the norm and approved by the powers that be at that time. Most of the nursing staff were recruited from the Highlands and Islands – big, dour, ill-educated folk who in the archive I read were described as 'warders' or 'keepers'. They had sparse medical knowledge and treated the inmates as non-persons. My last encounter was with a charge nurse called 'the Bosun', as he came from a fishing community in the Outer Hebrides. I caught him ill-treating patients on New Year's Day when he was drunk. Result, I thumped him and was suspended and confined to the nurses' home for two weeks.

I left nursing about 27 years ago with a heart attack, re-wired cheekbone and jaw – injuries incurred on duty.

I married again and changed career by joining a security firm. This was a notable date, as the day I drove down the motorway I was stopped by police and sent to the far lane, where I could see the full effects of the PanAm hit on Lockerbie.

During the first Gulf war, I worked in Bolton with the Ministry of Defence in a chemical warfare prevention factory. The hours were long and the regime strict but it was a job. My wife ran back to Glasgow to live with an old flame, leaving me with large debts which I eventually cleared. I came home and started again. I met a pal who played guitar and we formed a band called Route 66 which gave us a good income and a lot of enjoyment. I was struck with atrial fibrillation (irregular heart beat) and had to undergo treatment known as electrical cardioversion a few times. This slowed me down for a while. I went back to music on a lesser scale, but the damage was done. Hard upbringing, hard work, hard living had caught up with me.

◊ ◊ ◊

Everything I have said so far was just a preface and snippets which I feel at ease discussing openly, as they are almost public knowledge. The darker and more painful parts I will now mention, in the hope that anyone who reads them will perhaps identify with the range and intensity of emotions a person feels when they accept that they have this condition called dementia: it comes in many flavours, and none are pleasant.

I met my wife Moira 13 years ago and we married on my 60th birthday. The signs of dementia were there about seven or eight years ago, but not for Alex. He knew better!

The first sign was memory loss, which I put down to absent-mindedness and pressure. At that time I had pressure coming from all directions. I was using up savings to bail out wasters in our families, coping with anti-social neighbours and cardiac problems. I had many mood swings and depression. I felt suppressed rage at the world in general and a desire to lash out at some invisible force which was screwing up my thinking processes.

Alzheimer's was my biggest fear, after watching my father die in a painful and undignified manner, having been fleeced of all his money and left in penury by the family. I was working with the MoD in England at this time. I came up to visit and found him in a filthy old ramshackle hospital. He had no idea who I was and was covered in bedsores. I took a photo of him and was informed later on that evening of his death. After the funeral I returned to England and tried to come to terms with this trauma. As I write, his photo is in my desk drawer.

I self-diagnosed my dementia and kept it hidden with various ruses. I re-invented myself as an eccentric, outgoing man, full of fun – and at times full of ale and wine. Drink was no help, so I chucked it. I went through a lot of emotions. How long could I hide this condition? I went back to my old wish to be an investigative reporter and obtained a few stories and won some plaudits for exposing a few not so nice people. My mind had to be kept occupied to distract my thoughts from the big D – dementia.

At this time, Moira was working as a house-keeper for two Indian doctors. We socialised often and became close friends. The husband is one of the top plastic surgeons in the UK and renowned worldwide for his pioneering work in facial reconstruction. His wife is a consultant paediatrician. She was a member of an Alzheimer's specialist group in her spare time and spotted my symptoms, which I had been able to hide for about three years. She discreetly broached the topic with Moira, who still kept her own counsel as I was very volatile verbally. Never physically violent, just touchy.

When I had a coronary followed by a stroke I was sent to the falls clinic in a local psychogeriatric hospital. This puzzled me as I expected to go to a mainstream hospital. My father's fate was in my mind when I consented to MRI scans and other procedures. I was informed that I had cerebral atrophy, i.e. shrinkage of the brain and decline of cognitive functions, which I had known and tried to hide for several years.

My GP referred me to a so-called specialist – a quack who fed me strong medication which had many adverse effects. When I got frustrated and angry I would walk out and end up by the seaside or lochs. My loss of faith in religion and my affinity with nature drew me to these places as I often remarked that Mother Nature was more dependable than all the deities used as moral and mental crutches. Suicide was a good option, preferably the sea, as it is quick and I suppose painless. The deep blue water seemed to beckon me as it was a swift and merciful escape from a living hell. I was dragged out of the River Clyde twice and Loch Lomond once. Other times I disappeared into the mountains. I feared not death but the indignity of being a bed blocker at home or in some other place. Memories of my early nursing days are still with me, and a lot of the old bad medical habits are back in nursing homes.

I became angry at myself, the world and religion. 'Why me?' I asked, and a preacher replied that it was God's will. End of religion and start of my war against the three Ps: preachers, politicians and police. I had friends who were reporters and columnists who I gave stories to about police corruption, which was rife in Glasgow, to which I had returned. I was angry at all things official, political and the world in general.

This went on until I was contacted by social services. The lady was very nice but way out of her depth. I was a man with clinical knowledge who knew what was wrong but could not abide well-meaning do-gooders who had no clue what was going on in my brain.

I was still lost and went back to my GP to see if a milder anti-depressant would work, but after four days I dumped it. My rage was still burning at the self-styled psychogeriatrician. I had harsh words with her, which I do not regret. When my wife asked for answers and guidance the consultant curtly informed her that our consultation time had expired and there were other patients to see. I became withdrawn, which annoyed my wife and caused many arguments.

I had visits from several social worker types who had not a clue. They sent me to day centres where most were in very advanced stages of dementia. I abandoned them and eventually met another social worker who upset me at first but I can see the funny side now. In a chat she mentioned to Moira something about a respite holiday. My ears perked up. Aha, I thought, Blackpool or Benidorm. Her offer was two weeks in an old folks' home. I very curtly asked her if she had ever watched *One Flew Over the Cuckoo's Nest*. No, was her reply. I told her to get a copy and call me McMurphy from then on.

One day, I was asked to call in to see my GP, who is a great guy. He had six students and asked me if I would mind talking about my condition which had been confirmed by MRI and CAT scans. I was very frank, blunt, amusing, but shocked them all when replying to a question asked by a student. She asked me if I found any consolation in faith or religion and I popped my cork. I informed them that in my opinion all preachers were con men. I asked them why is it that when 10,000 kids die of AIDs, starvation etc., the Bible bashers say, 'It's God's will.' One timidly asked what would happen if I was wrong, and went to Heaven. My reply was that He would need Mick and the Archangels in body armour as I would give Him what is known as the 'Glasgow

Kiss' for starters. We shook hands and left in good humour, with my GP trying to keep a straight face. Poor wee students. They did get an education that morning.

◊ ◊ ◊

After a while I met someone who referred me to Alzheimer Scotland. That and having a support worker called Julie gave me the chance to recoup what strength I had, and my life now had a purpose. I discovered I was not alone or unique and unlike my late father did not have Alzheimer's but vascular dementia. I researched on that and found a glimmer of light.

Martin, Jenny and all at Alzheimer Scotland gave me tips and tricks which I adapted to suit my particular needs. I am realistic, quite optimistic and no longer pessimistic. My sense of humour is back in full swing as is my old rebellious self. I earn a few pounds every week or so by writing humorous and somewhat scathing letters to the press, national and local. I have many scrap books full of published letters which are a legacy and also proof that dementia is not a death sentence nor need one be considered to be a vegetable. We all have untapped resources which can be brought with a little stimulation and less medication. I still have down days like normal folks, but ride them out. I decline drugs which dull the mind and turn one into a facsimile of oneself. I count myself as being fortunate insofar as I can live with this condition. I do not hide it as there is no shame lurking in the back of my mind. I discuss it openly and people always seem surprised when they find out. There is no stereotype, and being Alex, I never was a stereotype or conformist.

I was taught to use my first iMac about six years ago and kept at it with college classes and weekly tuition from my Uncle Joe. I now have the latest iMac and applications to maintain it. I liken my brain to a hard drive. It has to be de-fragmented and optimised regularly with the tools I have borrowed from others.

I go out Tuesday mornings with an ex-prison officer called Brian who is one of the lads and fun company. Thursdays I have the afternoon with Julie, whom I regard as a daughter, and we go to Loch Lomond and the seaside to enjoy nature and banter.

To summarise: I am Alex. Take me as I am or as you wish. I live for two things only: my wife, Moira and my Yorkshire terrier, Muffin. If I took my life I would hurt them and that is a selfish act I decline to do. Now I prefer to do what I like best, helping others and keeping an even grip on my life.

◊ ◊ ◊

Postscript: The angel on my shoulder

Soon after I had written my chapter for this book, Moira was diagnosed with cancer.

Her first thought was for me. While she was undergoing treatment she made an odd remark. 'Alex, I hope you go before me, as I worry as to how you will cope alone.' I said, 'I wish that I could take the cancer for your sake.' That is love at its utmost.

All I could focus on was giving her palliative care and trying not to cry, though I was crying inside. My dementia had to be put on hold, and old skills recalled, to make her last days and hours as painless and comfortable as possible.

Seconds before Moira passed away, one of her sons pointed out of the window and there was a rainbow.

When you lose someone who was an integral part of your life it is hard to get back into the mainstream. Moira and I were a matched set who never went out without each other. She was a great support with my ailment, although it took her a few years to understand my condition and memory lapses. Eleven years into vascular dementia, I coped with the help and compassion of a loving wife. She was my rock in difficult times and I owe her my life, such as it is without her presence. I would like to dedicate my chapter to Moira, and all the unsung heroes and heroines who care for people with my condition.

I dipped for a wee while when I lost Moira and I became a recluse. However, it is time to take small steps to regain some sort of normality. I still feel her presence or spirit. This keeps me going, as to throw in the towel would offend her. She is my guardian angel, and subconsciously I feel her guiding me.

I am coping, struggling at times, but still stubborn. I am still the same old Alex, but age is catching up with me and it becomes harder to bounce back. I always wonder if Moira and I will meet again, but there is only one way I will ever find out.

At present life is bearable. Muffin is my companion, and never leaves my side. I don't go out much but am adjusting to my new life. I speak to Moira each morning and last thing at night: I say a prayer at her monument in the garden and bid her goodnight as I go to bed.

Dementia and bereavement are not curable but with willpower and faith can be absorbed. I still have my faith, though it is a bit dented at times by the abundance of errant clergy. My rebellious nature has helped me to fight my type of dementia. My therapy is simple: keep the establishment on the run! To all those like myself, I say, 'Use all resources available, and keep on fighting.'

Chapter 18

The doors of perception

EDWARD MCLAUGHLIN

Edward McLaughlin *is a former engineer who has always loved painting and drawing. He was Chair of the Scottish Dementia Working Group (SDWG)*[60] *for two years, and drew the cartoons for the SDWG joke book* Why am I laughing?[61] *Edward received the MBE in 2011 for 'Services to people with dementia in Scotland'. I interviewed him by telephone. LW*

Edward McLaughlin and family at Buckingham Palace for Edward's MBE, 2011.

I first began to notice that something was a bit strange about 15 years ago. I used to work as an Instrument Engineer, calibrating and installing instruments in the oil and gas industries. I enjoyed my job and used to look forward to it, but at that time I had too much on my plate. I was too busy. I was divorced from my first wife, and my son was living with me. He was about 14, and I was bringing him up. I also had to travel and be away quite frequently. My mother used to come and look after him. And then I realised things like, I would be driving up from England back here to Scotland, and I wouldn't remember doing it. I couldn't even recall the locations in between point A and point B. I thought it was stress, or I was having a breakdown, or something like that. I was trying to do my job, trying to bring up my son, and run a house by remote control when I was away. It just added to my feeling of exhaustion, but I still had to go to work, because you've got to pay your way.

That went on for quite a while. Then eventually I married my second wife. My mother always said, 'You've been divorced, you've been living on your own for God knows how many years, it's time you settled down' etc.., and she met this lovely girl who she thought it would all work out very well with. She was a divorcee. And eventually, I just succumbed to it. But it didn't work out. It was a disaster.

It was my second wife who gave me my original diagnosis. She actually worked in the dementia area – she was the manager of a dementia unit. She recognised the signs from my general demeanour. I would forget lots of things. I would go away, and sometimes I would phone up and say, 'Right, I'm on my way back' – and I would turn up maybe about two days later. In the meantime I'd went to visit other people. So my wife done quite a lot of testing and enquiring. I just felt confused and curious. I mean, I had no idea what Alzheimer's was. We eventually went to my GP, who sent me to have an examination, and then I was taken into hospital and they gave me various brain scans. I had had some head trauma, many years before. I had quite a bad injury. But I don't know if that was a contributing factor. The doctor wouldn't go one way or the other. He wouldn't commit himself. But he eventually gave me a diagnosis of Alzheimer's disease. The whole process took about three years.

When I got the diagnosis, of course I had to stop work. Came home, and my wife told me she wanted a divorce. I asked her why, and she came out with this story. Then she told me she had this boyfriend, that she'd been having an affair with this last three years. And she says, 'I can sympathise with the diagnosis, but I'm not going to live with it.' So it was more or less: find somewhere to live, find a new life, and just get on with it.

I was idiotic. I thought we were actually quite happily married. And then I realised of course, we weren't. To turn round and say, 'I feel quite sympathetic towards it,' wouldn't be totally accurate! It was not a particularly nice thing to do. I mean, her friends virtually deserted her. They thought it was absolutely outrageous.

After my divorce, I got assigned a CPN (community psychiatric nurse), to help me run my affairs. I had to find another house to live in. And she had a hard time working me out, because besides coping with a new diagnosis, I also had anger, off my second wife.

When I got a house and moved into it – I lived in cardboard boxes. At the beginning, you're just looking out of the window, watching people going to work, eating, going to your bed – you sleep, get up, walk round the house, look out of the window again, watch people going to work – I mean, what the hell do you do with yourself? You feel redundant as a human being.

My CPN says, 'Let's get some of these boxes sorted out.'

You could hardly move in some of the rooms, there was so many boxes. And what to keep, and what to get rid of? And a lot of it was from my academic life. And we came across one which was a thesis I'd written on Yagi lasers. I knew it was mine, my name was on it. You know how you see these things, you think, 'Och, I'll hang on to this, it's interesting, it might come in handy some time,' etc.. So I opened it up – and I couldn't understand it. Not only could I not understand it, I couldn't pronounce half the words. And I thought, 'My God, how far have I slipped!' It really was like a brick coming through the window.

And then I realised, if you're going to change your circumstances, you're going to have to take all this and get rid of it. Because you can't go back. The place isn't there for you any more. And you're not totally void of things that you want to do, or ideas or anything else. Take all that energy, and negativeness, and try and turn it round. And that was hard.

My CPN was fantastic. I wouldn't have survived without her. I'd have committed suicide. I think she was a farmer's daughter. She was about six foot – she was not taking any nonsense from me! She was a 'can do' sort of character. It didn't matter what the problem was, she would find a way round it. And we got all my affairs sorted out, banks and bills and all these sort of things, and we tried to develop routines. And then eventually we went out shopping. I got a new kitchen, got a new bathroom, furnished the house, and now I think, I'm actually quite happy here.

It was my CPN who first took me along to the Scottish Dementia Working Group (SDWG). The good thing was, you're in a room that's full of the same type of people as yourself. So there's no need for analysing everything or being self-conscious. You can just speak your mind, and somebody will say, 'Oh yeah, I recognise that. I went through that myself.' And there's a certain relief that you're not an oddity. It's like being in a room full of – not necessarily friends – but people who recognise your situation without having great big explanations. You're suddenly all speaking the same language, which is more comfortable. People in the group aren't fearful of asking a question or looking for assistance. They're not shy in coming forward and saying, 'Look, I've got a problem, can you help me with it?' And everybody's quite happy to do that.

I was Chair of the SDWG for three years. What the group has achieved is incredible. From the original concept and the group itself, if you were there on day 1, you'd say, 'Yes, I recognise these people have all got a diagnosis.' If you came back ten years later, you'd think, 'There's nothing wrong with these people,' because they're all coping with all sorts of events, and talking all round the world, and actually hitting the nail on the head every time. And it's only because they're inside the game – they're not outside looking in – they understand the frustrations and things that need to be looked at.

The SDWG has got lots of laws enacted in Scotland. We helped put together the National Dementia Strategy for Scotland, and the Charter of Rights for People with Dementia and their Carers. A lot of finance has been invested by the Government – it's really, really changed. And there's a very positive dementia awareness campaign in the NHS, north of the border.

The DVDs that we made are used by lots of different countries as training aids. They now give them to people who have nearly had a diagnosis, because they've discovered that it actually empowers them. They think, 'My God, my life's not at an end. Look at these people there, what they're doing.' And that's a great piece of investment.

Alzheimer Scotland have been very supportive of the SDWG. They have said to us that they'll never see us short of funds. And we've also had the same type of commitment from the Scottish National Party, that they'll be willing to add to the coffers. This gives you confidence, looking forward. You don't have to look over your shoulder the whole time.

All the people I've spoken to in different countries use the SDWG as the basic model to build on. A lot of them are still very gobsmacked as to how far we've moved forward politically and socially – actually conquering the politics, and also the medicine area, and the universities.

When you're involved in something like this, I think you become hyperactive in some areas. It throws up challenges to you, to find new roads to travel and new techniques to discover, and to cope with certain situations. It brings on the endorphins, or whatever the term is. And that in itself can energise you. Once you've finished whatever it is you want to do, you just want to go and lie down! Pretty much everybody says they have full energy in the morning, and they start to wane a little bit in the afternoon, and once they have a rest, they're up and running again. It's difficult to pace yourself because you become so enthused, you want to get on with it.

Not everybody has the energy, or is at such a stage in their diagnosis, to take such an active part. There are people in the group who seem to be balls of fire, and there are others who just want to sit back. And the majority sit back. And that's fine.

I talk to lots of groups round here, and go to local surgeries and hospitals in my own area. I take a lot of active interest in the dementia clinic up here.

I say to doctors, 'You've got the power in your hands. Either bring us into the light, or push us into the darkness.' The right people can really give you your life back, but there's people whose lives are totally ruined, and I'm sure there's people who could commit suicide, because they're so depressed – because it's been a bad diagnosis.

I went to one doctor, and I had Bell's palsy at the time. And I thought it was a stroke. And I went to Casualty, and the doctor said, 'Just lie up on the table. I'll have a wee look.' And I said, 'By the way, I've also got Alzheimer's.' 'Ah,' he says, 'right. Count from 20 backwards.' Which I did. 'You don't have Alzheimer's!'

Now, that lack of awareness – this goes on all the time. This is one of the things we're trying to change, which is very, very difficult.

I talk to groups of people with a diagnosis, and just make everybody laugh! Laughter – some people can laugh, and it's a total shock to them. I don't go in with the intention that this is going to be a joke session, but lots and lots of funny things happen to people with a diagnosis, so it's more, 'This happened to me last week,' or 'This happened to someone I know,' and all due to dementia.

For example, there's a big central area in Glasgow called George Square. And I've lived in the place for years. And I walked through there one day, and I got halfway across the square, and I realised that I didn't know where I was going, I didn't know what I was doing there, and I didn't know how to get out of it, which was quite scary. My solution was, I saw a newspaper sitting on a seat, so I picked it up and pretended to read it. And an old woman came past me and said,

'You realise, son, your paper's upside down!' Then she said, 'What's your problem?'

So I just opened up: 'This is what happened, I'm in the square, I haven't got a clue how to get out of it,' and she got up and took me down to where I wanted to be, and went on her way. People can be quite amazing.

On another occasion, I got really quite confused on a place called Victoria Road. And all these guys with chains hanging off their jackets, and cockatoo hairstyles came along, and one of them said, 'Are you all right?' and I said, 'No.' I don't know why

I said no, I should have just said yes and let them walk on. But I told them, and we all buggered off together, and they bought me a meal! And the proprietor of the café saw us sitting round the table, and he nearly fainted. I thought, 'Oh my God, what's going to happen here?' They looked horrendous, absolute villains, but somewhere underneath all that, they were somebody's children!

I have a problem with reading and writing. If I'm reading black print on a white page, I can read maybe the first half dozen lines, and then they all just merge, just like straight black lines across the page.

When I'm writing, I will write something, and think I'm writing what I'm thinking, and then when I go to review it, I find things like two or three 'this', and two or three 'and's added into it. But while you're writing, you're totally convinced that it's a normal sentence.

I do a lot of painting, and I find my colour sense has changed. The colours I use now are quite outrageous! Looking at drawings and paintings I done years ago, you just wouldn't think it's the same person.

It also affects the way I perceive other people's paintings. I go to the galleries quite a lot. I enjoy being there, seeing the work, but my interpretation is just a bit different. I see colours that I never saw before. For example, Canaletto's 'Regatta in Venice': the colours in that are now more alive than they were before.

I like Van Gogh. I can see why he painted the way he done, and I think it's phenomenal. He was bipolar, and the colours that he used – they're vibrant, they're alive. Whereas before, I might have looked at them and thought, 'That's an interesting technique,' now I don't – I can actually see what he was aiming at. I can understand his diagnosis – let's put it that way.

The last time I was away, I was in Dortmund in Germany. I was meant to be giving a talk at a dementia conference, but I had a long journey from the airport, and I collapsed when I got off at Dortmund train station. I was taken into hospital and I went into seizures, and they found out that – I think it was my gallbladder, I'm not too sure – had gone septic. I think if I had been half an hour later getting to hospital, I'd have been dead. So I needed an immediate operation. And I didn't have time to tell them that they shouldn't give me a particular type of anaesthetic, simply because they're absolute poison to anybody with a diagnosis. Anyway, I went in and got the operation, with the wrong anaesthetic. But while I was having the operation, I had these hallucinations. I was in this really bizarre place, where everything floated. And rather than be fearful, I was absolutely fascinated.

Eventually I was conscious again, up on the ward, and one of the earliest things I can remember was saying to a nurse, 'Get me a piece of paper and a pen!' and I started drawing what I'd seen in this hallucination. I was so fascinated by it, the colours and everything else. After I got home, about three or four months later, I was going through a drawer, and I came across this little drawing, and a sort of light bulb came on, and I started to draw what I had seen. And this became the Dortmund obsession. I've done a series of paintings, and there's still lots of stuff there that I've had from it. And people have been saying, 'How the hell did you come to the conclusion of that?' They're actually quite taken by it.

But that anaesthetic done me a lot of harm. There's nothing for nothing! When I went back to work with the group (the SDWG), I had to stand down from being Chair.

About six years after I got my diagnosis, I got involved with a new partner. We already knew each other in passing. We'd say, 'Good morning, how're you doing, blah blah blah,' – and we'd done that for years. And then one day I was in a restaurant somewhere, and she walked in, and I said, 'Hi, hallo. I'm just sitting here myself. Do you want to sit down?' and we just started talking, and it sort of built up from there. And apparently, she'd been wanting to ask me out for years, but was too shy!

It was a revelation. We're both into very much the same things, like painting and music. We're a wee bit like the left and right hand of something.

She's an absolute open book. She's had her hiccups and problems and marriages and divorce in her life, but – she's a more courageous, honest person than I could ever be. She can tell me things which I don't even know about myself! She just doesn't want me to be anything else. The truth is there all the time. You just have to accept it.

I'm full of optimism. The optimism in the full glass.

For five or six years, I really just functioned. I just kept going. But I think, at some point, I came round a corner metaphorically and bumped into my own self, and I thought, 'You ain't so bad after all. You ain't so complicated, or whatever.'

I don't quite know what it was. I think I was in Glasgow or Edinburgh, and it was one of these little cafés with tables out on the pavement, and I stopped there, got a coffee, picked up a paper, sat down and started to read it. And I became aware of thinking, 'My life ain't that bad!' I'm quite content to be content.

Chapter 19

Journey into Alzheimerland

PETER MITTLER

Peter Mittler CBE *is Emeritus Professor of Special Needs Education
at the University of Manchester. He trained as a clinical psychologist, and
devoted his career to championing the rights of people with intellectual
and developmental disabilities to education and citizenship. He is a former
President of Inclusion International, a UN consultant on disability and*

education and is active in promoting the UN Convention on the Rights of Persons with Disabilities.

He was diagnosed with 'early, very mild Alzheimer's' in 2006, and the article which follows this Prologue, 'Journey into Alzheimerland', is an updated and revised version of a piece which first appeared under the same title in the journal Dementia.[62]

Prologue

Overleaf are extracts from a memoir which Peter Mittler published in 2010, Thinking Globally, Acting Locally: A Personal Journey.[63]

On reading his memoir, I was struck by the fact that as a young Jewish child, he was forced to flee his native Vienna after Hitler annexed Austria; he then spent his professional life in research and teaching on intellectual disability and campaigning for the human rights of people who have intellectual disabilities. In later life, he has begun to experience the symptoms of dementia, an intellectually disabling condition which often leads to social exclusion.

We know that not only were six million Jews murdered by the Nazis, along with gypsies, communists and gay people, but that adults and children with physical or learning disabilities, or with mental illnesses, were the first to be sterilised, experimented on, and killed, often by members of the medical profession, as part of the Nazi quest to produce a so-called 'master race'.[64] I am not aware of specific research into numbers of people with dementia who may have been put to death during this reign of terror, but it seems clear that people displaying symptoms of dementia would have been regarded as part of the target group for this programme of extermination.

There is a continuous thread in Peter Mittler's life: against *exclusion and persecution, against those attitudes which dehumanise (and ultimately seek to annihilate) people who are perceived as 'other'; and* for *inclusion, aspiring to a world where every human being is accorded their human rights, regardless of their intellectual abilities or any other factor.*

(Lucy Whitman)

◊ ◊ ◊

Peter Mittler aged 7 in Vienna, 1938.

Extracts from the introduction and first chapter of *Thinking Globally Acting Locally: A Personal Journey*

On 11 January 1939, my mother was one of hundreds of parents who took their children to the railway terminus in Vienna. I could see that some parents and children were crying, but had little inkling of the seriousness of what was happening. My memory is one of excitement rather than fear or sadness. It was all a great adventure, and there seemed to be quite a few adults to look after us. Of the 10,000 children who travelled on these trains, 9,000 never saw their parents again. I was one of the fortunate ten per cent.

We were all travelling without parents. Each of us wore a huge label with our name, destination and identification number. Everyone carried the minimal belongings allowed to us in almost identical small suitcases. Everything had to be counted, checked and signed for. As the train pulled out of the station, handkerchiefs fluttered in all directions and there was more crying.

My only memories of the train journey are that it seemed never-ending, but that the warmth of the welcome from Dutch people as we finally crossed the border, bringing hot drinks, cakes and chocolates and much cheering and wishing us well, made us feel like heroes.

I also remember arriving at the Hook of Holland late at night; someone helping me to walk up the long gangplank and being overwhelmed by the size of the ferry – this was my first sea trip. When I got to the cabin, I was baffled by what I later learned were blankets, which seemed to be tied to the mattress. I was only familiar with loose duvets, unknown in England at that time. We reached Harwich the next morning and were given our first English breakfast of eggs and bacon (the latter providing either a new experience or a conflict of loyalties for the more orthodox children) before joining the waiting boat train to London. This provided my first exposure to row after row of seemingly identical houses, something completely new to those of us brought up in cities consisting almost entirely of large apartment blocks...

[Peter was fostered by a kind and supportive couple, and both his parents also managed to reach England and safety, but it was some years before his family could all live together.]

Although I absorbed English like a first language, I remained very conscious of my origins and was frequently reminded of them. My surname sounded German and rhymed horribly with Hitler, Britain was at war with Germany and a German invasion seemed imminent. As an 'enemy alien', my father was automatically suspected of being a German spy and spent many months in internment camps, with long-term effects on his morale and mental health. It is hardly surprising that I followed the progress of the war with special attention, knowing that European Jews would be the first to be rounded up in the event of a German invasion. My interest in psychology, politics and international relations must have had their origins in this critical period of my development.

As an eight-year-old, I did not spend much time thinking about what I might become, far less what I might be capable of becoming. But whatever sense of security I had must have been undermined by the manner in which I was daily confronted with disturbing evidence that I now belonged to an unwanted and persecuted minority...

When I was a child, I did not think of myself as a *Kindertransport*[65] child, since the term did not then have the resonance which it has today; I was too busy living in the present to spend time thinking about the past.

I am now trying to confront the question of why I never really asked my parents about their experiences of National Socialism in action – not only at official level but also from neighbours and colleagues. With hindsight, I wish I had asked my mother how it felt to be alone in Vienna at the time of the *Anschluss*[66] and how she survived the persecution, humiliation, arrest and even suicide of so many of her friends and colleagues. How did she cope with the Kafkaesque nightmare of bureaucratic imperatives to secure the countless sworn affidavits, guarantees, tax and bank statements which she needed to leave the country of her birth? And what did she have to do to ensure that I was on that Kindertransport train only two months after *Kristallnacht*?[67] How did she and other parents cope with the trauma of putting their child on a train to safety, realising that they might never see them again?

My failure to ask these questions is all the more astonishing in the light of my long-standing interest in history and politics and my later work as a psychologist interested in the impact of deprivation and disadvantage on children. The subject was not taboo and I think my parents would have been willing to provide more information had I asked them to do so.

I now realise that I was part of the long, universal silence which started during the war and which continued for decades beyond... Despite the unforgettable films of the death camps which were shown in 1945 and the publicity given to the Nürnberg war crimes trials of the surviving Nazi leaders, there was little open discussion of the Holocaust for some 20 years. There was general awareness that millions of people had been systematically exterminated but the sheer horror of these events seemed to cast a veil over the whole subject, at least until the Eichman trial[68] in 1961, followed some years later by the film *Schindler's List* and later still by the 50th anniversary of World War Two and the erection of Holocaust Museums in the 1990s. It is only in the last 20 to 30 years that the Holocaust has been widely discussed in the media and in schools and that Holocaust Studies has become an academic discipline, with its own research centres, learned journals and specialist libraries...

There is now a monument to the *Kindertransport* at Liverpool Street station,[69] in which the sculptor has managed to convey the bewilderment of a small group of children of varying ages, each with their small suitcase, waiting to be collected: when and by whom?

◊ ◊ ◊

Journey into Alzheimerland
Then

I would probably not have asked for a referral to the local memory clinic if I had not had previous experience of assessing people for dementia in my first job as an NHS clinical psychologist. I remember my discomfort at that time in realising that test findings did not necessarily reflect what people could or could not do in real life situations. That lesson is now part of my own story.

I went to the clinic because my wife and I were concerned about an increasing number of memory lapses, such as not bringing home the right shopping and forgetting to do routine things like switching off lights and closing cupboard doors. I knew that early diagnosis was important and that drugs were now available which could at least slow down the deterioration associated with the disease.

The experience of being on the 'other side of the table' at the age of 76 was a bit strange at first, especially when I realised that I had used some of the same memory tests 50 years earlier. My psychological test results showed average or above average functioning in most areas, with the significant exception of tasks involving immediate recall of strings of unrelated words or pictures. I half expected this finding, because when my children were small they could always beat me at games requiring the recall of large numbers of upturned pictures, but a series of brain scans also revealed a greater degree of cortical atrophy ('holes in the head') than might be expected at my age. After reviewing all the evidence, including a detailed account of the concerns expressed by my wife, the consultant told us that although Alzheimer's could only be fully confirmed at autopsy, the balance of probability lay with a diagnosis of 'early, very mild Alzheimer's disease'. I trusted his experience, politely declined his offer of a second opinion and arranged to donate what was left of my brain to the Brain Bank research programme.

When I first told people about my diagnosis, most were incredulous, dismissing examples of my memory lapses as mere 'senior moments' and capping them with more serious examples from their own experience. However, the fact that I do not display 'obvious' symptoms of dementia does not mean that the diagnosis is wrong – that I am a 'false positive', in the medical jargon.

Now

The good news is that eight years later, the rapid deterioration which I was expecting has not materialised. My psychological test results have not changed over many re-assessments: in fact, the most recent reflects a slight improvement on the first. Even the tests of immediate recall on which I feel I do very badly are now just within the average range for my age.

My day-to-day functioning in most areas seems to me to be about normal for my age and background. I still sometimes forget to shut drawers or put things back where they belong, but claim to get it right more often than not. I can look after myself if necessary and undertake complex journeys. I feel reasonably competent in driving in familiar areas but am now more watchful and slower at decision making and worried about the annual renewal of my licence.

In many ways, my intellectual and cultural horizons have expanded since I retired from full-time university work 20 years ago. My reading has been enriched to include 20th century history and politics, as well as travel books and modern literature and I now have a fuller appreciation of music and the visual arts, especially since acquiring a second home in Florence. I have published a memoir,[70] edited a selection of my papers for publication[71] and contributed several new papers to academic and professional journals on the implementation of the new United Nations Convention on the Rights of Persons with Disabilities, which could greatly improve the quality of life and support for all disabled people, including those living with dementia.[72] Nevertheless, I have decided to stop academic writing because I now find it more difficult and because it takes up too much time which can be better spent in more rewarding activities.

An A* in GCSE Italian in 2008 provided welcome independent evidence that I could still learn, while the high marks that I later received for an Open University degree level module in Italian did more for my self-esteem than my doctorate several decades earlier. Despite my good examination marks and competence in reading and speaking Italian, my ability to understand and follow a conversation is disproportionately low, even under ideal acoustic conditions when I am wearing headphones to listen to a studio-recorded disc. This could be due to Alzheimer's, old age, or some complex combination of the two. Be that as it may, it is frustrating for me and confusing for Italians who assume that because I can speak the language, they can talk at their normal speed – and all at once.

It is difficult to draw a clear line between the effects of 'normal ageing' and Alzheimer's disease for people at my end of the dementia spectrum. The difficulty is overshadowed in my case by severe deafness which now deprives me of some 70 per cent of normal hearing. My particular combination of dementia and deafness is more than doubly debilitating because it affects the quality of my life and relationships. Although digital hearing aids can amplify sound, they are not yet able to strike a balance between essential foreground information and background noise in social situations and restaurants. Irrelevant and intrusive music makes it particularly difficult for me to follow a story line on radio or television, though I can still do so in reading. It is also difficult for me to use the telephone because although I may be able to hear the speaker, it takes me much longer to understand what is being said. Worst of all, even one-to-one conversations in quiet conditions can become frustrating because I have misheard or misunderstood what has been said when I thought I had been listening hard to avoid communication breakdowns. These 'processing difficulties' are associated with dementia but there is very little knowledge or understanding about their impact on people who also have a significant hearing loss.

Nevertheless, there are times when dementia does seem to be the most likely explanation of behaviours which are completely out of character. One notable example occurred in Italy several years ago when I forgot to move our car from the town square before market day, only to come across it the next morning surrounded by fruit and vegetable stalls and with a policeman bearing down on me, notebook in hand. I had always remembered to move the car in good time, so this lapse was quite uncharacteristic. Furthermore, I had already spent some time in another part of the market that morning without anything triggering a reminder that I should have moved the car on the previous evening.

These episodes are mercifully rare, and I do what I can to prevent them by making a list of day-to-day tasks. But there are times when a new mistake makes me wonder whether the deterioration slope is about to become steeper, even precipitous, as happened with a friend of ours. Examples include the misreading of a timetable which caused us to arrive at a railway station an hour too early and another day when I made five small mistakes, each of which could be mistaken for 'professorial absent-mindedness' but which, taken together, might be the first sign of a more rapid decline.

Next?

Like autism, dementia is on a spectrum. I am fortunate to be at one end of that spectrum but how long can this continue? Annual health checks show that apart from hearing, all my other systems are functioning well for my age but how long will my addled brain be able to keep pace as I go through the second half of my 80s or 90s? When I put this question to my consultant after four years, I was encouraged by his statement that there was no reason why the next four years should be any different. I was sceptical about this prediction but relieved that it seems to have been confirmed.

Although I am now more interested in prognosis than diagnosis, I later asked him if he had considered the alternative classification of 'mild cognitive impairment' which was by that time beginning to be more widely used. I also asked him to imagine a scenario in which he is acting as an expert witness on my behalf in a court of law where I am on a serious criminal charge. What evidence would he use to support his diagnosis of Alzheimer's disease against another expert witness who insisted that I was within normal limits for my age and therefore fully responsible for my actions? After reviewing my tests and brain scans, he stood by his diagnosis, adding that I had 'plenty of reserves in my spare tank' and that the medication which I have been taking deserves some credit for the absence of deterioration.

What about the next four years? Time will tell.

Impressions about Alzheimerland

Despite a lifetime of experience in the wider disability field, I soon realised how little I knew about dementia. I joined the Alzheimer's Society, read books and articles by people living with dementia and carers and was greatly influenced by Tom Kitwood's ground-breaking book *Dementia Reconsidered: The Person Comes First.*[73] I have since tried to follow professional and service developments through the *Journal of Dementia Care*, accessible summaries of research developments on the international Alzheimer Forum Weekly Newsletter and public lectures arranged by the UK Alzheimer's Research Forum. I am fortunate to be living in Manchester, which is recognised worldwide as a centre of excellence for research and teaching in ageing and dementia and promoting improvements in policy and practice locally and nationally.

I have learned most by becoming a member of the Alzheimer's Society Research Network Volunteers, which is made up of people living with dementia, carers and former carers and has been running for 15 years.[74] We have a major role in reviewing research grant applications, as well as opportunities for joining two other volunteers in personally monitoring projects in which they have a special interest. The research which I am monitoring is exploring ways of investigating the impact of dementia on the individual's sense of identity and 'self' – a topic in which I have a personal as well as a research interest.

As a former director of a research and dissemination centre on intellectual disability, I welcome the commitment to research by the Society and the increase in government research funding. But as a person with Alzheimer's, I am concerned about the degree of priority given to biomedical research in comparison with research which could improve the day-to-day experience and quality of life of people affected by dementia, especially those in residential care. The Society has now created two parallel research streams, one focusing on biomedical research and the other with care, services and public health research. Network volunteers work with both.

My experience of national and international dementia conferences has been mixed. Having attended many conferences on disability during the period when public services were still largely provided by trained health and local authority professionals, I was unprepared for the large number of staff from private and voluntary organisations and the many examples of sponsorship and prizes from the pharmaceutical industry. I was particularly troubled by a pervasive complacency about the high quality of services being provided, as well as by the naiveté of politicians who seemed unaware of the gap between good policies and their patchy implementation on the ground.

At one conference, I resented having to wear a coloured name-tag which labelled me as a person with dementia, though I understood the intention of the organisers to signal that some of the participants might need help in following the proceedings or in finding their way around the vast conference centre.

At another conference, although people living with dementia had an important part in the programme, it was clear from several private conversations that some of them felt patronised and disappointed that their demands for a more proactive role and 'voice' were not being met. At a private pre-conference welcome, one of the organisers seemed to anticipate trouble by asking us to 'behave as proper ambassadors.'

Following a video message from the Care Minister about the National Dementia Strategy, a few people living with dementia (now known as 'experts by experience') and several care partners gave examples of drastic cuts to local services and support. I initially got the impression from the chair of that session that these concerns would be sent to the Minister and the media, but when I spoke to him afterwards, I was less sure that this would happen. If this had been a conference of people with other impairments, including those with intellectual disabilities, there would have been a vociferous demand for a meeting with the Minister to insist on their full participation in the development of better policies and above all in their implementation on the ground.

The disability movement has raised awareness about the power of the words we use to reflect our values and attitudes towards people with disabilities. Consequently, we use 'people with disabilities' in place of 'the disabled' and 'Down's syndrome' in place of 'mongolism'. Although 'idiot' and 'imbecile' have been abolished as diagnostic categories, they survive as insults in common parlance. But what message is conveyed by the widespread use of 'dementia time bomb', and why has it not been more strongly challenged?

None of the speakers at these conferences referred to the opportunities presented by the UK's recent ratification of the United Nations Convention on the Rights of Persons with Disabilities. My research into the impact of this Convention indicates that governments are not including people with dementia in its implementation, despite clear guidance to the contrary from United Nations agencies and the definition of the scope of disability in the Convention.[75] Their exclusion could have been prevented if disability and dementia NGOs had joined forces to advocate for their common rights. It is not too late for them to do so.

The Convention marks a watershed in the slow and painful struggle of people with disabilities to be 'allowed' to speak for themselves rather than having to listen to others speaking for them. A powerful consortium of international Disabled Persons' Organisations, committed to the principle of *Nothing about us without us,* took a full and equal part in the detailed negotiations that created the Convention, and remains active in working for its implementation at national and local level.

The time is now ripe for people living with dementia and their supporters to become part of this movement, so that '*us*' can finally become '*all of us*'.

Chapter 20

Who's afraid of the flying bombs?

LORNA MOORE

Lorna Moore and husband Lawrie, 1992.

Lorna Moore *was born in East London in 1927 and her family suffered severely during the Great Depression of the 1930s. She was a pioneer of computer science and an active Labour Party member in Margaret Thatcher's constituency in Finchley, North London. I interviewed her in the presence of her daughter Jane, who helped to fill in some of the* *details. Jane told me that when they first noticed that Lorna was showing signs of memory loss, about ten years previously, the consultant who tested her said there was nothing wrong, as she had scored so highly on all the puzzles and mathematical tests. It was only when they went to see another consultant who took a full history, and learned about Lorna's career as a computer scientist, that she was given an accurate diagnosis of Alzheimer's disease. Sadly, Lorna died in May 2014, soon after this interview was conducted. LW*

I've always been interested in politics. I joined the Young Communist League when I was a teenager. It was a time when Russia was an ally, and Mrs Churchill started the Aid to Russia Fund.[76]

Afterwards I left the Young Communists and joined the Labour Party. I used to go out canvassing, and delivering leaflets, and I ran the committee rooms during election times. If people had said they were going to vote Labour, you'd knock them up and see if they needed a lift. I live in Finchley, which was Mrs Thatcher's constituency. We never had a Labour MP until she retired. I'm still a Labour party member. I don't agree with everything the Labour Party does, but on the whole, I think their heart's in the right place!

I think my attitude to politicians started very early, because when I was a small child, my father was out of work for three years. It was a terrible time. We couldn't afford a good diet. I lost all my teeth by the time I was in my late teens, because I just hadn't had the right food. We lived in a very poor housing estate in Essex, and we only survived because our relatives helped us. We belonged to a big family, so there were all sorts of aunts, uncles and cousins, and they all helped. The family was always very much a unit. And we were able to do things for them later, like look after them when they were old. It was a two-way thing.

I very much admire my Aunt Jessie, who was also my godmother, because she joined the St John's Ambulance Brigade, and she went to France as a volunteer. And she saw some terrible things. And she told me all about them, and she said, 'Never let yourself get involved in a call for war. Because war is terrible. And the human race have to learn to settle their differences without having wars.'

My grandfather used to help out at a Dr Barnado's home. He was one of Dr Barnado's young men. When I was a little girl, I was taught that a tithe of my pocket money must always go towards helping other people, so it went to Dr Barnado's. I used to go there and read to the children too, when I was old enough to read. It was a thing that the family as a whole cared about.

One of my great aunts told me my family were immigrants from Denmark. That's probably how my father came to work in the shipping business. I can't remember how many generations back they came. I think it was earlier than my grandfather. But quite a long time ago, they were immigrants from Denmark, and they came to England, and they were out of work for a long time, because there was a recession going on. But my father's father got work in the docks. He knew about cargoes. And he became a cargo planner.

And when my father was a young man, there was a lot of unemployment, so because there were no jobs to go to, my grandfather took my father to work with him. And when my grandfather died, they wrote to my grandmother and said, 'Where is young Jack?' and offered my father his job. So my father became a cargo planner too, and this meant he was exempt from going to war, because he worked at the docks.

During the war, I was an evacuee twice. The first time was very brief. It was in Ipswich but I can't remember anything about it, except that I wasn't happy there. I missed my parents. Then they moved, so that they could get me back home again, because I was quite young. We lived in Ilford, but Ilford was unsafe. It was too near the docks. So they moved to Orpington in Kent, and my father went on working at the docks.

When the flying bombs came, I was evacuated for a second time. I was a teenager by then.

I wasn't afraid of the flying bombs. Teenagers found them exciting! I used to climb up on to the roof and catch bits of shrapnel. I had to keep a wet rag in my bag, because I kept licking my fingers, when I was picking up hot shrapnel. So I took a damp rag and wound it round my fingers. All teenagers collected shrapnel in those days. And then when they needed metal, and they asked people to donate their shrapnel, I had a whole lot to donate. I didn't want it. I enjoyed climbing around to get it.

Anyway, I was evacuated again and this time I was very lucky. My billet was with the County Surveyor of Leicestershire. And he took me everywhere with him – because I asked questions. He had several children, but apparently they weren't terribly interested in what he was doing. And so because I asked questions all the time, and wanted to know how everything worked, he took me round with him and I learned a lot about how the countryside works, and how it's financed and everything. He said I asked interesting questions. It was the first time I'd met a grown-up who didn't mind how many questions I asked.

I had a wonderful time there. I enjoyed it, because they really drew me into their family, and I played my part. I did my share of whatever was being done, and roamed the countryside, and we collected fruit and made jam and all sorts of things.

While I was in Leicestershire, I spent a very happy year or two in a boys' school, because the girls' school wasn't doing the same A level subjects that I was already doing. I was doing physics, chemistry and pure and applied maths. At first I used to have to tear across the grounds to the girls' school, if I wanted to go to the lavatory. Then one of the women teachers in the boys' school gave me the key to the women's staff lavatory.

I didn't really miss my parents while I was there, because I could write to them, and talk to them on the phone and all that. What I really missed was that I had been helping my father do his cargo-planning. He had got lung cancer. He didn't die until after the war, but he just gradually got less able to do things.

He smoked a pipe. The connection between smoking and lung cancer wasn't known at that time, and by the time he knew it was too late.

So when he got ill, I did his cargo-planning for him. I used to take the plans to the dock gates and say, 'My father sent these.' I never told them that I'd been doing them. But there were no mishaps. You see, he checked them, as long as he could, and by the time he couldn't check them any longer, I knew my own way around these things. I had worked my way through his text books.

And it was good for me, because I was doing a responsible grown-up job, even when I was a teenager, and that taught me that you had to be sure you were right – people's lives depended on it. You had to know the properties of all the cargoes, what could safely be put together with what, and what couldn't – if there was any danger of the cargoes interfering with each other, or a chemical reaction – and how to balance the ship. You had to learn the mechanics of balancing a ship, and that was very good for my applied maths. I really enjoyed it too.

What amused me was that I would be taking the plans to the dock gates and saying, 'My father sent these,' and they didn't realise that I had done them. My writing was quite like my father's, so all I had to do was sharpen it up a bit, and no loops.

I enjoyed it. I really enjoyed learning a new skill. And I enjoyed being useful to my family. And then the flying bombs came, and I was an evacuee, and I couldn't do it any longer.

After the war I did a part time degree in maths and computer science, and got a job at the Institute of Computer Science, which was one of the research institutes of the University of London. I met my husband Lawrie when I was president of the students union at Birkbeck College. I spent most of my working life at the Institute until it was closed down in the early 1970s and I was transferred to Imperial College. I ran the advisory service, advising anybody who wanted to use the computers. I had to sign the Official Secrets Act, because of some of the things I was doing. I also did some lecturing, to first year students. At the same time I was bringing up my family, a daughter, two sons and a stepson.

A few years ago, I noticed that my memory was getting bad. Other people noticed as well. I can remember having a memory test, but I can't remember how it happened.

I found I gradually had to write more things down. I use a desk diary. I can easily find it because it's got a maroon cover. I might write down a television programme that I want to watch, or a book I want to get out of the library. I write it on a bit of paper, put it in my pocket, and then transfer it when I've got the desk diary.

I was really sorry when I couldn't drive any longer, but I don't approve of old people meandering about on the roads.

We used to have a bungalow in Dorset, a holiday home, but we've sold it now. We used to go there for weekends, but there's no point when I can't drive. I still like to go walking, wherever there's open countryside. I like hills and climbing and things like that. I have no intention of losing the use of my legs!

I don't drive any longer. Apart from that, I can do anything.

Chapter 21

Time to break the taboo

RUKIYA MUKADAM

Rukiya Mukadam and husband Mahomed
on their wedding day, 1973.

Rukiya Mukadam *was born in Kashmir, India, in 1951, and practised as a GP in Malawi for more than 30 years. Now based in London, she has recently been diagnosed with young onset Alzheimer's disease. I interviewed her at her home in the presence of her husband Mahomed Mukadam, also a GP. He told me he is finding it quite hard to adjust to his wife's condition. In his mind she is still 'that Superwoman that I married 40 years ago.' LW*

My childhood was very nice. You know, in Kashmir, or generally in Asian communities, they give preference to the male child. And though my mother had more preference to my brother, my dad was very much for me, and he always wanted me to study, and always wanted me to do something in life. If I did something wrong, I was afraid of my mother – I wouldn't tell her. But I would say to my dad, 'Tell her you did it!' I was very much encouraged to study. And from my childhood, I was a very blunt type of child, I wasn't timid. And still up to now I am very blunt. People can tell me anything – but I'll do what I want to do! I'm a bit stubborn!

So then, when I went to medical school, my mother knew that I'm a stubborn type of child, so she told me that if you meet somebody, don't run away with him, just come home and tell me, and I'll get you married. And that is where I met my husband, in the medical school. So then I told my mother, and my mother convinced my dad to get us married, so we got married.

And after that, life has been a struggle. I had my first child, a son, when I was in the fourth year of medical college. But my mum and dad were a great help in that, because we still continued to do the study, and fortunately we finished with very good results – he came first in the university, and I came second!

His family was in Malawi, so we went there. Then I had my daughter, six years after the first child. And we established our practice. We were both doing general practice in separate places, in the same town, about five kilometres from our house. He was in one place and I was in another place.

The work was very rewarding – not in money, but in satisfaction. Because in Malawi, there is not a different department for everything. We were basically general practitioners, but we were doing a lot more work! What general practitioners do here is nothing compared to what we were doing there. Because we were doing minor surgeries, we were doing gynaecology, paediatrics, counselling, psychiatry – everything. We were about 32 years in practice, so we treated three generations of people there, and it was very, very satisfying. Because you heal a person. And you see that.

There are no emergency services in Malawi, and hospitals are few and far between, and not well equipped, either. And there are some private hospitals which are rip-offs! I feel sorry for the people who go to them – especially the African people there, the Malawians. Some of them are well to do, and can afford the treatment. But believe it or not, in a day, at least ten or 20 people we would not charge anything, because they couldn't afford it. We were not there for profiting. We were not there as a mercenaries. We just wanted to give them the best care. Most of the people would say, 'I'll pay you the day after tomorrow.' It never came. But we didn't mind. And we didn't stop that. Especially my husband – he is very kind in that.

We were in a town. But people would walk ten, fifteen kilometres to come to see us. So that way we felt nice, because they would appreciate. And sometimes, if they didn't have fees, they would bring some eggs, or a chicken or something. We wouldn't want to take it, but we didn't want to break their heart either. It's a cultural thing. And when my husband had an accident – it was a terrible accident, the doctors told him to rest for six months, but he was still going to work on crutches – you won't believe how many people were coming there, some with chickens, with eggs, whatever they could afford. So we felt very well appreciated and loved.

Then our children grew up, and they wanted education. Unfortunately, Malawi didn't have a good standard of education, so we sent them here to England after their A-levels. My son went to university in Bath, and then after him my daughter came. She came to Cambridge first and then Oxford, studying medicine. She is a psychiatrist by the way – and she's also researching dementia.

We tried to persuade her not to become a doctor, because it is very stressful, but she just was adamant. It's a very committed job. It's not like accountancy, or something else, where you just come home and forget it. It takes a lot out of you. And in the middle of the night, if a patient comes and says, 'I am sick,' you can't tell him, 'Can you go away, I don't want to see you.' If you have gone through that yourself, you don't want your child to go through that.

We didn't want her to become a doctor. We told her, go in finance or something. I said, 'You won't get much money in medicine.' She says, 'I don't want money.' But she is stubborn like me, and her father is also very stubborn. So she's got genes from both sides! So eventually we gave up. We said ok, she wants to do it; let her do it.

And she is doing now a PhD in psychiatry, on dementia. And she is very happy in her profession!

We came to England in 2009, because after eight years, my son got a baby girl – and my husband went berserk! He wanted to come straight away, leave everything there. I wasn't ready to come, but because he was so adamant to come, so we came. We enjoyed seeing our granddaughter, but in 2010, I was diagnosed with breast cancer, and my husband had a heart attack the same time.

When we decided to come, we expected it was going to be six months here, and six months in India with my mother. So that we can have both worlds – company of my mother and also company of my children. While we were living in Malawi, we used to visit my mother often, and I was coming here also to visit my children.

Anyway, it didn't work out like that, because I was very ill. Then I had treatment, and he had operation. So we ended up staying here.

When I had the breast cancer, and they put me on chemotherapy, initially I didn't realise, but I was leaving keys in the door. Twice or thrice I nearly burned the house, because I forgot the food on the cooker, and I didn't switch it off. One day I had put the food on the stove, and it got burnt. I had fallen off to sleep. All the people from the whole building came in here. I hadn't locked the door either!

Also, I was getting lost. Even going to places I had been to many times before. The orientation has gone.

And then many times, when I used the credit card, I would go, take the money, and leave the card inside. And it was fortunate that my husband used to come with me all the time, so when I left the machine, he would say, 'Did you take out the card?' 'Oops, I haven't!' And many times I left the money also, and the card. Then I told him, 'Look, you cash money for me. I don't want to do this any more.'

So I was having these problems, and then my husband realised, and my daughter, because she's a psychiatrist. She realised that I'm forgetting, and maybe I should go for a check-up, and ask the GP to send me to the memory service. This was much later, in 2013.

When I did my medical training, in those days – I'm talking about 35, 40 years ago – there was only one chapter in the medical book on psychiatry. Dementia was mentioned very briefly. There was not so much information as there is nowadays. And because we were not dealing with it so much, we didn't really pay much attention.

So for a couple of years, I was thinking, this is just my forgetfulness, because I am sick, and this and that. And any time I asked my friends – I know how Indian people react. I would say, 'I keep forgetting things.' They would say, 'Oh no, we also forget.' So they don't pay much attention to it. Then in 2013, my daughter said, 'No, you must go and have the memory test.' So I went in 2013.

I had to wait six months for an appointment. And after that, when contact had been established, unfortunately the appointment they gave me was at a time when I was going to India to see my mother. I went there, and I got stuck, because floods came in Kashmir, so we were nearly four months there. The floods came towards the end of our journey, and we couldn't leave, so another month was wasted. When I came back, it was September 2014.

They gave me a variety of tests. I don't remember what tests they gave me. They also did an MRI scan, to establish my diagnosis, which is early onset Alzheimer's.

When they gave me the diagnosis, they didn't give me much information. I saw the specialist nurse, and they took me once to see the peer support worker, a lady who had also early Alzheimer's, and she talked to me. She was very positive, and she did arrange for few things which helped, to keep myself occupied and all that. They gave me an introduction to Alzheimer's, and I think there's going to be a group session. But not a lot of information. That is a problem.

But in the meantime, I also did a lot of research on Alzheimer's because I have got a family history also of Alzheimer's: my dad, my aunt from my father's side, my uncle from my father's side all had Alzheimer's. And my mother's two sisters, who are right now alive, they also have Alzheimer's.

In my father's case, and my paternal aunt and uncle, it came early, when they were in their 50s. By the time my father was 62, 63, he didn't remember me. When I came home after two years of marriage, he didn't recognise me.

When I got my diagnosis, I felt very upset. Because you know, with cancer and with all the other problems I have had – I have had facial paralysis, I have had a hysterectomy, I have had too many things in my life – that didn't upset me so much. But this upset me because I imagined myself in few years' time, people calling me 'loony'. That upset me quite a bit. Because I don't want people looking at me and thinking, 'She is mental.' I don't want that. I'd rather be dead than be like that.

In Asian families, if someone gets Alzheimer's, they want to cover it up. They don't want the person to come out.

As a child in Kashmir, I remember that in many families, if there used to be an old lady or old man, they wouldn't let them come into the sitting room where anybody is sitting, because they thought they might say something embarrassing. You know how Alzheimer's patients are, they don't talk sense sometimes to other people. I'm not saying they don't talk sense to themselves. But sometimes they forget who they are talking to, or they might ask questions many times.

Families feel embarrassed for them to come out in public. So they cover it up. They say 'Oh, he's not feeling well today.' Even my own uncle, when he had Alzheimer's, every time I went to visit him, his sons, his wife, they would say, 'Oh no, he has forgotten today only. He's not feeling too well. He's got a headache. He's got this, he has got that. Don't worry. He remembers everybody.' Which was not true.

It's a taboo. You don't talk about it. Within Asian communities, the taboo is very strong, very powerful. They feel they have got this problem because he must have done something wrong in his life.

When something bad happens to people, Indians or Asians don't think, 'It's part of living,' or 'You are sick,' or 'It can happen to you.' It's not like that. They say, 'Oh, she must have done something bad.' When I had cancer, a close relative told me, 'You must have done some bad sins in your life.' That's the type of thing. That is what scares me more.

And sometimes the finger is pointed towards the daughter-in-law, and they say that the daughter-in-law must have cast an evil spell.

I have been very strong, because it didn't matter to me, when I had cancer, when I had chemotherapy, but this has affected me. I would like to have sympathy from people, but they don't give sympathy. They say 'Well, you have overcome everything else, you will overcome this also.' You can't overcome this if it is Alzheimer's! People do not believe me. Every person that I tell I have got early Alzheimer's, they keep telling me that, 'You will get better.' How will I get better I don't know!

And then they say, 'We all forget. Just now I left my keys there, I did this there…' They say, 'I have also got this memory problem, I have also got dementia.' They don't accept that a diagnosis of dementia is a different thing from mere forgetfulness.

I hope something can be done to help raise awareness in the Asian community about dementia, to break down the taboo and get rid of the stigma. I'll be very happy if that happens.

Although I said that I didn't want my daughter to be a doctor, the most rewarding thing is that she's the one who is understanding me the most. In fact her husband gave me some exercises, some brain exercises. Those are helping me. And she is very supportive. She is telling me, 'Look, don't worry. Do the exercises, do this, do that, go to memory service.' She has been very supportive. And now I feel glad that she became a doctor!

Chapter 22

Something better

MARY TALL

Mary Tall *does not wish to give her real name. In this chapter she celebrates some of the unexpected benefits of living with dementia. LW*

When we were in junior school us girls used to run around the playground shouting: 'Once a wish, twice a kiss, three times something better!' I hadn't a clue what the 'something better' was, and had to wait to get married before I found out! And it was much better – not a dream or a thrill but a deep loving relationship to another person.

Since the onset of dementia, my experience has been that both my spirituality and my sexuality have grown stronger. My husband Jim says I have lost my sexual inhibitions but retain my loyalty to him and our marriage. My best friend Julie tells me that she likes me even more with Alzheimer's than in earlier years, because I am more relaxed, my sense of humour has improved, and being with me is delightfully unpredictable. They are both right, but the changes are so substantive that I sometimes cry when I see how much I have changed. My daughter Angela has offered me a balanced and helpful perspective: 'Your perceptions have shifted, Mum.' I guess Jim is right when he marvels at my willingness to tackle any problem that arises. He tells me, 'You're

Batman. You solve every problem everywhere.' But I tell him, 'No, I'm not Batman. I'm Batwoman, or rather batty woman, winging my way through life.'

Jim takes good care of me, but we both experience that being husband and wife is what matters, especially because I also take good care of him. I have coined the term 'cuddle care' for the sensitivity with which Jim looks after me; and he says that he needs 'cuddle care' just as much as I do. When you are in love with another person, giving and receiving become one, so that you are no longer aware whether you are giving or receiving. However, I have always been a person who prefers to give rather than to receive, so I struggle at times to accept that in the midst of dementia my needs are greater.

The other day, Jim said to me that we all live our lives on five levels – physical, emotional, sexual, cognitive (or intellectual) and spiritual. I thought for a minute and replied, 'Well, there's nothing wrong with me sexually!' 'No,' he laughed, 'or spiritually or emotionally either. You can't control the physical or cognitive parts of your life, but you are an absolute delight.'

I have come to the conclusion that the best medicine for dementia is love itself – what the doctors professionally and unfeelingly call a 'non-pharmacological intervention'. I recognise that the physical and cognitive changes linked to dementia do cause a certain emotional volatility, but the brain is plastic. Our ability to think and to feel changes in the course of our lives. In his book *The Social Animal: The Hidden Sources of Love, Character, and Achievement,* the writer David Brooks has reflected: 'We suffer our way to wisdom,' and 'the essence of that wisdom is that below our awareness there are viewpoints and emotions that help guide us as we wander through our lives. These viewpoints and emotions can leap from friend to friend and lover to lover. The unconscious is not merely a dark, primitive zone of fear and pain. It is also a place where spiritual states arise ... where brain matter produces emotion, where love rewires the neurons.'[77] This seems like an incredible claim, and yet it is supported by recent discoveries in neurology. Books such as *The Plastic Mind*[78] by Sharon Begley and *The Brain that Changes Itself*[79] by Norman Doidge offer convincing evidence that neurons do change, that the brain can adapt, that what is lost may not be lost forever.

So how can love rewire neurons? The scientific evidence is not yet clear, so we can only develop hypotheses. Sexual joy helps, but then so does sexual abstinence, as we learn to balance sexuality as simply one of the experiences of life. Referring to an account by Anna Young, who cared for her husband with dementia, Jim points out to me that in my head, 'time and space are fused, thoughts and ideas don't follow a logical pathway' since 'clumps of brain cells are dying' so that 'the thought has to jump over the clump and, of course, who knows where it will land'.[80] However, Jim and I have both become aware of how much control I do retain over the sexual, emotional and spiritual dimensions of my life, even in the midst of dementia.

As far we both can tell, the key to managing dementia is avoiding anxiety or at least trying to stop being anxious when a sense of inadequacy begins to rise up. As long as we both can avoid anxiety, each day is a growing experience, unpredictable but joyful. I have found that alternative therapies can help, especially reflexology, which brings together the brain and the body through movement of the hands and feet in an integrated fashion. Unfortunately, avoiding responsibility now looks to be part of my life with dementia, because I often find explicit responsibilities, such as cooking a big meal, cause anxiety. I can no longer multitask, but I can still achieve quite a lot.

You can see that I am not exactly a passive sufferer of dementia, wandering around as if I lived in a Shakespearean tragedy telling anyone who will listen, 'Woe is me! I have Alzheimer's. Take pity on me!' OK, there is presently no 'cure' for dementia, but we can all live in such a way that we minimise both the possibility and the impact of dementia through exercise and diet and relaxation. No, that will not stop everyone from experiencing dementia, but it will save a lot of people from a lot of suffering. Shortly after

I was diagnosed with Alzheimer's my husband mentioned my condition to a mutual friend, a doctor who was a radiologist and knew quite a lot about dementia. 'Well,' she said, 'if it was me, the first thing I would do is make sure my cardiovascular system was in order.' 'You mean, you would exercise?' he said. 'That's right,' she said, 'whatever exercise Mary herself decides to do.' It was good advice; and I try to follow it by walking and swimming and playing table tennis.

Since Jim and I are both in our 70s, we have to pace ourselves and limit our emotional and physical exertions. He tells me that while I have my memory limitations, he has his sexual limitations; and we have to accept each other as we are, equals in living out our final years. There is certainly nothing comfortable about having dementia for the patient, the carer or the doctor. However, instead of focusing on such clearly defined roles, I find that life is best lived simply by being human and by relating to God.

I have always been aware of God's presence in my life, but now that I have dementia, I am more aware of the sufferings of Jesus. His crucifixion resonates with me more deeply now that I have less control over my own thoughts and emotions. I pray to God for healing, but I recognise that the future is in his hands, not mine. Just like every person who experiences life through the lens of dementia, I live largely in the present moment. Although my thoughts at times turn to the past, I am committed to the sacrament of the present moment – the awareness that God blesses us as we are, in the midst of our very personal fears and hopes.

For me and for Jim, relating to God is a day-to-day experience in which we thank God for the gift of life, while accepting the challenges that life brings. I guess that 'something better' has now become a deepening discovery of love, involving both sexuality and spirituality, possible even after years of dementia.

Chapter 23

A psychiatrist with dementia

DAPHNE WALLACE

Daphne Wallace *is a retired old age psychiatrist based in North Yorkshire. She is an ambassador for the Alzheimer's Society and contributed to the preparation of the National Dementia Strategy in England. She was co-chair of the External Reference Group, monitoring the progress of the Strategy. Daphne was diagnosed with vascular dementia in 2005. She is*

involved in a variety of research projects, and frequently travels on her own across the UK and beyond. I interviewed her at my home in London. LW

From an early age I wanted to do medicine. When I was about 11, my form mistress asked if we had any ideas what we wanted to do. I said I wanted to be a nurse. And she asked a very significant question. She said: 'Have you ever thought of being a doctor?' And of course the answer to that was 'No.' It had never occurred to me before. But from that day, I never wanted to do anything else.

I studied medicine at St Andrew's University, and enjoyed it very much, and I did quite a lot of extra psychiatry. We still had long summer holidays in those days, and we were expected to go and get some work experience. Through some family friends, I'd met the superintendent of a mental hospital in Sussex, so I went and worked there for part of the summer holidays. It was a big old asylum, but it was very progressive really. Although all the consultants came from different perspectives, they had a shared vision of what they were basically trying to achieve, which was very refreshing (and very contrasting to one of the jobs I had subsequently).

I qualified in 1965, and started working in the same hospital and training in psychiatry, in 1967. And it was very good, because they did things which a lot of hospitals didn't do at that time – it really was quite ahead of the game. And while I was there I had the advantage of working with Klaus Bergmann, who became one of the pioneers of old age psychiatry. (He went on to work with Martin Roth and his ground-breaking team in Newcastle, and later worked at the Maudsley Hospital in London.)

Then my husband decided to be ordained, so we moved to Durham, where he trained. And I got a locum job at the big asylum in Sedgefield – and I absolutely hated it! It was such a contrast! The consultants were all at one another's throats, and as far as I could tell, the junior doctors spent the afternoon with their feet up in front of the telly – it was just awful. And I came home one day and said I would rather go and work in Woolworth's! I then worked in learning disability for several years in a hospital outside Durham, two years as a locum consultant.

After that we moved to Bradford, and I've been in Yorkshire ever since. After a spell working in addictions, I filled in on various jobs until I got a senior registrar post, and trained in old age psychiatry. And then I was appointed consultant, in 1979, in Leeds, and I worked there for a little over 20 years.

We were the first old age psychiatrists they'd ever had in Leeds, so we were sort of pioneers, which was amazing. We had a philosophy that we wanted it to be the sort of service that people wanted, looking at the particular needs of older people with mental health problems, and it should be tailored to their needs, and be local and so on. And by the time I retired, we had really quite a nice set-up, with three purpose-built units. My team was based in one of these units, and I did an outpatient clinic and had a day hospital there, and I had an assessment ward for people with dementia with challenging behaviour.

I didn't work full-time most of the time, and I did a diploma in psychotherapy at Liverpool, and had a private psychotherapy practice from 1992 until I retired from that in 2007. I actually retired from the Health Service in 2000, when I was 60, and retired gradually from private practice after getting my diagnosis.

What happened was that at the end of 2004, I did some locum work for five months to help my former colleagues. They wanted two half-day sessions from me, and I decided I would do the two sessions in one day, because it was too far to travel. One half day was an outpatient clinic with new patients and follow-up patients, and the other half day was a ward round in the acute ward in the hospital. And I had to drive across Leeds in the lunch hour. I had to leave home about half past seven in the morning, and I didn't get home until half past seven at night, and in between that, I was trying to liaise with the community team, as well, and some of the time I didn't have a junior doctor with me. It was all quite difficult actually, and quite stressful. It wasn't that different from the kind of pressures that I'd had before, and it was only one day a week, but by the end of the five months, I was really quite depressed. And I can account for that with hindsight, because it accords with some of my beliefs about what happens to people with very early undiagnosed dementia.

I'm someone who has always been a very busy person, and I've never found that difficult. We adopted four children, and we also took another two young people under our wings, and although we've never actually had all six of them at home at once, I did have four children at home for quite long periods of time, and if you're a vicar's wife, and you're working, you have to be organised. So it wasn't new for me to have to be organised and to be under pressure, but I actually got quite depressed.

Well, I came out of the depression. But once I was no longer depressed, I thought – I'm not functioning quite properly. There are things that I used to be able to do, that I don't seem to be able to do properly. So I talked to two friends, both quite senior old age psychiatrists, and when I described the things that I'd noticed, they both said, that if that was happening to them, they would want to have tests done.

The things that I'd noticed were – well, in the past, if I'd been to a place once, I could usually find my way again. But one of the things that alarmed me, that happened to me round about that time, was that one day I ended up doing a ten mile detour over Saddleworth Moor, and I thought, there's something wrong – this isn't me!

I was also having terrible problems with anything involved with arithmetic. Now, maths was my best subject at school. But I could no longer do simple arithmetic, and I really can't now. And it isn't just ordinary sums. For instance, if I'm setting my oven, or setting my bread-maker, I find it very difficult to work out how many hours or minutes it has to be. I can't convert recipes. I have to write it out as a sum, to do quite a simple conversion of quantities.

I've never been good at remembering names, so it doesn't bother me that I can't remember people's names, but the other thing that I used to be very good at was recognising people's faces, even years after I had last seen them. I found it very disturbing that I suddenly met people, who obviously knew me – 'Oh, lovely to see you, blah,' – and as far as I was concerned they were total strangers. It's really quite frightening, when people obviously know you very well, and you might just as well have never seen them before.

One of the things I always say when I give lectures is that it's not actually helpful to say to someone who has dementia, 'Well, I've never been able to do that,' (for example, recognising people, or doing mental arithmetic), because the whole point is, that if you have lost it, and you were once very good at it, then it is a very real loss, and it's quite upsetting. And some of the things that I used do very well, a lot of people can't do very well – but I used to be able to!

So anyway, I went to my GP, and told him all the things that I was noticing, and he referred me to the neurologist at the local hospital. The neurologist arranged for me to have a scan, and said he would see me afterwards.

After I had had the scan, the neurologist rang me up. It was the August bank holiday weekend, and he said, 'You've got minor changes, very early vascular changes, showing up in the scan. So it's early vascular dementia.' And I've had an MRI scan since then, and there are signs. There is a little patch that's obviously damaged.

I've had two re-assessments. I may say I had three and a half years with nothing, because the neurologist emigrated, and I was just left. And it was a colleague on the Reference Group when we were writing the National Dementia Strategy who said, 'You need to be a patient,' and encouraged me to insist on regular follow-up, and I am now seen every six months by a consultant. At the moment, because I have no evidence of continuous deterioration, they think that it's definitely only vascular. But I didn't know that for three and a half years

It's seven years since I was diagnosed, and I don't think the dementia symptoms have got worse, but I've got seven years older. I think being tired affects me a bit more – which is what you would expect anyway. One of the things I have noticed is that my vision is also affected, and not just in facial recognition. My husband is forever putting his specs down somewhere and not being able to find them. In the past, if we were looking for something in the house I would go into a room, and scan it, and pick out the item. Now, if I'm looking for something that I've put down, I walk past it, unless I actually look straight at it. I've lost that sort of broad sweep of picking out things. And that's definitely a loss. My husband notices it, because he's never been good at that. I used to be forever trying to find his things. And now we're both trundling round the house trying to find things. And it means also that I walk into things and misjudge distances. I bump into the door-frame or bits of furniture because I think there's room for me to go through. I wouldn't have done that in the past.

The other thing I have difficulty with is finding words. When I was a student, I was once described as 'a professional athlete of the tongue'! So I've changed! It takes me longer to write things. It's harder for me to write a lecture or to revise a chapter of a book for a second edition for example.

I can hear myself that my language use is much less rich. My expressive vocabulary has shrunk. I don't have difficulty when I'm reading. I know what words mean. People use words and I think, yes, that's a lovely word, a useful word, and I know what it means, but it never comes spontaneously.

But people don't notice when I lecture. I used to be able to do it from PowerPoint slides, with just the key points on them. But now, although I don't actually read it, I do have to write it all out in advance. I have it there to refer to. It gives me a bit of reassurance if I'm struggling to find the really important word. And the mere fact of having it written down helps me to remember it as well.

On one occasion, I gave a lecture on the spiritual needs of people with dementia. I was one of three speakers. And they decided to record all the talks, and afterwards they asked if we could let them have our talks in writing. Now none of us had got much in writing, so they gave me the tape of my talk, and I asked my former secretary to listen to the tape, and I said, 'I've got to re-jig it, but just type exactly what you hear.' And when I listened to it, I could tell when I had gone round and found another way of saying something, because I couldn't find the word I was looking for. Nobody noticed there was anything wrong, but I could tell where it was that I was struggling to find some alternative.

People tend to say, 'I can't believe you've got dementia.' You get two different kinds of reactions. When people say, 'Oh, I can't believe it,' that is almost denigrating really, because I'm a professional. I spent a lot of my professional life diagnosing dementia. I should know if I can't do things that I used to be able to do.

Then there's the other kind of response. The Royal College of Psychiatrists was running a session preparing for retirement, and I was there as someone who is retired. In fact I do still do a limited amount of work, sitting on mental health tribunals, and one of my former colleagues said, 'Should you be working? What happens if you make a mistake?' Which I felt was really quite insulting – both to me and the people I work with. If they thought I wasn't capable, I'm sure they'd do something about it. I'm appraised regularly – at the tribunal service we all are – and people would know. And I certainly wouldn't have got re-appointed three times, over the age limit! I've actually just been re-appointed for another year. I was supposed to have retired at 70.

The thing is, different people experience dementia differently. That's one of the things that I've always been concerned about, and it informs a lot of what I've written and what I talk about. We are all different, and even if you have the same pathology as the person sitting next to you, it won't manifest itself in exactly the same way. Because the substrate of the personality is there and that interacts with the disease process. And I always used to say when I lectured, 'People are not like cans of beans. They are not predictable.' But some of the management that we've had over the last 20 years – they seem to think people are always alike.

Everything is a tick box approach. And it's not just my psychotherapy training – my way of practising, and my religious beliefs and everything else, all rebel against tick boxes and pigeon holes. People don't fit in pigeon holes. So that informed the way I worked, but also, when people tell me, 'You're doing too much, you should slow down, give up some of these things you do,' I've got a stock answer to that: 'Well, you didn't know my mother!' Because my mother, at 94, was attending a course in local history, and giving talks about what it was like to be a governess in India and Egypt in the 1930s.

I think it's very important to help people recognise the early signs of dementia. I write an occasional blog on the NHS Local website, where I describe some of my symptoms. I recognise some of my symptoms in a way that most people might not, because I'm used to thinking in that way and I can make sense of them, so I think that that's instructive. (Particularly as I'm now donating my brain to the brain bank.) I also try to do this when I talk to groups of people.

I gave a talk on Woman's Hour, and described some of my symptoms, and a listener wrote to me, and said how helpful she had found it in one way, but unfortunately it was a bit late. Her mother had been attending a vascular clinic for years, with angina I think, and for the last six months of her life she became quite different, and recognised that she wasn't functioning properly and became quite distressed. And it was difficult for her daughter to understand what was going on. But having heard me talk, she said she realised that it must have been vascular dementia. Her symptoms weren't the same as mine, but the fact that there were some changes – no one in the clinic had suggested that it could be the arteries in her brain causing the problem. She said she was just so sad that she didn't understand this when her mother was still alive.

I've always been a great believer in 'whole person' medicine. For many years I belonged to an international organisation, Médecine de la Personne (Medicine of the Person), founded by Paul Tournier, a Swiss physician and psychotherapist who believed that part of the healing process was the relationship between the doctor and the person – he believed in person-centred medicine. And I was also chair of the Dementia Group of the Christian Council on Ageing, which was concerned with providing spiritually conscious care for older people. We were very much concerned with people with dementia, because we felt they were the ones who lost out most, but we believed that what we were saying applied to everyone, including people with a learning disability. And we published some things which said, 'Whatever you do, if you're caring for someone, foster the spirit of the person.' We're not just talking about religion. Religion is a particular expression of the spirituality of a person, but other people have spiritual needs just the same. So whether you're giving them a bath, or feeding them or whatever, do it in that sort of way.

I used to judge the homes I went into, for example, by how they responded if you were having a conversation with them in the office, and someone with advanced dementia wandered in. Would they chivvy them out? – 'No, no, no! We're busy in here.' The ones who I really thought were good said, 'Oh, have you come to help us today? You can sit on that chair.' And I used to talk also to relatives, who might say, 'What's the point in coming to visit – they don't know who I am.' I would say, 'They'll know that you're someone important. They will feel that. And the good feeling of having had a nice time with you will last far longer than your visit.'

I don't call myself a campaigner, because I don't go on protests and that sort of thing. I do campaign, but in a different sort of way. I get invited to speak at lots of conferences, to talk about what it is like to have dementia. And I get very upset because I also get all these notices for other events about how to carry out the aims of the National Dementia Strategy, and so on, where all the speakers are professors, and that's all – there's no one on the programme who is either a carer, or a person with dementia, so there is nobody *living with dementia*, in either sense. Yet all the people with dementia I know who do talks of this sort have been told, on numerous occasions, 'Your talk was the most inspiring, and helped me to understand.' 'It was the one thing that made a difference.' So, when I'm given an opportunity to go and talk, that's why I do it.

Postscript

Daphne Wallace adds:

Three years later, I am fortunate that the progression of my dementia is slow and most people do not perceive any changes. I have more support now which also helps me to support my husband who has early Parkinson's disease. As I get older I get more tired, and I have to curb my enthusiasm for 'spreading the word' about living with dementia.

What clinicians can learn from people with dementia

As can often be the way, life takes a turn, stuff happens and a moment arrives. The day before I sat down to write this Afterword I was invited to give a seminar to GPs and healthcare workers, entitled *Managing Dementia in Primary Care*. I said I was unhappy with the title, but was told this is what it had to be, as the seminar was specifically aimed at educating healthcare professionals on how to best manage dementia in primary care. I told the organisers that unless the title was changed to reflect that we don't manage dementia, but instead we care, support, advise, empower or are just there for people living with dementia, then I would not participate, for I was not prepared to be party to an event that perpetuated the myth that dementia was more about pathology than it is about people.

I cannot recall when I first wrote, 'We work with people, not pathology,' but it was some years ago — yet it seems we still have some way to go. Having read the compelling stories that make up *People with Dementia Speak Out*, there is no way you can avoid being touched by the words of these storytellers whose lives are affected by dementia in ways that are unexpected, sometimes cruel, on occasions uplifting but always life-changing. Ordinary people telling us about their extraordinary lives with dementia. Stories that are humbling and compelling in equal measure.

I first started working with people with dementia 31 years ago – and what an admission that is, for I didn't always work with the *people*. Rather I worked with dementia. During my training and in the immediate years that followed my qualification it did not cross my mind that I might be working with people. Was a person with dementia not first subsumed under layers of intellectual devastation, and then destined to one day disappear? Alzheimer's disease was a terrible condition; it destroyed the person but forgot to take the body away. A body that thereafter solely played host to signs and symptoms of disease. How wrong we were.

Since those early days, what has working with people living with dementia taught me? First, people with dementia can be a puzzle, but why should it be otherwise? We are all complicated. Our partners, family and friends may at times be mystified by what we do or say. We at times may surprise ourselves, asking 'Why did I do that?', and sometimes being equally mystified by the answer. So why should a person with dementia be anything other than similarly complicated in what they say and do?

Second, the closer you get to people with dementia, the longer you take seeing and listening – rather than skimming a conversation, looking and hearing but learning nothing – the more you appreciate that each person embarks on their *own* journey with dementia. Each is resourced differently to cope with a progressively worsening intellectual disability – for that is what dementia is – and as such, some cope less well than others, while on occasions we are given the opportunity to wonder at the extraordinary fortitude of the human spirit. And these stories reinforce this view like no other I've read. How can you close your eyes to these people? Their fears, their worries, their sense of injustice, sometimes their determination not to let dementia bring them down, the sheer 'everydayness' of them all. They cannot be ignored. Instead, in all instances and at all times, knowing who people with dementia are must be the guiding principle that governs whatever we do to help them negotiate what will one day be a harrowing journey into a world of not knowing.

All of us are unique, but our personalities and life histories are psychosocial phenomena superimposed upon what we all share in common, and we share *more* in common than what separates us. And this is not affected by dementia. A shared need to be safe, to belong, to be in receipt of tenderness and affection, to have occupation, to have meaningful not cursory human contact, to experience self-respect and to have peace of mind. And to truly appreciate this we must not be seduced by what is obvious. Yes, a person with dementia's intellectual powers are failing, that is clear. People who relate their stories in this book talk about their early struggles with memory loss and other intellectual symptoms, but no one is all disability, hence we must never become preoccupied with a person's dementia to the exclusion of all else. If we do, all we see is difference, and if all we see is difference, then we know we share nothing in common, and the danger is that we start to act and react to people with dementia in ways that are insensitive and unthinking to the point that we disregard them as people like ourselves.

The person may often present as different, but it is misguided to take this as evidence that the person has disappeared, leaving behind nothing more than a shell or shadow of little consequence. Instead, understand the person as trying to communicate who they are and who they have always been whilst they are losing the capacity to remember what once anchored them in context, place and time, as their language crumbles and conversation is challenged, and as their ability to think and reason slips away and risk and vulnerability surfaces. Frustrating, upsetting and bewildering symptoms the person will have to negotiate. Their behaviour and feelings may present as strange and disproportionate but this is not testimony to the person having been lost. While appearances may support such an assertion, appearances can be deceptive!

The discovery of the *person* with dementia was not the consequence of an elegant scientific breakthrough. It came about through appreciating the experiences of people attempting to live their lives in the face of debilitating brain diseases that were causing their dementia, most commonly Alzheimer's disease. People who only years previously were living lives indistinguishable from our own, blissfully ignorant of the fact that before too long they were to face a life affected by dementia. People like those whose stories have been captured in this wonderful collection. And having discovered the person, we are conscious that it is they who are the true experts, for dementia is their experience, it is not ours.

For some who read this book the experience will be an epiphany. Thereafter might it be possible that what we do to help a person with dementia, in some way to be kind to them, is diminished only by the limits we place on our ambition, imagination and humanity.

Professor Graham Stokes
Global Director of Dementia Care, Bupa
Honorary Visiting Professor of Person-Centred
Dementia Care, University of Bradford

P.S.: The title of the seminar was changed. Someone somewhere had been educated!

Frequently asked questions about dementia

See also the Glossary on page 265.

1. What is dementia?

Dementia is a clinical condition that may be caused by a number of different physical diseases of the brain. Most people with dementia experience a progressive decline in their mental abilities, including memory, concentration, reasoning, judgement, understanding and communication skills. Most people with dementia experience confusion, and some experience perceptual problems or hallucinations, or find they no longer recognise familiar faces or places. Some people with dementia start to behave in ways that seem 'out of character', losing inhibitions, lacking empathy, becoming aggressive, excessively anxious, or apathetic. As the illness progresses, physical abilities are also affected, and people gradually become more dependent on others to help them with everyday activities and functions. The most common types of dementia are *Alzheimer's disease* and *vascular dementia*.

2. What is the difference between dementia and Alzheimer's disease?

Alzheimer's disease is one kind of dementia; there are many other kinds such as vascular dementia, Lewy body dementia, frontotemporal dementia and so on. Everyone with Alzheimer's has dementia; but not everyone with dementia has Alzheimer's.

It is important to make this distinction, because not only do some of the symptoms differ, but also some drug treatments may be safe and effective for people with Alzheimer's disease but dangerous or ineffective for people with other types of dementia.

3. Is dementia a normal part of ageing?

Dementia is not a normal part of ageing, although the risk of developing dementia increases the older you get. Dementia is a disabling condition caused by damage to the brain. Not everyone who grows old develops dementia, and some people develop dementia before they grow old.

4. Is dementia just about memory loss?

With most types of dementia, people experience memory loss, which usually becomes increasingly severe as time goes on. However, most people with dementia also experience other symptoms that may be just as distressing as memory problems, if not more so.

These symptoms vary from person to person and may include physical, intellectual and emotional changes such as altered sleep patterns, lack of vitality, restlessness, confusion, loss of judgement, progressive loss of language skills, anxiety and depression. People with dementia may experience perceptual problems (for example not being able to distinguish between a shadow on the ground and a hole in the ground), delusions (believing things that are not true), and hallucinations (seeing, smelling or hearing things that aren't real). Hallucinations are particularly common in Lewy body dementia. Eventually most people with dementia lose the ability to carry out everyday tasks without help.

In some cases, the most noticeable symptoms are not to do with memory loss at all, but to do with behaviour – for example when a person starts to behave in a surprisingly unreasonable, uninhibited or aggressive way, causing great distress to family and friends, while seeming not to realise or not to care about the hurt that is caused.

If other symptoms appear first, before memory problems become apparent, neither the person experiencing the symptoms nor the clinician who is assessing them may recognise that these are the first signs of dementia, particularly if the person is under 65.

It is therefore important for us all to recognise that although dementia is usually accompanied by memory loss, other symptoms may appear first, or may have a greater impact on the quality of life experienced by the person with dementia and those closest to them.

5. Is there a cure for dementia?

At present there is no cure for dementia. Research is ongoing, but there is no likelihood that a cure will be found in the near future.

However, just because there is no known 'cure' does not mean that 'there is nothing that can be done' to make life better for people with dementia. Certain drug treatments may help to slow down the progression of the disease. Most important of all is the support that is offered by family, friends and professionals to help people with dementia to remain as active and independent as possible for as long as possible, and, when the advanced stage is reached, to live in comfort, safety and dignity, embraced by love and compassion.

6. Is dementia inherited?

This is a complex issue and research is ongoing. So far, we know that:

- Some extremely rare types of Alzheimer's disease (early onset familial Alzheimer's disease) can be passed down through the family.

- Other very rare conditions that usually lead to dementia, such as Huntington's disease, can be inherited.

- Having a close family member (parent, sister or brother) with Alzheimer's disease, particularly young onset Alzheimer's disease, may increase your risk of developing dementia.

See Alzheimer's Society Factsheet 405 'Genetics of dementia' at www. alzheimers.org.uk/factsheet/405.

7. Am I at risk of developing dementia?

All of us are at risk of developing dementia, but for some people the risk is higher than for others.

- For the majority of people, the greatest risk factor for developing dementia is age: the older we are, the greater the likelihood of developing dementia. It is estimated that one in fourteen people aged over 65, and one in six aged over 80, has dementia.

- Lifestyle factors can increase our risk of developing dementia: poor diet, lack of exercise, smoking and excessive alcohol intake all increase the risk of developing dementia. Uncontrolled high blood pressure, high cholesterol levels and being overweight can not only increase the risk of heart disease, stroke and diabetes, but also increase the risk of developing dementia.

- Family history may play a part in increasing our risk of developing dementia (see question 6 above.)

See Alzheimer's Society *Factsheet 450* 'Am I at risk of developing dementia?' at: www.alzheimers.org.uk/site/scripts/documents_info. php?documentID=102

and NHS Choices at: 'Can dementia be prevented?' www.nhs.uk/ Conditions/dementia-guide/Pages/dementia-prevention.aspx.

8. What can I do to reduce my risk of developing dementia?

There is no guaranteed way to prevent dementia developing. However, we can reduce our risk of developing certain types of dementia by trying to live as healthy a lifestyle as possible.

What is good for the heart is also good for the brain, so we should all try to follow these tips:

- Get plenty of exercise.

- Eat plenty of fresh fruit and vegetables.

- Cut down on sugary, salty and fatty foods.

- Do not smoke – smoking increases the risk of developing dementia as well as other serious conditions such as cancer and lung disease.

- Try to keep your blood pressure, cholesterol levels and weight under control.

- If you drink alcohol, drink in moderation.

- Try not to be isolated; stay involved socially.

- Stay involved in things that interest you and that keep your brain active.

The good news is that if you follow these tips you are also reducing your risk of other serious conditions such as heart disease, stroke, diabetes and cancer, and increasing your likelihood of living healthily for longer.

Glossary

Alzheimer's disease: the most common cause of *dementia*. An illness that alters the chemistry and structure of the brain, causing brain cells to die. Alzheimer's disease usually begins with mild symptoms, typically memory loss, and progresses gradually. People with Alzheimer's disease often live for ten or more years after symptoms first become apparent. Alzheimer's disease was first identified by the German neurologist Alois Alzheimer in 1906.

Antipsychotic drugs: major tranquillisers or sedatives, normally used in the treatment of schizophrenia. They are sometimes used to sedate people with *dementia* who are displaying aggressive or restless behaviour. There are major concerns about the side-effects of these drugs (including drowsiness, dizziness, unsteadiness, reduced mobility and coherence, increased risk of stroke and heart attack), and there is evidence that they may accelerate the rate of decline in people with dementia, and lead to premature death. For people who have *Lewy body dementia*, antipsychotic drugs may be particularly dangerous. In recent years, since these concerns have been publicised, there has been a reduction in the prescription of antipsychotic drugs for people with dementia in the UK.

See Alzheimer's Society Factsheet 408 *Dementia: drugs used to relieve depression and behavioural symptoms* (www.alzheimers.org.uk/factsheet/408) and the Alzheimer's Society position statement on antipsychotic drugs: www.alzheimers.org.uk/site/scripts/documents_info.php?documentID=548.

Aricept: see Cholinesterase inhibitors

BAME: black, Asian or minority ethnic.

Brain scans: CAT, CT, MRI, PET and SPECT scans are different types of scans that may be used to help diagnose dementia by revealing that the brain has been damaged in some way. Brain scans create images of the brain and may show, for example, that the small blood vessels in the brain have been damaged, or that parts of the brain are shrinking.

CAT scan (or CT scan): a 'computerised axial tomography' scan. See *Brain scans.*

Cholinesterase inhibitors: (also known as acetylcholinesterase inhibitors) are drugs that may alleviate the symptoms of *Alzheimer's disease,* or help to slow down the progress of the disease, usually for a limited amount of time. The three main cholinesterase inhibitors are: donepezil (Aricept), rivastigmine (Exelon) and galantamine (Reminyl). They all work in much the same way but have somewhat different side effects, and some people find one of them easier to take than the others. Current *NICE* guidance suggests trying donepezil first. They are often prescribed for people with mild to moderate dementia, but may also be effective for people experiencing more severe symptoms. These drugs are not prescribed for *vascular dementia.* See www.alzheimers.org.uk/factsheet/407.

Dementia: is a clinical condition that may be caused by a number of different physical diseases of the brain. Most people with dementia experience a progressive decline in their mental abilities, including memory, concentration, reasoning, judgement, understanding and communication skills. Most people with dementia also experience confusion, and some experience perceptual problems or hallucinations, or find they no longer recognise familiar faces or places. Some people with dementia start to behave in ways that seem 'out of character', losing inhibitions, lacking empathy, becoming aggressive, excessively anxious, or apathetic. As the illness progresses, physical abilities are also affected, and people gradually become more dependent on others to help them with everyday activities and functions. The most common types of dementia are *Alzheimer's disease* and *vascular dementia.*

Early onset dementia (also known as young onset dementia): *dementia* that develops before the age of 65.

Exelon: see Cholinesterase inhibitors.

Frontotemporal dementia: a rare form of *dementia*, caused by damage to the frontal lobe and/or temporal parts of the brain. At an early stage, memory usually remains intact while personality and behaviour – including social skills and the ability to empathise with others – may change radically. Language skills may also become damaged. At a later stage, symptoms are usually similar to those of *Alzheimer's disease*. Frontotemporal dementia may develop at any age, but is more likely to affect people under 65.

Galantamine: see Cholinesterase inhibitors.

Lewy body dementia: (also known as dementia with Lewy bodies) is a type of dementia in which abnormal protein deposits, known as Lewy bodies, develop inside nerve cells in the brain, interrupting the brain's normal functioning. A person with this type of dementia typically fluctuates in their mental abilities from day to day, and may experience hallucinations. Some symptoms are similar to those of *Parkinson's disease*, including tremors and slowness of movement.

LGBT: lesbian, gay, bisexual and transgender.

Memantine: is a drug that may be prescribed for moderate to severe *Alzheimer's disease*. It may be used to treat someone who does not respond well to the *Cholinesterase inhibitors.*

Mini mental state examination (MMSE): a series of questions and instructions that are designed to assist in assessing a person's level of cognitive functioning, and that may be used to reach a possible diagnosis of *dementia*. The questions test functions such as short-term memory, ability to name familiar objects, being aware of the current date and the day of the week, recall of personal information such as own address, etc.. Each question in the *mini mental state examination* is scored. Correct responses to all questions or instructions attract a score of 30. With most types of dementia, the more advanced the disease, the lower the score on the MMSE will be.

Until recently the MMSE was the test most commonly used by clinicians to assess cognition, but a number of other tests are now available and the MMSE is not used so often.

Whichever cognition test is used, it is normally only one element in a series of techniques and procedures (including talking at some length to the patient and their family) that may be used by a clinician before they arrive at a diagnosis of dementia (or a conclusion as to whether cognitive functioning has improved, stabilised or deteriorated since a previous test).

Mixed dementia: is the name given to the condition where a person appears to have symptoms of both *Alzheimer's disease* and *vascular dementia*.

MRI scan: a 'magnetic resonance imaging' scan. See *Brain scans*.

NICE: The National Institute for Health and Care Excellence, which provides national guidance and advice to improve health and social care in England. NICE guidance and recommendations are made by independent committees. NICE publishes guidelines on the use of new and existing medicines and treatments, including recommendations as to which drugs should be prescribed for certain illnesses and conditions. NICE also publishes guidelines on clinical practice, health promotion and social care.

Parkinson's disease: a progressive disease of the nervous system that affects the ability to coordinate movement. It is characterised by a pronounced tremor, slowness of movement and stiff muscles that may lead to an expressionless face. People with Parkinson's disease have a higher than average risk of developing *dementia*. The illness was first identified by the London doctor James Parkinson in 1817.

PET scan: a 'positron emission tomography' scan. See *Brain scans*.

Pick's disease: a type of *frontotemporal dementia*.

Reminyl: see Cholinesterase inhibitors.

Rivastigmine: see Cholinesterase inhibitors.

Sectioning: the terms 'sectioning' and 'being sectioned' are commonly used to mean being admitted to a psychiatric hospital under compulsion. The term derives from the various 'sections' of the Mental Health Act 1983, which give the authorities the power to detain someone in a psychiatric hospital against their will. Two doctors must agree that the person is 'suffering from a mental disorder of a nature or degree which warrants the detention of the patient in a hospital for assessment or treatment for at least a limited period', either for their own protection or for the protection of other people.

SPECT scan: a 'single photon emission computed tomography' scan. See *Brain scans*.

TIA: is a 'transient ischaemic attack' or mini-stroke, which interrupts the blood supply to the brain, and may cause sudden temporary weakness or numbness in the face or limbs, visual disturbance and/or inability to speak or think clearly. A person may not be aware that they have had a mini-stroke. It may occur in their sleep, or may cause momentary discomfort that does not seem to be significant at the time. A series of mini-strokes can lead to *vascular dementia*.

Vascular dementia: is *dementia* caused by interruptions in the blood supply to the brain, usually following a stroke or a series of small strokes. Many of the symptoms of vascular dementia are similar to those of *Alzheimer's disease*, but whereas the progression of Alzheimer's disease tends to be gradual, and is usually pictured as a downward slope, in vascular dementia it is usually pictured as descending staircase, where sudden noticeable deterioration occurs at intervals. At present the drugs typically prescribed for people with Alzheimer's disease are not thought to benefit people with vascular dementia and are not usually prescribed. People with vascular dementia are more likely to be prescribed treatment, which may help to reduce the effect of underlying conditions such as high blood pressure.

Young onset dementia (also known as early onset dementia): *dementia* that develops before the age of 65.

Suggestions for further reading and other resources

Books

People with dementia in their own words

Dancing with Dementia: My Story of Living Positively with Dementia by Christine Bryden. Jessica Kingsley Publishers, 2005.

Living in the Labyrinth: A Personal Journey Through the Maze of Alzheimer's by Diana Friel McGowin. Mainsail Press, 1994.

Tell Mrs Mill her Husband is Still Dead: more stories from the Trebus Project compiled by David Clegg. Trebus Projects, 2010. (Out of print, but electronic edition available at Amazon.co.uk).

The Things Between Us: Words and Poems of People Experiencing Dementia compiled by Living Words. Shoving Leopard, 2014.

Welcome to Our World: A Collection of Life Writing by People Living with Dementia edited by Liz Jennings. Forget-Me-Nots, 2014.

Understanding dementia

Alzheimer's and Other Dementias: Answers at your Fingertips (Fourth Edition) by Alex Bailey. Class Health, 2014.

And Still the Music Plays: Stories of People with Dementia by Graham Stokes. Hawker Publications, 2008.

Understanding Alzheimer's Disease and Other Dementias by Nori Graham and James Warner. Family Doctor Publications, 2009.

Living well with dementia; caring for someone with dementia

Can I tell you about Dementia? A guide for family, friends and carers by Jude Welton. Jessica Kingsley Publishers, 2013

Dear Dementia: The Laughter and the Tears by Ian Donaghy. Hawker Publications, 2014.

Dementia Positive by John Killick. Luath Press, 2013.

Dementia: Support for Family and Friends by Dave Pulsford and Rachel Thompson. Jessica Kingsley Publishers, 2013.

Hearing the Person with Dementia: Person-Centred Approaches to Communication for Families and Caregivers by Bernie McCarthy. Jessica Kingsley Publishers, 2011.

Living well with dementia. NHS Health Scotland 2014. Download at www. healthscotland.com/documents/15.aspx

Personal accounts of caring for someone with dementia

Caring for Kathleen: A Sister's Story about Down's Syndrome and Dementia by Margaret T Fray. BILD Publications, 2000.

Inside the Dementia Epidemic: a Daughter's Memoir by Martha Stettinius. Dundee Lakemont Press, 2012.

Keeper by Andrea Gillies. Short Books, 2009.

Losing Clive to Younger Onset Dementia by Helen Beaumont. Jessica Kingsley Publishers, 2009.

Telling Tales About Dementia: Experiences of Caring edited by Lucy Whitman. Jessica Kingsley Publishers, 2010.

Leaflets, videos and online resources

Alzheimer's Society

The Alzheimer's Society website contains a wealth of information about all aspects of dementia care, including *Factsheets* on a wide range of subjects, for example: No. 500 *Communicating*; No. 524 *Understanding and respecting the person with dementia*; No. 523 *Carers: looking after yourself*; No. 467 *Financial and legal affairs*, etc.. All the *Factsheets* may be downloaded at www.alzheimers.org.uk/factsheets.

Printed copies of the *Factsheets* and versions in other formats are also available.

The Alzheimer's Society have produced a comprehensive *Dementia Guide*, which can be downloaded here: www.alzheimers.org.uk/site/scripts/documents_info.php?documentID=2227.

A series of videos to accompany the *Dementia Guide* can be viewed on the Alzheimer's Society YouTube channel along with many other helpful videos: www.youtube.com/user/AlzheimersSociety.

The *Dementia Guide* and video series have been translated into a number of community languages and there is a video version available in British Sign Language. See www.alzheimers.org.uk/site/scripts/documents_info.php?documentID=2612.

NHS Health Scotland

NHS Health Scotland in partnership with Alzheimer Scotland and the Scottish Dementia Working Group have produced a video, *Living well with dementia*, for people who have recently received a diagnosis of dementia: www.healthscotland.com/topics/stages/healthy-ageing/dementia/living-well-with-dementia.aspx.

Information about dementia for people with learning disabilities and their carers

The Alzheimer's Society and BILD (the British Institute of Learning Disabilities) have produced an Easy Read factsheet 'What is dementia?' available to download here: www.alzheimers.org.uk/site/scripts/download_info.php?fileID=2369.

The Down's Syndrome Association website has information about Down's syndrome and dementia, including a booklet in their Health series on 'Alzheimer's Disease', which can be downloaded here: www.downs-syndrome.org.uk/download-package/2-alzheimers-disease.

The Down's Syndrome Association has produced three DVDs on Down's syndrome and dementia: *Fighting for Andrew, Forget me Not, Philosophy of Care*, which can be purchased here: www.downs-syndrome.org.uk/shop.

Other websites offering information, advice and ideas about dementia, carers, social care and related topics

Age UK www.ageuk.org.uk/publications/age-uk-information-guides-and-factsheets

Carers Trust www.carers.org/money-benefits

Carers UK www.carersuk.org/help-and-advice

Dementia Challengers www.dementiachallengers.com

Glorious Opportunity www.gloriousopportunity.org

Independent Age www.independentage.org/advice

NHS Choices: www.nhs.uk See especially the sections on *Dementia* and on *Care and support* www.nhs.uk/conditions/dementia-guide/pages/about-dementia.aspx

www.nhs.uk/Conditions/social-care-and-support-guide/Pages/what-is-social-care.aspx

The Trebus Project

Stories collected from people with dementia can be read on the Trebus project website www.trebusprojects.org, and you can also listen to recordings of actors such as Alison Steadman, Maureen Lipman and Paul Whitehouse reading some of these stories. For latest updates see the Trebus Project Ltd Facebook page.

Helpful organisations

England and across the UK

Admiral Nursing DIRECT
Helpline: 0845 257 9406
Email support: direct@dementiauk.org
www.dementiauk.org/information-support/admiral-nursing-direct

Age UK
Advice line: 0800 169 6565
www.ageuk.org.uk

Alzheimer's Society (supports people affected by
all types of dementia, not just Alzheimer's)
National Dementia Helpline: 0300 222 11 22
Enquiries: 020 7423 3500
enquiries@alzheimers.org.uk
www.alzheimers.org.uk

British Institute of Learning Disabilities (BILD)
Enquiries: 0121 415 6960
enquiries@bild.org.uk
www.bild.org.uk

Care Quality Commission (CQC)
Enquiries: 03000 616161
enquiries@cqc.org.uk
www.cqc.org.uk

Carers Direct
Helpline: 0300 123 1053

Carers Trust
Email support: support@carers.org
Enquiries: info@carers.org
Head office: 0844 800 4361
www.carers.org

Carers UK
Adviceline: 0808 808 7777
Email support: advice@carersuk.org
Enquiries: 020 7378 4999
www.carersuk.org

Dementia Action Alliance
www.dementiaaction.org.uk

Dementia Adventure
Enquiries: 01245 237 548
info@dementiaadventure.co.uk
www.dementiaadventure.co.uk

Dementia Engagement and Empowerment Project (DEEP)
Enquiries: 01392 420 076
www.dementiavoices.org.uk

Dementia UK (Admiral Nurses)
Enquiries: 020 7697 4160
www.dementiauk.org

Down's Syndrome Association
Helpline and enquiries: 0333 1212 300
info@downs-syndrome.org.uk
www.downs-syndrome.org.uk

Family Carers Involvement Network (for carers of people with dementia)
Enquiries: 0151 237 2669
www.lifestorynetwork.org.uk/family-carers-involvement-network

Frontotemporal dementia support group
Enquiries: frontotemp@aol.com
www.ftdsg.org

Healthwatch England
Enquiries: 03000 68 3000
enquiries@healthwatch.co.uk
www.healthwatch.co.uk

Independent Age
Advice line: 0800 319 6789
advice@independentage.org
Enquiries: 020 7605 4200
www.independentage.org

Innovations in Dementia
Enquiries: 01392 420 076
www.innovationsindementia.org.uk

Jewish Care
Helpline: 020 8922 2222
helpline@jcare.org
Enquiries: 020 8922 2000
www.jewishcare.org

Life Story Network
Enquiries: 0151 237 2669
enquiries@lifestorynetwork.org.uk
www.lifestorynetwork.org.uk

Mental Health Foundation
Enquiries: 020 7803 1100
www.mentalhealth.org.uk

National Council for Palliative Care
Enquiries: 020 7697 1520
www.ncpc.org.uk

NHS 111 (England)
Telephone advice and information about health
issues "when it's less urgent than 999"
Dial: 111

Parkinson's Disease Society
Helpline: 0808 800 0303
Enquiries: 020 7931 8080
hello@parkinsons.org.uk
www.parkinsons.org.uk

Young Dementia UK
Enquiries: 01993 776 295
mail@youngdementiauk.org
www.youngdementiauk.org

Northern Ireland

Age NI (Age UK)
Advice line: 0808 808 7575
Enquiries: 02890 245 729
www.ageuk.org.uk/northern-ireland

Alzheimer's Society, Northern Ireland
Northern Ireland Helpline: 028 9066 4100
Enquiries: nir@alzheimers.org.uk
www.alzheimers.org.uk/northernireland

Carers NI (Carers UK Northern Ireland)
Adviceline: 0808 808 7777
Email support: advice@carersuk.org
Enquiries: 02890 439 843
www.carersuk.org/northernireland

Carers Trust Northern Ireland
Email support: support@carers.org
Enquiries: info@carers.org
Head office: 0844 800 4361
www.carers.org/northern-ireland

Down's Syndrome Association: Northern Ireland Office
Enquiries: 02890 665 260
enquiriesni@downs-syndrome.org.uk
www.downs-syndrome.org.uk

Regulation and Quality Improvement Authority (RQIA)
Enquiries: 028 9051 7500
info@rqia.org.uk
www.rqia.org.uk

Scotland
Age Scotland (Age UK)
Helpline: 0845 125 9732
Enquiries: 0845 833 0200
www.ageuk.org.uk/scotland

Alzheimer Scotland – Action on Dementia
Dementia helpline: 0808 808 3000
Email helpline@alzscot.org
Enquiries: 0131 243 1453
Enquiries: info@alzscot.org
www.alzscot.org

Care Inspectorate
Enquiries: 0345 600 9527
enquiries@careinspectorate.com
www.scswis.com

Carers Scotland (Carers UK Scotland)
Adviceline: 0808 808 7777
Email support: advice@carersuk.org
Enquiries: 0141 445 3070
www.carersuk.org/scotland

Carers Trust Scotland
Email support: support@carers.org
Enquiries: 0300 123 2008
www.carers.org/scotland

Down's Syndrome Scotland
Enquiries: 0131 313 4225
www.dsscotland.org.uk

Scottish Dementia Working Group
Enquiries: 0141 418 3939
sdwg@alzscot.org
www.sdwg.org.uk

Scottish Partnership for Palliative Care
Enquiries: 0131 272 2735
www.palliativecarescotland.org.uk

Wales

Age Cymru (Age UK)
Advice line: 08000 223 444
Enquiries: 02920 431 555
www.ageuk.org.uk/cymru

Alzheimer's Society Wales
National Dementia Helpline: 0300 222 11 22
Enquiries North and West Wales: 01248 671 137
Enquiries South Wales: 02920 480 593
www.alzheimers.org.uk/wales

Care and Social Services Inspectorate Wales

Enquiries: 0300 7900 126

www.cssiw.org.uk

Carers Trust Wales/Cymru

Enquiries: 02920 090 087

Enquiries: wales@carers.org

www.carers.org/wales

Carers Wales (Carers UK Wales)

Adviceline: 0808 808 7777

Email support: advice@carersuk.org

Enquiries: 029 2081 1370

www.carersuk.org/wales

Down's Syndrome Association: Wales Office

Enquiries: 0333 121 2300 or 07834 987 421

wales@downs-syndrome.org.uk

www.downs-syndrome.org.uk/about-us/wales

Republic of Ireland

Age Action

Enquiries: 01 475 6989

info@ageaction.i.e.

www.ageaction.i.e.

Alzheimer Society of Ireland

Helpline: 1 800 341 341

Enquiries: 01 207 3800

www.alzheimer.i.e.

Carers' Association

Freephone careline and enquiries: 1800 240 724

info@carersireland.com

www.carersireland.com

Down Syndrome Ireland

Enquiries: 01 426 6500

Low call number: 1890 374 374

www.downsyndrome.i.e.

Irish Association for Palliative Care

Enquiries: 01 873 4735

info@palliativecare.i.e.

www.iapc.i.e.

International

Alzheimer's Disease International

Enquiries: +44 20 7981 0880

info@alz.co.uk

www.alz.co.uk

Editing challenges

The following is an edited extract from an article[81] *that first appeared in a special edition, edited by John Killick and Susanna Howard, of* Writing in Education, *the journal of the National Association of Writers in Education (NAWE), which was devoted to the theme of 'Writing and dementia'. In this article I discussed some of the challenges of editing the contributions for* People with Dementia Speak Out.

Whether I am editing a written text or the transcript of an interview, I try to retain the authentic voice of the authors, their rhythms and cadences, and their distinctive use of language. I aim to be respectful, sensitive and not patronising. But when does 'editing' someone's heartfelt first-person narrative constitute unwarranted interference? And when does non-intervention become patronising?

In my briefing notes for potential contributors, I stated:

All the contributions that are accepted for the book will be edited in a professional way. That is:

- I will correct spellings and punctuation.

- I may shorten your chapter.

- I may ask you to expand certain sections.

- I may ask you to explain certain passages more clearly.

- I may re-arrange the order of the paragraphs.

I will do my best to retain your personal style, so that it still sounds like 'your voice'.

I will keep in touch with you while I do the editing, so that we can agree on any suggested amendments. I will show you the revised version of the text and get your approval. I will not include your contribution without your express permission.

The question I have wrestled with is to what extent I should alter the language used by the contributor in order to make it more like conventional standard written English. There are two aspects to this. One relates to the use of regional or cultural varieties of English, many of which have historically been seen as 'inferior' forms of English, signifying a lack of education or 'low' social status. The other relates to the occasional use of unorthodox sentence construction, or an apparently misremembered proverb or saying, which is likely to reflect the way the author's language use has been affected by their dementia.

I am very clear that I want the book to reflect the cultural diversity of the contributors and their individual personalities. The language we use is an intrinsic part of our identity, and to 'sanitise' people's grammar and vocabulary, forcing it into the straitjacket of standard English, would in my opinion reveal a lack of respect for the contributors' cultural and linguistic heritage, as well as constituting an assault on each author's uniqueness. This is all the more important at a time when, because of their dementia, the contributors may be fighting to preserve their own sense of who they are. Not to mention the obvious fact that if you insist on changing 'wouldnae' to 'would not', and 'Then my dad pass away and my mum left alone' to 'Then my dad passed away and my mum was left alone,' you will end up with a chapter that does not sound anything like the person it purports to represent.

All the same, this is a sensitive issue. I am well aware of the stigma associated with non-standard varieties of English, (for example, British Black English, and its antecedents in the Caribbean), and I don't want anyone to feel 'exposed' in any way.[82] I hope that the contributors feel that through their distinctive use of language, their personality and unique identity is being celebrated.

Like any editor, I don't want the reader to get bored or confused, so, as in the radio show *Just a minute*, I aim to eliminate repetition, hesitation and deviation. Except of course that sometimes it is the repetition, hesitation and deviation that tells us more about the experience of living with dementia than a pared-down, totally coherent and well-organised piece of prose would. So I have to decide how much to intervene.

If I was editing a piece by someone who did not have dementia, and they appeared to be struggling to express themselves clearly, I would certainly offer some editorial advice, and would not deliberately leave untouched any syntax that I considered garbled. I do take a slightly different approach in editing prose produced by a person with dementia, which I hope is not patronising. As we know, in many types of dementia, the ability to use language conventionally becomes progressively compromised, and this is part of the lived experience of dementia for many people. Therefore, if a contributor uses syntax that 'doesn't quite make sense', in conventional terms, it seems to me legitimate to leave it unchanged, even if the rest of the piece is written in conventional standard English. In fact, very often, these unexpected turns of phrase add depth and richness to the text.

Here are some examples, all from different contributors:

'*In some ways you get caught in a devil and the dark blue sea.*' (Alex Burton, 'Are you sure you've got Alzheimer's?')

This sentence was spoken aloud in an interview. Written down, it makes you do a double-take, in case you have misread it. On further consideration, this form of words seems to convey more fear, desperation and helplessness than the familiar cliché.

'*Socially, I was perceived as somewhat extrovert, and known as a "party animal". Dementia has taken that personality from me. I now live a lifestyle of almost complete opposite.*' (Carol Cronk, 'Riding the rollercoaster'.)

At first I thought it was my editorial duty to rephrase that last sentence, but eventually I decided not to, having realised that the meaning is perfectly clear, and that the unusual sentence structure reveals some of the huge effort and struggle the writer is going through.

'I'm full of optimism. The optimism in the full glass.' (Edward McLaughlin, 'The doors of perception'.)

This was said in a telephone interview, and I queried it at the time. 'Do you mean, being an optimist, seeing the glass as half-full, not half-empty?' 'No. The optimism in the full glass.' I picture a glass full of champagne, an incredibly powerful image of irrepressible optimism – which of course most people would not expect to hear from someone who is living with dementia.

Appendix II

Narrative based medicine

After my previous book,[83] was published, I was introduced by Dr Graham Stokes to the concept of narrative based medicine. I was thrilled to discover this concept, as it confirmed for me the importance of the work I was doing in gathering together first-person accounts from people affected by dementia.

Narrative based medicine is a holistic and person-centred approach to medicine, which (put simply) recognises the importance of what the patient tells the doctor. This approach aims not only to validate the experience of the patient, but also to encourage creativity and self-reflection in the physician.

'Medicine', for our purposes, can be taken to mean the whole gamut of health, social care and support services for people with dementia; 'the physician' can be taken to mean all the people involved in delivering that care, not just the doctor or psychiatrist.

Rita Charon, the leading proponent of this approach in the USA, defines it as: 'Medicine practised with the narrative competence to recognise, absorb, interpret and be moved by the stories of illness.'[84]

In the UK, Trisha Greenhalgh and Brian Hurwitz compiled a marvellous anthology, *Narrative Based Medicine*, in which clinical practitioners and other writers explore various facets of this approach. Greenhalgh and Hurwitz assert[85] that a narrative based approach can help in four ways: in diagnosis, in the therapeutic process, in education and research.

The stories in this book can help to illustrate their theory.

Diagnosis

It may seem self-evident that during the process of diagnosis (and when deciding on appropriate treatment), clinicians should listen to what the patient has to say about their own illness, but all too often, patients feel intimidated and silenced by the doctors and specialists who are examining them. There are numerous instances in this book where a doctor dismisses the patient's concerns, or doesn't believe what they say – see for example, the chapters by Alex Burton ('Are you sure you've got Alzheimer's?') and Jennifer Bute ('A doctor in search of a diagnosis').

The therapeutic process

Greenhalgh and Hurwitz also assert that for a patient, the very act of telling the story of their illness, to an attentive listener, is therapeutic. 'I have found writing this piece helpful,' says Sylvia Kahn at the end of her chapter for this book ('Down with dementia!'), 'because it makes me feel more of a person.'

Education

Greenhalgh and Hurwitz point out that all the great teachers in history have used stories as a means of making important ideas accessible and memorable. Listening to a story may be more likely to bring about an 'aha moment' of sudden illumination than studying reams of data. I commend the stories in this book to all who are striving to improve the care and treatment of people with dementia – whether they are novices or eminent practitioners and researchers of many years' experience.

Research

Greenhalgh and Hurwitz suggest that listening to patients' stories can enrich formal research and may suggest new lines of enquiry. The subjective accounts of living with dementia that have been collected together in this book may complement, confirm or call into question some long-established practices in dementia care and some of the findings of formal research.

Appendix III

LGBT people with dementia

A progressive 'biographical approach' to health and social care recognises not just the importance of the individual's own unique life story, but also how that individual's experiences may have been affected by the culture and shared history of the community to which they belong – for example, family expectations, social networks, faith traditions, experiences of migration or of persecution.

Lesbians and gay men now in their 70s, 80s and 90s grew up in an era when homosexuality was classified as a mental disorder, when sex between men was a criminal act, when lesbian or gay relationships, however faithful or long-lived, had to be disowned in public. Older LGBT people have experienced, collectively, if not always individually, persecution by state, religious and medical authorities as well as the fear – or the reality – of rejection by their families of origin, their colleagues and neighbours. Many have had to pass as straight in order to survive.

Laws have changed and attitudes have softened to some extent in recent years, particularly among the younger generation, but deep scars remain from earlier wounds. Past experiences of discrimination within the health service – for example, being subjected by psychiatrists to brutal 'aversion therapy' – have left an indelible impression upon some LGBT people, making them reluctant to access the support they need as they get older and frailer. Yet they may need these services more than most because, 'Older LGBT people are more likely than their heterosexual peers to rely upon formal care services as they age, not least because they are less likely to have children and more likely to live alone.'[86]

Those LGBT people who fought to change social attitudes, and carved out a place for themselves within their own communities, may now find that if they need care and support, they have to fight some of the battles for recognition and against discrimination all over again. A recent discussion paper gives the example of 'staff in one care home who, having supported a burgeoning friendship between two older residents, were horrified to discover they were gay and beginning a relationship. They stopped seating them next to each other and threatened to tell the family of one of the men.'[87] Some older LGBT people receiving home care services 'have reported being given religious texts by staff and being treated in an openly hostile and even abusive way.'[88]

It is not surprising therefore that LGBT people with dementia and their carers may be wary of disclosing their sexuality to service providers. One gay man said: 'When social care staff are in my home I sometimes feel like a stranger because I have to hide photos, literature, etc. which use the words "gay".'[89]

And yet, while people from these communities remain invisible, all sorts of wrong assumptions may be made about their lives and what matters to them.

The Opening Doors London project[90] recognises 'the transformative power of using biographies and life stories for training purposes', and invites older LGBT speakers to talk about their experiences at the awareness-raising workshops they run: 'Hearing personal stories helps to open minds in a way that more abstract or theoretical training and written case studies can never achieve.'[91]

Work is afoot to offer support to LGBT people who have dementia, and to make health and social care services more LGBT friendly,[92] but there is much more to do before it will be easy to find people who are relaxed about sharing their experiences as an LGBT person who has dementia.

Notes

1. Life expectancy varies significantly according to which type of dementia a person has, as well as individual factors including age and general state of health. On average a person with any type of dementia will live for at least five years after their symptoms begin. People with Alzheimer's disease or dementia with Lewy bodies often live for up to ten years after their symptoms begin. See Alzheimer's Society Factsheet 458, *The progression of Alzheimer's and other dementias.* Available at www.alzheimers.org.uk/site/scripts/documents_info.php?documentID=133, 27 April 2015.
2. Alzheimer's Society (2014) *Dementia UK, Second edition,* Overview. London: Alzheimer's Society, p.17. Available at: www.alzheimers.org.uk/site/scripts/download_info.php?downloadID=1491, accessed 27 April 2015.
3. Alzheimer's Society (2014) *Dementia UK, Second edition,* Overview. London: Alzheimer's Society, p.5. Available at: www.alzheimers.org.uk/site/scripts/download_info.php?downloadID=1491, accessed 27 April 2015.
4. Examples of first person narratives by people with dementia are included in Suggestions for further reading and other resources on page 269.
5. MMSE: mini mental state examination; the test commonly used by clinicians to help diagnose dementia and assess its severity.
6. Singing for the Brain, founded by Chreanne Montgomery-Smith, is a service provided by many branches of Alzheimer's Society that uses singing to bring people with dementia and carers together in a friendly and stimulating social environment. See www.youtube.com/watch?v=epKPyOR0joM, accessed 27 April 2015.
7. The Scottish Dementia Working Group (SDWG) is a national campaigning group run by people with dementia. It is the independent voice of people with dementia within Alzheimer Scotland. See www.sdwg.org.uk, accessed 27 April 2015.
8. Whitman, L. (ed.) (2010) *Telling Tales About Dementia: Experiences of Caring.* London: Jessica Kingsley Publishers.
9. Greenhalgh, T. and Hurwitz, B. (eds) (1998) *Narrative Based Medicine: Dialogue and Discourse in Clinical Practice.* London: BMJ Books.

10. For further information about life story work see: www.lifestorynetwork.org.uk, www.dementiauk.org/information-support/life-story-work, www.alzheimers.org. uk/site/scripts/services_info.php?serviceID=193, all accessed 27 April 2015.

11. Moriarty, J., Sharif, S. and Robinson, J. (2011) *Research briefing 35, Black and minority ethnic people with dementia and their access to support and services.* London: Social Care Institute for Excellence, pp.4–5. Available at www.scie.org.uk/publications/briefings/briefing35/index.asp, accessed 27 April 2015.

12. All-Party Parliamentary Group on Dementia (2013) *Dementia does not discriminate: the experiences of black, Asian and minority ethnic communities.* London: House of Commons APPG on Dementia. Available at: www.alzheimers.org.uk/site/scripts/download_info.php?downloadID=1186, accessed 27 April 2015.

13. Kindertransport: (Children's Transport) the name given to the rescue mission that brought thousands of Jewish children to Great Britain from Nazi Germany, Austria and Czechoslovakia between 1938 and 1940.

14. Clarice Hall and Pearl Hylton contribute to the short film about the Healthy Living Club, which is available at: https://hlclc.wordpress.com/videos, accessed 27 April 2015.

15. See www.meriyaadain.co.uk, accessed 27 April 2015.

16. Pugh, S. 'Care Anticipated' in Ward, R., Rivers, I. and Sutherland, M. (eds) (2012) *Lesbian, Gay, Bisexual and Transgender Ageing: Biographical Approaches for Inclusive Care and Support,* p.40. London: Jessica Kingsley Publishers.

17. Whitman, L. (ed.) (2010) *Telling Tales About Dementia: Experiences of Caring.* London: Jessica Kingsley Publishers.

18. Department of Health (2015) *Prime Minister's Challenge on Dementia 2020.* London: Department of Health. Available at: www.gov.uk/government/uploads/system/uploads/attachment_data/file/414344/pm-dementia2020.pdf, accessed 27 April 2015.

19. Department of Health (2009) *Living Well with Dementia: A National Dementia Strategy.* London: Department of Health, p.47. Available at: www.gov.uk/government/publications/living-well-with-dementia-a-national-dementia-strategy, accessed 27 April 2015.

20. Alzheimer's Society (2014) *Dementia UK: Second edition,* Overview. London: Alzheimer's Society, p.22. Available at: www.alzheimers.org.uk/site/scripts/download_info.php?downloadID=1491, accessed 27 April 2015.

21. Concerns about home care visits of 15 minutes or even less have been widely reported in the British press over the last few years. For example, this piece in the Daily Telegraph 15 February 2015: www.telegraph.co.uk/news/health/news/11302534/Revealed-more-than-500000-home-care-visits-last-less-than-five-minutes.html, accessed 27 April 2015.

22. DEEP is funded by the Joseph Rowntree Foundation, and managed through a collaborative partnership between the Mental Health Foundation, Innovations in Dementia and Alzheimer's Society. www.dementiavoices.org.uk, accessed 27 April 2015. A report of the first phase of the project is available at www.jrf.org. uk/publications/stronger-collective-voice, accessed 27 April 2015.

23. www.dementiavoices.org.uk/deep-groups-alphabetical-order, accessed 27 April 2015.

24. www.lancashiredementiavoices.org, accessed 27 April 2015.

25. United Nations Department of Public Information (2006) *United Nations Convention on the Rights of Persons with Disabilities.* Available at www.un.org/disabilities/convention/conventionfull.shtml, accessed 27 April 2015.

26. Department of Health (2010) *Equity and Excellence: Liberating the NHS* p.3. London: Department of Health. Available at: www.gov.uk/government/uploads/system/uploads/attachment_data/file/213823/dh_117794.pdf, accessed 27 April 2015.

27. www.dementiavoices.org.uk/hope-group, accessed 27 April 2015.

28. www.lancashiredementiavoices.org, accessed 27 April 2015.

29. Rivastigmine: a drug that may temporarily improve or stabilise the symptoms of Alzheimer's disease. See www.alzheimers.org.uk/site/scripts/documents_info.php?documentID=147, accessed 27 April 2015.

30. Metastasis: the spread of a disease, especially of a malignant tumour, from one part of the body to another via the bloodstream or lymphatic system, or across a body cavity; a new area of cancer that has spread from the primary site.

31. See www.goldstandardsframework.org.uk, accessed 27 April 2015.

32. The fifth edition of this booklet has now been issued, and has been renamed 'Looking after someone with cancer'. Available from: www.be.macmillan.org.uk/Downloads/CancerInformation/InfoForCarers/MAC5767Lookingaftersomeonewithcancer E05.pdf accessed 27 April 2015.

33. This group lasted until 2014, but has now been closed down.

34. 'You have the right to be involved, directly or through representatives, in the planning of healthcare services commissioned by NHS bodies, the development and consideration of proposals for changes in the way those services are provided, and in decisions to be made affecting the operation of those services.' Department of Health (2013) NHS Constitution for England, p.9. London: DoH www.gov.uk/government/uploads/system/uploads/attachment_data/file/170656/NHS_Constitution.pdf, accessed 27 April 2015.

35. 'Joint planning should include local service users and carers in order to highlight and address problems specific to each locality.' National Institute for Health and Clinical Excellence and Social Care Institute for Excellence (2007) The NICE-SCIE Guideline on supporting people with dementia and their carers in health and social care (National Clinical Practice Guideline 42) (2007) p.11. London: The British Psychological Society and Gaskell. www.nice.org.uk/guidance/cg42/evidence/cg42-dementia-full-guideline-including-appendices-172, accessed 27 April 2015.

36. www.petergarrard.co.uk, accessed 27 April 2015.

37. An 'olfactory hallucination' otherwise known as 'phantosmia' is the sensation of smelling an imaginary odour. According to the NHS Choices website: 'The smell is unique to the person and is usually unpleasant.' www.nhs.uk/Conditions/phantosmia/Pages/Introduction.aspx, accessed 27 April 2015.

38. www.gloriousopportunity.org, accessed 27 April 2015.

39. https://vimeo.com/40513833, accessed 27 April 2015.

40. www.alz.co.uk/ADI-conference-2012-presentations, accessed 27 April 2015.

41. www.sdwg.org.uk/, accessed 27 April 2015.

42. www.falkirk.gov.uk/services/social-care/adults-older-people/dementia-services.aspx, accessed 27 April 2015.

43. See www.nhs.uk/Conditions/Epilepsy/Pages/Symptoms.aspx, accessed 27 April 2015.

44. *Facing Dementia* is no longer available but you can download another publication by the SDWG, *Don't make the journey alone*, here: www.alzscot.org/assets/0000/0269/dontmake.pdf, accessed 27 April 2015.

45. An edited extract from Kayleigh's piece 'How I see dementia' In JDI Mutual Support Group (2008) *In The Mists of Memory – A Celebration of the Circle of Life.* *Falkirk: Joint Dementia Initiative.* The book is a collection of poems and prose by people with dementia and their grandchildren.

46. See www.greenhamwpc.org.uk/

47. Contadini: peasant farmers.

48. Ferrovia: railway.

49. La casa: the house.

50. Nella campagna: in the countryside.

51. Bryden, C. (2005) *Dancing with Dementia: My Story of Living Positively with Dementia,* London: Jessica Kingsley Publishers, and Bryden, C. (2012) *Who Will I be When I Die?* London: Jessica Kingsley Publishers.

52. Flaouna: a type of pastry from Cyprus.

53. Myra Hindley was a notorious murderer jailed for life in 1966. She died in prison in 2002.

54. The Healthy Living Club is in Stockwell, South London, and is coordinated by Simona Florio. Clarice contributes to the short film about the Healthy Living Club, which can be found at: https://hlclc.wordpress.com/videos, accessed 29 April 2015.

55. Clarice and her daughters Joanne and Valerie also appear in a film made by the Alzheimer's Society for Dementia Awareness Week 2012: www.youtube.com/watch?v=VvxEXWV1ShI, accessed 29 April 2015.

56. June and Brian Hennell's three booklets, endorsed by NHS Gloucestershire Clinical Commissioning Group and Gloucestershire County Council, are: Booklet 1: *Hello I'm Me – Our Early Days with Dementia.* Booklet 2: *Hello I'm Still Me – Living with Midterm Dementia and Mistress or Wife?* Booklet 3: *Hello and Goodbye Brian.* They are available at £4 per set of three booklets, or may be ordered in larger quantities. Please contact June Hennell: June@jacsplace.co.uk.

57. For information about registering as a brain donor, see: www.alzheimers.org.uk/site/scripts/documents_info.php?documentID=1103, accessed 29 April 2015.

58. June launched the Hennell Award for Innovation and Excellence in Dementia Care, in memory of Brian Hennell, in May 2014. Full details are available at: www.worcester.ac.uk/discover/the-hennell-award-2014.html, accessed 29 April 2015.

59. The Healthy Living Club is in Stockwell, South London, and is coordinated by Simona Florio. Pearl contributes to the short film about the Healthy Living Club, which can be found at: https://hlclc.wordpresss.com/videos, accessed 29 April 2015.

60. www.sdwg.org.uk, accessed 2 May 2015.

61. The Scottish Dementia Working Group (2010) Why Am I Laughing? Glasgow: Waverley Books.

62. Mittler, P. (2011) 'Editorial: Journey into Alzheimerland.' *Dementia: The International Journal of Social Research and Practice 10*, 2, 145–147, reproduced by kind permission of the editor and Sage Publications.

63. Mittler, P. (2010) *Thinking Globally Acting Locally: A Personal Journey.* Milton Keynes: AuthorHouse and Amazon (ebook). www.mittlermemoir.com, accessed 2 April 2015.

64. See for example, www.theholocaustexplained.org/ks3/life-in-nazi-occupied-europe/non-jewish-minorities, accessed 2 April 2015; also Burleigh, M. (1994) *Death and Deliverance: 'Euthanasia' in Germany c.1900–1945.* Cambridge University Press.

65. Kindertransport: (Children's Transport) the name given to the rescue mission that brought thousands of Jewish children to Great Britain from Nazi Germany, Austria and Czechoslovakia between 1938 and 1940.

66. Anschluss: the annexation of Austria by Germany in March 1938.

67. Kristallnacht: the 'night of broken glass' in November 1938 when Jewish people throughout Nazi Germany and Austria were attacked and their homes and shops destroyed in a frenzy of violence.

68. Otto Adolph Eichmann was a Lieutenant Colonel in the Nazi SS, and one of the major organisers of the Holocaust. He was captured in Argentina in 1960, tried in Israel and hanged in 1962.

69. Photos of this monument, created by Frank Meisler, can be seen at: www.talkingbeautifulstuff.com/2013/05/23/the-kindertransport-statue-liverpool-street-station-london; further information is available at www.frank-meisler.com CitySculpture.html, accessed 2 May 2015.

70. Mittler, P. (2010) *Thinking Globally Acting Locally: A Personal Journey.* Milton Keynes: AuthorHouse and Amazon (ebook). www.mittlermemoir.com, accessed 2 April 2015.

71. Mittler, P. (2013) *Overcoming Exclusion: Social Justice Through Education.* London: Routledge World Library of Educationalists.

72. Mittler, P. (2015) 'The UN Convention on the Rights of Persons with Disabilities: Implementing a Paradigm Shift.' In Iriarte, E., McConkey, R. and Gilligan, R. (eds) *Disability in a Global Age: A Human Rights Based Approach.* London: Palgrave Macmillan.

73. Kitwood, T. (1997) *Dementia Reconsidered: The Person Comes First.* Maidenhead: Open University Press.

74. Alzheimer's Society (2014) *15 Years of the Research Network: Celebrating the Impact of Public Involvement in Dementia Research.* London: Alzheimer's Society. www.alzheimers.org.uk, accessed 2 May 2015.

75. World Health Organization and Alzheimer's Disease International (2012) *Dementia: A Public Health Priority.* Geneva and New York: WHO.

76. See www.caringonthehomefront.org.uk/search-the-library/aid-to-russia-fund, accessed 3 May 2015.

77. Brooks, D. (2011) *The Social Animal: The Hidden Sources of Love, Character, and Achievement*, p. xvii. New York: Random House.

78. Begley, S. (2009) *The Plastic Mind: New Science Reveals Our Extraordinary Potential to Transform Ourselves.* London: Constable.

79. Doidge, N. (2008) *The Brain that Changes Itself: Stories of Personal Triumph from the Frontiers of Brain Science.* London: Penguin.

80. Young, A. 'Half a World Away.' In Lucy Whitman (ed.) (2009) *Telling Tales about Dementia: Experiences of Caring*, p.69. London: Jessica Kingsley Publishers.

81. Whitman, L. (2013) 'Caught in a devil and a dark blue sea.' *Writing in Education* 61, pp.22–24. Reproduced by kind permission of NAWE.

82. In the 1980s I taught English in a further education college in inner London, and collaborated with colleagues in the Afro-Caribbean Language and Literacy Project to produce a compendium of teaching and learning materials called *Language and Power*. This book explores the social history of standard and non-standard varieties of English in depth, and celebrates the eloquence and creativity of varieties of English that have sometimes been derided as 'defective' or 'broken'. See: Afro-Caribbean Language and Literacy Project (1990) *Language and Power*. London: Harcourt Brace Jovanovich.

83. Whitman, L. (ed.) (2010) *Telling Tales About Dementia: Experiences of Caring*. London: Jessica Kingsley Publishers.

84. Charon, R. (2006) *Narrative Medicine: Honoring the Stories of Illness*, p.vii. New York: Oxford University Press.

85. Greenhalgh, T. and Hurwitz, B. 'Why study narrative?' In Greenhalgh, T. and Hurwitz, B. (eds) (1998) *Narrative Based Medicine: Dialogue and Discourse in Clinical Practice*. London: BMJ Books.

86. Ward, R. 'Making space for LGBT lives in health and social care.' In Ward, R., Rivers, I. and Sutherland, M. (2012) *Lesbian, Gay, Bisexual and Transgender Ageing: Biographical Approaches for Inclusive Care and Support*, pp.201–202. London: Jessica Kingsley Publishers.

87. The National LGB&T Partnership, *et al.* (2014) *The Dementia Challenge for LGBT Communities*, p.5. National LGB&T Partnership, National Care Forum, Voluntary Organisations Disability Group and Sue Ryder. www.nationalcareforum.org.uk/spp-resources.asp, accessed 3 May 2015.

88. Knocker S., Maxwell N., Phillips, M. and Halls, S. 'Opening Doors and Opening Minds: Sharing One Project's Experience of Successful Community Engagement.' In Ward, R., Rivers, I. and Sutherland, M. (2012) *Lesbian, Gay, Bisexual and Transgender Ageing: Biographical Approaches for Inclusive Care and Support*, p.160. London: Jessica Kingsley Publishers.

89. Knocker S., Maxwell N., Phillips, M. and Halls, S. 'Opening Doors and Opening Minds: Sharing One Project's Experience of Successful Community Engagement.' In Ward, R., Rivers, I. and Sutherland, M. (2012) *Lesbian, Gay, Bisexual and Transgender Ageing: Biographical Approaches for Inclusive Care and Support*, p.161. London: Jessica Kingsley Publishers.

90. The Opening Doors London (ODL) project for older LGBT people is based at Age UK Camden and works across London boroughs. A short film in which LGBT people between the ages of 68 and 91 talk about their lives can be found on the home page of the ODL website www.openingdoorslondon.org.uk, accessed 3 May 2015.

91. Knocker S., Maxwell N., Phillips, M. and Halls, S. 'Opening Doors and Opening Minds: Sharing One Project's Experience of Successful Community Engagement.' In Ward, R., Rivers, I. and Sutherland, M. (2012) *Lesbian, Gay, Bisexual and Transgender Ageing: Biographical Approaches for Inclusive Care and Support*, p.163. London: Jessica Kingsley Publishers.

92. In addition to projects and articles already mentioned, see Peel, E. and McDaid, S. (2015) *Over the rainbow: report on the LGBT people and dementia support and advocacy project.* Worcester: University of Worcester Association for Dementia Studies, Birmingham LGBT Centre for Health and Wellbeing, and PACE Health London. www.dementiavoices.org.uk/2015/03/over-the-rainbow-report-about-lgbt-people-and-dementia, accessed 3 May 2015.

READING WELL

Reading Well Books on Prescription helps you to understand and manage your health and well-being using self-help reading. The scheme is endorsed by health professionals and supported by public libraries.

For more information, see http://reading-well.org.uk/books/books-on-prescription/dementia.

These books have been selected by dementia healthcare experts as part of the 'Books on Prescription' collection.

JKP is proud to have published 7 of the 25 selected titles.

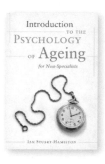

Introduction to the Psychology of Ageing for Non-Specialists
Ian Stuart-Hamilton

Paperback: £16.99 / $26.95
ISBN: 978 1 84905 363 1
Large print: 978 1 84985 838 0
Ebook: 978 0 85700 715 5
Audio digital download: 978 1 78450 081 8
240 pages

A comprehensive introduction to the psychology of ageing for non-specialists. It covers all the key issues, from definitions of ageing and life expectancy to the aspects of ageing that have the most impact on people's lives. It draws on the latest research in the field and offers practical information for those working with the older population.

Professor Ian Stuart-Hamilton is Professor of Developmental Psychology at the University of Glamorgan, Wales. He has over thirty years' research experience in a wide variety of psychological techniques and settings. *The Psychology of Ageing* is now translated into 16 languages, and was awarded a British Medical Association Book of the Year award in the Geriatric Medicine section in 2008.

Can I tell you about Dementia?
A guide for family, friends and carers
Jude Welton, illustrated by Jane Telford

Paperback £8.99 / £14.95
ISBN: 978 1 84905 297 9
Large print: 978 1 84985 842 7
Ebook: 978 0 85700 634 9
48 pages

Meet Jack – an older man with dementia. Jack invites readers to learn about dementia from his perspective, helping them to understand the challenges faced by someone with dementia and the changes it causes to memory, communication and behaviour. He also gives advice on how to help someone with dementia stay as mentally and physically active as possible, keep safe and continue to feel cared for and valued.

With illustrations throughout, this useful book will be an ideal introduction to dementia for anyone from child to adult. It will also guide family, friends and carers in understanding and explaining the condition and could serve as an excellent starting point for family and classroom discussions.

Jude Welton is a freelance writer, writing mainly on the arts and originally trained as a child psychologist specialising in autism. **Jane Telford** is a childhood friend of the author. She is an artist and illustrator, who has exhibited paintings and drawings widely in the UK and also internationally. The book is dedicated to Jude's late father, and Jane's father, both dementia sufferers.

Dementia – Support for Family and Friends

Dave Pulsford and Rachel Thompson

Paperback: £13.99 / $24.95
ISBN: 978 1 84905 243 6
Large print: 978 1 84985 843 4
Ebook: 978 0 85700 504 5
240 pages

For friends, family members and carers of people with dementia, understanding the condition and coping with the impact it has on their lives can be extremely challenging. This book, written specifically for these groups, explores each stage of the journey with dementia and explains not only how it will affect the person with the condition, but also those around them, and how best to offer support and where to get professional and informal assistance. It focuses on the progressive nature of dementia and the issues that can arise as a result, and gives practical advice that can help to ensure the best possible quality of life both for the person with dementia and the people around them.

A comprehensive and practical introduction to the condition, this book is essential reading for anyone who has a friend or relative with dementia.

Dave Pulsford is Senior Lecturer in Mental Health Nursing at the University of Central Lancashire, UK. Rachel Thompson is Dementia Project Lead for the Royal College of Nursing (RCN) and is an Admiral Nurse with Dementia UK. Both have significant experience of nursing in dementia care in practice, research, teaching, and professional writing in this field.

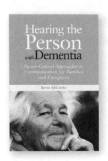

Hearing the Person with Dementia
Person-Centred Approaches to Communication for Families and Caregivers
Bernie McCarthy

Paperback: £12.99 / $18.95
ISBN: 978 1 84905 186 6
Large print: 978 1 84985 839 7
Ebook: 978 0 85700 499 4
112 pages

Losing the ability to communicate can be a frustrating and difficult experience for people with dementia, their families and carers. As the disease progresses, the person with dementia may find it increasingly difficult to express themselves clearly, and to understand what others say.

Written with both family and professional carers in mind, this book clearly explains what happens to communication as dementia progresses, how this may affect an individual's memory, language and senses, and how carers might need to adapt their approach as a result. Advocating a person-centred approach to dementia care, the author describes methods of verbal and non-verbal communication, techniques for communicating with people who cannot speak or move easily, and strategies for communicating more effectively in specific day-to-day situations, including at mealtimes, whilst helping the person with dementia to bathe or dress, and whilst out and about. Exercises at the end of each chapter encourage the carer to reflect on their learning and apply it to their own circumstances, and guidelines for creating a life story with the person with dementia as a means of promoting good communication are also included.

This concise, practical book is essential reading for family caregivers, professional care staff, and all those who work with, or who are training to work with, people with dementia.

Bernie McCarthy is the founder of McCarthy Psychology Services, and is a registered clinical psychologist with a Master of Arts in Clinical Psychology from Melbourne University. He is also a Member of the Australian Psychological Society and the College of Clinical Psychologists. Bernie is a trainer in Dementia Care Mapping and conducts staff training in dementia care and other aspects of psychological wellbeing and culture change in health and aged care throughout Australia.

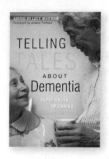

Telling Tales About Dementia
Experiences of Caring
Edited by Lucy Whitman

Paperback: £14.99 / $24.95
ISBN: 978 1 84310 941 9
Large print: 978 1 84985 841 0
Ebook: 978 0 85700 017 0
224 pages

How does it feel when someone you love develops dementia? How do you cope with the shock, the stress and the grief? Can you be sure that you and your family will receive the support you need?

In *Telling Tales About Dementia*, thirty carers from different backgrounds and in different circumstances share their experiences of caring for a parent, partner or friend with dementia. They speak from the heart about love and loss: 'I still find it hard to believe that Alzheimer's has happened to us,' writes one contributor, 'as if we were sent the wrong script.' The stories told here vividly reflect the tragedy of dementia, the gravity of loss, and instances of unsatisfactory diagnosis, treatment and care. But they contain hope and optimism too: clear indications that the quality of people's lives can be enhanced by sensitive support services, by improved understanding of the impact of dementia, by recognising the importance of valuing us all as human beings, and by embracing and sustaining the connections between us.

This unique collection of personal accounts will be an engaging read for anyone affected by dementia in a personal or professional context, including relatives of people with dementia, social workers, medical practitioners and care staff.

Lucy Whitman is a writer, editor and trainer, and a former teacher in further education. She cared for her mother who had dementia, and this inspired her first anthology, *Telling Tales About Dementia: Experiences of Caring*, a collection of person accounts by people who have looked after someone with dementia. Lucy has worked extensively with family carers, and writes regularly for the *Journal of Dementia Care*. She works as Community Engagement Officer for Healthwatch Enfield.

Losing Clive to Younger Onset Dementia
One Family's Story
Helen Beaumont

Paperback: £13.99 / $24.99
ISBN: 978 1 84985 840 3
Large print: 978 1 84310 480 3
Ebook: 978 1 84642 862 3
144 pages

Clive Beaumont was diagnosed with Younger Onset Dementia at age 45, when his children were aged just 3 and 4. He had become less and less able to do his job properly and had been made redundant from the Army the year before.

Clive's wife, Helen, tells of how she and the rest of the family made it through the next six years until Clive died: the challenge of continually adapting to his progressive deterioration; having to address the legal implications of the illness; applying for benefit payments; finding nursing homes; and juggling her responsibilities as a wife, a mother and an employee. She also describes the successful founding and development of The Clive Project, a registered charity set up by Helen and others in a bid to establish support services for people with Younger Onset Dementia.

Younger Onset Dementia is comparatively rare, but not that rare. This story is for the family and friends of people with the condition, for the people themselves, and for the professionals working with them.

Helen Beaumont is a founder member of The Clive Project (www. thecliveproject.org.uk), a registered charity based in Oxfordshire and named after her husband. She lives in Oxfordshire with her two children.

Dancing with Dementia
My Story of Living Positively with Dementia
Christine Bryden

Paperback: £13.99 / $21.95
ISBN: 978 1 84310 332 5
Large print: 978 1 84985 837 3
Ebook: 978 1 84642 095 5
Audio digital download: 978 1 78450 079 5
200 pages

Christine Bryden was a top civil servant and single mother of three children when she was diagnosed with dementia at the age of 46. Since then she has gone on to challenge almost every stereotype of people with dementia by campaigning for self-advocacy, writing articles and speaking at national conferences.

This book is a vivid account of the author's experiences of living with dementia, exploring the effects of memory problems, loss of independence, difficulties in communication and the exhaustion of coping with simple tasks. She describes how, with the support of her husband Paul, she continues to lead an active life nevertheless, and explains how professionals and carers can help.

Christine Bryden makes an outspoken attempt to change prevailing attitudes and misconceptions about the disease. Arguing for greater empowerment and respect for people with dementia as individuals, she also reflects on the importance of spirituality in her life and how it has helped her better understand who she is and who she is becoming.

Dancing with Dementia is a thoughtful exploration of how dementia challenges our ideas of personal identity and of the process of self-discovery it can bring about.

Christine Bryden has worked in the pharmaceutical industry and as a senior executive in the Australian Prime Minister's Department. Following her diagnosis with Alzheimer's Disease in 1995, she has been instrumental in setting up local support groups for people with dementia and has addressed national and international conferences. In 2003 she was the first person with dementia to be elected to the Board of Alzheimer's Disease International. Her first book *Who will I be when I die?* is also published by JKP and has been translated into several languages. She lives in Brisbane, Australia.